www. bookcross
BCID: 690-16269

The Time

~ Haston Lee ~

Copyright © 2018 by Haston Lee

All rights reserved. No part of this publication may be reproduced, stored in a retrieval system, or transmitted, in any form or by any means, electronic, mechanical, photocopying, recording, or otherwise, without prior permission of the author. Any person, who does any unauthorized act in relation to this publication, may be liable to criminal prosecution and civil claims for damages

This is a work of fiction. Names, **characters**, businesses, places, events and incidents are the products of the author's imagination. **Any** resemblance to actual persons, living or dead, or actual events is purely coincidental.

Acknowledgements:

Thanks to Sarah for the name Fubbyloofah. She kick-started a lot of fun dreaming up other fantastical names for magical creatures. Thanks also to Ash, whose dream provided me with the Deathly Shadow and to Alex who reminded me of the fun of magic by dressing up as Harry Potter all those years ago. Most of all, thanks to mum who filled my childhood full of books!

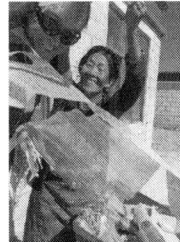

Haston Lee got tired of breathing stale corporate air and swapped his commute for a pen, paper and a rucksack. When not tangled up in Tibetan prayer flags he divides his time between London, the Lake District and the M6 northbound. He can often be found poking around Caesar's Well on Wimbledon Common hoping for a time splinter to free him from the latter.

The Time Splinter

1. The Waking of a Shadow-sylph
2. A Time Splinter Opens
3. Fubbyloofah
4. The Journey to Waftenway and what happened with Spiced Tea
5. Drowning in Stars
6. The Attack of the Puddies
7. The Return to Rascal Howe
8. The Puddies and the Pool
9. On the Wings of a Swan
10. The Chamber of Moths and the Creatures of the Night Shade
11. The Conference of the Wing
12. The Moth-Man
13. The Chamber of the Grand Assembly
14. Of Groundluggs & Sakratts
15. The Guardians of Life & Death
16. Flabblehogg gets Burnt
17. Fire-Cat Magic
18. Jassaspy's Welcome
19. The Daughter of Nobody
20. Secrets of the Time Splinter
21. The Trial of Tanglestep
22. Jassaspy's Triumph
23. Burnt Gold....and a Kiss!
24. Epilogue.

~ Glossary ~

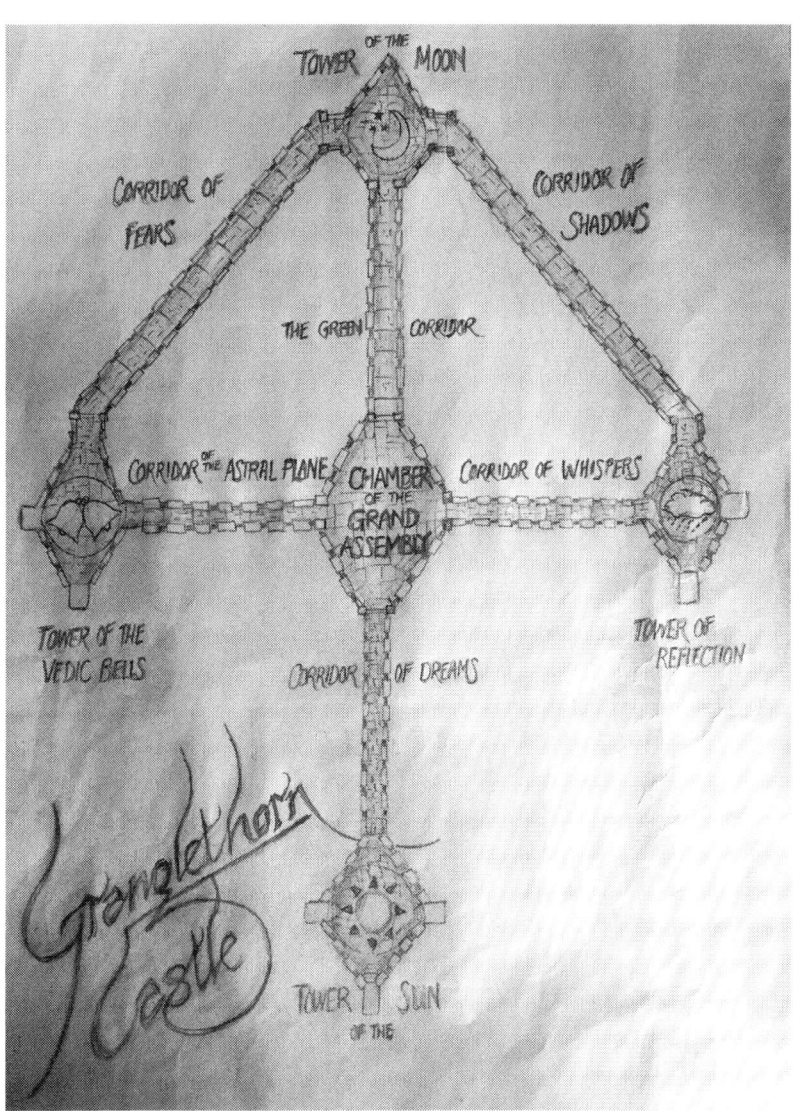

1. The Waking of a Shadow-Sylph

It was the burning of the gorse that awoke the shadow-sylph: a vile essence lying dormant between the dusk and the dank mouldering undergrowth. The boys responsible were unaware of what they had done, yet a scout from the Tower of the Moon could recognize the signs. He quickly set to work.

The colours of the day drained painfully away as the moon primed the land with its watery grey eye. Peek swirled his golden ale round his glass, taking comfort from its warm amber hues. Outside, the night was laying its mantle over the land and he shuffled closer to the roaring log fire by the bar. The colours reminded him of fire-cat magic. Why did he feel the need to surround himself with reminders of this after all these years? He shrugged in confusion as his gaze wandered across the pub. The tables were all adorned with flowers, and he leant forwards to drink in their scent before going for another beer. When he returned, a thin man with straggly black hair was sitting at his table.

"Snarklepike's the name. Pleassse to meet ya." The man slimed a smile and Peek nodded back noting how odd he looked drowning in his shirt with his hands half-covered by the cuffs and the collar sticking up.

"Evening!" said Peek with deliberate brevity. Sharklepike smiled again before hunching over his glass of pitch black ale which he stared into intently. Peek felt uneasy. Something bothered him, but what was it? He looked around in confusion before it struck him. It was right under his very nose: the flowers on his table. They had suddenly wilted and within the last few minutes. He glanced across to the other tables. They were all still fresh. What was going on?

Moonlight cut through the window and Snarklepike raised his head and sighed softly as it caressed his cheek. A small centipede wriggled out from under his up-turned collar and across his neck to disappear into his left ear. But Peek didn't see this. Snarklepike opened his eyes and exhaled slowly as if recovering from a moment of intense pleasure. Again, nobody noticed. Peek stared into his beer lost in his thoughts. What was it about this man?

"Aren't ya gonna tell me ya name then?" Snarklepike held out a slippery hand but Peek recoiled instinctively. The man withdrew his hand sharply and in his haste jolted the table. "Oops. Sorry about that," he said as both their ales slopped over. He reached out to steady Peek's glass. In a flash, the golden colour in the beer leached away completely. Peek gasped and their eyes locked instantly. Down on the table the golden ale and the pitch black stout swirled around on the table testily, refusing to mingle; like oil and water.

"Like the Tower of the Moon and the Tower of the Sun: forever at odds," said Snarklepike, pointedly.

There was a split second of silence before Peek shot to his feet, sent both pints tumbling and bolted for the door fingers scrabbling for the handle.

"It's too late. I've received a 'gorse-sign'," Snarklepike shouted as the door clattered shut behind him.

Peek felt his skin prickle but was it from fear or the frost of the night? He knew he was most vulnerable when out under a night sky. The man who had tracked him down could easily summon the Creatures of the Night Shade. His eyes flickered around nervously. Was he, even now, being watched: but which creatures should he look out for? Many of them were so tiny. His mind flashed back to the pub. In his mind's eye he saw the three centipedes that he had squelched underfoot as he had jumped to his feet. There could easily have been more that had wriggled across to him without him knowing. He frantically dusted himself down. He shook his arms and legs vigorously and ruffled his hair in case any had crawled up into it. If these things came home with him they would act as a beacon and lead other creatures to him: creatures even more dangerous that could … His mind flashed to the fire-cat's safety and into a patchwork quilt of horrors that settled around his imagination too heavy to cast off.

"They mustn't track me back here," he muttered as he got to his front door; then froze on the threshold. The doormat was peppered with yellow blossom: a 'gorse sign!' He had more sense than to question how it had got there. He'd seen one before. He lunged for the phone.

"Hi Marj…it's me.. Peek," he said, breathing heavily, as his friend's wife answered.

"Peek...what are you doing ringing so late? Is everything alright?"

"Listen Marj...I've just had a sign. You gotta help. I don't..."

"Oh Peek: not this again. How many times have you worried about this? There's -"

"Marj, PLEASE! It's the same as when Ron disappeared".

There was a silence at the mention of her husband who had disappeared a few years ago on the Common. At the time he was heavily involved with Peek and the 'fire-cat magic', but Marj knew nothing of this.

"What do you mean?" she asked flatly.

"You know: the gorse signs," he said softly.

There was an overlong moment of silence before Marj spoke again.

"Peek, I can't come over now."

Her mind swam with images from the night her husband disappeared: her son Jack, huddled in a corner clutching a key, the doormat strewn with yellow gorse and the sound of footsteps running away.

"I'll be round tomorrow," she said quietly before ringing off.

Peek put the phone down. Memories seeped back through the hour-glass of his mind: memories of the old fire-cat magic: memories of when Ron was still with them and when - he broke off his reverie. The curtains were still open. The gaping black night mouthed silently at him. Anything could be out there. Anything could be looking in. He shot forwards and dragged them together.

A 'gorse sign.' The memories returned: memories of how time splintered, memories of a land resuscitated: brought back to life, from the brink of a slow anaemic death: a land saved by fire-cat magic. But who or what had triggered the gorse-signs? Was it the Guardian-Priests of Granglethorn: and what about the fire-cat? His mind raced over a million possibilities. Soon a time splinter would occur: but when? Where? ...and how could he possibly be of any help now, after all these years of lying fallow?

"Careful, or you'll lose an eye!" A whorl of branches swung past: inches from his face.

"Scott, you prat. Pack it in or I'll -"

"You'll do what? Teach me a lesson? You'd mess up your hair if you tried." Scott grinned over to his brother.

Jack was broody, bookish and fashion-conscious as hell, whereas his younger brother, Scott cared nothing for those things. As long as he was outdoors and active, he was happy. He breathed deeply and shook his tousled blonde mop as they put the finishing touches to a tree den close to Caesar's Well: an ancient well on the edge of the Common. It was earlier on the very same day that Peek met Snarklepike in the pub, and they had chosen this spot because of the weirdly shaped evergreen trees that shot up hundreds of feet into the air. The boys put the last branch in place and sat back.

"Right, now we can see out but no one can see in," said Jack.

" - says the guy who's wearing a bright yellow top. You 'dumb-ass'," laughed Scott.

"Ah crap!" muttered Jack as he turned his back to his brother to hide his sheepish look. Why had he put on a stupid yellow top?

"Hey, how about we use some of that yellow gorse as camouflage? Your top won't show through that, will it?" Scott suggested helpfully.

"Not like you to come up with something so sensible!" grumbled Jack, still smarting from the 'dumb-ass' jibe. Scott pulled a face in response, but was quick to forget it.

The gorse was perfect. The yellow blossom was powerfully fragrant, and the thorns would be an ideal deterrent. They set about it eagerly: kicking at branches to break them free and covering their hands with the cuffs of their Jackets for protection. It was tough going but finally they had something to work with. A couple of crows flapped down to roost on a tree nearby as they positioned the branches over the den and after ten minutes it was almost done.

"Hey, it's gone spookily quiet all of a sudden," Scott said whilst catching his breath. His eyes glinted as his imagination went into overdrive and he waved his hands about in a ghostly manner. Jack's faced creased in irritation.

"Stop messing around, you big kid and give me a hand finishing this," he said, anxiously, aware of how loudly his words reverberated. He shot a glance around him. The Common *was* strangely quiet. His eyes darted across to the surrounding trees before he realised what it was. "Hey, there's no birdsong!" he muttered. He looked vaguely troubled but then shrugged. Scott hadn't heard him and was busy dragging the remaining branches over. Over by the tree a few more crows had gathered.

"Hey, why don't we burn these extra branches?" Scott said whilst rubbing his hands to stave off the winter chill. Jack started suddenly as his dad's words suddenly came back to him.

"No; better not. The light's fading and you know what dad used to say about twilight."

"Oh, not that 'dark magic' rubbish? That was just to get us home in time for dinner. Come on! It's getting really chilly." He nudged a branch with his foot.

"Oh I don't know. It does -"

"Come on. Why do you have to over-think everything?"

"I guess it does seem a bit far-fetched," muttered Jack, as Scott turned towards the gorse bush purposefully. It wasn't long before a smoky fragrance was wafting over them.

"Stag-man! Stag-man!" yelled Scott.

Jack whirled round in alarm. Scott was laughing and holding a branch of gorse over his head giving himself antlers. He was so caught up in the moment that Jack suppressed his instinctive annoyance and relaxed into a grin. They laughed together and both sat back to enjoy the scent of the burning gorse and watch the shadows twitch and jerk in the twilight. The smoke swirled over them, caressing, smothering. It was warm and strangely comforting. Happy memories of holidays by campsite fires settled around them. Times spent with cousins when - Jack jolted awake. He must have fallen asleep. He looked round at Scott who was slumped against the gorse, the branch of antlers by his side. Then, out of the corner of his eye, he saw it: an inky black essence. He became dimly aware of his breath quickening.

"Scott: look! Over there! That shadow!"

Scott opened a bleary eye. It was over by the fire: a tall, wiry creature with jagged antlers in the half-light. It seemed to twitch. Was it looking at them? Suddenly it darted forwards.

"IT'S COMING FOR US!" They kicked and punched but fought nothing but air. Suddenly, rivulets of frost whipped around Jack's forearm and his skin soaked up the icy essence like blotting paper.

"ARRGH, its got my arm!" Through a scream of fire and ice he heard a terrifying yowl.

"Mine too! It's completely numb!" wailed Scott, rubbing his arm frantically.

Then, as quickly as it had come, it had gone: darting off, zig-zagging in the half-light, before jumping down to disappear into Caesar's Well. For a second all they could hear was their own heavy breathing but they knew that each had caught a glimpse of the darkness and it was something they would never forget.

"Let's get outta here! I knew we should never have hung around here at twilight." Jack staggered to his feet and half dragged his brother out of the den.

The gorse fire was now almost out; the twilight was turning into night. But something was different now and they could both feel it. Behind them on a nearby tree the number of crows had gathered to over a hundred.

"Listen Marj," said Peek, the following day as he ushered her to a seat and thrust a cup of tea into her hands. "I don't want to alarm you, but I'd really appreciate it if you would look after Lava for a while. You can see how much Chloe loves him." He nodded towards her daughter as she cradled a small ginger cat on the floor.

"We'll be good for ever and ever. Amen," said Chloe with a cheeky grin and looking cow-eyed. Angel impressions generally allowed her to hoodwink her mum. She threw a cheeky wink to Scott. Chloe was Scott's twin and with an attitude as sparky as her spiky hair.

"It wouldn't be for long," he urged. "It's just that after everything that happened last night and with the 'gorse sign' too."

"GORSE!" Jack blurted out as he stepped into the room. He immediately blushed at the alarm his outburst had caused. "We had a totally weird experience with gorse on the Common yesterday," he said.

"What do you mean, Jack?" asked Peek, tensing suddenly.

We were making a den from gorse branches and had too many, so Scott suggested we burn the leftovers -"

"It was your idea too!" said Scott, anxious to avoid the blame.

"Whatever, dude! Anyway, we started burning it, when this shadow - it came alive and -," Jack broke off and suddenly winced as he felt an icy tingle run up his arm. He rubbed his arm vigorously and frowned. It was as if the mere memory had triggered it again. "We were just messin' about. You know, making antlers out of the branches. It wasn't -" Suddenly he started swaying. Peek quickly darted to his side.

"Step back everyone!" He said as with one hand he helped Jack collapse onto the sofa. Beside him Marj stiffened before rounding on Scott.

"You should have both known better! What did your father say about gorse and twilight before he disappeared?"

Scott stared back sullenly but was saved from answering as Jack suddenly spluttered to.

"Mum, my arm: it's so cold!" His eyes were wide with unanswered questions. "What's happening to me?"

Several hot cups of tea later, Peek led the boys up towards his study with a real sense of urgency.

"You shouldn't have messed with the gorse, boys. It's imbued with an ancient power." They trudged in silence not daring to meet his gaze. "Gorse signs always coincide with a time splinter," he explained, as he approached the study door. "That's when time is ruptured," he said simply by way of an explanation. The boys looked anxiously at each other. "Come: in here quickly!" He opened the door to a sudden flash as a maelstrom of flickering colour exploded in their faces.

"Whoa, look out, Scott!" Jack thrust his brother back out of the room as orange and black flashes transmogrified into an iridescent blue.

"Boys, there's no need -" Peak's words were drowned out as an eye-blinding yellow subsided into a shower of pure brilliantine white. "BOYS, THEY'RE JUST PLANTS," shouted Peek. His words hung in the air just long enough to overpower the visual explosions going on all around them.

"PLANTS?" Jack gaped open mouthed; yet Peek was right! Small tiny shoots were flowering repeatedly with a 'pop' that sent coloured petals shooting several feet into the air like confetti; and they were everywhere: on top of his pile of books, on the chair where he sat, and on the table where he worked. There was even one on the rim of his tea-cup!

"Wow! What? How do they do that?" Jack was intrigued.

"They're poppletons: only started flowering today!" said Peek, with a half smile on his face. "They got stuck here the last time that time splintered, but I'm guessing that you half-expected that by -" he broke off, noticing that Scott was frowning.

"I see them popping but I can't see any colour." His voice wavered. "All I can see are shadows - and my arm has gone icy cold like Jack's!" He rubbed it furiously and looked beseechingly towards Peek who quickly beckoned him forwards.

"Stand here under the light for a moment," he urged.

Scott shuffled forwards. Peek looked intently into his eyes and rubbed his arm vigorously. Eventually the inky blackness behind Scott's eyes began to fade and Peek let out a sigh of relief.

"Listen boys, I know what's happening. I need to give you both something important that you must promise to look after and keep with you at all times, is that understood?"

They nodded mutely as he started rummaging through a mountain of trinkets of all shapes and sizes. It seemed to be taking forever so the boys soon started nosing amongst the stuff themselves whilst they waited. Peek found what he was looking for just as Scott let out a whoop of delight.

"Just let anyone try and mess with me now," he laughed as he held aloft a curved and heavily bejewelled Turkish dagger. Peek looked up and laughed, relieved at the change that had come over him.

"It's only a letter opener, but it's yours, if you want it."

Jack looked up and smirked. "Expecting letters from your girlfriend, Scott? You'll probably need that, dragon that she is," he quipped. His smile died instantly as Peek beckoned him over and he saw what he was holding.

"An ancient time-key," said Peek, as he handed Jack a black gothic wrought-iron key with a head as large as a matchbox and strange symbols carved into it. Jack went as white as a sheet.

"Oh, not a key. Of all things: not a key. No I can't. Really, I can't." He waved Peek away as the memories flooded back.

"Open the door Jack. It's me, your dad. Just open the door."

These were the last words his father had said to him. In his mind's eye he was crouched on the floor, his father silhouetted against the window, hammering to get in, pleading with his young son. It was still so vivid: him clutching the key tightly, too scared to act, before yellow gorse drifted in under the door. He never saw his father again.

Peek pressed the time-key into his hand before pointing to a tiny hand-sized frame on the wall by the door. "No time for this, Jack. Pass that to your brother," he said. Confused and shaken, Jack did as asked.

"What's so special about a picture of an old woman in black?" he said as he handed it over. Scott took it and immediately stiffened.

"You mean a young blonde?"

"Eh? No; it's an old woman in black." Jack glanced over Scott's shoulder before his jaw dropped in astonishment. "Hey, where's she gone? Here, pass it back for a moment." He lunged for the frame and got half a hand-hold on it before Scott twisted away. Together they tumbled to the floor and Peek's head jerked up from what he was doing.

"For heaven's sake, what's going on?" he shouted.

"It's the picture. It keeps changing. LOOK!" Jack thrust the frame up to Peek. For a second, the frame showed an old woman in black before Scott grabbed it back and it changed to a young woman with blonde hair. Peek stared at it in silence."Well? What do you see: the blonde or the old woman?" asked Jack in frustration.

"Nothing! There's no image here except my own. It's a mirror. It happens to be the Mirror of Aggraides: although it appears strangely tarnished."

"MIRROR? it's not a mirror! There's a woman in it. We both agree that much." Scott and Jack exchanged looks. Peek felt his pulse pound furiously.

"A time splinter," he muttered under his breath. There was a pregnant pause whilst he stared at the ground between his feet. When he looked up again, it was with an air of deadly seriousness. "Listen boys! I know what it was that touched you both when you burnt the gorse." He paused wondering exactly how much more to tell them. The boys looked tense yet Peek sensed a resilience that could be relied upon. He decided to continue. "It was a shadow-sylph," he said simply. Their eyes owled.

"A shadow-'what'? What's that?" they echoed. Peek brushed the question aside.

"Listen carefully! Soon something odd will start to happen to time and you'll find yourselves in a strange dimension where some things will look the same and others not. You must remember to seek out the Guardian-Priests from the Tower of the Sun. Do you think you can remember that?" The boys looked alarmed but nodded solemnly.

"Can't *you* help us Peek?" pleaded Jack after a moment's silence.

"Boys, it's been too long. I'm stuck in this time now. Seek out the Guardian-Priests. They can help you, and just remember to keep these talismans with you at all times." Both boys swallowed hard then Scott responded for both of them.

"We'll be fine Peek. You can rely on us," he said, puffing his chest out with a bravado that Jack couldn't help feel slightly irritated by.

Peek's brow briefly furrowed before he ushered them out of the study. They trooped downstairs in silence, their heads buzzing with unanswered questions. Peek glanced through the window at the approaching night. It would bring nothing but the risk of discovery. He stepped into the lounge and saw that Marj was ready to go.

"Here, un-zip your coat and carry Lava back inside," he said as he bent down to scoop him up from the hearth. Marj smiled at his fussing, but played along. "You'll keep each other warm this way," he added unnecessarily.

They were half way down the garden path when the stillness of the night was shattered.

"Hang on! Hang on! You can't leave yet," Peek cried. They whirled round to see him beckoning frantically.

"What now?" they asked apprehensively.

"It's Chloe; she also needs a talisman," he said through a relaxed smile. The boys groaned in unison.

"But Chloe loses or breaks everything," said Scott dismissively.

"'*Chloe loses or breaks everything',*" said Chloe in mimicry. She screwed up her face in Scott's direction before walking back towards Peek.

"Ignore them Chloe. Go on! Pop up to my study. Open the green trunk and choose anything you like."

Chloe's eyes flashed as she bounded off up the stairs. Moments later she returned, her eyes full of silent wonder. Scott took one look at what she had chosen and snorted with derision.

"I don't believe it! What a wasted opportunity!" he said.

"*Scott!*" His mother cut him short.

"It doesn't bother me. He's just a noodle!" said Chloe as all eyes turned to see her holding aloft an orange. She tossed it up and down into the air catching it each time it fell earthwards. "Somehow, this just felt right," she said wistfully.

"Yes, something from nature. That'll cause quite a stir. Keep it safe until you need it most," said Peek. Chloe looked quizzically at him before running to catch up with the others.

As they walked off into the dusk, everything around them seemed to change: but not in an obvious way. The trees were the same trees that they had passed earlier in the day, and the grass verges looked identical too. No: it was if the inner essence of the land was changing. The trees started to take on a threatening demeanour: their branches stabbing like forks into the sky in all directions, as if looking to skewer something. The grasses, which they had earlier brushed through, now snatched and snagged at their ankles. Three crows suddenly flapped by with a rasping caw that startled them. Marj put a comforting hand against the warm pulse of fur within her jacket and laughed in embarrassment. She never thought of herself as someone who startled easily. Five minutes later, she was surprised to see the three crows again. The crows' heads turned as they walked by. Were they being watched? Again, she put it out of her mind as silly nonsense. But then suddenly Scott yelled out.

"Uggh…mum! Look out!" She caught him looking at her feet and to her horror saw them crawling with bugs. Worms, spiders, centipedes, wood lice; her shoes were covered. In a panic she shook her feet and dragged them through the long grass. *Thank God most of them came off!* Her eyes quickly scanned upwards from her ankles in case - A large garden spider was just above her knee and crawling upwards. She knocked it off with a yelp and a shudder, then there were more: two centipedes, wriggling up the back of her calves! She tore off a handful of long grass and frantically started dusting herself down, until two voices broke through.

"Mum, mum. It's alright. They've gone now." It was Jack and Scott, both looking anxious and concerned. She flashed them a weak smile whilst she caught her breath, then nodded and set off again towards the bus stop. She tried desperately to put it out of her mind. They were only a few minutes away but the light was fading fast and it was taking her peace of mind with it. Her eyes started flickering nervously at the ground around her feet as if expecting another up-surge from an underworld of all things rotten and dank: but it didn't come from the ground this time. Veering up out of nowhere and screeching raucously in their faces, flapped the same three crows that they had noticed earlier. Their large ragged wings beat the air with a powerful rhythm as they hovered only inches away, blocking their path. They were close enough to see their pitch black, lifeless eyes staring blankly out at a world where beauty meant nothing, and weakness meant death. Jack staggered back in shock and cursed as his hair became entangled in brambles at the side of the lane. Scott simply stared open-jawed before Chloe, in a fury, tried to scare them off by waving her arms wildly.

Then it happened. The enclosing blackness of the night suddenly receded as they found themselves in a pod of golden light, just large enough to envelop them all. The light pulsed and throbbed with a powerful energy. The crows shrieked and whirled off, back into the bosom of the night and Marj looked down. Her face flickered through a whole range of conflicting emotions. Afraid she would cause alarm, she masked what she could, before slowly unzipping her coat, half in wonder and half in fright.

"I don't know what's happening: really, I don't. I mean, I -" She never finished her sentence.

"It's Lava!" shouted Chloe as the golden glow radiated outwards from the folds of her mum's open coat.

"Peek said Lava was special, but this is -" Marj zipped up her coat gently and muttered something about getting to the bottom of it all. Behind them, and watching furtively from under the shadow of a splintered tree, were three black crows; and underneath them: Snarklepike, the scout from the Tower of the Moon.

2. A Time Splinter Opens

The next day the sky was black and the trees in the school playground stood guard menacingly as if the kids were there to serve time as punishment. An eerie silence over-hung the place as one by one the children trooped in their heads dropping with dejection as they passed through the school gates. As expected, the Puddleton brothers, or Puddies as they were known, were standing just outside the gates. These were the school bullies hanging about to administer a kicking to whoever it was that they had it in for. Flan, short for Flan-face, was a pimply youth whose fleshy face flapped in the wind whenever he was made to move faster than his vast bulk would permit. He was also the younger of the two. The older brother was known as Dog Bottom, after slipping one day on a patch of wet grass and landing on a pile of dog poo. He'd spent the rest of the day trying to get it off his pants and threatening to punch anyone who mentioned it. The whole school was in stitches behind his back and spent days holding their noses and starting up conversations about dogs and house-training whenever he passed by. Today, however, they were distracted from their usual bullying by a woman with a permanently sour face and dressed in an enormous bear-skin coat. She was jabbering at them in a very excitable manner. It was clear from their expressions that they were eager listeners.

"- any talk of a ginger cat, anything at all: find a way to get it for me."

"Sure thing, Hagratty." The boys nodded furiously, aware that she had something in her hands that she was about to give them.

"Here: these will help you when the time is ripe." In one hand she held a ball of tightly bound thin leather strips and in the other something that looked like a sticky black plum. "It's a 'worm-sponge' full of insect larvae. Whatever you squeeze it over, will rot," she said, as she passed the plum to Flan. His face lit up with wonder before a spiteful leer settled over it.

"- and what's mine then?" asked Dog Bottom impatiently, feeling suddenly short-changed.

"A centipede ball," snapped Hagratty.

"You mean these thin strips are actually centipedes?" He peered more closely at what he held in his hand.

"They are sleeping at present, but throw the ball at someone, and they will wake, scatter and latch on to them, so that you will know exactly where they are."

"Cool!" His mind raced with possibilities.

"To be used only in pursuit of the fire-cat, you understand. I won't have my gifts wasted." She flashed them a look which meant business. He swallowed hard and nodded vigorously but then a commotion over by the school gates distracted him.

"It's happening again. I think I'm gonna faint. Scott, wait!" wailed Jack. But his words weren't heard as Scott was already through the gates. He shot Chloe a desperate look before staggering badly.

"Scott, wait! Jack needs help - oomff!" cried Chloe as her arm cracked painfully against the iron railings and a blast of bad breath filled her face. She recoiled as Dog Bottom leant into her.

"Oops sorry," he sniggered as she rubbed her elbow. To her left Jack was wobbling, barely able to stand. She had to play for time.

"I think you've broken it," she mumbled, doubling up to feign a greater injury.

"Hope you're not gonna blub now," he sneered. Out of the corner of her eye she saw Jack steady himself and move towards the school entrance. She waited a couple more seconds then lunged forwards. A cushion of belly fat enveloped her shoulder and Dog Bottom let out a roar before she twisted free and bolted for the entrance. Behind her, she heard him crash to the ground.

"Yeeooww! You're such dead meat!" He bellowed, as she turned back from the school entrance grinning.

"I might have a bruise, but what's this?" she paused dramatically, to sniff the air in his direction. "I'm sure I can smell another problem in the -PANTS department!"

"You're DEAD!" He snarled.

"Don't think so! You'll have to catch me first, and don't forget -" she paused again, to dramatically sniff the air, "I can smell you a mile away!"

Dog Bottom didn't respond. His eyes met Flan's and together they gazed at the worm-sponge. Slowly, a malicious smile creased his lips.

The morning's lessons seemed to drag on for an eternity. Jack couldn't help but wonder what the shadow-sylph had done to him. To black out without warning was really freaking him out and as for the icy numbness in his arm... Meanwhile, Scott was doing art and the teacher was not amused.

"Are you deliberately trying to provoke me?" he said on seeing Scott hopelessly reaching for the wrong colours.

"Sorry sir. It's my eyes they -"

"Don't be a fool all your life; have a day off!" he said cuttingly. He shuffled off and Scott cursed inwardly. All he could see were shadows and shades of grey whilst at the same time the icy grip was beginning once again to penetrate him to the very bones. What the hell was happening? The seconds dragged on. Would the lesson never end? It felt like years before it eventually did and when the bell finally did go, he shot out like a coiled spring, eager to hook up with Jack and Chloe. It didn't take him long.

"Pick on someone your own size!" cried Chloe. Scott rounded the corner just as Dog Bottom flung her to the floor and kicked her hard in the back.

"Arrgh! Help! Scott!" She shot him a desperate look as Flan grabbed her lunch box, opened it and squeezed the 'worm-sponge' over the contents. Scott's heart pounded. His legs carried him forwards to help her, or at least he thought they did.

"SCOTT!" She cried again but it was no use. He was rooted to the spot. What was happening? Why wasn't he helping? The black viscous liquid dribbled all over her lunch as Flan shot a glance over to him.

"He's too chicken to help. You're on your own little girl." He smirked and Chloe could only watch as the contents of her lunch box heaved and wriggled with larvae.

"Oops... sorry," sniggered Flan as her apple rolled out onto the floor. "Let me help you." He bent down before giving the apple an almighty kick.

"Job done!" laughed Dog Bottom as Chloe choked with anger and frustration.

"You won't get away with this. You blubber-bellied bullies! You won't! You'll see!" she cried. Their laughter reverberated as they sauntered off. A split second later, she whirled on Scott in fury.

"Get away from me, you spineless git. What sort of a brother are you? Don't ever come to me for any help or support after this: ever!"

Scott mouthed something silently before she stormed off in a mixture of tears and rage. He just couldn't understand what had happened. Why hadn't he tried to help? Had he been over-awed by the dark magic of that sponge that Flan carried? Was this the start of a time splinter as Peek had foretold? After this, the afternoon's lessons were a torture for Scott who was now totally obsessed.

"Well time is certainly dragging even if it isn't quite splintering," he muttered to perplexed looks from his classmates. Eventually, the end-of-school bell rang and he darted out to meet up with the others at the school gates. Chloe was just about to give him another piece of her mind when Jack pointed frantically at the last thing they wanted to see: the Puddies. Once again, they were with Hagratty who was now accompanied by Snarklepike, the spindly man who had confronted Peek in the pub, and had been present with the crows when they had taken Lava home. Hagratty was clearly furious.

"Fool! Did you think I wouldn't know whether you had used my gift frivolously?" She stared, waiting for a response. Flan said nothing hoping to let her fury wash over him.

"I see that I shall have to watch over you," she said, as she dug amongst the contents of her bag. After a few seconds, she pulled out a cluster of tiny white eggs the size of pin heads.

"Here: rub these into your hair!" she barked.

"Why? What are they for?" Flan shot her a reluctant glance before wilting under her ferocious glare. He reluctantly did what she asked.

"Good! When those fleas hatch, they'll ferry messages back and forth between us. Make sure they have something positive to report, or the next thing I'll give you will be a spleeworm, which will lay an egg inside you so sulphurous that people will smell you from miles around!"

"Ha! Nice one!" snorted Dog Bottom, amused by the idea.

Jack gestured frantically to the others and they took advantage of their distraction to dart past.

The woman's presence had definitely triggered a change in the landscape. The same dark, brooding sky was hanging over the school again, and although they were walking through the same streets that they had gone through a thousand times before, nothing seemed the same any more. The people that they passed en-route to the bus-stop looked strangely vacant. One guy stopped mid-stride and turned a deathly white face towards them and stared open-mouthed in their direction. Jack found himself staring back, first at the face, then at the eyes and then at the mouth which got bigger and bigger. The mouth was cavernous. He felt himself drifting, falling into it. He jolted back into himself and gasped in shock. Where had the man gone? He swung his head from side to side but the street was empty in all directions.

"Scott; Chloe; did you see that pale-faced -?" he stopped, as their blank expressions showed him that they hadn't. Was this something to do with a time splinter? His mind flashed back to the weird happenings of the night before and he trudged on, deep in thought. Before long they were at the bus-stop and true to form, Chloe and Scott were arguing again.

"Can't you two shut it for a second? This is boring the -" Jack's words tailed off as the colour drained from his face.

"What's up, Jack?" asked Chloe as she noticed his shock and forgot her grudge against her twin for a second.

"It's - I don't believe it," he pointed weakly. Their eyes followed his finger before they all instinctively hunched together. "It's that ball of a woman and that scarecrow again! How on earth did they get here before us?" They stared in horror at Hagratty and Snarklepike waiting amongst a crowd for the same bus that they needed.

"We can't afford any more mistakes. We can expect a time splinter anytime now," said Hagratty before scanning the horizon. "We must find the mirror and the fire-cat before the sun is revived."

Snarklepike nodded agreement and muttered something incomprehensible before reaching into his mouth. He fished a dead wood-louse out from under his tongue and held it gently in front of him. Hagratty's gaze softened in sympathy.

"Grieve not! Our little friends of the dank and dark will not suffer a life under stones for much longer. I see a time soon, when they will scurry freely, feeding on fresh bark," she said. His eyes soaked up her words gratefully.

Jack's mind raced. Should he steer Scott and Chloe deeper into the crowd where they wouldn't be seen? Yet - he needed to hear what else they were saying. Snarklepike was now getting quite agitated.

"I've lost three centipedes," he said bitterly.

"Just stop them before a time splinter occurs," Hagratty insisted as they got onto the bus in deep animated discussion. Jack and the others followed as close behind as they dared. He heard the words "fire-cat" and "kids" along with various words such as "spores" and "smothered" which set alarm bells ringing in his over-active imagination. His heart pounded. He really wanted to get a good look at them; but what if he was recognised? The bus snaked its way up from the town centre and they huddled deep into their hoods grateful for the crowds of people who were constantly getting on and off. Snarklepike and Hagratty were sitting at the back, and Jack was sure that each time he felt the hairs on the back of his neck bristle it was because they were looking at him. It took all of his strength not to give into temptation and turn round and check. The bus rumbled on, and then his heart skipped a beat; Chloe suddenly shot to her feet and turned to face the back of the bus.

"Sit down for heaven's sake!" hissed Jack in desperation, aware that this risked an equally emotive response. He wasn't wrong.

"For God's sake, Jack, who do you think you are: our dad?"

Jack blanched as the sound reverberated around the bus, and then froze as Snarklepike stopped spluttering. There was a deathly moment of silence.

"The sooner we're off this darned bus, the better," he muttered in irritation.

"What now? Bothered by a shrieking kid are we?" taunted Hagratty, with a sneer that even the reflection failed to diminish. "Well, you'll soon escape the wretch, and then we have a busy night ahead of us. It's a full moon tonight."

The bus sailed past the Telephone Exchange, where Snarklepike and Hagratty got off. Jack turned to stare, as Hagratty lumbered down the street like an overweight bear in need of shedding its winter coat with Snarklepike's every wriggling step overcompensating for her clumping gait. He waited for them to disappear out of sight before he whirled on his sister.

"What is it with you? It's as if you darned well wanted them to see you!" he said in exasperation.

"Oh, stop fussing! We're getting off at the next stop ourselves. What could they have done? I just wanted to get a good look at them," she said defiantly, though not without a tinge of sulkiness. Jack sighed and filled them in all he had managed to over-hear. When he had finished, Scott piped up with a grin.

"Can't say I noticed anything bro. But what's the problem? They were probably just a couple of old dinosaurs coming up to the Telephone Exchange to make a phone call."

"Very funny, Scott. Keep on making jokes. It's about all you're good for," snapped Chloe. His chuckles died in his throat as the earlier events in the playground flooded back.

Soon, they were home and after a carefully edited account of the day, were banished to their rooms whilst mum did the hoovering and cleaning. Scott, in particular, never did understand his mum's obsession with hoovering. After all, once the dust was down it wasn't as if you noticed any more, and nobody had yet invented a device to *measure* the amount of dust. With a feeling of having discovered something profound, he snuggled down into his bed with his book and at some point later that night drifted off into dreams where monsters became mixed up with hoovers, and Jedi knights with mop-wielding mums.

When the 'gorse-sign' arrived it was accompanied by lashing rain and a thin eerie howl. Scott woke up in his bed and froze. His eyes darted towards the window. Dawn had only recently broken. For a split second he considered waking Jack but then thought of the stinging rebuke should it turn out to be nothing.The rain pounded the windowpane insistently and then he heard it again: a hideous yowl. He felt his throat tighten as he pulled on a dressing gown and crept forwards. Then a nerve-jangling screech shattered the room and five razor sharp claws scraped down the windowpane. With heart thumping, he fumbled for something, *anything* that might serve as a weapon: but then, whatever it was, moved. It was bristly and fast. First it thumped against the pane then it reared up. His breath quickened as his knuckles whitened around a candlestick. There it was again! A red russet blur smeared the window: or was it a burnt gold? His mind whirled through a kaleidoscope until it dawned on him. It couldn't be: it was!

"Lava! What are *you* doing out there and what's…?" He opened the window and his voice trailed off as he dusted the yellow gorse from Lava's back and Peek's words suddenly flooded back to him. But Lava made no attempt to come in. Scott stared at him in confusion. "What do you want? Do you want me to follow you somewhere?" he asked, as Lava stepped away from the open window and paused to look back at him.

"OK, OK, just let me get dressed," he said with one leg already in his jeans. He considered waking Chloe, but only for a second. "Pah! Let her sleep on. Maybe she'll wake up in a better mood than she went to bed!" he muttered, before grabbing a coat, his talisman and a handful of grapes as the only thing edible to hand. He darted out just in time to see Lava heading for the Common.

"Oh no: not here!" he wailed involuntarily as his eyes nervously darted about Caesar's Well. Thankfully, there was no sign of the shadow-sylph this time and he certainly wasn't going to start burning gorse again. He had just enough time to catch his breath before Lava shot into a nearby bramble bush.

"Wait. Come back! I can't follow you in there," gasped Scott. The bush was dense and prickly and not helped by the moonlight which cast strange shadows over his imagination. He walked around the brambles pleading inwardly for it to release Lava and how in return, he would never pick fruit again, or at least not until it was well and truly ripened. The bush yawned contemptuously and gave nothing back, and certainly nothing of a ginger nature. He returned to the well then caught his breath in alarm. A sudden darkness had descended. What was wrong? There were no storm clouds. It was almost as if it was dawn or dusk again. Peek's words suddenly reverberated around his head. Was time breaking up? Was this a time splinter? His heart raced and he looked down into the well in front of him. It was only a couple of feet deep and completely sealed up, yet…

Before he knew what he was doing, he had stepped down into the well. He gasped in shock as water soaked his feet, yet when he looked down it was the same dried up well as before! But his foot *felt* wet and his jeans were sodden. He took another step. This time he walked into deep crunchy snow: again his eyes told him otherwise. Suddenly, he remembered his talisman. He glanced into the mirror. The woman's image was blurred but he could just make out that she was smiling. Encouraged, he walked into the centre of the well and into a ring of fire!

"What the -?" He looked around with a gaping mouth that mirrored the bramble patch that had mocked him a moment ago. He was standing in the middle of a beautiful meadow which was groaning under a mass of wild flowers, above which butterflies and insects swarmed; yet there were also bare patches of earth where nothing grew. He briefly pondered the reason for this before he jolted with realisation. The ghostly shades of grey that had afflicted him since his encounter with the shadow-sylph had totally gone! In front of him a kaleidoscope of multi-coloured puffleflies exploded into the air: small six-winged creatures that reflected a different colour of the rainbow with each successive beat of their tiny wings. He laughed as they danced around him in a sparkle of colour. But then, just as quickly as they had appeared, they vanished. Why? The meadow was still basking in the gentle warmth of the sun and the flowers were filling the air with scent, or were they? His nose twitched as he caught the smell of something else, something nasty. His breath choked off sharply. Ammonia: and it was getting stronger!

"Hide! Hide, you fool!"

He dropped into the long grass, his heart pounding. Who had spoken? Out of the corner of his eye, he saw the image in the mirror signalling frantically. He cursed himself for not waking Jack. Why hadn't he done so? Next time he would: he would! The stench got stronger and stronger. Now he was gagging. Then he heard it: stems breaking with a crisp, crackling noise and the dreadful smell of burning. He looked up and choked as a tall cowled figure glided through the meadow, leaving a wake of putrescence behind him. The figure paused and looked back in his direction. His face was hidden deep within his cowl from which a noxious green fume leached out into the surrounding air. He surveyed the meadow through which he had come as if sensing the presence of another. Scott froze and the colours started to drain away from his world as shadows returned to swirl around him. He could feel that now familiar ice racing through his veins again as the shadow-sylph's grip on his arm intensified. "Keep still, stay down!" He told himself as his head started spinning. Moments later, he blacked out.

He woke to twilight. The shadow-sylph's grip had weakened and he rubbed at his arm before peering through the shadows that blurred his vision. The meadow had been decimated. The figure had left a trail of slimy mucus in his wake which had burnt and singed all it had touched. Huge tracts of meadowlands were left dissected by these noxious trails that reached like a virus, worming its way into every patch of healthy ground. But Scott could only think of one thing now. Where was Lava and was he alright?

"Come out before that cowled *thing* returns," he hissed urgently. It was half an hour later and Scott had made his way across the meadow and was standing besides a bush from which he could hear scratching. "LAVA! If I have to come in there and get you, I'll, I'll - turn you into - erm - gingerbread," he added lamely. Nothing happened and he sighed deeply. There was only one thing for it and whether he liked it or not, he would have to go in. Covering his exposed flesh as best he could, he groped like a blind man, deeper and deeper into bushes so dense that he couldn't see the nose in front of him. Finally, his face creased into a grin as his fingers closed over fur. "At last!" he yelled with a huge grin. Seconds later, branches whirled, sunlight flashed from all angles and he found himself on the floor staring at the sky and fighting for breath. Something had shot out, thudded into his chest and sent him crashing to the ground. His mind raced until the sky blotted out. This was no cat looming over him as he clutched at lungfuls of air. It was covered in fur alright but the fur was black and white, not ginger. It also had a huge snout full of razor sharp teeth.

"Get up now!" the creature roared.Scott didn't have time to respond. A huge paw jolted forward, grasped his collar and yanked him to his feet. In front of him stood a huge bear-like creature covered in black fur but with a broad band of white fur running from the tip of his snout and down his back. Scott wailed involuntarily as the size of the creature became apparent as his head came no higher than its huge chest. "Who or what are you; and what in La-Kelisland are you doing out here?" It snarled, with its teeth glinting in the light.Scott mumbled vague nothings as his mind raced for ideas.

"Lost your tongue eh? Well, we'll see about that. Get moving!" said the creature as it pushed him back onto the path. The sharp prod in his back told him not to argue, and as for those sharp fangs? Why, oh why, hadn't he woken the others? He stumbled on down the track feeling thoroughly wretched. Twenty minutes later the sky whirled again as he lost his footing, fell and cut his knee.

"Can we please rest for a while? I'm exhausted," he said whilst rubbing his knee. He glanced up but saw nothing encouraging in that face full of fangs.

"Found your voice now have we?" Another sharp prod concluded the discussion and Scott just had time to scan the hillside for Lava before he found himself shunted forwards again. He groaned inwardly as he saw no sign of anything except the spires of a distant castle. They trudged on through a canopy of trees festooned with giant cobwebs that made Scott shudder and feel strangely grateful that he was not walking beneath them on his own. He was now desperately tired but more worried about Lava. Where was he? Was he safe? He looked around anxiously, hoping to see evidence of his gingery friend, but it was hopeless. They must have covered miles of rough, wild terrain. Lava could simply be anywhere. He shuddered at the possibilities and with a herculean effort tried to reassure himself that cats were lucky and had nine lives. Then he snapped back to his current predicament and quickly hatched a plan.

"Can't go on," he mumbled as he slumped once more to the floor with a groan. There was a pregnant pause before the creature reacted.

"WHAT? Get up you fool. Do you know what will happen to you if you don't."

Scott moaned sleepily then yelped in pain as a flurry of jabbing blows rained down on his ribs but he held firm and stayed on the ground. The creature stared at him for a moment.

"Fool! You are moving whether you want to or not." A paw flashed out and with a wrench and twist of his collar Scott suddenly found himself airborne again. With a thump, he landed onto the creature's back and for the second time that day had the breath knocked out of him. It was all he could do to cling on for dear life as the creature suddenly dropped down onto all fours and bounded off down the track.

"Here we are. Now get off my back," grunted the creature with a sudden shake of his body.

"Arrgh! My arm!" cried Scott as he fell to the floor inside the doorway of a house in an old slate mining village.

"Be quiet and don't touch anything," said the creature as it moved passed a staircase festooned with hop vines into the back of the house leaving Scott to nurse his arm and his pride. Moments later he heard a huge clattering of pans, more cursing and the sound of a great gushing of water. He was alone at last but he was also trapped. He pulled out the Mirror of Aggraides but the image in it was now much fainter and a shadowy glaze still affected his vision. Eventually, the creature returned and thrust a steaming pewter cauldron towards him which gave off a rich earthy tang. Scott felt a wave of rebellion surge within him.

"No fur ball's gonna poison me!" he cried rashly.

"Don't be stupid now, it'll do…Arrgh!" yelled the creature. The hot liquid arched upwards as Scott kicked out and sent the vessel spinning. Tiny droplets of scalding liquid splattered down over them both.

"Aooww! You idiot! It was only tea."

"WHAT?"

"YES! I am not trying to harm you. Why do you think I rescued you?"

"RESCUED ME? I thought you were gonna -" Scott's eyes flashed to his fangs and the creature chuckled.

"- eat you? Hardly! You're all skin and bone for starters."

Scott felt a blush of embarrassment. But then the creature shot forward, his snout only inches away from his face. Its mouth opened and its sharp teeth glinted in the light. Scott caught the word 'introduction' then realised that the creature was only grinning.

"I'm Fubbyloofah, a beluga-bear," he said with a mock bow, "and very pleased to welcome you to my home: Rascal Howe." He waved a paw towards the rustic interior with a flourish. "Now can I get on with making more tea and then we can sit by the fire. I am sure you have just as many questions for me as I have for you."

3. Fubbyloofah

"Scott, my name's Scott and I'm sorry if I burnt you with that hot tea," he added red faced.

"Mmm quite!" added Fubbyloofah testily. "Well the less said about that the better." He still looked a little put out but shuffled back to the kitchen to prepare more tea. Scott looked around at his surroundings with more wonder than fear. Even with the touch of the shadow-sylph on him, Rascal Howe looked as mysterious as its name evoked. What a marvellous house it was. The ceiling was covered in humungous old oak beams and there was a gigantic craggy slate chimney breast with a cast iron fireplace. For the first time in a long time he broke into a grin. Just wait 'til Jack and that sour-faced sister of his heard all about this! A sharp tang of spice hit his nostrils.

"Here, drink this!" Fubbyloofah thrust a pewter goblet at him and then moved over to the fire, turned his snout to look directly up the chimney and whistled for a few seconds. Scott was perplexed. What on earth was he doing? There was a faint scrabbling sound and the next minute, three spindly black figures no longer than his forearm, with heads the size of a large pine cone, poked out from the chimney.

"Oh, hello stranger," one of them said whilst winking at Scott. "Snuffmeakin's the name. Pleased to meet ya! Now, what's your poison?"

"Huh? Poison?" Scott shot a look of alarm towards Fubbyloofah.

"We'll have a bit of cherry please," said Fubbyloofah waving a reassuring paw in Scott's direction.

"Right you are, Mr Fubbyloofah, right you are." Snuffmeakin turned to his companions, "Come along, lads. You heard what he said. Now let's get crackin'." He gave Scott an acknowledging nod and then they all disappeared back up the chimney, where Scott could hear them scraping and scratching away. Scott looked questioningly at Fubbyloofah but got no explanation as something else was puzzling him.

"So why you are so different to the other groundluggs?" he said as he sniffed the air around him intently.

"Eh? What are you on about and what the heck are groundluggs?" said Scott, acutely embarrassed at being sniffed at and keen to move the conversation on to something other than any perceived bodily odour. Before Fubbyloofah could answer, there was a sudden loud scrape and a clump of powder dropped into the flames from the chimney. A powerful cherry fragrance filled the room. Fubbyloofah shot Scott a grin.

"Since giving a home in my chimney to these crocklepips, I've never had a dull fire yet," he smiled. "They mine the sooty deposits from inside the chimney and extract the aromatic particles. I've had sandalwood, fresh pine, apple and cedar. I've even had treacle, though that must have been a blend of something, as I've never put that into the fire!"

Scott sat back to enjoy the scent and Fubbyloofah soon started up with his questions again. "So if you're not a groundlugg, what are you? You don't come from round here, that's for sure."

Scott filled him in and when he got to the part about time going crazy and Lava's disappearance at Caesar's Well, Fubbyloofah interjected.

"Stop, stop!" he said raising a paw. "Time fractured, eh? My grandfather talked about this. You know what this means, don't you?" Scott looked blank. "A time splinter must have happened. But you were so unfocused that you arrived in the most inconvenient of places." He reached for his dressing gown and stood up. "Follow me," he said as he went towards the staircase. Scott trudged up behind him until they entered the bathroom.

"Glow-worm heating" said Fubbyloofah to Scott's grin as he felt the heat under his feet. They were standing in Fubbyloofah's stone tiled bathroom and several worms scurried back under the tiles to continue with the job in hand. Fubbyloofah pointed to a large brass porthole that hung behind the bathroom door: the type you see on ships.

"You could have come through there," he said. "My grandfather put it there at the time of the last time splinter all those years ago." He shot Scott an embarrassed glance as he dusted off the cobwebs then he unscrewed it and swung it open. "I think it's time we had another look inside," he said, before sticking his nose in. He gave a grunt of satisfaction before Scott also put his head inside. He was astonished to find that the porthole was a dark cavernous void far bigger than the width of the door should permit. Inside, bands of colour swirled about in suspension.

"Is it real? I mean, how is it possible? And .. those colours.." He babbled excitedly as colour started to seep back into his world again.

"All in good time, all in good time. Now where did you say you came in: brambles was it?"

"Yes, near Caesar's Well; a huge patch of them." He sighed in relief as the shadow-sylph's touch ebbed away and he could finally take in the vibrant lustre of Fubbyloofah's fur and the rich warm shades of the stone tiling. He grinned oafishly as Fubbyloofah continued.

"That's it! Had you been a bit more single-minded when in this Sissy's Well -"

"*Caesar's* Well," laughed Scott.

"Whatever," said Fubbyloofah. "Don't you see? Stay focused whilst in the well and time will splinter in such a way that you can find yourself here. With your mind half on brambles, you arrive half way up a mountain; in the rock-troll's backyard. You're lucky I found you before he did. Many's the groundlugg that he has put to work on his mountain road."

"BUT I'M NOT A GROUNDLUGG!" Scott blurted before wincing with embarrassment at the force of his voice.

"Steady on! Steady on! No need to be cantankerous," said Fubbyloofah, looking down his snout disapprovingly, before casting a further wistful look at the porthole for a few seconds.

"One day someone will get it right. It can get quite wearisome spending your days repairing the damage done to the land by those corrosive slime trails. Everyone's too afraid to pop out and visit anyone like we used to do in the old days." He paused to savour the nostalgic memory before remembering that he had a guest. "Back to the fire with you, young Snot."

"Scott" he corrected.

"Eh, what did you say? Oh never mind -"

They were just settling back down by the fire when there was a sudden knock on the door and a voice murmured outside. Fubbyloofah's ears twitched in recognition and he leapt to his paws to open up. In the doorway stood a lumbering oaf of a being. He was not unlike a large man, only with ears twice as large and with a grin to match. But it was only when he crossed the threshold that Scott saw that his arms extended well beyond his knees to hang loosely around the middle of his calves.

"I'm a sorry to disturb an all, Mr Fubbyloofah," he said, as he was waved to a seat. "- but I has got to speak to someone. You see, they've taken 'er: mi darlin', Florabunda: just like as what happened to 'ole Tub's missus".

"Slow down, Cob and start from the beginning please," said Fubbyloofah, as he handed him a cup of tea and another clump of powder came tumbling down the chimney. A fresh waft of cherry filled the air.

"Thank you, crocklepips," said Fubbyloofah. "That'll do for tonight. Save the rest for another day."

A little black head popped out from under the chimney breast and sniffed the aroma appreciatively, before grinning proudly.

"OK, Mr Fubbyloofah, but don't forget there's still that bundle of hazel and wychwood to burn. That should make for an interesting aroma, if you can find time to chop it up."

Fubbyloofah twitched his snout in acknowledgement, before turning back to Cob.

"This is the second of us groundluggs to be taken in only two weeks," said Cob. "'Ole Prod, the wax-pie maker, says the same thing 'as happened over in Yakshead and also in Crambleside where five groundluggs have gone since the start of the month. 'Time to serve the slygorm now you is nice an fat,' that's what the sakratts said before they took 'er away!"

"Slygorm?" asked Fubbyloofah quizzically. Cob just shrugged and gawped back in response.

"Nobody knows, but we 'ave lost enough of our folks to it!"

Fubbyloofah suggested he put his feet up by the fire, whilst he prepared him a soothing head wrap. Scott, too fascinated to be offended at being mistaken for one of these groundluggs, watched as Fubbyloofah returned with what looked like a huge ivy pot-plant.

"Sit back and relax, Cob. This wipwaffle should help." He placed the plant just behind Cob's head. The ivy tendrils snaked out and wound themselves round Cob's head. The room then filled with groans of delight as it started squeezing and tightening until all the tension in Cob had gone. With Cob now calmer and quieter,

Fubbyloofah put the wipwaffle to one side and introduced the two of them properly.

"Cor, I've never seen any folk as tiny as you," said Cob with affection. "'ave you been starved or something'?"

"NO! I'm perfectly normal, thank you," said Scott indignantly, before suddenly remembering what he was here for. "Look, I need to find Lava and the Guardian-Priests. Do you know -?"

"Guardian-Priests? What do you want with them?" interrupted Fubbyloofah noticing out of the corner of his eye that Cob had taken advantage of the distraction to move the wipwaffle back behind his head for another massage.

"I don't know. Apparently it's all because I've woken a shadow-sylph and something to do with fire-cat magic," faltered Scott.

"Fire-cat magic!" cried Fubbyloofah with such a start that poor Cob bolted and up-rooted the wipwaffle in the process. A sharp whine filled the room as the poor plant loosened its grip round Cob's head and rapidly wilted.

"I'm so sorry, Mr Fubbyloofah. I was asleep. I just couldn't help it," he apologised.

It took a few minutes of gentle fussing over the root ball for which Fubbyloofah had to pop outside to make a special mulch of moulted fur and beetle juice, before it started to spring back to life.

"I think I'd better put this away for the night," he said, with a sharp glance at Cob. "Now then, where was I?"

"Shadow-sylphs and fire-cat magic?" said Scott expectantly.

"Ah yes. I'm not sure how much is true, but legends speak of a fire-cat, called Rama, that saved La-Kelisland many years ago from a dying sun. We could certainly do with Rama now"

"Really? Why?" asked Scott, fascinated.

"Oh, you'll see tomorrow morning when the sun comes up," he said, dismissing the question with a wave of his paw. "According to legend, Rama went to World's End with a time-ward and revived the sun with burnt gold but - wait a minute -" Suddenly his jaw dropped with astonishment. "You've travelled through a time splinter. *You're* a time-ward! Bless my berriblods! Are *you* here to find burnt gold?"

"Eh? No. I've never heard of burnt gold, or any of this. How could I find burnt gold, I spend half my time these days looking at the world through shadows."

Scott hated to admit it but something told him that having everyone's hopes pinned on him was a bad idea. But it was no use.

"Fabulous! Wonderful! We'll soon have our sun back, Cob!" Fubbyloofah chuckled. "Just wait 'til everyone hears of this."

"No, you got it wrong. It's these Guardian-Priests that we need to find: not me." Scott felt wretched.

"Eh? What's that? Oh you're talking of the Hebradaigese. Yes, maybe. They are schooled in this stuff, and their primary function is to look after the land." He paused as Cob suddenly became quite animated.

"Does you think these 'ebradaigese will rescue our missing groundlugg folk from them sakratts?" he asked expectantly. Fubbyloofah fixed him with a concerned look.

"I don't know Cob. They spend most of their time having political in-fights with each other in Granglethorn Castle. You may have seen the castle from the track where I found you," he added to Scott as an aside, before turning back to Cob. "I don't how much use they'll be to anyone. I mean, they don't seem able to stop the sun leaching away," he said as Cob suddenly looked downcast. "The only Hebradaigen who regularly emerges from the castle, and is to be avoided at all costs, is Jassaspy."

"**Jassaspy, Jassaspy Jassaspy Jassaspy Jassaspy Jassaspy,**" chimed a voice from the wall.

"What an unfortunate moment to utter his name," said Fubbyloofah. "Don't be alarmed. It's only the 'mime-clock'.It repeats the last word said on each hour. Shame it had to be his."

Cob looked around in confusion, whilst Scott couldn't stop grinning at the fun he could have were Jack and Chloe ever to come here.

"Who *is* Jassaspy?" asked Scott after the clock had finished.

"If you mean what does he look like? Nobody knows for sure, because nobody has seen him. He is a cowled figure that lurks in the shadows, and leaves a slime trail and a noxious smell wherever he goes," said Fubbyloofah. Scott jolted.

"Oh, my God! I saw him - in the meadows - leaving trails of green slime everywhere."

"Yes, that's him," added Fubbyloofah. "High-Lord Hebradaigen of the Tower of the Moon, and no friend of anything that flourishes under the sun.Thankfully, we still have the waxenwaifs and Featherfae to counterbalance his poison. You must meet Featherfae; life simply springs from her footprints!" He left this unexplained, as he reached towards a framed picture and a pair of half-moon spectacles which he perched on the end of his snout.

"Me and my grandfather," he said, as he passed the picture around, "and just *look* at those trees dripping with berriblods. The whole valley was covered with them *and* the air was full of birdsong *and* the streams ran crystal clear." His voice was beginning to crack and his eyes were moistening. Scott and Cob exchanged alarmed glances.

"Don't you be worryin' 'bout this, Mr Fubbyloofah," said Cob. "We'll all fight this together, eh? Aint no groundlugg gonna let Jassaspy poison our lands no more. What say you, Scott?"

"Absolutely, and once my brother and sister get here, there'll be three of us to contend with."

"Three of you, eh? Well, climb a tree and eat my berriblods! You're sure to find burnt gold if there are three of you." He threw a hopeful look at Scott, who flinched but decided to let the comment go. "Do you think you could bring them through my bathroom porthole?"

"I can certainly try," grinned Scott before the photo once again exerted its pull and a sob welled up in Fubbyloofah again.

"Just look how things have changed," he wailed.

"Well, maybe it's time to put that picture down and think about how we are going to find these people you wanted me to meet," said Scott, keen to pull Fubbyloofah out from the emotional well he was stuck in.

"Eh? I don't remember saying anything about meeting people," said Fubbyloofah, momentarily distracted.

"Yes, you did. You said something about feathers and waifs or something like that," said Scott.

"Ahh yes, Featherfae and the waxenwaifs. Yes, absolutely. Not sure we'll find waxenwaifs though. They can't exactly be summoned. They're small visceral fairies that appear at moments of great peril to save something precious. Think of them as the guardians of the natural world."

"Well, I'm glad there's something to help in the fight against Jassaspy," said Scott with a yawn as the emotion of the day suddenly caught up with him. Cob took this as a sign he should go and rose to leave.

"Well, I best be off," he said as he made for the door.

"Don't go, Cob; there's plenty of room. Besides, we were hoping you'd come with us tomorrow to find Featherfae," said Fubbyloofah, suddenly feeling a need to be surrounded by friends. Cob paused briefly before breaking into a grin.

"OK. I'll be glad to. Anything I can do to help get my missus back, I'll do," he said earnestly.

So within ten minutes of them all retiring to their bedrooms, they were fast asleep. This time, Scott dreamt of rock-trolls and castles accompanied by a constant rumbling of thunder, that were he awake, he would have ascribed to Cob's rhythmic, if unsettling, snores.

4. The journey to Waftenway and what happened with spiced tea

"Come along then, grab your Jacket. We're off to find Featherfae and burnt gold." Fubbyloofah stuck his snout outside and wrinkled it in disapproval. "This is the second time this week that the sun has refused to rise. We journey by moonshine only I'm afraid," he added with a shake of his head as he peered carefully at the horizon. Scott and Cob looked at the sky. The sun was nowhere. What light there was, came from a leech-green hue that was strongest down on the horizon. It was as if the sun was sickening down there, too weak to climb into the sky. "It's dying on us," said Fubbyloofah, in response to Scott's quizzical look.

"But can't it be saved?" asked Scott concerned.

"Yeah, we needs our sun back. Can't get nothing to grow when it's like this," added Cob ruefully.

"That's what you're here to do, isn't it? Save it with burnt gold?" added Fubbyloofah expectantly.

"Please! Stop it, or you're going to be very disappointed. I know nothing about burnt gold. I'm just here to find my ginger cat," said Scott mournfully. Fubbyloofah started suddenly.

"Ginger! Did you say the cat was 'ginger'? If this is true then -" he stopped mid-sentence, his eyes flickered up to the heavens, as if he expected to see Lava descending from on high like a heavenly being. "Is he - erm - very gingery?" Scott nodded earnestly as Fubbyloofah broke into a hearty chortle. "Well, crush my berriblods and turn 'em into wine! Come along then! Let's not dally. If he's that colour there'll be sun-threads to gather!"

"Sun-threads?" Cob looked blank as Scott shrugged in exasperation. Fubbyloofah offered no explanation though as with a whoop of delight and a hop and a skip, most unusual for one of his bulk, cantered off down the lane.

"Just look at it," said Cob. "Many's the bird that's dropped out o' the sky since that appeared. Nobody knows where it's from. It's yet another worry we have."

"It seems to be getting thicker as the sun gets weaker," said Fubbyloofah. "Thankfully, it is still high above the roof tops. But if it sinks down to ground level -" He shook his head gravely and Scott looked up at the thick band of green mist hovering above the chimney pots. It looked claggy and noxious. Onyx-Stone was an otherwise picturesque village of slate buildings, which Scott presumed had been mined from Dragmines valley. Grey woodsmoke curled out of their chimney pots adding to the charm. A couple of crocklepips waved down to Fubbyloofah.

"Good day to you sire. Give our regards to Snuffmeakin."

Fubbyloofah flourished a paw in response. He was well liked amongst their community for providing a chimney for three of their kind to call home. Suddenly a voice rang out.

"Move: you muppets!"

A host of dandelion seeds streamed past them, followed by a large bird careering out of control. There was a flash of lime green feathers as he clipped the side of a small bush before spinning to the ground breathlessly.

"Now, why did you have to get in the way like that," said a green woodpecker, dusting himself down with a huff. "I've been rounding up those dandelion seeds all morning. *Now* where are they? That's my bedding that's gone missing. Makes a lovely pillow does a dandelion seed. As if we birds don't have enough to worry about with that stuff up there," he said, nodding towards the claggy green smog.

"Terribly sorry," said Fubbyloofah, "Here, let me help." He lunged clumsily in the air but only served to scatter the dandelion seeds further.

"Enough! Enough!" The woodpecker fumed.

"Sorry, but don't be angry. We're here to help. You see my friend here is going to find burnt gold and revive the sun." He said excitedly. "He'll soon get rid of that green smog."

"FUBBYLOOFAH!" cried Scott in exasperation.

"Burnt gold? Burnt gold'? I thought we birds were the flighty ones. For the Sun's sake, take your head out of the clouds and stop dreaming. All that fur has woollied up your brains. Burnt gold? What stuff and nonsense! Now where's my pillow?" he said as he gave Fubbyloofah an indignant look.

"There they go!" cried Scott, pointing to the dandelion seeds floating off over the roof-tops.

"Jolly good. At least one of you has something positive to contribute," he said, throwing Fubbyloofah another withering glance. "Well; goodbye then! Oh, by the way, Tappletock's the name, but I must be off. Can't let them get away again. Tally ho! and keep out of the flight paths!" he said, as he launched himself skywards, dipping low over the chimney pots and sending the crocklepips scurrying for cover.

After leaving the village, their next stop was at the famed beauty spot of Yuletree Tarn where they were all reduced to feelings of despair and horror. The whole area had been contaminated with green slime. The grass had withered under its onslaught and the pool shimmered with an oily viscous hue of purple and green, which might have been considered attractive were it not for its toxicity. Scott's face creased in disgust.

"Uggh, this must be that Jassaspy's work," he muttered as Fubbyloofah's long furry ears began to twitch back and forth.

"Ssh! I can hear something," he said, signalling for silence. He crept forwards gingerly, paw by paw then froze as his snout wrinkled in the direction of some large boulders.

"Mind yourself Fubby, there's slatherwelts round 'ere," warned Cob. Fubbyloofah tensed at the mention of these six legged bloated blood-suckers. Once under your fur they were devilish to remove and could keep a wound open for weeks.

"You approach from the opposite side, Cob. Scott, cover my back. If it is a slatherwelt, then remember to cover your eyes if it springs at you," said Fubbyloofah, as he heaved a large boulder to one side. Suddenly he bellowed in pain and bolted deep into the surrounding woodland.

"Fubbyloofah come back!" Scott's jaw dropped and he whirled round in a panic. Should they also run; whatever it was had to be bad if it could drive off the 7 foot Fubbyloofah? A deep moaning sound suddenly rang out. He whirled to find Cob crouching with his hands over his eyes and groaning in fright. This was all he needed. "That's really not helping, Cob! Why don't you - ?" He never finished his sentence. For a moment he was a frantic scrabble of fingers.

"Why didn't I think of this before?" he muttered to himself as he took out and started frantically shaking the Mirror of Aggraides.

"I'm worried about mum. Is there anything we can say to make her feel better?" A splatter of orange petals hit Jack's cheek as the poppletons danced out their lives around them. Peek was making tea for him and Chloe and put the teapot down to let the leaves settle. Chloe sat sullenly to one side: a mess of mixed feelings. Part of her was still mad as hell with Scott for standing by whilst the Puddies attacked her, whilst the rest of her just felt guilty now that he had disappeared.

"Not unless you think she'll be comforted by our talk of a time splinter," said Peek doubtfully.

"Mmm, I think she would more likely think we'd gone mad," said Jack. Peek passed them something that throbbed with a calming light.

"Baked to shine a light on your troubles," he said as they started to nibble slices of pulsecake thoughtfully. Chloe reached to give the teapot a stir but then gave a jolt.

"Hey! There's a message here!" She stared into the pot and Jack motioned to Peek not to engage. Chloe had made these bizarre references before, usually in connection with their missing father. It was her way of coping with her loss, or so Jack assumed.

"Do you know whether he took the Mirror of Aggraides with him when he disappeared?" Peek asked, turning back towards Jack.

"He must have done," replied Jack, as he felt a flush from the cake travel to his face and caught his reflection glowing like a beacon. "I've had a good look around his room and it's nowhere to be found."

The light filled his head with calm. It was wonderfully relaxing. Peek nodded thoughtfully before turning to Chloe who simply kept staring into the teapot.

"What *are* you so obsessed with, Chloe?" he asked before leaning forwards to look over her shoulder. He drew back sharply.

"What is it?" asked Jack in mild alarm. Peek beckoned him over and they all peered into the pot. At first, Jack thought there was nothing there but tea leaves and boiling water but then; there at the bottom of the pot, as plain as anything; the tea leaves had settled into clearly defined letters: T - O - C - T - S.

"It's a fluke. Pure co-incidence," said Jack, reaching across to give the pot a stir and breathing heavily. "This is just to show you both," he muttered before letting out a cry as the leaves settled once more into the same letters, but which this time spelt: C - O - T - T - S. He swallowed hard and looked questioningly at Peek. Chloe just sat and stared into the tea in a state of calm communion.

"Mmm, very odd. I've seen messages in tea leaves before, but they have always been *after* the tea has been drunk, and they are never letters, only suggestive shapes and patterns," said Peek with his head down in thought. When he lifted his head again, his eyes reflected a certain resolve. "We need to visit the Keeper of the Ancient Runes," he said simply.

"It's moving! it's coming for us!" Cob squeaked in panic. Scott froze and caught a flicker of coarse bristly hair from behind the rocks, before everything in front of him mulched into murky shadows. He felt the shadow-sylph's icy fingers caress his arm again. He groped forwards breathing heavily. The mirror was no help now.

"You first!" said Cob as he pushed Scott forwards.

"Oh, thanks for that, Cob, very noble of you." Scott fumbled to his left and grabbed hold of a sharp branch. He hung his head for a moment, breathing deeply. The shadows were subsiding slowly: just a few more seconds was all he needed.

"It's 'eard us, Scott," said Cob, as a sudden high pitched whine filled the air.

It was now or never! In an instant Scott was at the rocks, kicking them over, and raising his makeshift spear high above his head. His charging cry echoed back from the boulders, then wilted in his throat almost immediately. He was dumbstruck! In the den and inches away from being skewered by his lance were two small furry creatures: the most miserable helpless specimens that he'd ever seen. Their eyes had shrunk, as if in self-defence and their fur had hardened and matted as if in response to the surrounding pollutants. They looked up and mewled weakly. How could *they* have driven off Fubbyloofah? It just didn't make sense. He looked down at their den, now destroyed, and realised that there was only one thing he could do for these creatures that he'd just made homeless. He scooped them up, tucked them inside his Jacket and called out to Cob.

"Don't you be distracted by my moans and all," said Cob, as he caught Scott up, wheezing a little from the effort. "They were old groundlugg 'war-cries'. I was just about to wallop 'em. Honestly, I was."

"Pull the other one Cob and be quiet will you. There's something weird about this place," said Scott looking around furtively.

The overhead tree canopy cast a dark shade yet, despite the shadowy film across his eyes, Scott couldn't help but notice trails of flowers leading deep into the woods.

"Guess we may as well follow these trails and see where they go," said Cob, anxious to chatter normally again. Scott grunted in response and together they trudged along the flower trails wondering how on earth they could have flowered in such shade. He thought back to the slime trails he had seen when coming down the mountain track. It seemed as if these were the diametric opposite: each making its mark on the world but in totally different ways. A sudden moaning cut short his musings.

"Fubbyloofah!" he cried as there in front of them rolling and wriggling on a huge mossy bank was their friend.

"Oh, bless your berriblods for coming after me. I got so terribly burnt by that slime: got it into my fur when I shifted those boulders. I just had to find a grassy bank to rub against. Most of it is off now." He gave himself a final vigorous rub. "There, that's better," he said standing up. He was a full 7 feet in height and Scott had to stand on tip-toe to show him the two little fur balls curled up asleep in his Jacket.

"Ahh, smoggilars!" he said. "Cute, aren't they? Increasingly rare round here you know. It's all due to habitat loss," he added, "and with that slime on the pool, I wouldn't have given these more than a day or two at most: lucky that we came along when we did. Are you alright to keep them in there for a while?" Scott nodded and gave the little creatures a stroke under their chins causing them to curl up even tighter.

They emerged from Shackledown woods with Fubbyloofah babbling excitedly about the flower-trails. "Didn't you notice them? They're the signs that Featherfae has passed by. Hopefully we'll spot her soon."

They walked alongside a cascading river and up towards a waterfall that was just big enough to inch behind. Once behind the wall of water, they took a small clearly defined track through a grotto and out towards a tarn: and what a tarn it was! God had clearly dropped his palette from the heavens and here was where it had fallen. "Waftenway! We're here at last" said Fubbyloofah.

The foliage was a stunning display of red, orange, green and yellow. The tarn itself was snuggled neatly into a basin atop the ridge separating Yakshead from Onyx-Stone and was daubed with a gentler more forgiving light than the lurid green that they had suffered all day. A persistent but gentle drizzle bathed the whole area, as if soothing old wounds.

"But it's so vibrant and healthy," stuttered Scott.

"That's because it's never been found," explained Fubbyloofah before Cob interrupted him with a sudden cry.

"Down by the lake! Flowers!" he shouted excitedly. They all turned to look and Fubbyloofah let out a low chuckle.

"Ahh, yes, but that's a *clump* and we need to look out for a *trail* of flowers. Follow the trail to find Featherfae!" he said as they continued around the headland marvelling at how the islands stood like crowns in the tarn with their tall dramatic fir trees garbed in autumnal shades.

"There she is!" cried Fubbyloofah, suddenly. A figure was moving along the ridge above them and as she got closer, Scott could see that she was hopping and skipping joyously. But what absolutely astonished him was the fact that small tiny flowers started to spring up from every footprint that she left behind. She was literally leaving flowers in her wake! He rubbed his eyes in disbelief.

"Featherfae! Featherfae!" Fubbyloofah cried as he set off towards her at a pace Scott found difficult to match. A moment later, they were met by a beaming smile.

"Fubbyloofah, how lovely to see you again."

Facing them was a winged wood nymph: only she looked a little different to most wood nymphs on account of her father being a time-ward like Scott. Her hair was long and had love-lies-bleeding trailing through it along with a scattering of leafy twigs. But she exuded such warmth and affection that within seconds Scott didn't notice this and as for the fact that flowers sprung up from her every footstep, well, anything could be overlooked for that. Scott was dimly aware of Cob making a groundlugg greeting gesture, as the temptation to close his eyes and drift off, enwrapped in the emotion that she radiated, was intense. She leaned forwards, and her aura seemed to frisk the surrounding air with affection, whilst those large eyes just shone - and shone - and shone!

"Ahh, we have a djinn in our midst," she said as she stepped back. Scott suddenly looked worried

"A what?" he asked nervously.

"A djinn: one of the three sentient creations of God. Together, the djinn, humans and angels make up the three. You have the essence of the djinn inside you. Can't you feel it?"

"Feel what? What are you talking about?" Scott whirled round anxiously looking for support.

"The smokeless and scorching fire inside," she said.

"Great fat berriblods!" interjected Fubbyloofah, his attention now grabbed. "Are you sure Featherfae? This would change everything! A djinn would be a powerful ally," he said, hopping up and down in his customary excitement. "He's here to find burnt gold, you know."

"Please, Fubbyloofah. Stop raising everyone's hopes. I spend half my time looking at the world through shadows. I wouldn't be able to see the colour gold if it was right there under my nose. I'm - sorry to disappoint you," said Scott falteringly, as Fubbyloofah's excitement fell. "I also think I'd know if there was any fire inside me, too," he said, glancing awkwardly at Featherfae. In response, she simply smiled before letting out a squeak of delight as two scratty little heads suddenly popped out of his Jacket and started wriggling.

"Smoggilars! Such sweet little creatures," she cooed with an expansive grin.

In the same way that Scott was so taken by Featherfae's inner radiance that he didn't notice her dishevelled hair, so with Featherfae, who instantly saw past the matted fur and the shrunken eyes of the smoggilars.

"We need to feed you up on some forest irrebies don't we my little friends?" she said, tickling them under their chins. The smoggilars jumped down, scampered over and were soon running rings round her legs, rubbing their heads against her and arching their backs with pleasure. Featherfae raised her head and beamed with joy, and Scott could swear that at that moment a ray of sunshine burst forth from her eyes to mingle with the soft golden glow that Waftenway bathed in. When the smoggillars finally allowed her room to move again the flowers shot up in her footprints to such a height that they blocked the view of the tarn.

"I won't be a minute," she said with a laugh, as she skipped off into the forest with the smoggilars at her heels. Fubbyloofah chuckled.

"Those smoggilars don't know how lucky they are," he said. "Featherfae can sniff out what few forest foods still exist from a distance that the rest of us could barely see with the naked eye."

Scott felt strangely comforted. All the pervading fears that had been building up in him since the time splinter, had ebbed away in her presence. With Featherfae at large, he knew that Lava, wherever he was, stood a chance. When she returned, Fubbyloofah filled her in on what had happened. As soon as she heard about Lava, her face lit up and she produced a small tuft of golden threads which Scott identified immediately.

"That's Lava's fur, but where did you find it, and is - Lava - OK?" he asked hesitantly; a million frightening scenarios flashing across his mind. But it was a question he knew no one could answer.

"Sun-threads! I knew it! Just look at the golden glow they give off," chuckled Fubbyloofah. Scott remembered well: that very first evening they'd taken Lava home and how he'd astonished them all with his golden glow. "- and do you know what's even more amazing?" Fubbyloofah continued whilst pausing for effect. "They'll never fade. They'll keep the light in places where plants and animals need it most."

"I have already started to lay them down as way-markers," said Featherfae. Scott was impressed, though worried that with everyone thinking of Lava as the fire-cat, expectations of him finding burnt gold would be raised again. To his relief, the conversation moved on to other things that included the shadow-sylph and his need to get help from the Guardian-Priests.

"Ahh, you talk of the Hebradaigese. You won't get far without an introduction and most are too busy squabbling with each other in Granglethorn castle," said Featherfae sadly. "But there is one I know who is untainted by all the in-fighting, but it's a long and arduous journey to reach him." At these words Fubbyloofah's ears pricked up.

"Well, what are we waiting for? Our friend here needs all the help he can get." He nodded assertively before indicating the way back. "I wonder if we can help wake the djinn. It's bound to help with finding burnt gold," he muttered to himself as he bounded off in front. Scott groaned at the mention of his supposed inner powers. Would it never end?

They set off on their return journey with pockets full of autumnal leaves which Cob was convinced contained burnt gold and steeled themselves for the return of the lurid green hue. Scott felt the sickness in the land almost immediately on leaving Waftenway and was grateful for the first rest stop on the fringes of Shackledown Woods. There was a sticky mess in his pocket and he wanted rid of it.

"I guess this wasn't the best idea." He moved to toss away the squishy bunch of grapes that he had brought from home, hoping it would stem the nausea he'd felt since leaving Waftenway but it didn't.

"What? Quick! Pass them here!" shouted Fubbyloofah excitedly. "I remember bunches hanging from trees in the days when the sun was so bright that you couldn't look directly at it. Where did you get them from?"

But Scott wasn't listening. Hunched over in a ball at their feet, he suddenly started twitching erratically.

"I - can't – see," he panted breathlessly. The shadows were melting and merging again. His breath started to constrict as his veins iced up. His breath rasped in panic. What if everything stayed like this? He'd be virtually blind, living in shadows. Images of death flashed by followed by a soothing stream of warmth and then - flowers - trails of flowers. Was it Featherfae? He couldn't tell. "Arrgh!" His arm fizzled as a final rush of heat flooded back. He shook it frantically. "It's the shadow-sylph. Since it touched me, I get these attacks. Now you must understand. How can I possibly find burnt gold for you?" he said, panting heavily at the sea of concerned faces surrounding him.

"The sooner we get him to this Hebradaigen that you know, the better. I don't like this one little bit. Did you see the blackness in his eyes?" asked Fubbyloofah. Featherfae nodded gravely.

"I'm Ok now, I think. Let me get rid of these." Scott took a deep breath then tossed the grapes aside. "They're well past their best."

"Yup! 'orrible lookin' things," said Cob, his nose wrinkling with distaste.

"No; you silly fool, don't you know about their healing powers?" Featherfae could barely contain her excitement. "We'll extract the juice then plant the pips."

Healing the land was her speciality, and she was not going to pass up on this. She rummaged through her bag and took out a small stoppered flask.

"Steady on, steady on!" squeaked the cork-bug, as it eased itself out of the neck of the flask. "Don't put too much in, mind. I don't want to get mi bum wet." He scowled at their laughter, before Featherfae proceeded to add the juice.

"This is agrappa. It heals burns, and is especially valuable now that Jassaspy has left his corrosive trails everywhere."

"Ohh, well if you'd said that's what it was I wouldn't have made such a fuss," the cork-bug said, looking from one to the other expectantly.

"Perhaps Fubbyloofah would like some for his paw," said Scott thinking of the slime burns he had got by the pool.

"Never mind him; I was just about to say," said the cork-bug, as Fubbyloofah declined the offer with a shake of his head, "that I don't mind if you fill her up to the top. I quite fancy bathing my bits in agrappa."

"Oh, do be quiet, cork-bug," said Featherfae. She pushed him back down into the neck of the flask. They all heard a squeal of delight as the juice washed around him and she replaced the flask in her bag and turned to look for the smoggilars.

"Fumblepaw? Tumbleweed? Hurry back please. We need to plant these pips."

The two smoggilars were busy snuffling round the undergrowth and in his haste to get back little Fumblepaw lived up to his name. He tripped over his paws and rolled, rather than ran, back to her. Featherfae helped the dishevelled little fur ball to his feet with an affectionate laugh before they all approached the task in hand. As 'Master of Ceremonies', Featherfae was in her element directing operations with military precision. Scott was to plant some pips near the moss, as this area was damp enough for the pips to germinate, whilst she and the smoggilars would plant the others by the sun-threads that she had previously laid as way-markers. She reasoned that the light from the sun-threads would guarantee germination. Meanwhile Fubbyloofah was to be here, there and everywhere, ready to use his sharp claws to dig up the soil and remove any pernicious weeds or awkward rocks that might threaten the project. They set about the task with keen abandon, and within half an hour, the pips were securely planted and the party back on the way to Onyx-Stone and the comfort of Rascal Howe.

5. Drowning in Stars

It took about 10 minutes for Peek, Jack and Chloe to arrive at 'Sticky Wicket', a shop of curios and keepsakes, tucked down a cobbled side-street of the Village. They opened the door and a brass bell chimed delicately. Inside, they found ceiling to floor bookcases and stuffed animal heads jutting out from every available alcove.

"Oi, did you see that stag's head just wink at me?" Jack said as he jumped back in shock causing Chloe to squeal.

"Ow! Watch it, you clumsy git!" She bent to rub the foot that he'd just trodden on.

"Sorry," he muttered before he started again. "Look, it's smiling now!" He stared back intently before footsteps distracted him. A distinguished looking Indian gentleman wearing an elaborately embroidered waistcoat appeared before them.

"Good afternoon, Mr Khan," said Peek warmly.

"Ahh, Peak, how delightful to see you again, and who, pray tell me, are your erstwhile companions?" he asked, as he beckoned them in past strange-looking antique curios of unknown origin or purpose. Before Peek could respond, Chloe blurted out:

"I've seen you before. You worked with my dad didn't you?"

The man jolted and knocked one of the pewter tankards hanging from the ceiling. "Good heavens. I - well - yes, we did, but it was on a matter of - " A shower of dust and small creatures chimed in the air as they fell, before fluttering up to roost by the ceiling again.

"Fire-cat magic?" finished Chloe, refusing to be distracted by what had just happened. "Yes, we know all about that." She eyed him carefully. "I have a hunch we'll find our father again. What do you think?" There was a moment's pause as the man swallowed hard.

"Erm - please, come in for tea," he said, his eyes darting towards Peek, not quite knowing how best to respond.

He led the way past a collection of coloured glass vials. One contained an iridescent beetle whose wings would flutter whenever you removed the stopper. Others contained powders that were so volatile that they constantly ricocheted around inside the glass bottle. Finally he waved them to some seats and Peek explained all that had happened earlier with the teapot.

"Extraordinary," said Mr Khan, "and you say this - what's-his-name - Scott, went missing a few days ago?" They all nodded. "You'd better come through to the Chamber of the Tree Wain."

Jack and Chloe shot each other a look of pure intrigue as he slippered the way towards the back of the shop which was even more magical than the shop itself.

"Good afternoon, Twitchetty-poos. Reading anything interesting?" asked Mr Khan. On top of a huge stack of books sat a bespectacled white mouse reading a copy of 'One nibble and your nobbled: the discerning rodent's guide to real cheese.' He nodded in acknowledgement but Mr Khan had already passed by and now had his back to him. Over the rim of his spectacles he caught sight of Jack staring up at him.

"Don't you know it's rude to stare?" he squeaked before flicking a piece of cheese rind towards his gaping mouth.

"Wake up!" chuckled Chloe as she pushed Jack forwards. The rind missed the open goal and passed harmlessly over his shoulder.

Further along the corridor was a cauldron full of pink liquid bubbling away merrily in the corner. Rose petals were floating on the surface and an array of punch glasses were laid out as if for visitors. But it was right in the middle of the room that the biggest surprise was to be found. A giant hazel tree: growing up from the ground and through the floor! Hosts of twittering birds were nesting in its branches amongst the books stored there. Mr Khan weaved his way round the trunk, and reached into the upper branches to take down a very large and incredibly dusty leather-bound tome. He blew off the dust which started Jack and Chloe off into coughing fits.

"Cor blimey!" said a voice out of nowhere. "What's an 'umble book-worm got to do to get a good night's kip round 'ere?"

"Sorry, didn't realise you were in there, Mr Bagwapple," said Mr Khan as he carefully swept up the dust and an irate bookworm too.

"Saying sorry's no good now. That's my beauty sleep, you've just gone and ruined. There I was deep in the Pleistocene era and delighted to finally catch up on my sleep, when you come along and do your hurricane impression. Do you know how long it took me to find something that boring?"

"Terribly sorry. Do let me put it right. Here, there must be other equally dull books," said Mr Khan, as he rummaged around the bookshelf. "How about this? '17th century military leather wear: what any aspiring cavalier ought to know'." But Mr Bagwapple just grimaced. "Ok, what about, 'Family, fools and friends: an entrepreneur's guide to fund raising'?" asked Mr Khan, eyebrows raised optimistically. "No? Aha! How about this then: 'Algebraic calculus for the modern man'?"

"I suppose I could give that one a try," Mr Bagwapple said sniffily as he wriggled towards the large dusty volume. It wasn't long before he was snoozing away deep in chapter one.

Mr Khan lifted the heavy cover of the book he had been seeking, and peered inside. "It's written here that tea-leaves normally communicate through shapes and patterns. But there's nothing here about the use of letters." He looked gravely at Peek. "We need to consult the Lost Runes of Rapgallion," he said quietly.

Several dust clouds later, Mr Khan suggested they break for tea.

"Here are some examples of messages coming through," said Peek as Mr Khan clattered about in the kitchen. "Some are spelt out in animal scratchings whilst others appear in gravel pathways. All are opportunities to respond if you know what to do"

"But we *don't* know what to do," blurted out Jack, "and we don't know how to help him either, do we?" A chink of glass and a loud burp prevented Peek answering. A knot of toads now sat on the rim of the cauldron, each holding a glass of the pink bubbling liquid.

"Your good health!" One of them raised a glass in their direction. It fizzed and frothed before disappearing down its throat. It burped loudly again before its bleary eye settled on something else. Chloe grinned then turned away as Mr Khan reappeared with the tea.

"Apparently, cinnamon if thrown at a mirror enables the beholder to see a world beyond, whilst cloves and cardamom if added to a hot broth, can induce visions," he said as he put the teapot down. "I wonder what will happen if we add it to hot tea instead. Shall we try?" They all nodded vigorously. "OK, one, two, three!" He flipped the teapot lid and tipped in the spice. Four pairs of eyes dived in scouring it for answers. The spices swirled in the water and slowly settled.

"Nothing's changed! It's the same as before," Jack exclaimed as the letters reappeared at the bottom. Peek closed the teapot lid slowly and they all sipped their tea lost in silent thoughts.

"Just leave the teapot and cups by the sink," said Mr Khan some time later as he thumbed through yet another volume. Jack gathered the cups and disappeared into the kitchen to rinse out the pot. Seconds later he let out an almighty yell.

"QUICK! Get in here!"

Peek was the first into the kitchen. "Eureka!" he shrieked as Mr Khan and Chloe appeared on either side. The kitchen was full of steam from the open teapot and shimmering in the air was an apparition.

"It's him!" cried Jack, pointing at the image in the air.

"And look in the teapot!" Peek shouted.

Now there was no doubt about it as the letters at the bottom spelt out the name in everyone's mind: SCOTT

"Your favourite dish, Featherfae!"

Fubbyloofah emerged from the Onyx-Stone grocery with the same cheeky grin on his face as he had when he went in. He thrust the shopping bag under her nose with obvious delight.

"I don't know what you could possibly be referring to," she said, in mock ignorance, knowing full well and conscious all of a sudden of her slightly rotund curves.

"Creamy mushrooms," he said with a chuckle. Featherfae smiled guiltily and her one imperfect tooth peeped over her lower lip cheekily.

"Tish! tish! Time to go. Scott will be wondering where we are," she said and made as to cross the road. Behind her she heard a sharp intake of breath.

"Stop!" Fubbyloofah shot out a restraining paw. "SAKRATTS!"

Across the road and lolling slovenly against the pub doorway were two slobby, thick-necked, beer-swilling hulks with grey, wrinkled skin. Once human in form, these creatures had mutated over the years to adapt to the polluted service of Jassaspy. As was usual with sakratts, they were adorned with tattoos and one had a claw tattooed across the left side of his face. The other's discerning feature was his long pigtail at the end of which was a knot of barbed wire pieces. These had been skilfully woven in with the hair, and over time had matted into an unpleasant spiky clump. Both had short patchy stubble over the rest of their heads and they each carried a large club and a long metal implement called a drowl with a huge spiked claw on the end which they used for digging up plants and trees. They hated all plant life and would instinctively uproot all living things they came across.

"Gerr 'orff my drowl," grunted Hackweezle whilst taking a huge swig from his tankard.

"I wasn't ruddy touchin' it," Spittlewhip snarled in response.

"You were just! Do it again and I'll 'ave you!" he threatened.

"Oh, yeah? I'd like to see you try." Spittlewhip put down his tankard and was squaring up for a fight when he caught sight of Fubbyloofah across the street. "Wadda you staring at you great big lummox?" he said, his lip curling.

"Yeah, are you looking for trouble?" joined in Hackweezle, catching the direction of his gaze. Fubbyloofah bristled up like a brush in response.

"Quick, find Scott. Check he's OK!" he muttered to Featherfae. She nodded but couldn't help feeling a twinge of resentment against the sakratts: less for where their loyalties lay than for curtailing all thoughts of creamy mushrooms.

Scott, meanwhile, had wandered over to a couple of cottages that overlooked the river. He was leaning over to stare into the inky waters. How hypnotically black they were! Eventually, he pulled back but then caught his breath sharply. Was someone watching him?

"Who's there?" he asked, staring into the shadows as he felt the hairs rise on the back of neck.

"Of course, why didn't I think of it before?" exclaimed Mr Khan. "The spice mix *does* induce visions, but only after you consume it." He replaced the tomes on his shelves, taking care not to disturb Mr Bagwapple's doze in 'Algebraic Calculus'. "Jack, Chloe, go home at once and make sure you both keep your talismans with you at all times. A time splinter is imminent. Watch out for time beginning to go crazy. Once it starts you'll find yourselves caught up in it and you must have them with you and - don't look so worried!" he said, as Chloe's brow furrowed.

Jack nodded and led Chloe back through the shop. The knot of toads were still there wobbling on the rim of the cauldron. They were holding empty punch glasses and looking decidedly the worse for wear. A large red-eyed one cursed and burped loudly as they passed.

"Pardon my French," he said as he swayed and staggered along the rim.

"Oh, shut up!" snapped Chloe from the sudden build-up of tension. She knocked him off the rim and he plopped under the bubbling pink liquid before re-surfacing to a chorus of belching laughter from his fellow toads.

"By 'eck, that's strong stuff!" he spluttered, whilst eyeing the empty glass.

"Hi Mum, we're back."

The plan was to appear bright and breezy. There was no way they could share their fears with her. But the words died in their throats. Standing awkwardly in the middle of the living room were mum and two policemen. Their mother seemed unnaturally calm as if in a dream world. She hadn't even noticed them come in. At the same time, the police were looking down and holding their hats. One of them held a dripping garment which was slowly pooling up on the floor. Odd words and phrases broke through, like: "found in Queensmere pond," and "very deep, you know". Jack took one look at the garment and felt his legs wobble. His mind pieced everything together in a flash: the letters that spelt out his brother's name had appeared in the teapot *under* water, the vision in the cloud of steam showed Scott *under* water. He looked again at what the police were holding and heard them utter the word "drowned", as they passed a Jacket, *Scott's Jacket,* over to his mother who clutched frantically at thin air, as one of the policemen helped her to a seat.

Featherfae saw it all. "Scott look out! Behind you!" Twigs shot from her hair as her little wings helped propel her forwards even though they were not large enough to sustain flight. The sakratts whirled round and grabbed their drowls. A second later they were in the air as Fubbyloofah sent them tumbling with a single bound. Scott turned but just saw a whirl of limbs in which the only discernible thing was the colour of Fubbyloofah's fur. Out of the corner of his eye he could see Featherfae homing in on him frantically. What was going on? Then the figure in the shadows stepped out. Scott took one look, spotted the cowl and froze in horror. Jassaspy! The slime trail confirmed it. His head turned in panic. He was trapped, hemmed in with only the river behind! He dashed back to the balcony overlooking the river and whirled round. The cowl was inches away from his face.

"Hold your breath Scott. Don't breathe in!" Featherfae shouted as she rounded the corner. He fumbled for the mirror, as one would a crucifix.

"HELP!" he choked. He flung it a desperate glance. The blurred image waved frantically.

"The Mirror of Aggraides. Give it up: now!" hissed Jassaspy. A rabble of moths streamed out from his open cowl just as a shower of glitter rained down over Scott's head. He blinked furiously as an ammonic plume leeched from the cowl, gripped his throat and blistered his eyes. Reeling backwards, he bumped against the balcony, arms flailing helplessly, and toppled over. Featherfae rounded the corner at the exact moment he fell into the river.

"NO - Scottt!"

All sound was cut off as he plunged beneath the surface. Then the darkness closed in and he sank deeper and deeper towards the river bed.

"Gotta get to the surface. Gotta get -" He fought like crazy but it was as if the water was treacle, and wouldn't give him up. He was dimly aware of a host of shimmering lights around him as he tried and failed to fight the current. Soon he was bobbling along the river bed. It seemed like hours but could not have been more than a minute. The water was pitch black and so icy cold, or was it? He was no longer sure. He gulped a mouthful of water and felt himself choking on stars. He opened his eyes. The black water had gone, all he could see were lights that stung his eyes. Then, slowly, the pain ebbed away as he floated in an amniotic sac down by the river bed. With no fight left in him, he drifted in a shimmering cloud of gold and silver, to a gentle voice calling his name.

6. The Attack of the Puddies

The family stared at the Jacket that the Police held in front of them. It was sodden and muddy from the banks of Queensmere pond where they had found it. There was no mistaking it was Scott's. Mum nodded curtly to the policeman then turned on her heel and left the scene of her loss behind. Jack was left to bear witness to the fragments of a life that was.

"I don't believe it! Look who's back!" said mum a few days later. Jack nearly dropped his coffee cup.
"LAVA!" he cried in unison with Chloe.
"Come here you little chump," said mum as he entered through the flap with a plume of radiant gold. "I don't suppose you know what happened to poor Scott," she added under her breath as she picked him up. She closed her eyes, buried her face in his fur, drew in his warm comforting scent and squeezed his furry body as tightly as his little rib cage would allow: he squeaked when she reached that point. With Lava back, the atmosphere in the house lightened immediately and the rest of the afternoon was spent laughing and joking for the first time in what felt like ages.
"Oh no, you don't," laughed Jack later that day as Lava made a playful grab at his shoelaces. A chewed lace could lead to a chewed trainer, and that could easily lead to social ostracism from his fashion-conscious circle. He took them off and put them under the sofa. But Lava wouldn't stop, and pushed his trainers towards the door. Jack stared for a second before it hit him. "I think he wants us to follow him somewhere," he said whilst glancing over his shoulder to check that their mum hadn't reappeared downstairs.
"Mum'll flip her wig," said Chloe before an eager glint appeared in her eye. "But anything's better than moping round here day after day."
"Yeah, you're right. Mum's gonna go spare." His heart sank at the thought of causing her any more worry and of stepping into danger himself. "We'll leave her a quick note and take our talismans, something to eat and -" his head swung around abstractedly, "- there must be other things we need to take with us."

"Oh, stop fussing. Are you coming or what?" Chloe grinned as she reached for the doorknob. Down by the floor, Lava had already slipped out into the open courtyard.

"I mean: up here in the Village of all places!" said a woman in exasperation. "We pay for the upkeep of this Common. How can hooligans like that be allowed to spoil our enjoyment?" Her husband mumbled rote noises of assent before the family walked out of earshot.

"I wonder what's going on?" Jack mumbled.

"Dunno, but there's definitely an aura of unrest out there," said Chloe.

"Oh, you and your 'auras'. You'll be saying dad's coming back next," said Jack bitingly.

"I *do* believe we'll find dad again, Jack. I just can't believe he's gone for good. That would be too awful to contemplate."

Jack felt rotten and wished he'd kept his mouth shut. Once Chloe got started on their missing father, there was no saying where her thoughts would go. He looked over at the paths leading into the Common. They were so confusing: so easy to get lost in. Thankfully, Lava seemed to know the way and they soon came across a couple of golfers, or 'red-breasts', as they were known locally, because of their red jumpers which chimed with the winter bird.

"I'll report him!" said one, clearly upset.

"He's not right in the head. Still; it's not -" The rest of his sentence was drowned out by an awful caterwauling and from round a huge holly bush came a middle-aged woman looking very harried. Her hair was dishevelled and she was breathing heavily.

"Stay away from there!" she said to Jack and Chloe. "He's just thrown something at me. The warden needs to hear of this." She hurried off, stumbled over a tree root, and yelped assuming she was under further attack.

"What are you doing?" asked Jack as Chloe bent down to pick up a large stick.

"You can never be too sure," she said tapping it against her free hand. They inched their way closer to the source of the commotion.

"LEAVE ME ALONE! BOG OFF!" a voice rang out.

Jack instinctively ducked as seconds later a pine cone whizzed past his left ear. Chloe raised her stick like a baseball star primed for the next pitch. Another pine cone flew past and landed behind them. Chloe heard a sharp intake of breath from Jack.

"It's grown legs!" he cried.

She whirled and sure enough as soon as the pine cone hit the ground, it grew legs and scuttled into a nearby holly bush. The same thing happened to the next one that glanced off his Jacket. It fell to the ground, sprouted six legs and, like an over-sized bug, scurried off.

"This has to be connected to fire-cat magic." Jack stood up excitedly, forgetting his fear for a moment. He swung his head frantically to and fro looking for where they were coming from.

"Get down!" Chloe hissed as more pine cones came whistling through the air.

"BOG OFF, YOU GIT!"

The voice was closer now and Chloe quickly hatched a plan. Zig-zagging her way forwards in the belief that erratic movement was the best defence against a shower of pine cones, she spotted a figure 30 feet off the ground nestled in a huge pine tree. How had he got up there? There was nothing but a vertical trunk for the first 20 feet. But even this paled into insignificance with what she saw next. Thinking that the pine cone that had bounced off her head was inducing hallucinations, she turned to Jack.

"Jack, look up there in the tree and tell me I am not going crazy," she urged. He peered up before ducking back as a hail of projectiles came flying over. Then he stood and stared again and this time his voice carried Chloe up, up, up to the heavens, as he shouted out a name that she never expected to hear again except in hushed tones of painful remembrance: the name of the brother they all thought was dead!

"SCOTT! SCOTT! It's us! Aowww!" A pine cone bounced off his head. "Scott. It's me: Jack." He rubbed his head furiously. "What are you doing up there? We thought you'd drowned."

"GIT!"

"Scott come down! Don't you recognise us?" There was a moment of silence then more pine cones rattled down on them. The pine cone bugs were now so numerous that they were bumping into each other like dodgem cars at the fair.

"Scott. Stop it. It's us!" They retreated out of range to the other side of Caesar's Well.

"He's gone completely ape," huffed Chloe.

"I don't care how bonkers he is. He's alive. That's all that matters," grinned Jack.

"Outrageous and SO embarrassing!" laughed mum. "We'll NEVER be able to set foot on that Common again after this. Are you coming, or are you just going to stand there looking gormless?" she asked Jack as she grabbed her coat before making for the door. Jack closed his gaping mouth and, with a twinge of concern that she might be referring to his appearance, checked his hair in the mirror before following.

They certainly heard him well before they saw him. "BOG OFF!" he yelled as mum tried to talk him down from the tree. She retreated to avoid the same treatment that Jack and Chloe had received.

"Well, there's no shortage of the life-force in him is there?" Her smile said more than her words.

"I suppose we could try and get the ranger to help us," said Jack. There really was nothing else they could think of, so Jack was dispatched to his cottage by the windmill. Eventually he returned with the ranger who did not look well pleased.

"I've got a good mind to refer this to the police," he said as he put his ladder against the tree. "Do you know how many complaints we've had about this?" He didn't expect or receive an answer as he steadied the ladder to bring Scott down. Two minutes later he scrabbled down, red faced and extremely irritated. "That boy has had it," he fumed. "He's armed with a stick and what's more, he knows how to use it." He rubbed his head ruefully. "There's nothing for it I'll have to get a group of us together to bring him down. Mind the ladder until I get back." That said, off he went off accompanied by a barrage of abuse from the canopy above. Twenty minutes later and after much kicking and screaming, the ranger and his two assistants dragged a wriggling and wild-eyed Scott from the branches.

"Oww, the little devil caught me on the shin," said one of the men as Scott made his final kick count. Mum apologised on his behalf as the ranger and his men withdrew sulkily leaving the family alone together in a way they never expected to happen again.

"Something's not right." said Chloe after a moment. Her eyes flashed concern and found it reflected back. Scott was hunched in a ball on the ground. Suddenly, he heaved, jerked, drew a deep breath and sneezed.

"My God! Look at -" Chloe's voice died with Jack's warning glance as a cloud of tiny gold and silver particles twinkled in the air before dissolving into nothingness. But mum didn't comment because at that moment Scott spoke.

"Mum? Jack? Chloe? I thought - Where's Jassaspy? What's - ?" Scott looked up to three grinning and ecstatically happy faces.

The journey home, the dinner in front of the fire and the family bonding in front of the TV all happened as expected. The tension of late had gone and mum was back to massacring operas whenever she had a task to do in the kitchen. Amidst the caterwauling, Jack nudged Scott sharply in the ribs and with his eyes indicated that all get up stairs prontissimo.

"You got caught up in a time splinter didn't you?" he asked as soon as the bedroom door closed behind them. "There's no way those gold and silver stars you sneezed out were normal." Scott looked shifty but it was no use. He sighed with relief, desperate to get it off his chest and gave them a quick potted account of what had happened: meeting Fubbyloofah and Featherfae and his encounter with Jassaspy on the bridge.

"Jeez: and you wanna go back there?"

"Oh don't be like that, Jack. They need our help and besides, we've got magic talismans," said Chloe cheerfully. Jack winced at the weight of expectation this provoked.

"Ok, then we stick together as much as possible so that when a time splinter occurs again, we *all* get caught up in it at the same time. Oh, and it goes without saying that we keep Lava and our talismans with us at all times."

"And some fruit too," said Scott softly, thinking of Featherfae and how happy it would make her.

"We should have had breakfast," moaned Scott, hungrily.

They were up at the Common a couple of weeks later and he was starving. He broke off from his moan as he eyed the chocolate shop enviously. Jack caught his glance.

"Ok, go on. Get three croissants then." Why the same shop specialised in both chocolate and bread he never could fathom.

Scott stepped inside. The clock struck 9 as he entered the shop and his heart thumped as he remembered how strangely pressing the shopkeeper had been on a previous visit.

"Go on boy," she had said in a sugary voice, "try a little choccy-woccy." Scott was not normally one to refuse chocolate; and they had some fabulous ones: hearts in red wrapping and towering cakes of such exquisite beauty that you expected them to take off like a rocket in a celebration of their own glory. However, even he had instinctively said 'no' before heading for the door confused and angry about why he had refused. This time too there was an ominous air to the place. The shop was empty and he idly picked up one of the red wrapped chocolate hearts. Eventually the shop assistant came: a drooping, stooping excuse for a man, far too thin to work in a chocolate shop and with a permanent half-smile fixed to his lips that didn't look at all happy to be there.

"How can I help you, little fella?" Each word slithered out from lips that caressed them like the fleshy arms of a masseur. Scott baulked.

"Three fresh croissants please and - no chocolate because I need to save money and anyway it's - not good to eat too much chocolate," he said, aware that he was babbling.

"OK, but a little tiny piece wouldn't hurt. Tell you what, why don't you keep that piece in your hand and save it for later. Don't worry about paying for it. It's my treat, cos we're friendsssss." He hissed on the final 's' as he passed him the croissants. Scott stared and failing to see any evidence of a forked tongue flickering between the lips, glanced down at the chocolate heart he was holding. It was wrapped in an attractive red foil but at the same time looked strangely misshapen as if something was trying to burst out from it. Suddenly thorns pierced the foil and pricked his fingers.

"Ouch! What the -?" He dropped it in fright and turned to leave, aware of the man sniggering behind him. He glanced down as he left. The red foil-wrapped heart was on the floor, but there were no thorns. It was just as he had found it: as good as new! He frowned as he closed the door behind him, too preoccupied to notice the clock strike 9...again!

"God; that was quick," said Jack as Scott came out with the croissants.

"Yeah, bit of a weird guy in there," he muttered. Jack peered through the window and did a double-take.

"Quick, that's the creep from the bus stop. Let's move it!" he said as they turned sharply towards the Common. Behind them, Snarklepike slowly replaced the receiver of the telephone and, with eyes, if not tongue, flickering furtively, slithered out of the back door. A sign in the window read, "Closed for the day."

"Fancy going ape again, Scott?" said Jack, with a grin and a nod at the old pine tree where Scott had thrown his wobbly. The sky looked strangely dark above it.

"Ha! Ha! Very funny. We'll see how you cope when you meet Jassaspy, shall we?" he replied as Lava wriggled to be put down.

"Where's he going? And why's it so dark all of a sudden?" asked Chloe as Lava set off deeper into the Common.

"I dunno, but we'd better follow him before we lose him," said Scott striding ahead. Chloe glanced down at her watch.

"Crikey! It's only 8am."

"WHAT? NO WAY!" Jack whirled to face her. "We left the house at 8.15" Their eyes locked together knowingly.

"A time splinter! It must be! Time's breaking up." Chloe's eyes were wide with excitement.

"It's happening again. Scott, wait!" Jack sprinted after his brother, his fingers fumbling for the time-key.

A solitary red rose was in the middle and ashes were sprinkled all around the rim as if some strange ceremony had recently taken place. Would druids or ghouls suddenly emerge to claim territorial rights? Jack bumped into Scott breathlessly as their fevered imaginations ran riot. Lava was over on the other side and Chloe just a few paces behind them. They were standing on the rim of Caesar's well. Jack noted that the time was 7.45. They all looked around nervously clutching their talismans.

"Come on Scott what happened last time?" asked Jack tentatively.

"I dunno. Lava darted into that bramble patch over there and I just walked into the well," said Scott whilst staring into the Mirror of Aggraides hoping for answers.

Jack walked up to the well and peered into it. He took out the time-key and prodded the stone carved lettering around the rim in the hope that he might find a concealed keyhole. He didn't.

"This isn't much of a well is it? It's completely filled in."

The sound of twigs snapping underfoot made him spin round. His eyes roved the bush but nothing moved. That's when it happened.

"Quick! One of you grab the key and the mirror, the other get the cat!"

There was a rustle of leaf and branch and out of a bramble patch to their right jumped Snarklepike. At the same time another figure bulldozed his way from left field and ran straight for Lava. It was Dog Bottom and he was half way there when he hurled a small fibrous ball. The centipede ball hit the ground in front of Lava and a shower of wriggling centipedes rained down.

"NO!" yelled Scott, throwing himself forward. He fell flat on his face but not before grabbing Dog Bottom by the ankle. At the same time, Flan appeared and with his vast bulk brought Jack crashing down. Hands scrabbled frantically for the talismans. There was a frenetic blur as a big stick moved through the air and Chloe charged in.

"Give up before something happens which you'll regret," yelled Snarklepike. Dog Bottom's hand clawed for Lava whilst he tugged to free his ankle. Scott held firm and grappled his way up his leg. But Dog Bottom was pulling himself away and was only inches away from Lava now. Was this how it would end? A yell in his ear distracted him. Jack wriggled free, grabbed the talismans and stamped on Dog Bottom's fingers. They crunched under his heel just as Chloe's stick thwacked against his head. He bellowed with pain, grabbed someone's ankle and kicked back. Scott held on grimly, aware of Lava in the middle somewhere. Flan's belly loomed close and he caught a glimpse of Chloe holding on grimly to a fistful of hair. Then everything became a flailing heap of limbs as they all tumbled into Caesar's Well.

Jack felt something slam into his head. It was probably someone's foot but he wasn't sure. He saw Lava slip from Dog

Bottom's grip like a fish and hover a few feet away. He kicked himself loose and felt himself glide towards Lava. Something told him to go with the flow, but where was Scott? He let go and glided after Lava feeling totally confused. Moments later he saw a neat round beam of light.

"Arrgh, Chloe get off me," he yelped. They had tumbled through a time splinter into Fubbyloofah's bathroom. A couple of glow-worms emerged from under the floor tiles.
"You great big lummox! Spare a thought for us little glow-worms or we'll move out and you can watch your toes turn blue." They were rubbing their bruised heads at their thunderous entry. A moment later footsteps rushed up the stairs. It took all of a second for them to recognise who it was.
"Uhh, hello, you must be Fubbyloofah," said Jack rubbing his head and acutely aware of the ungainly manner of the introductions.
"Ahh, Jack and Chloe, I presume," said Fubbyloofah warmly. They nodded and scrabbled to their feet and looked around. Fubbyloofah's bathroom was full of mosaic travertine which exuded a comforting golden glow augmented by the efforts of the disgruntled glow-worms. Behind the door was the brass porthole that Scott had described. Fubbyloofah caught their glance. "Yes, that's where you entered. Glad Scott had the sense to heed my words, though you might want to try a little more speed and less haste next time." His snout wrinkled disdainfully at the sprawled heap that they made on the floor. "But where's Scott? Didn't he come with you?"

When Scott heard Dog Bottom howl in pain, he felt euphoric but it was all too brief. The next thing he knew, he was in the air, had landed on top of his brother and the whole lot of them, Flan and Lava included, had rolled into Caesar's Well in an untidy mass of limbs. Only Snarklepike was left hopping around on the edge of the well, a spectator to the main show. Gradually they disentangled or floated apart to be more exact. Scott knew they were all caught up in a time splinter. He saw Lava, Jack and Chloe drift off towards a bright window of light whilst at the same time the Puddies were pulled far away in another direction towards a luminous green light. But *he* wasn't moving at all. He was stuck, floating in limbo. What's more, he was not alone. He saw a figure sitting on a chair, floating and surrounded by soft glowing light. He drifted closer. There was something about her which was familiar.

"Who are you?" he asked, thinking all the time that he already knew the answer. "And what are you doing here?"

The woman smiled a warm smile that made him feel safe and secure. "My name is Willow," she said calmly, "and I'm waiting for the key-holder. I'm afraid I'm trapped in this time splinter."

"How did that -? I mean, how does it work: this time splinter?" He paused, confused. "I'm not sure I can help," he added weakly. She smiled softly but said nothing so he continued. "Of course, I'll do what I can, but – hey - wait a minute." Sudden realisation struck him. "Maybe I can help after all. My brother Jack has a time-key. Perhaps he can help you."

The woman nodded wistfully. "He may hold the key at the moment, but whether he is *the* key-holder remains to be seen. There have been many key-holders over the years. You must help him. You hold the Mirror of Aggraides. That is the window through which you can find the keyhole." The figure smiled warmly again. "Go now to your friends and I will try to guide you."

"Guide me? How can you if you're stuck here?"

"But I have been helping already. Don't you recognise me?" He stared back and then it dawned on him. OF COURSE! His eyes flashed with recognition: the woman in his mirror. But he was already being pulled away, as if the mere fact of recognition had severed something.

"Willow! Willow!" he cried into the void as he drifted away.

7. The Return to Rascal Howe

"What took you, bro?" Jack said with a grudgingly admiring nod as Scott landed acrobatically. Scott grinned, gave his brother a "high five" and shot Fubbyloofah a welcoming smile.

"At least *he* didn't give us concussion," said Glob, one of the glow-worms. He shot a withering glance in Jack's direction. "We've got a floor to heat and we'd appreciate being left to do it without all these constant high-impact interruptions. We'll be wanting danger money if this carries on."

"Don't worry, Glob, there'll be no more visitors tonight," said Fubbyloofah.

"I should hope not or I'll quit the private sector and go and work up at Granglethorn Castle," he said whilst soothing down his segments and slipping back under the tiles with a grumble. The boys chuckled as Fubbyloofah led them downstairs.

A clump of powder hit the fire and exploded into an aromatic cloud. There was a sharp crackle as the fire took and a bristly mass of wiry hair moved closer to peer at a radiant pulse of gold down on the hearth.

"Hope you like apple and cinnamon," said Fubbyloofah as the aroma enveloped them.

"Should we make it stronger?" a voice piped out of the haze, followed by anxious looking glances directed towards the throbbing golden light curled up beside the fire.

"It's perfect as it is, Snuffmeakin, and don't go worrying about the fire-cat. He's not about to make you redundant. He has far more pressing uses for his glowing coat than making my house cosy," said Fubbyloofah. The crocklepip grinned with reassurance before winking and nodding at all the visitors.

"Right you are. Right you are, Mr Fubbyloofah. If you need anything else just drop a small piece of cherry wood on the fire. That'll bring us scurrying. Well: toodle-oo!" He waved before darting back up the chimney.

In front of the crackling log fire were Lava and the two smoggilars who were snuggled up to him as if his gingery fur might impart some of its glow to their coarse bristly coats. Scott sat back in the sofa and immediately felt an inviting tickle at the back of his neck. His head snapped back into a mass of tendrils and a massage from the wipwaffle. A few minutes later, he opened his eyes to strands of love-lies-bleeding, the odd leafy twig and a smile of radiant joy.

"Featherfae!" he cried out in joy.

"My dear, dear, Scott. We were all SO worried when you fell in the river by the bridge."

"Yeah, I don't really know what happened," said Scott, freeing himself from the wipwaffle's soporific clutches. "One minute I felt like I was drowning, the next I was caught up in a cloud of gold and silver stars and the next, I found myself up a tree fighting off Jassaspy - except that it wasn't Jassaspy, it was any innocent passer-by and - it's all a bit confusing really and VERY embarrassing."

"I'll say!" muttered Jack under his breath.

"Waxenwaifs" said a voice from the kitchen.

"Waxen-what?" said Scott.

"It was the waxenwaifs that saved you my boy," said Fubbyloofah again as he returned with a steaming cauldron of spiced tea. Chloe pointed excitedly at the pot plants as they shimmered and danced to the scent of spice given off from the tea. "The gold and silver stars, as you call them, are waxenwaifs: small visceral fairies that are the soul and spirit of the land. I told you they couldn't be summoned but they do have a knack of appearing at times when you need them most - normally when something natural and beautiful is being threatened," he continued. Chloe snorted in derision at the association but Scott was too fascinated to rise to the bait.

"When we saw the waxenwaifs light up the black river water around you," said Featherfae, "our priority became to distract Jassaspy so that he didn't notice them. We wanted him to assume you'd drowned."

"- and it worked!" said Fubbyloofah.

There was a moment's silence as he passed everyone a cup of spiced tea. They sipped it in silence for a few moments enjoying the warmth of the aromatic spices.

"What's in the bowl by the fire? Whatever it is seems to be soaking up the colour of the flames," asked Jack eventually.

"They're leaves from Waftenway," sighed Featherfae fondly.

Just the mention of this magical place seemed to trigger something in Lava. From being curled up in a tight ball by the fire, he suddenly moved to touch the tip of the leaves with his damp nose and Scott grinned broadly.

"Burnt gold?" he asked expectantly. Jack was about to tell him not to be so stupid when tendrils reached out and the wipwaffle went to work on his head.

"No, it's not, but look!" said Fubbyloofah. The leaves had dissolved into multi-coloured fluorescent liquid which filled the bowl with swirling colour. "Just you wait until I put it in an oil lamp," he winked.

By the time the second cup of tea was ready, they were all admiring the rainbow in a bowl and wondering what else Lava was capable of. It was then that Featherfae noticed something.

"I thought I recognised him! Can't you see it?" she stammered. Heads turned and suddenly everyone was staring at Jack.

"Hey! Stop it! What've I done?" Jack pulled away. Suddenly the fire seemed far too hot. Away to his left the wipwaffle's tendrils wavered in search of another client.

"Look at his hand! He carries the mark," she said.

Scott looked at his brother bemused and Fubbyloofah raised a reassuring paw, before beckoning him forwards.

"No, no, no," Jack stuffed his hands in his pockets. What was she on about: as if he didn't have enough to worry about with the key that he carried? Featherfae smiled reassuringly and took him by the hands.

"You're the Elven Prince of Oswithiel," she said simply.

"NO!" Jack pulled his hand back in fresh alarm. He heard a laugh beside him.

"I'll say!" said Chloe. "Prince of 'No'-thing!"

"But, you are. You carry the mark." All eyes turned to stare at the red birthmark on Jack's finger.

"Well, that makes two of us then, because apparently I'm a djinn, with the fire within!" said Scott, miming flames with his fingers.

"Fat lot of good that is," Chloe said bitingly. "If you hadn't let those Puddies kick me in the back, I wouldn't have these!" she indicated a couple of large lumps on her back. Scott blanched. Fortunately, just at this moment, Fubbyloofah launched into a monologue about Granglethorn, Waftenway and the problems the land faced. Then suddenly Scott realised the one thing no one had yet mentioned.

"We haven't yet shown you our talismans," he blurted out excitedly as he scrabbled for the Mirror of Aggraides. Jack followed suit and soon both items were in Fubbyloofah's paws.

"This looks Hebradaigen," he said on fingering the time-key. "I wonder what it's for."

"Tanglestep will know," said Featherfae. "After all, he's a Hebradaigen of the Tower of the Sun."

"They're the Guardian-Priests," explained Fubbyloofah to Jack's puzzled look. "Here, take it back and keep it safe."

"No, you keep it. I really don't want the responsibility." He thrust the key at them both but they shook their heads.

"No, Jack. Whether you like it or not, it's been given to you for a reason."

"But I'll mess up. I just know that when the time comes I won't be able to use it."

Visions of his father banging on the locked door flooded back: him sitting on the floor, clutching the key but unable to act. Why this: an accursed *key* of all things?

"And this is the Mirror of Aggraides. Look Fubbyloofah! Look how tarnished it is!" Featherfae was waving the mirror excitedly.

"Well, crush my berriblods and use them as a foot balm! The lost Mirror of Aggraides!" mused Fubbyloofah as he turned it over in his paws.

"Yeah, and there's a woman called Willow trapped in there and we've got to set her free, somehow." Scott quickly recounted his conversation with Willow but his beseeching eyes found no answers to the myriads of questions he still had.

"But how can someone be in a mirror?" they both asked when he'd finally finished.

"WHAT? Not you two as well? She was there just now as I passed her over. See - there she is again!" Scott took the mirror back and Willow's image appeared again only for it to disappear once more in the paws of Fubbyloofah.

"Humpf" Fubbyloofah handed the mirror to Featherfae who shook her head and sighed.

"Sorry, Scott, I can't see anything either."

"Wait a minute. Here, Jack, tell me if you can still see that old lady." He passed the mirror over to his brother.

"Yes, there she is in her rocking chair, all dressed in black. This is *so* weird."

Fubbyloofah and Featherfae peered over his shoulder and shrugged uneasily before Fubbyloofah gathered up the crockery to take to the kitchen.

"We'll, there *are* people in there, even if *you* can't see them," said Scott in frustration. "And at least I didn't waste my gift like Chloe did."

"I did NOT waste my gift. Peek said it was special."

"He was just trying to be kind," said Scott smugly. There was a sudden blur of movement before he yelped. "Ouch! What did you do that for?" He glared at her and rubbed the arm she had punched.

"Don't be so patronising!" She glowered and then pulled out her orange proudly. A moment later there was a crash from the other side of the living room followed by a moan. They rushed round to find Fubbyloofah flat out on the floor. Broken crockery was everywhere, but oddly enough he was smiling.

"A sunfruit!" he gasped from down on the floor.

"A 'what'?" they cried in unison.

"A sunfruit! There has only ever been one tree that produced fruit like that and that withered away years ago. I won't even ask where you found it but step outside. Let's see if it will wake the earth."

"*Wake the earth*?" muttered Jack in confusion. "It's an orange. It doesn't *do* anything. In fact it doesn't even taste that good."

Crockery crunched under paw as Fubbyloofah bounded towards the door. It was dark and chilly outside and nobody could see a thing, or at least not until Chloe came out and held up her orange. Then it started to pulse and throb with a powerful golden light.

"Got any more quips, lads?" she beamed.

"What are we expecting to happen?" asked Jack, turning to Fubbyloofah.

"Look: fireflakes: particles of fire that lie dormant in the earth and are woken by the sunfruit." Fubbyloofah pointed down in the valley below the cottage. There they were: tiny sparkles of crimson. They were very faint and seemed to disappear once you looked at them directly, but out of the corner of your eye, they sparkled magically.

"And over there in the trees!" said Scott. Tiny glints of diamond winked back at them.

"Those are the frostflakes. They await the courtship of the fireflakes. When they are united in dance, fire and frost will return to heat and cool the land," Fubbyloofah was practically hopping with excitement.

"So why aren't they dancing now?" asked Chloe.

"They need to be airborne and the sun is too weak to revive them," explained Fubbyloofah.

"- and that's why I'm here," said a strange voice from behind them. Everyone whirled round in surprise.

"LAVA!" Chloe laughed in delight. Fubbyloofah just stood and stared. There was a pregnant pause in which everyone slowly adjusted to the fact that Lava was talking.

"Yes, we still have time to save the sun but first I have to find burnt gold and then get to World's End. It won't be easy but it's not impossible."

He spoke with such a quiet confidence that they returned to sit by the fire with more hope than they'd felt for a long time.

"Chloe," shouted Jack, "are you up there?"

It was later that evening and a sudden crash had everyone sprinting upstairs. They had the bedroom door open in a moment to find Chloe in front of a huge pile of shoes that had tumbled out of the wardrobe.

The shoes were jumping about and making a terrible racket like dogs pent up in a kennel for too long.

"Jeez, how weird is that?" cried Scott as a pair of pointed shoes stabbed the air in front of her.

"Calm down, Blahnicks!" Featherfae eased her way in front of everyone, her one imperfect tooth peeping over her lower lip as she grinned sheepishly. "Yes, yes, I know I have rather a lot," she said as she placated her footwear. Fubbyloofah looked both relieved and embarrassed.

"She filled her own wardrobe years ago and, well, it just seemed right for me to offer. But they don't half make a racket when they tumble forth. I'm going to have to secure that door,

Featherfae," he went on. "I can't be doing with this when we have a houseful of visitors."

"Of course, of course. Whatever you want," said Featherfae consciously avoiding everyone's gaze as she replaced the last pair back inside the wardrobe. "Hope they didn't alarm you too much Chloe. It's just that I can't resist lovely shoes and I don't find too many opportunities to give them the outing that they all deserve. As you can see, they can get a bit tetchy about it." They all exchanged amused glances but at the same time felt her embarrassment.

"Those green suede shoes with the bow on the toe look divine Featherfae," offered Scott kindly.

"Do you really think so? Thank you, Scott." she said, brightening up instantly.

"Yes, but I preferred the beige strappy ones," said Jack.

"Oh, I think I know what you mean," said Featherfae. "The beige ones cut more of a dash in the summer whereas the green ones are -"

"- perfect for winter!" finished Scott.

"Exactly!"

They all laughed heartily, pleased that her joyful spirit was once again restored.

"Now don't get your hopes up. What with our waning sun and the slime trails everywhere, the veg that does grow is in a pretty sorry state."

It was time for dinner and Fubbyloofah was bringing out the evening meal. He wasn't kidding either. The carrots were not only purple but unbelievably wrinkly. It was as if they'd been in the veg rack for far longer than they'd ever been in the ground, and as for the broccoli: a few anaemic sprouts in a fetid pool of sauce that had fallen out of favour with its roux.

"Been saving these up for a special occasion," he said proudly as Jack paled at the contents. The sauce was so watery, it was as if - no - surely not!

"I'm so sorry Mr Fubbyloofah, I tried ever so hard. I really did," a voice from the window sill broke through. The boys stared in disbelief. "I used to be so proud of my head of florets, but these days I just can't get enough from the soil. I'm afraid they're my tears of frustration that you can see seeping out of them. I hope they don't make your dinner too watery."

"Gross! There is no way I'm gonna eat veg that's weeping into the sauce," said Jack. Fubbyloofah shot him a disapproving look before offering reassurance.

"Now, now, Podwhiffle, don't you go a-worrying. I know perfectly well what you are up against. We always enjoy your fancy florets no matter what."

"Do you really? That's very kind of you to say so, sir. I do try my best. I really do. Oooh, oooh, get ready Fubbyloofah. I feel a flush of pride coming on," he said excitedly.

"Ooh lovely!" said Fubbyloofah. "I'll have a floret of the old purple-sprouting if you don't mind." He sprang forward and quickly nipped off the sprouting bud.

"Ohh, that's better." Podwhiffle was panting heavily. "I do overheat if those purple flushes aren't seen to straight away."

Needless to say, dinner was not a success.

"I'm sure we can re-heat them tomorrow morning," said Fubbyloofah to the mass of excuses that the three of them made for their sudden lack of appetite. "Though I do have a special treat saved up for breakfast," he added mysteriously.

"That's ok. Scott can have my portion of tonight's veg. He likes a large breakfast," said Jack with a wicked grin. Scott glared back but then quickly lit up at Fubbyloofah's next words.

"OK; carrots and broccoli soup for Scott and Jack can have the fried beetle wings."

"Fried what?" Jack stammered.

"Beetle wings," said Fubbyloofah, "and a rare delicacy they are too," he added. "Do you know my uncle only ever had them on his wedding day and they were more common in those days than they are now. It's all down to the waning sun and the polluting slime you know."

"It's such an honour for you, Jack," grinned Scott.

"Indeed it is. A breakfast fit for the Elven Prince!" laughed Chloe as Fubbyloofah put up his paw to quell what he mistook for protestations of false modesty.

"Just remember to take them right to the back of the mouth and taste them with the back of your tongue. That way, you'll avoid them getting stuck between your teeth."

Scott could contain himself no longer and a burst of laughter suddenly camouflaged itself into a mock coughing fit. This was getting better by the second. Then Lava spoke again and his words sobered the mood instantly.

"It's time for me to leave. It won't be easy finding burnt gold and we don't have much time."

"What? You mean leave right now?" Jack and Scott echoed each other in alarm.

"In the middle of the night?" said Chloe looking upset. He shook his ginger fur. The golden sun-threads flashed with the glow of the fire and the sunfruit in her hands began to pulse again with a fresh flush of heat.

"Burnt gold rarely takes the same form twice. It could be present in anything. It won't be easy to find," he said.

"But surely it's a mineral and will be found underground?" said Fubbyloofah. Lava shook his head.

"You mean, it could be right here under our noses and we wouldn't know?" asked Featherfae.

"Yes, if it contains the right colour pigment," Lava said. Featherfae looked shocked.

"So, Cob was right in bringing those leaves back from Waftenway?" Scott added.

"In a way, yes. As it happens, they don't contain burnt gold but he was right to pick them for their colour."

This gave everyone lots to think about, and the next few minutes saw all sorts of suggestions being made, from hot coals in the fire to the golden oak of the ceiling beams.

"Well, at least stay the night," said Fubbyloofah eventually. "We can all set off in the morning. We need to show the talismans to this Hebradaigen that Featherfae knows. If what we know is true, then having both the key to the time splinters and the window through which to find the keyhole could be very significant."

"Besides, you're a cat and I know what you need more than anything else?" Chloe beamed. Lava blinked and they all looked at her quizzically. "Sleep!" she added quickly. Amongst the groans from the boys and Featherfae's laughter, Fubbyloofah started rearranging cushions.

"Boys, you're down here by the fire with Lava. Chloe, you're in the back bedroom with Featherfae. But for heaven's sake, don't forget to keep the wardrobe door closed!"

8. The Puddies and the Pool

"Arrgh!" Coughing and retching, Dog Bottom landed besides a fetid green slime pool deep underground. He fumbled as he tried to get up but a huge lardy lump was crushing the life out of him. Panic flooded through him. God! It was huge. What was it?

"Can't breathe. Got to break free!" With all his strength he lurched and heaved, until finally he wriggled free. He panted at the effort and flopped back exhausted, dimly aware of a wet slapping sound as he did so. It was then that he felt it.

"Something's burning me!" He sprang to his feet in panic as the corrosive slime burned through his clothes and ate into his skin. He pulled his sleeve over his hand and wiped frantically, but only succeeded in smearing it everywhere. He winced and looked around wretchedly. It was then that he felt his anger surge.

"I should have guessed!" The lump that had crushed him was groaning on the floor. "Look what you've done! Get up, you dork!" He kicked out at Flan's prostrate form then he remembered and looked round frantically. "Where's that cat?" But they were completely alone. It just didn't make sense; he had grabbed it by the tail. He looked around dejectedly. "Where on earth are we?" he muttered weakly.

They appeared to be in an underground chamber dimly lit by an eerie green glow. The walls were made of huge cobs of stone that glistened with something damp and foul smelling. Flan was sitting up in the half-light now and was fidgeting comically.

"What are you up to now, you idiot?"

"It's Hagratty's fleas. They've hatched and set up home in my hair," said Flan, scratching crazily. Dog Bottom guffawed with laughter.

"Well, this is no underground hair salon so when you've finished maybe you can think about how to get out of here."

Flan glared back in response before stumbling to his feet. Together, they groped their way into the shadowy tunnels. The patchy burns caused Dog Bottom to lurch spasmodically and it was enough to put him in a foul mood.

"This is nothing compared to the fury I plan to wreak on those three brats and their ginger cat when I catch up with them". His mind raced over recent events. He remembered Hagratty and Snarklepike inviting them both to their chocolate shop after school. His ears had pricked up at the mention of a time splinter but he hadn't paid much attention, as a strawberry fondant had squelched all the way down his shirt at that time and he was more preoccupied with getting another one before his brother got there first. Now, he was starting to wish he had listened more carefully, as it might help in their current predicament. He looked at his brother.

"How on earth are we going to get out of these never-ending tunnels?" he moaned.

"How the hell should I know?" shrugged Flan sulkily. They trudged on through the clammy dank passageways before Dog Bottom could tolerate it no longer.

"Arrgh! It's stinging to the bone. I've got to wash it off."

"Well, how about using that then?" said Flan pointing to a small stream trickling down a rock face.

"At last, something that isn't 'glow-in-the-dark' green," said Dog Bottom, splashing it over his burns before stooping down for a drink. "Tastes sour though," he grimaced. Flan wasn't listening. He was too busy scratching like fury at the fleas but then he started giggling. The trickle that Dog Bottom had drunk from was coming from the lip of a pool and what was more, they could glimpse the top of someone's head in there.

"Looks like you've just drunk someone's bath water," he chuckled. Dog Bottom glared back sullenly but decided not to retaliate. They needed to get out of this cavern and starting a fight when someone was within ear-shot was not the best way of going about it. They crept closer before Dog Bottom let out a low groan. Floating in the pool was something with a large bloated belly and limbs too puny to support its weight. How it had got there was anyone's guess. Yet - a hand flashed to his mouth. Flan was right! The creature was wallowing in the liquid that he had recently drunk. His stomach heaved but he was quick to control himself: footsteps were approaching.

Four brutish creatures came into view full of tattoos and clothed in tatty strips of studded leather. Three of them carried a heavy vat that made made them lurch under the weight. Following behind them was a tall cowled figure.

"Careful you don't spill any of it," hissed Jassaspy, "or you'll spend the next few weeks on pack-horse duty."

"Yeah," said the female sakratt, who was supervising the males. "The slygorm needs 'em fat and sweaty, so treat this stuff wi' respeck."

Female sakratts made excellent supervisors. Being vast in bulk, they could throw their weight around with ease and indulge their naturally slovenly nature. She did so now by bawling loudly as she cuffed the hapless males around the head. Their grunts and groans echoed around the underground chamber before reverberating away down the dark chasms. The sakratts carefully lowered the vat to the rim of the pool as the creature in the pool sculled over towards them: its huge body bobbing around like a rubber raft. With a nod from Jassaspy, viscous white groatmeal dolloped into the pool. The effect upon the creature was startling. Its flabby body shuddered in anticipation then it sank below each floating blob like a huge white whale. Time after time the creature dived only to resurface directly under each piece of gloop, which it caught with open mouth. Dog Bottom grimaced at Flan and they lay back against a soft, clammy mound to watch. Moments later, an intoxicating smell wafted over to them.

"What's that?" asked Dog Bottom salivating.

"Don't know. But it smells divine!"

They craned their necks forwards. Flan's nose was twitching like crazy, aware that it was a long time ago since they'd had anything to eat.

"Time to go now," said the female sakratt as she threw her excessive bulk against one of the males. He staggered and wobbled precariously on the pool edge. A huge lurch of belly laughs echoed round the chamber.

"You nearly joined the groat, you half-wit," said his mate.

"If you're that hungry, you can lick out the bowl!" laughed another.

"If he did that he may as well stay here. It's addictive stuff," snorted the female. They trudged after Jassaspy back the way they had come and were soon lost to sight. The Puddies darted forwards. What was this sweet, sugary stuff? Dog Bottom's eyes glinted and a wicked smile creased his lips.

"What are we waiting for? I'm starving!" He bolted to the pool side. Flan wasn't far behind. The groat was sculling on the surface scooping up the groatmeal in an orgy of gluttony. "It's gorging itself silly!" Dog Bottom scowled.

"Yeah, at this rate there'll be nothing left for us. Damn! I can't reach. Here, take my other arm." Dog Bottom obliged and Flan stretched out over the surface of the pool. His fingers dipped into the white gelatinous groatmeal and he wound it stickily round his hand like thick treacle.

"We'll come on, let's taste it then!" said Dog Bottom impatiently as the sugary vapours dizzied their heads. Flan went first. Ever so cautiously he touched the groatmeal with the tip of his tongue. His taste buds exploded like shooting stars. His eyes flashed to his brother before his whole hand shot to his mouth. But it didn't get there.

"Not so fast, bro!" Dog Bottom had seen the glint in his eye and with a sudden lurch had grabbed him by the wrist. There was a blur of light as they grappled on the edge of the pool. Flan strained - just a couple more inches! He saw his brother's eyes crazed with lust as he lurched forwards desperate for the gloop, frantic for even a globule. Dribbles of saliva tricked down his forearm as Dog Bottom got closer and closer. In desperation, he slammed his brother towards the pool. Flan's grip loosened in shock.

"Wey, hey!" Dog Bottom grabbed his hand. The sticky groatmeal squelched through his fingers. YES! His tongue flickered out searchingly. Soon, soon, any second now! The vapour was dizzying. Flan's fingers flailed and clutched at thin air. Then he felt his collar twist sharply.

"WOOAAH!" He tottered wildly but the weight of his brother was just too much. "You idiot!" The pool liquid folded over them both like a warm sticky wrapper and their world closed down for a second.

"Pooh!" They resurfaced together and gasped for air. The water had a sour stink to it but all that mattered was the groatmeal. Dog Bottom grabbed at a floater in front of him and rammed it into his mouth. Wow! The sugar rush was intense. He swam over to another floating dollop whilst his brother propelled himself towards a thick curd of scum by the pool edge. Together they dived, gobbled and gorged for what seemed like an eternity. Then they turned onto their backs to float and catch their breath. Flan let out a huge belch which echoed around the cavern and Dog Bottom responded with a cloud of bubbles from below. They were almost too exhausted to laugh! The cavern seemed weird when viewed from their backs in this way and the pool surface was choppier than they expected. Was it a trick of the light? Dog Bottom felt a sudden sharp tug. Something had him by the ankle. The next minute, his eyes were on stalks, cheeks puffed out and limbs flailing in slow motion. Slowly but forcefully he was pulled under the surface. His head swung around. What was it? His lungs screamed. Above him he could just make out the luminescent green of the cavern percolating down towards him. The pool liquid was thick and viscous and dragged at his every move but he could just make out a large white mass. He fought like a thresher shark, kicked out viciously and somehow broke free. He burst through the gelatinous film rasping for breath. A sudden upsurge of liquid washed over him. He shook the globules from his eyes as the great white mass charged him again.

"Out! This is my pool and my groatmeal!" It was the groat and it was in no mood for pleasantries. It landed a punch squarely on Dog Bottom's nose. With a desperate surge and an exhausting whirl of limbs Dog Bottom made it to the pool side. Flan was close behind panting heavily.

"Uggh, what is it about this place: first the burning slime and now this?" They were back on the side of the pool and coated in a thin sheen of spittle. He glanced at Flan and smirked. His hair was all gunked up and he had a dribble of spittle stuck to his chin that made him look like a drooling half-wit. He decided to say nothing and enjoy the spectacle but even this small pleasure was curtailed. A small tidal wave of spittle washed over their feet. They looked up just in time to see the huge white groat launch itself at the pool side in an attempt to get out. It strained to support its great bulk but its withered arms were useless out of water and it flopped back into the pool exhausted.

"Ha! It's too darn fat to get out. Now who's the big guy, eh?" The groat tried again and this time Dog Bottom felt emboldened enough to put a foot on its head. With a dramatic heave, he kicked it back into the pool before his eyes flashed wickedly. "Hey, bro, pass me some of those rocks". Flan knew immediately what would happen next. "OK, let's see how you like this fatty." Dog Bottom half-juggled a small rock before taking aim. He squealed with sadistic pleasure as it hit target and the groat let out a small yelp.

"My turn now," piped up Flan before throwing one of his own. It missed.

"One - nil, to me," said Dog Bottom as he took aim for the second time. The groat floundered over to the far side of the pool but it was no use. It was stuck in its own watery amphitheatre as one by one the Puddies pounded it mercilessly in their own gladiatorial way.

"That'll teach you! No one gets away with trying to drown a Puddleton. No-one!" said Dog Bottom as he eventually flopped down with exhaustion.

"I'm knackered and *so* stuffed!" Flan said as he collapsed next to him. They were resting by the same large mound close to the pool. Flan sucked his stomach in to try and pop the button on his pants. A loud trumping noise from below the waist echoed around the chamber.

"Sorry bro, didn't catch that. Talking through your rear end again?" chortled Dog Bottom.

"Damn this button!" cursed Flan as he struggled to get his fingers round it. He looked at his waistline which flobbed over like a huge muffin top. Why was it so swollen? But then a groan from his brother caught his attention. "Strewth! What's happening to you?"

"YEARGGGHH!" The sound of strained stitching was everywhere as Dog Bottom's belly had suddenly doubled in size. He rocked from side to side, desperate for relief. There was a loud tearing noise before loose flaps of belly fat flopped to either side of him. He groaned softly as the stomach cramps subsided. A second later, Flan managed to spring his own waistband loose. What relief! Who cared if he'd never fasten it again! The awful pressure was gone and that was all that mattered now. Together they lay back on the mound panting with exhaustion.

Dog Bottom woke about 20 minutes later to the sound of a throaty rasp. Visions of creatures with sharp fangs and claws flitted across his mind. He lay perfectly still hoping it hadn't spotted them. He peered out of half-closed eyes, but could see nothing. Then it hit him: a fetid plume of gas, like bad eggs on a bad day. He caught his breath and prayed that his brother would keep still long enough for it to move off. The fumes settled around him and he couldn't avoid taking in another lungful as he heard it rasp again. It was getting closer: in fact - His brother turned over noisily in his sleep and then it dawned on him.

"You filthy GIT." He elbowed Flan in the ribs as he now knew exactly what he had just breathed in, Flan woke with a start, let out another cloud of gas and laughed as he rained off the flurry of blows from his brother.

"Steady on, bro," he said half-chuckling at Dog Bottom's fury.

"I got a lungful of that!" Dog Bottom glared as he motioned for them to get going. "We've been down here far too long. We need to get out into fresh air." He shot Flan another pointed look before he clambered down from the soft mound.

"Damn this spittle!" Flan tried to wipe the sticky mess away but only succeeded in smearing it further. His hair, in particular, looked as if it had been dipped in a very greasy frying pan.

"Come on, get a move on grease ball!" Dog Bottom gestured irritably and set off towards the path taken by Jassaspy and the sakratts. He took a couple of short comic steps before he crashed to the floor. Flan exploded into laughter as he passed him.

"Goddammit!" He got to his feet and pulled up his trousers. Without a button to hold them up this was not going to be easy. With a grunt of annoyance he grabbed firmly hold of his waistband and lurched off into the shadows still twitching from the effects of the slime burns.

Behind them, the soft mound stirred and the large maggoty creature they had rested against humpfed and bellied its way after them, its rings of fat oozing a clammy moisture.

9. On the Wings of a Swan

"Those green fumes are getting thicker by the day. When Scott was last here, they were above the roof-tops. Groundluggs are now falling sick with chest complaints," said Fubbyloofah, as he caught the direction of Jack's glance the next morning. Lava was outside on the garden wall soaking in what big of sun there was and Jack was staring through the window and frowning at the sky. He looked around at the plant life. What remained was etiolated: long yellowish stems with little strength to stand up-right. There was no doubt about it, La-Kelisland was a land that was suffering, ailing for something.

"It's on the table going cold" cried Fubbyloofah, cutting across Jack's thoughts. Jack went in to the breakfast table. Scott was already seated and halfway through a slice of homemade toast.

"Where's Featherfae?" he asked, through a mouthful of toast. A rush of warm air suddenly announced her presence.

"Good morning all!" she said, positively beaming. "You'll never guess what Chloe has done this morning."

"You mean apart from annoying everyone?" asked Scott. Chloe rolled her eyes and Jack laughed whilst crunching into a piece of pated toast.

"No, far from it! She has been directing the smoggilars with their planting. All the grape pips are now securely planted," said Featherfae with a satisfied air. Jack flung a confused glance around the table.

"But how does Chloe know what to do with those pips, she's never been here before?" he asked confused.

"Oh, didn't you know? Chloe can communicate with animals using their sounds," explained Featherfae as Chloe broke into a huge grin beside her. Jack took a huge bite of toast whilst his mind raced. It was ludicrous; though in a place with a seven foot creature like Fubbyloofah, anything was possible. He looked questioningly at everyone.

"There's only one other person that I know who doesn't have to wait for creatures to speak in our tongue," added Fubbyloofah, turning to Featherfae with a twinkle in his eye. She caught his glance and blushed a little. "That's how Featherfae is able to heal the land better than anyone I know. They cry out when they need help and Featherfae hears and responds."

"Oh stop, stop! I'm only doing what anyone else would do." She blushed an even deeper shade of red with all this praise. "It's everyone's duty to care for this land."

"I wish the Hebradaigese would remember that instead of spending their time quarrelling with each other," muttered Fubbyloofah under his breath.

Suddenly, and without the slightest sign of provocation, Scott shouted out, "JACK'S A TWIT". There was a split second of astonished silence, before a voice sounded out from behind them:

"Jack's a twit, Jack's a twit, Jack's a twit, Jack's a twit, Jack's a twit, Jack's a twit."

"What the...? Who ..?" Jack's head swung around in total confusion. Behind him Scott exploded with delight.

"It's just the mime-clock chiming the hour," laughed Fubbyloofah as everyone joined in merrily before eventually returning to their breakfast. After a few minutes of silent eating, Featherfae spoke up.

"So, what do you think of the beetle wings, Jack?"

Jack spluttered and coughed and instantly forgot all thoughts of revenge with the mime-clock. Beetle wings! How could he have forgotten? His eyes roamed the table in a panic. But, wait a minute, he couldn't remember eating any. Featherfae must be mistaken! Yes, and now that she had reminded him he could feign a full stomach. He was conscious of having a delirious smile on his face, when he caught sight of Scott. His smile vanished instantly. Scott was leaning across the table towards him with a devilish grin all over his face. He was also proffering something on a plate.

"Another piece of toast and pate: fried beetle-wing pate?" Glee was emanating from his every pore. Jack twinged with annoyance.

"Thanks, but no thanks. I think I've had enough for one day, bro," he said, striving hard to keep his voice level. The desire to whack his brother on the shins under the table was overwhelming.

"Well in that case, Featherfae will you pass the rest over here. Unless I can persuade you to abandon your vegetarianism that is," said Fubbyloofah, who then proceeded to nibble away as if in pate-heaven. Jack sat back and mentally kicked himself. Why hadn't he thought of that? Vegetarianism! It was too late now. He sat back in morbid fascination as Fubbyloofah licked his chops and preened his whiskers in naked delight at the fried delicacies which Jack imagined were already lodged between his back molars.

The beetle wings marked the zenith of the breakfast, and it wasn't long before the party was thinking of the journey ahead. Featherfae had already been out scouting ahead for the best route, and could confirm that the valley bottom was the most direct route with plenty of tree cover should sakratts be spotted. Once at Crambleside there was no alternative but to tackle the Striver. This was a relentless up-hill slog, but at least once at the top you would be at Treadmail Tower, Tanglestep's current posting. It wouldn't be an easy journey but they had little alternative and they had each other for company and moral support.

"Aren't we going to invite Cob to come along?" asked Scott feeling guilty that he hadn't mentioned him before now.

"I'm afraid not," said Fubbyloofah locking the front door behind them all. "Cob himself has now disappeared. As with his wife before him, we suspect he has also been taken to serve the slygorm. Three other groundluggs have also disappeared. Once they reach a certain size and weight the sakratts whisk them off. Virtually every village in La-Kelisland, is reporting the same."

"Well at least he might be able to find his wife now," said Scott hopefully as they set off.

"The way to the valley road is via the bridge. No lingering by the river this time please," Fubbyloofah said pointedly as they all headed down towards the river. Scott averted his eyes in embarrassment. It was strange to find himself back where he had nearly drowned. He looked anxiously at the shadows, half expecting to see Jassaspy secretly watching them, and couldn't help peering down into the deep black water into which he had fallen. It was just as black as ever. He pulled back to the comfort of his companions, and noticed Featherfae watching him carefully. He shuddered and put it out of his mind.

"It's so much worse than it was on my last visit." Scott said, eyeing the green smog. He choked as he pulled his collar up and tried to breathe through the fabric. The density of the green vapour that hung over the houses was wet and claggy and thick tendrils were drifting down to the ground making them all cough and splutter.

"All the more reason we don't delay. If it gets any worse the villages will soon become ghost towns," said Fubbyloofah.

They were soon out and beyond the village boundaries but their presence had already disturbed things. Behind them, tendrils of the green vapour were probing the air as if looking for something. Featherfae was disturbed.

"I know we mustn't dally but we can't go on like this," she said, noting how strung out the party was. Lava was way out in front and Chloe was lagging behind at the rear: she was clearly struggling already. The fall through the porthole, had added to the bruises she had got from the Puddies. The lumps between her shoulder blades were now quite prominent and very painful.

"We need to get to Roughrigg Tarn," said Fubbyloofah. "Once there we'll have more options."

They waited for Chloe to catch up then trudged on, but each footstep was getting heavier and heavier and slower and slower. The mist was down and visibility was poor. Somehow they all knew they weren't alone.

"What's that tearing sound?" asked Scott eventually as they tramped over a grass field together. Nobody knew but it had been going on for a while now and was very rhythmic as if in tandem with….

"Our feet!" yelled Jack suddenly. Their eyes flashed down. Tendrils of green vapour were snaking round their ankles. The other end seeped down into the turf, gripping it tightly. Jack pulled his foot up sharply. The turf underfoot tore away. To his left Chloe screamed. Plumes of green vapour danced and swirled around them. Her fingers dug into his shoulder with fear.

"No, no, no!" she yelled as she waved her arms to clear the air. Jack blinked and staggered through stinging eyes. Up in front Scott coughed violently, staggered once, twice, then wailed loudly and fell. A huge piece of turf ripped up with his fall and a host of darkling beetles emerged to scurry off into the mist waving their antennae. Fubbyloofah stiffened with alarm.

"Quick. There's no time to lose! Those beetles will put out the alert," he said. "Chloe, Scott, climb up on my back. We're not far now."

There was a scrabble of limbs and with a huge effort, he bounded free of the green tendrils. Jack and Featherfae had to manage the best they could. The tendrils snaked after them, menacing their every step until a sudden blast of light streamed forth.

"We've made it!" Fubbyloofah cried. The light from the lake lanced the green smog like a sulphurous boil, causing it to fizzle and crackle. It shrank back and dissipated. But the beetles had already done their job. Over on the horizon a cloud of fruit-bats were already winging their way back to Granglethorn.

Lava looked worried and so did Fubbyloofah. But what could they do about it? They paused to regroup and savour the beauty of their surroundings. It was a lovely spot, exquisitely flanked by a gentle rocky outcrop and with crystal clean waters. To top it all, swarms of puffleflies hovered over the water and all the colours of the rainbow showered down with every beat of their iridescent wings. Fubbyloofah took a deep breath. Chloe was clearly troubled by the bruises on her back and they had so much further to go. He looked over to the water's edge. A pristine white swan swam over towards Lava before tilting its slender neck towards Chloe in welcome.

"You're right about Chloe. She certainly seems to be in tune with the animals here," said Jack. Featherfae was watching her interact with the swan with a strange smile upon her face.

"She reminds me a lot of myself" she said wistfully. "I used to spend *so* much time down here with the swans at her age."

They all looked down at Chloe who, to their complete amazement, was now clambering onto the swan's back. The swan then shook itself a little to get used to its passenger, arched its neck upwards, and beat its huge wings several times before launching itself into the air. It glided up from the tarn and then went into a graceful swooping arc which took it right round everyone before landing a few feet away to their left.

"You've got some way to go before you equal that, huh?" exclaimed Chloe to Jack and Scott's gaping expressions. Featherfae and the swan made a series of strange clicking sounds before they both looked at Chloe.

"Come on Chloe, I know you understood that," said Featherfae. "How do you feel about what Silvertip suggested?" Silvertip twisted her neck to look at Chloe astride her back.

"I'll need some reins," she said simply. Silvertip nodded: but where to look? Fubbyloofah went down to the waterline where Lava was busy conserving energy for World's End by soaking in the sun on a hot rock. Scott and Jack looked in vain amongst the wildflowers in Featherfae's recently vacated footsteps.

"Wait! If I stand in the same spot for a while then stronger stemmed flowers will shoot up," she said determinedly.

Scott, Jack and Chloe looked on as Featherfae stayed rooted to the spot beaming joyously skywards. First to appear were a small ring of daisies, followed by buttercups and lupins. A minute or two later came the foxgloves. They were stunned to see how strong and fast they grew: in no time at all, they were waist height. But it wasn't until the hollyhocks appeared that Featherfae was satisfied.

"These are what we want," she said. "Once they get to about 4 feet in height, take a strip off each stem for the reins."

They watched in fascination as the hollyhocks shot up around Featherfae ready or harvesting. With the stem stripped out as Featherfae had suggested, it only needed Fubbyloofah to tie the ends in a reef knot before Featherfae was ready to present it to Silvertip for fitting. Silvertip bowed her proud head and murmured gentle sounds and reminiscences to her old friend Featherfae, who gently slipped the reins around her head and into her beak. Once fitted, Chloe was soon on Silvertip's back and Featherfae looked steadily at her.

"Silvertip knows how to respond to the reins. Don't worry, even sakratts think twice before messing with swans."

"Why does all the cool stuff happen to her?" grumbed Jack. Chloe giggled in response whilst Scott just stood there gawping open-mouthed like a fool.

"I'm not worried. I can handle myself. It's those noodles you should be worried about, especially him. Don't rely on him in a crisis!" She nodded towards Scott determined not to let him forget how he'd let her down with the Puddies. Then she pulled down sharply on the reins. "See you all in Crambleside!" she said, as Silvertip launched herself skywards.

10. The Chamber of Moths and the Creatures of the Night Shade

When the Puddies left the groat's pool, they seemed more concerned with holding up their trousers than with how to get out of the tunnels. They were also completely unaware that stalking them was a gigantic maggotty creature that was at least 20 feet long with a puckered mouth full of sharp teeth and hairy tendrils. They trudged silently along the tunnel that the sakratts had used earlier. But, half-hidden in a fissure hewn out of the rock face, a cowled figure was observing them with interest. He'd seen what they had chosen to rest against once they had come out of the pool and he could also see that it was tracking them. Jassaspy watched for a moment before his lips slimed into a smile and he faded back into the grey.

"I reckon as long as the path goes up-hill we've got to be going in the right direction," said Dog Bottom, as they came to a fork in the path. Flan nodded, more out of a sense of utter cluelessness. They trudged upwards taking the left hand fork, all the while unaware of what followed behind.

"Phew, it's stifling down here," moaned Flan, breaking out into a clammy sweat with the humidity.

"Tell me about it!" panted Dog Bottom. "Hey, is it my imagination or is this tunnel getting narrower?"

The tunnel was hot, dark and increasingly pokey and they kept stumbling over raised ridges that ran around the tunnel like gigantic gastric bands.

"It's not made any easier having to hold up our pants," Flan cursed. He looked at his huge distended belly. It was if that sugary groatmeal had permanently settled around his waist. Suddenly, a hand shot out and yanked them both into a crevice in the tunnel wall.

"What the...?" cried Dog Bottom.
"Get owwwfff!"

An oily rag stifled Flan's cry and he overbalanced as his pants fell round his ankles. He was dimly aware of his brother struggling with something too before a fetid plume of gas wafted over their heads.

"Careful you fools," hissed a voice. They felt their breath choke off with ammonia. "Look!" it said insistently.They squinted through tears at the tunnel they had left, and wailed in fear as the huge maggotty creature humpfed past leaving a stench of stale sweat in its wake.

"My God! What was that?" Dog Bottom turned to face a deep black cowl. He felt himself drown in its darkness. He thought he saw a smile on the shadow of a face there but he wasn't sure. "Who are you?" he asked hesitantly. The cowl hovered over his head for a split second before he answered.

"I am Jassaspy and that creature was the slygorm." He turned slowly on his heel before beckoning. "Follow me if you want to live," he said, before adding rather chillingly, "that tunnel you were in leads to its lair."

The Puddies stood open-mouthed in shock. Any questions about whether Jassaspy could be trusted were dropped. After all, hadn't he just saved them from that huge flesh-eating maggot? Dog Bottom recovered first and shot his brother a withering look of disdain, standing as he was in his underwear and scratching at his fleas.

"For God's sake, pull your pants up and let's get out of here," he snapped, before moving to catch up with Jassaspy who had already rounded the corner and was disappearing down, heaven knows which, tunnel. Flan grabbed at his pants, lurched forwards a couple of steps and then immediately bumped into his brother who had stopped dead in his tracks.

"What is it now?" asked Flan in frustration.

"That's what!" said Dog Bottom pointing to the fresh green slime that glistened on the path and seemed to secrete from under Jassaspy's robes.

"Best be careful of that stuff," said Flan. "It burns."

Dog Bottom whirled in fury. "Yes I know it burns, idiot, or have you forgotten how you knocked me into the stuff when we first arrived here?"

Flan didn't answer and both fell silent as they pondered the implications of following someone who was the source of the awful stuff. Still; what were the alternatives?

Twenty minutes of skirting around the slime and lurching through yet more tunnels, some of which, oddly enough, seemed to take them back downhill instead of up, they eventually arrived at a huge door set into a rock face and secured by large cast-iron bolts. Jassaspy rapped loudly with his staff and the door swung open with a creak. In his eagerness to be the first out of the tunnel, Flan shot forwards before letting out a howl of pain. A huge peal of raucous laughter met him from inside the room.

"Look who's stepped in Jassaspy's trail," said the sakratt that had opened the door. He didn't even try to conceal his malicious glee. Others were quick to join in.

"Ahh, who's a poor little runt then," said another, his eyes gleaming with amusement. "Here, let me wipe you down, eh?" he said, whilst grabbing an oily rag and shuffling forwards. He dabbed at the slime on Flan's foot then pressed the slime-coated rag tightly against Flan's leg whilst leering up into his face. Flan squealed in pain and the cavernous room echoed to a roar of malicious laughter. The pain burnt like crazy but then a crashing blow to the head sent the sakratt spinning and the rag flew into the air. Jassaspy brought his staff down onto the sakratt's skull a second time.

"Fool!" he hissed loudly. "You'll pay for this." The echo from his words had barely died away before the rag landed with a wet slap on the sakratt's face.

"YEEOOOWWW!" he squealed horribly as his face started to burn and the chamber erupted. The other sakratts couldn't remember as entertaining a time as this. He tore the rag from his face and with a manic look in his eye, darted from the room to a chorus of belly-heaving laughter. Flan limped after Jassaspy and did his best to ignore the burning pain and the 'now-you-know-what-it-feels-like' looks from his brother. The room they were crossing was humungous: a cross between a cellar and a baronial hall complete with a huge inglenook fireplace. The walls were indistinguishable from the rock face on the other side of the door, except for the aesthetic display of black metal weaponry pinned to it. Lolling around the base of the walls and within easy reach of the weapons were the sakratts who had been so recently amused by the incident with the slime. Jassaspy brushed past them and led the Puddies off towards an inner door in the opposite corner. The sakratts gawped and leered as they limped past but had the sense not to interfere: the memory of what had just happened was all too fresh. Once on the other side of the door, Jassaspy led them up a twisting stone staircase that seemed to go on forever. There were small slot windows through which the boys glimpsed sakratts torturing strange little mice with wings. On other levels they heard blood-curdling screams which reverberated around the stone chasm. Eventually they arrived at a room at the top.

"My chambers in Granglethorn," said Jassaspy with a sigh. He led them in and pointed to some chairs by a long narrow window. They flopped down exhausted as he turned to a cupboard in the wall. His chambers were full of dusty leather-bound books but what they noticed above everything else were the moths. There were hundreds of them, crawling over everything: on the table, on the window ledges, clinging to the spines of old books and dotted all over the floor. All sorts of weird and wonderful curios caught their eye whilst he rummaged in his cupboard. There was a giant spider mounted in a glass case with huge purple hairs all over it, a fish with a face-full of teeth that was mounted in a case on the wall, and a stuffed mouse with wings like the ones that they had seen through the window on the way up the staircase. Flan grinned to himself before taking down the glass case with the spider in it. Jassaspy turned just as he was putting it up to his face and scratching at his fleas.

"Let me solve that little flea problem for you," he snapped. He flung a handful of glittering powder over him and muttered some words in an ancient tongue. The glass case vanished into thin air and the spider landed softly on the bridge of Flan's nose, its eight legs spread right across his face from forehead to chin and from cheek to cheek. Flan's eyes opened in horror as the half inch fangs threatened to breach his focal point. Suddenly its abdomen twitched against his lower lip and the hairy creature scuttled up and over his face before burying itself in his hair. Flan froze, hardly daring to breathe, before his eyes darted over to Dog Bottom whose own shock only reinforced what he was feeling. Snatching gulps of air he started to wail in paralytic fear as he could feel it make sudden snapping movements as it made short shrift of the fleas.

"Relax. It won't hurt you now," said Jassaspy as he muttered some other ancient rune. "It has been fed and now sees you as its mother," he said smugly.

"But I don't want to be its mother. Can't you just get it out of my hair? PLEASE!" he wailed.

"It's called Sticklestabber. You'll get used to it…. in time. Just keep your hair well oiled. You wouldn't want it setting up home somewhere with more moisture, would you?" he said, sliming a smile. Flan recoiled from the image this evoked and Jassaspy smirked malevolently before bringing various phials of coloured liquid to the table.

"Now, who is going to tell me how you happened to be in the tunnels under Granglethorn?"

He turned to pour some smoking yellow liquid out of a phial into three short glasses, added a pinch of some musty-smelling powder, plucked a moth up from the floor, pulled off its wings, squelched it between his fingers and deftly drizzled the contents into each of the glasses. He swirled the concoction around until it started to fizzle, nodded imperceptibly at the result, and raised his glass to the brothers. They joined him in a toast and each took a tentative sip before Dog Bottom started to speak.

"Umm, well we kinda came here with a very fierce dog -" he suddenly started to choke and retch. "- and if we don't get back soon -" his stomach heaved with the effort of the words which were coming out all muffled as if talking with his mouth full. Suddenly a thick slimy black lugworm slithered out from between his lips, landed splat on the floor and wriggled off. Dog Bottom coughed violently and looked up at Jassaspy who indicated firmly for him to carry on. He composed himself before starting again.

"- the dog will attack anyone stopping us from leaving… ACKRAAGH!" He could contain it no longer. He let out a scream, and with it a spaghetti tangle of slithering worms wriggled forth from his mouth; some headed for his nostrils whilst others shot down his chin and made for the floor. "HELP!" he chocked as some of the worms took advantage of his open-throated cry to try and wriggle back down his throat. He retched them back up and in his eagerness accidentally bit into one. He felt the threshing in his mouth intensify and a noxious taste of worm oozed slowly over his tongue. Jassaspy watched with an expression of amused contentment.

"Shall we try again and this time without a mouthful of mealworm LIES!" he said, bristling with anger. Dog Bottom nodded pale-faced as the final few worms wriggled out. This time, he told the story with painstaking care, anxious to avoid anything he couldn't remember in case it be construed as a lie. It didn't take long before Jassaspy interrupted:

"Ahh, so they are both alive and on the other side of a time splinter," he said, on hearing about Snarklepike and Hagratty. Then, as the story unfolded, he fired more questions. "Who triggered a time splinter? Do you have the time-key?" But they were questions that they couldn't answer. "FOOLS!" he seethed as they floundering with unhelpful responses. But it was for Lava that he reserved the flint of his force. "So the fire-cat returns, eh?" He spat with venom. "Well this is one prophecy that won't be fulfilled. The sun is too far gone this time. He's too late. He should have come years ago. Soon the moon will light up this land and then the slygorm shall emerge from its lair."

He jumped to his feet and moved over to the window, his slime trail bubbling from his fevered imagination. He grabbed a handful of moths from the window ledge and without even bothering to remove their wings crunched them between his molars. Small spots of yellow pus dribbled out of his cowl and splattered his robe. The Puddies looked at each other in a state of exhausted terror. There was no doubt about it: they had exchanged the frying pan of the underground tunnels for the fire of Jassaspy. Flan now had a giant spider nesting in his hair and Dog Bottom couldn't say a word in case it was untrue and he started to choke on mealworms.

Jassaspy moved quickly. Using a mixture of strange lights and incantations he stood at the open window at the top of his Chamber of Moths and issued forth a summons and then sat back regally to await a response. First to arrive was a small delegation of rats. Their pack leader was a rag-eared creature with a patch over one eye. His two front teeth protruded sharply and would have glinted in the light were they not blackened by rot. Next to arrive were the crows. They swept in through the open windows and sent a cloud of moths scattering.

"Look out!" cried Dog Bottom. There was a purple flash as Sticklestabber reared up from Flan's hair to snatch them out of the air. The moths went hysterical and bounced around the chamber. By the time they'd settled, the Puddies were left smeared with the dust from their wings. The crows knew better than to go for any of Jassaspy's moths though and just cawed, cackled and ruffled their feathers whilst their leader picked at its beak with one of its razor sharp talons waiting for Jassaspy to address them. Finally, a pack of mangy wolves arrived: three large shaggy maned creatures and as motley a group of half-starved creatures that you could ever hope to find. Most of them were covered in open sores from their constant squabbles with each other and collectively their breath rivalled that of Jassaspy's for potency. Slowly the three groups settled down wondering why they had been summoned.

"War iz it 'ee wants?" muttered Grubgragga to his sidekick

"Ow should I know?" he responded "but it mus' be important if he's got those mutts and rag-wings 'ere," he said, nodding over to the wolves and the crows. "All I care about is us getting' a nice manky carcass to sink our fangs into. I'll be well 'appy wi' that," he chuckled, whilst salivating lasciviously at the thought. The Wolves pushed their way to the front snarling and drooling all over the heads of the rats as they did so.

"Got a problem rat-face?" said a huge hulking wolf with a black shaggy mane as the spittle from its jaws dribbled into Grubgragga's eye. It tensed its shoulders just itching for an excuse to pounce. Grubgragga looked disdainfully in the opposite direction and shook his head vigorously. The globule flew off and hit one of the crows on the head and started up a clattering racket of indignation.

"Creatures of the Night Shade," shouted Jassaspy, pausing to allow the commotion to die down. "I bring you news of a visitor: a most unwelcome visitor that I need you to find." The commotion started up again as wolf, bird and rat wondered what it could be.

"A groat has escaped," said one of the crows

"What would you know? When do you ever go underground?" said one of the rats.

"I bet you've never even seen a groat," replied another. "Everyone knows that all the groats can do is loll around in their own sweat-pool and wait for the slygorm."

"WHEN YOU HAVE QUITE FINISHED," proclaimed Jassaspy. A mantle of silence descended upon the gathering again. "I was speaking of a visitor from another time that you must find and bring to me."

"OK, but wots in for us?" leered Ripsnarl, the wolf, whilst casting sneaky sideways glances at his pack.

"I'll tell you what's in it for you," hissed Jassaspy malevolently as he grabbed the wolf by the scruff of its neck. A fetid plume of green gas escaped from his cowl. The wolf whimpered and wriggled violently chocked by the ammonic plume. "Your very survival, as you know it! That's what's in it for you." He threw the wolf to the ground in front of the pack. Ripsnarl yelped before retreating behind the rest of the pack to lick his wounds. Jassaspy surveyed the Night Shade who had gone very quiet on witnessing this display of power and were now hanging on his every word. "This creature that has returned is a creature from the old legends," he continued. "It is a creature that must be apprehended before it has chance to restore the power of the sun. I am talking of the fire-cat!" There was a moment's pause before the Night Shade erupted:

"We'll find 'im for you. Don't you worry about that!" shouted Grubgragga.

"Leave it to the crows, sire," said an inky black hooded crow eagerly.

"You shall ALL need to search in your own special way," said Jassaspy. "That is why I have summoned you," he continued. "Crows: take to the wing and scour the earth for flashes of his presence. His colour is not easily hidden in a land crying out for sunlight like this one. Rats: you are here because of your consummate skill under the earth. I want you to scurry deep underground in the tunnels under Granglethorn and Dragmines valley. Find any sign you can of his presence and you will be richly rewarded. These two," he nodded at the Puddies, "were found down there, so there is every chance that the fire-cat also materialised underground." The rats nodded eagerly. "Wolves…you are the most closely related to the fire-cat and a natural predator. Go; run like the wind through the forests and over the hills. Use your pack instinct and hunt him down. And remember, all of you, bring him to me ALIVE and UNHARMED!" The Night Shade erupted into howls, squeaks and cackles, as Jassaspy dismissed the gathering and they all set off to begin the search.

With the Night Shade dispersed, Jassaspy had to move quickly to convene a Council meeting with his fellow Hebradaigese. Hagratty had jeopardised the security of La-Kelisland. In her bungled attempt to catch the fire-cat another time splinter had been triggered. Here was a marvellous opportunity to marginalise his rival. All it would take would be for the Council to decide that

Hagratty had acted inappropriately in some way for her to be subjected to sanctions of the severest nature.

"Is there any chance we could get something to eat?" said Flan, cutting across his train of thought.

"- other than these moths," interjected Dog Bottom, conscious that all he could taste at the moment was worm. Jassaspy momentarily froze, looked across at them for a split-second before gliding over to the door.

"Stay here," he exclaimed before leaving the chamber and slamming the door behind him. Once alone, the Puddies collapsed in a heap feeling totally wretched.

"What now?" said Flan.

"I don't care. Just as long as he brings some decent food," said Dog Bottom. Moments later the door opened again.

"Take these fools to the sweat-pools. They are of no more use to me," Jassaspy hissed to the same sakratts that Fubbyloofah and his party had met by the bridge. Hackweezle lunged, grabbed Dog Bottom by the foot and dragged his bloated body towards the door, squelching moths as he went. Meanwhile, Spittlewhip grabbed Flan by the hair before shrieking in pain.

"ARRGH!" he withdrew his hand sharply as Sticklestabber waved its two front legs in the air menacingly. Blood trickled from the bite.

"Move!" spat Jassaspy unconcerned. He shoved both Flan and Spittlewhip towards the door. Hackweezle threw the door open and with an almighty heave kicked Dog Bottom out. He thumped and tumbled down the stone staircase. Flan fared better, as Spittlewhip simply prodded him in the back afraid that any undue cruelty on his part would trigger Sticklestabber's wrath.

"Gerra move on scum!" bawled Hackweezle, prodding Dog Bottom in the back with a black cast-iron spike once they were down at the bottom. They trudged back along the passage until, to their utter dismay, the sakratts opened a familiar door.

"Ahh, no. Not back here again!" cried Flan in despair. They were right back in the underground tunnels where they had started.

"Yeah, but this time you're gonna get your own sweat-pool," said Spittlewhip prodding him with his iron spike but from a safe distance in case Sticklestabber reared up again.

They snaked their way down into the bowels of the earth for what must have been half an hour before emerging in a huge underground cavern honeycombed with hollow pits deep enough to stop the occupants from clambering out. The first few pits contained groats swilling around in their own pool but as they got further into the honeycomb, they could hear voices calling out.

"Hey, you gotta help me get outta here. Please, you gotta help!"

"Who's that?" hissed Flan to his brother.

"Dunno, but it seems we're not the only ones held prisoner down here," muttered Flan glumly as they tried but failed to spot who was crying out.

Eventually they arrived at freshly excavated pits and, with a snarl and a face-full of bad breath as a parting gift, the Puddies were dumped, each into one of their own.

"Enjoy your new home, scum!" leered Hackweezle. They looked up to see him standing above them on the rim of the pit. "Ahh, come now," he jeered. "Cheer up! It's not that bad. Eat your fill and sweat until your pit fills up and becomes a pool. By that stage you won't know or care about anything except when your next serving of groatmeal is comin' and once you've eaten it, you'll sweat some more. And 'why' you ask yourselves? 'cos the slygorm needs your sweat: that's why!"

He snickered before nodding towards Spittlewhip who up-ended a cauldron of groatmeal that was positioned at the far end of each pit. The thick, sweet gunk flobbed down into the base of each pit. The sakratts waited until it started oozing towards the Puddies like an oil slick before retreating back down the passageway goading the occupants of the other pits as they did so. The Puddies were left staring at the impossibly high walls of their own private sweat-pool and the dawning realisation that they might never, ever, get out.

"Don't touch that stuff, bro," said Dog Bottom, as the groatmeal was about to pool around his feet. "You heard what he said."

"Yeah, I remember. Hey, you do realise that the reason we came out of that groat's pool all sticky was -"

"..yes; a sweat-pool. I worked it out too. I can't believe we were swimming in someone's sweat: how vile!"

They watched the approaching tide of gloop despondently.

"You know bro, we've been down here for hours now with nothin' to eat," moaned Flan dolefully later that day. "Perhaps if we just eat a little…" He inched towards the pool of groatmeal and scooped up a sticky handful. It was exactly the same as they'd had at the pool. It smelt divine! He dabbed at it with his tongue and felt instant gratification. "Hey, bro, just try a bit. It'll get rid of that worm taste in your mouth."

"Are you trying to be helpful or is that just a painful reminder?"

"Aww, don't be like that. I'm serious, just try a bit."

Dog Bottom glanced over to the groatmeal and sniffed the air tentatively. It was enough to start his head started spinning. Flan was right. A tiny amount would be enough to clear his mouth from the taste of the worms. He took a small nibble then heard his brother say something about "another small handful" when an irrational panic took over. Seized by a fear that Flan was ahead of him and that somehow that would mean less for him, he waded forwards. Soon he was in the deepest part of the pool. He lay back with a sigh of relief as it slowly globulated into his open mouth. He chuckled to himself as he swallowed five or six times in rapid succession. Ecstasy! The taste of the worms was now a distant foggy memory. He let it run over his body and its vapour fill his head with dizzy delight! If there was to be heaven on earth, this was it and to hell with the consequences!

11. The Conference of the Wing

Fubbyloofah's party left the shores of Roughrigg Tarn in trepidation. They knew that the fruit bats would have delivered their message by now and the roads into Crambleside were likely to be heavily patrolled by sakratts. Jack cast a final backward glance at the tarn and was struck by the large swathe of wildflowers growing from Featherfae's footsteps. As these led straight to her, he suddenly had an alarming thought.

"The sakratts will simply follow the trail of flowers and find us!" he exclaimed. Featherfae shook her head.

"No. The flowers that spring from my footsteps now contain poppletons. Within a short space of time, no discernible trail is evident. Look, its already happening," she said. Jack looked back to see that the poppletons were shooting their coloured petals and seeds everywhere so that the trail was very quickly blurred. He smiled in relief.

They returned to the road ahead feeling more comforted, though it snaked like a roller-coaster and was not made any easier by Featherfae's sudden detours.

"Won't be a second" she said as she sprinted off with the smoggilars to plant more pips. Whenever this happened, Lava would seize his chance to curl up in the sun to soak up energy for World's End by catching what warmth it could give. The boys were equally keen to grab a breather.

"I'm knackered. Are we nearly there yet?" asked Scott. Jack murmured in sympathy. Fubbyloofah scrutinised both of them as if weighing something up.

"One more up-hill stretch and then we'll take a detour down to Ye Olde Dungeon Creek. There's a rustic hostelry at the foot of the crags run by a friend of mine," he replied. "Just wait 'til you taste his lovely pastries," he exclaimed with a twinkle in his eye.

They took to the road with new-found enthusiasm and the next half an hour or so was spent going through the alphabet naming foods and drinks which they hoped to find there. By the time they had got to the letter "Q" their expectations had been raised to such a ridiculous extent that nothing but a king's banquet would have satisfied them.

"Quaggles," said Featherfae after several seconds of stumped silence.

"What on earth are quaggles?" asked the boys intrigued.

"Jumping nuts!" she explained. "You can't enjoy a feast without quaggles. They're about the size of a walnut, and as soon as you crack the shell they jump out as if they're on springs. Everyone has such fun on a feast day with quaggles." Fubbyloofah smiled and nodded in agreement and reassured the boys that Ye Olde Dungeon Creek held plenty of surprises, not least of which was the owner himself.

It wasn't difficult to spot the hostelry. It was nestled down at the head of the adjacent valley and gave itself away with a wisp of blue smoke that curled up for all to see. The boys broke into a sprint, eager to be the first to arrive. It had been quite a tiring walk and they both felt envious of Chloe travelling in style with Silvertip. A few minutes later, they were at the door to the hostelry. It was suitably imposing: a huge old oak door that must have been at least 12 inches thick, covered in large black cast-iron studs and finished with a pair of impressive gothic hinges. Scott looked up to Fubbyloofah who turned the old door ring and, with his weight behind him, pushed hard. It creaked slowly open to reveal a dark interior lit by a couple of twinkling lights. The room was a former stable and had been converted into a couple of snugs. The snug by the bar faced an impressive black range which was growling out a wall of heat from the logs that spat and crackled there.

"What do you fancy boys?" asked Fubbyloofah as they pushed their noses up against a glass counter full of cakes and pastries a moment later.

"I like the look of that one. What is it?" asked Scott, pointing to a rich brown tower of layered flakes and crumbling buttons.

"That's the Mouse-house" said a voice from round the back of the bar. "It's a real delicacy but only for those with a VERY sweet tooth," he added whilst shuffling forwards.

They peered into the gloom hoping for a glimpse of whoever had spoken. A leg came into view. It was clad in a pair of green moleskin trousers exquisitely finished with a tiny row of gold buttons that ran down the side of the calf and which disappeared into a pair of blue leather boots with bright yellow stitching that ran around the junction of the upper and the sole. Their eyes travelled up to see a body dressed in a waistcoat made of the same green moleskin as the trousers and draped with a gold chained pocket-watch. Beneath the waistcoat was a crisp white shirt and a bright red tie. But what really shocked Scott and Jack was the sight of who, or what, was wearing the clothes. The figure was huge; at least as tall as Fubbyloofah, but it wasn't so much its size that was the issue. Facing them across the bar was an enormous tawny owl and it was wearing a gold monocle in one of its enormous eyes.

"Professor Cornelius Flapbaggles, or just 'Flapbaggles' to my friends. At your service!" said the figure with a stiff bow. "Now what can I get you all to eat? The Mouse-house , the Feather-bed Flurry or a piece of Dingle Bell Pie?" He indicated a filo pasty of what looked like pink candy-floss and then pointed to a caquelon of pink jewels peeping out from below a hearty crust. Their eyes were on stalks.

"Could I change to the Feather-bed Flurry, please Professor Flapbaggles?" asked Scott positively salivating at the sight of all that pink fluff which he could just imagine dissolving on his tongue.

"Nothing could be too much trouble for our burnt gold seeker," said Flapbaggles with a wink.

"WHAT? Oh not this again. It's not true! Lava, is looking for burnt gold. I'm afraid I don't know anything about it." Scott looked round in distress. This rumour had to be scotched once and for all. He glanced at Fubbyloofah, who shrugged his shoulders in a gesture of innocence. "This is your fault. If you hadn't -"

"Steady on, steady on. It wasn't Fubbyloofah. I heard it from Tappletock the woodpecker. But are you telling me that it isn't true?" asked Flapbaggles in concern.

"Of course it's not true. What do I know about burnt gold? I can't even see proper colours anymore; not since the shadow-sylph touched me. I'm the last person you could rely on to spot burnt gold."

Flapbaggles' feathers flattened in disappointment. "Oh I see. How unfortunate. We really were hoping -"

"Yes, I know...I'm sorry." Scott muttered. No matter what he said or did, he seemed destined to dash everyone's hopes.

"Ah well, all the more reason for cake," said Flapbaggles with a sigh, before turning to Jack, "- and what about you? I can recommend the Mouse-house if you like the taste of sweet summer dew or the Dingle Bell Pie if you prefer something savoury but with the sharp sweet surprise of dingles."

Jack chose the Mouse-house and Flapbaggles ruffed up his feathers in pride as he personally saw to the order himself whilst the party settled themselves at the table by the fire. When the various plates arrived, the boys fell upon them with ravenous delight. The Feather-bed Flurry was simply exquisite and popped and fizzled upon the tongue to the extent that Scott sporadically jumped from his seat like a firecracker. Jack meanwhile was slowly working his way down the Mouse-house, each layer of cake contained thicker and more gelatinous layers of sugary gloop so that by the time he had reached the bottom it was solid.

"That's why I call it the Mouse-house said Flapbaggles. "It's built on solid foundations but is only big enough for a mouse. I like to add a dead one to the cake as a special treat, though I don't suppose you would appreciate that would you?"

"It's the most divine cake that I've ever eaten, though you're quite right to leave out the rodent," said Jack relieved that at least someone thought to ask before proffering nibbles of the animal and insect world.

"Thank you my friend, but you mustn't over-indulge," said Flapbaggles. "It's made of carbalix and we all know what that has done to the groundluggs, don't we?"

Scott's ears pricked up. What *had* it done to the groundluggs? Had this anything to do with Cob? He looked towards Fubbyloofah expectantly but he had his eyes closed as he warmed his paws by the fire. Flapbaggles continued.

"With crops failing due to the weakness of our sun, Granglethorn supplies the carbalix as famine relief. Unfortunately, they didn't warn the groundluggs about the effects of excess consumption. However, don't worry, the occasional cake won't do you any harm, providing you have the willpower to resist that extra helping."

Jack didn't really know what to make of this. He certainly didn't want to turn out looking anything like the Puddies, but then again, he wouldn't want to live on the sort of food that Fubbyloofah served up either. He'd had enough beetle wings and fetid broccoli to last him a lifetime. By the time he'd ruminated on the implications of all this, the conversation had turned towards the rest of their journey.

"You must be careful in Crambleside", said Flapbaggles. "It's not the place it used to be. A few months ago a hostelry was set up to cater specifically for sakratts and they're making their presence felt in so many ways. Only last week, beehives were turned over, rabbits were smoked out of their warrens and a family of robins had their nest destroyed and their eggs used as projectiles in one of their infantile squabbles."

"But surely the groundluggs will have something to say about that," said Fubbyloofah. "After all, it's their village. The sakratts belong in their garrison."

"Not these days old chap. It seems that as long as the groundluggs get their carbalix, anything goes; and the sakratts always make sure they deliver that," he finished.

This was sobering stuff for Fubbyloofah to hear. He certainly knew that the groundluggs had been suffering from a poor diet but he didn't know they'd stopped caring about their villages.

"Flapbaggles, I wonder whether your feathered friends can help," he began thoughtfully before a deep moan beside him caused him to start. Scott was waving his arms out searchingly and his eyes were black and soulless.

"What's *wrong* with him?" asked Flapbaggles, feathers ruffled in alarm.

"Quick: before he hurts himself." Featherfae jumped up, as Flapbaggles fluttered to the bar for a calming glass of water. Suddenly, a great commotion erupted outside.

"Where's Lava?" cried Jack in a panic. In all the excitement they'd forgotten he was still outside soaking up the sun on the wall. For a moment they froze and just stared at each other then they shot to the door. It slammed shut behind them and there was a blur of activity as they all bolted forward. Facing them all was a whirling black and ginger fireball. Suddenly, the whirlpool stopped mid-cycle and Lava emerged head first only to be dragged back into the spin-cycle a second later. Finally, he managed to break free and dart towards Fubbyloofah, eyes as wide as saucers..

"He's terrified!" Jack yelled; his hand at his mouth. Fubbyloofah lunged forwards to help, but he was too far away. The black mass split into five black shards that honed in on Lava from the air. Crows: five vicious, nasty carrion crows! Before anyone could even think of how to fight back, they swooped down and like a giant black claw, plucked Lava off the ground and spiralled skywards. His claws flashed and caught the air and then.... There were several seconds of painful silence as they all gaped helplessly up from the ground.

Scott was sitting with his head in his hands and panting as the others filed back inside in a state of shock. He looked groggily up. Featherfae was clutching a handful of sun-threads shed in the recent attack and was looking grim. What had happened and why was Flapbaggles hooting at various octaves through the open windows?

Soon a couple of chattering magpies bounced up to the door of the hostelry. They were quickly followed by a pair of swifts that skimmed into the bar and perched high up on a roof beam. Next, came a whole host of smaller birds: sparrows, bullfinches, starlings, thrushes, larks and nightingales. They streamed in through the open windows and swarmed around the bar until everyone was left dizzy by trying to keep up with their movements.

"Stop it! No!" laughed Featherfae as a robin tried to make a nest from the twigs in her hair. It burrowed its way in and no amount of grooming on her part could encourage it out. "Tish! Tish! Ok, stay then, but at least tidy up those twigs for me," she asked, beginning to think there could be advantages to this arrangement.

Next, came the larger birds. Pigeons and parrots were followed by a gaggle of geese who were honking loudly in an attempt to upstage the muster of peacocks behind them. The peacocks entered one by one. They paused in the open doorway and fanned out their tails with panache. Finally, just as Flapbaggles was clearing his throat to address the conference a sharp pecking was heard on the door.

"Come on in, whoever you are," said Flapbaggles eager to get going before the smaller birds started tucking their heads under their wings for a quick kip. TktTktTktTkt... the pecking sounded again. "Oh for goodness sake," grumbled Flapbaggles.

A couple of magpies obliged and in through the open door came a woodpecker, with a hop, a skip and a delicate pirouette that chimed perfectly with his resplendent dash of green plumage.

"Tappletock!" shouted Scott in delight at being re-united with the woodpecker they had met on the fringes of Onyx-Stone.

"Ahh, the dream cheaters!" said Tappletock. He clearly hadn't forgotten that they had nearly cost him a nice pillow of dandelion seeds. He smiled to show no hard feelings and bowed formally to Flapbaggles before announcing that he was not alone.

"I should have guessed," said Flapbaggles as, seconds later, in walked a beautifully resplendent Jay: his pink chest puffed out with pride and offset with a pair of gold breeches and a matching waistcoat. He carried a gold topped cane in his left wing which he twirled for dramatic effect as he surveyed the gathering before announcing rather sniffily.

"Darlings, darlings, we simply *are* slumming it these days, aren't we?" He strutted over to the bar whilst casting a withering look at a couple of house sparrows who retreated behind the thrushes suddenly ashamed of their drab plumage. "But If I *must* endure this interminable beak-wagging, then, by heavens, let it be with a G&T."

"Good to see you again, Raffles." Flapbaggles gave a nod to the bar staff and then formally announced the Conference of the Wing open. The boys watched in fascination as one by one, various birds took the perch to have their say.

"Crows are just born nasty," said a thrush with a bare patch on her back which seemed to indicate that she was talking from personal experience.

"Let me summon a murmuration. If those crows are anywhere in this valley, we'll flush 'em out in no time," said a young starling eagerly. His head darted from left to right hoping to find a spark of interest in his idea.

"The crows have obviously carried him off somewhere, but the question is where?"

"Oh Lordy!" exclaimed Raffles as the pigeon raised a wing as if to compensate for his inane comment and drab appearance. Raffles beckoned the bar staff over for a top-up in exasperation.

The swifts in the rafters chirped up that they were the fastest on the wing and could cover the greatest distance which only provoked the swallows. The house sparrows said they didn't think they could do much to help against birds as large as crows to which the robins took umbrage, and we got into the old chestnut of whether size mattered. Soon the whole of Ye Olde Dungeon Creek was a cacophony of squabbling twitters.

Jack looked anxious. "This isn't getting us anywhere and meanwhile those crows are carrying Lava further and further away."

He stood up and approached Flapbaggles. "Please, professor, can I address the conference?"

Flapbaggles adjusted his monocle and blinked his very large eyes slowly before turning towards the chattering democratic excess.

"Colleagues…A moment please…I have received a…a most unusual request from this time-ward here. He, erm, wants permission, to.... address the conference."

The squabbling died down amongst the birds at the front but then spread rapidly by nudge of wing to the furthest rafters of the hostelry.

"This is totally against convention," said a duck that had walked in half way through the discussion.

"Ahh, shut it, waddler!" said a bullfinch. "I say let him talk. If it stops us all squabbling for just a few minutes it would be a blessed relief. My head's splitting." Murmurs of assent rippled through the crowd and Jack looked up at Flapbaggles who gave assent with a brief but perceptible nod of his head.

"Er, thank you all…for this opportunity," started Jack hesitantly.

"Ahh, get on with it!" said a voice from the back.

"Yes, right..well..mm. I just wanted to start by asking something. When was the last time any of you enjoyed fruits or irrebies?"

"Ages ago: they've all died out. What of it?" said another voice over to his far left. Jack soldiered on undeterred. It was time to get specific.

"Do any of you remember cherries or agrappa?" A hushed tone told him that many did. "Well hey…look!" he put his hand into his pocket and pulled out a handful and waved then in the air for everyone to see.

A peacock perched at the front screeched a lungful at him before the parrots, being amongst the oldest present, started squawking emotionally with tears of remembrance in their eyes. Jack waited for the crowd to calm down. He definitely had their attention now.

"Well, the crows have taken Lava, the fire-cat, and he's our only hope of reviving the sun. And if we can rescue him, he will travel to World's End with burnt gold. So the question is, will you at least try and help us?" he looked round the conference at the mass of birds gathered there, but nobody moved or spoke up. Then he had a sudden spurt of inspiration. He waved the fruits in the air again.

"Sign up for a search party now and get to taste the fruits and irrebies of yesteryear".

A ripple of excitement ran around the room. Before it had fully died down, volunteers were coming forwards, beaks-a-drooling. First up were a flight of swallows chirruping rapidly and eyeing the bunch of cherries greedily.

"OK, swallows. You are the fastest of all the birds," he said as their little chests puffed up with pride. "I need you to act as messengers or go-betweens, passing messages from one area of La-Kelisland to the next." They nodded eagerly and then fell into raptures as Jack passed them some cherries to feast upon.

There couldn't have been a better advert for recruitment than those swallows tossing the cherries up in the air to gobble them down greedily. The geese quickly waddled up to be next in line to volunteer their services.

"OK geese…thank you! But it's time to stop being a gaggle and become a skein. Fly north where the wind blows coldest and then sweep the skies by following the line of the sun. Keep in touch via the swallows who will ferry your messages back." They honked enthusiastically before tucking noisily into some grapes. Further offers of help flooded in and Jack quickly agreed for the peacocks to head towards Treadmail Tower, whilst the magpies were assigned to cover the skies over Crambleside. That just left Granglethorn Castle, arguably the most dangerous place that Lava could be taken.

"Who can offer to cover Granglethorn for us?" asked Jack. An argument at the back of the hall that had been simmering with a iow intensity for a while suddenly flared up between two parties, both eager to be chosen and both equally keen to point out the short comings of their rivals. Flapbaggles was quick to step in.

"Larks and nightingales! Calm down please," he exclaimed in exasperation. "There is sakratt activity at all hours of the day in Granglethorn. Either one of you can't possibly cover this alone. It will be best if we employ two teams on this posting. Gather all your friends together and let's have an exaltation of larks to cover the castle at daybreak and, as a relief force, we'll have a watch of nightingales to cover dusk." This seemed to satisfy the pride of both sets of birds and the squabbling died down. Flapbaggles then distributed the remaining cherries before turning to Fubbyloofah and his party. "Prepare to let your tastebuds explode" he said as he shared out the last few with them.

Fubbyloofah was grinning away in anticipation. He dropped the cherry into his mouth and his eyes gleamed with pleasure. The boys watched as his face ran the full gamut of emotions. Suddenly his jaw jolted and his eyes closed and for a split second he was transported to a parallel universe of pure pleasure. Gradually he came back to his senses, opened his eyes and swallowed hard. "Who's next?" he said. Scott quickly popped one into his mouth ready for the roller-coaster to begin. At first all he could taste was the firm outer skin of the fruit, and thought this was another example of Fubbyloofah getting over-excited about another unpalatable "food", but then, ever so slightly, he felt a slight sparkle at the back of his tongue. This was suddenly showing promise and he was about to urge Jack to try one too when the sparkle at the back of his tongue started to spread across the rest of his mouth. Suddenly his whole mouth was fizzing and he could feel sparks going off and hitting the roof of his mouth like an oral firework display. Suddenly, without warning, there was a very definite audible "POP" and the fruit burst open, hit the roof of his mouth and an incredibly sweet liqueur seeped out to coat his tongue with a velvety softness. It was unlike anything he had ever tasted before and he was conscious of his eyes rolling upwards and inwards in pure pleasure. The liqueur lingered for longer than he could have hoped and every time he moved his tongue he could taste it. It was simply divine. He opened his eyes again, looked at Jack, Featherfae and Fubbyloofah one by one and silently mouthed the word "WOW!" Who would have thought that a tired old cherry from back home would taste like this? What on earth had happened to it?"

For the next ten minutes, Ye Olde Dungeon Creek resounded to the murmurs of gastronomic delight that had not been heard since the hostelry had been known as the New Dungeon Creek. Eventually the feast was over and after a chorus of coos, bills, and tweets of appreciation, the birds flew off to commence their mission.

12. The Moth-Man

"Idiot!" bawled Jack. "Why haven't you asked Willow?"

They were on the road to Crambleside after bidding a reluctant farewell to Flapbaggles and his delicious assortment of snacks.

Scott was an instant scrabble of fingers which collapsed into a look of relief as she drifted into the frame. A quick look up told him that Fubbyloofah and Featherfae had seen nothing. This was something he had to do alone.

"Willow, we've lost Lava. He's been grabbed by crows and they've flown off with him. We have no idea where they've taken him or even if he's still alive. Can you.... help?" He shook the mirror anxiously until she responded.

"The fire-cat is not without powers of his own. You must continue to Treadmail Tower as you will not succeed without the help of the Hebradaigese. One of them must be present at the finding of the keyhole. Do not fail, or Jassaspy will rake the sun from the sky like a dying ember."

Scott felt the colour drain from his face as he looked up and shakily recounted the news.

"Quick: a slice of Dingle-bell pie for the lad," said Fubbyloofah, who tore off a huge slice of pie for Jack too in the hope that they would regain their strength and make swifter progress. It seemed to work as they covered the next couple of miles without a break, but then disaster struck. They can't have been more than an hour outside Crambleside when they stumbled into a pea soup of green vapour. Scott and Jack doubled up coughing.

"Ugghh, damn these fumes! Orgoooooph!" Scott's chest heaved and racked and he felt Jack stumble into him.

"Arrgh, my eyes!" He rubbed them frantically. "Featherfae, Fubbyloo- ugghackkk!"

"Put your sleeve to your face. Breathe through the fabric," said Featherfae urgently.

Above them a high pitched whine sounded. The sound quickly morphed into an angry buzzing and Fubbyloofah started waving his arms around frantically. Then a cloud of black biting insects fell upon them: huge flying ants with globular black bodies and razor sharp jaws.

"Yeoww!" yelled Scott, as first one limb then another welled up under the assault. "Fubbyloofah!" he cried in response to a desperate howl of pain. He turned to see the poor thing under a black cloud being half-bitten to death. They all bolted for cover but then Jack fell over, his eyes widening in horror as the swarm engulfed him.

"Featherfae!" Beseeching eyes met hers through the angry cloud but she could only look on helplessly.

"This way! Head for the road!" she shrieked as the robin in her hair snapped frantically at the swarm around her. Jack grasped for anything and everything until finally he staggered up from his knees. All around him insects zapped and darted. Fubbyloofah squealed again, his paws flapping helplessly as he bounded past. Scott was right behind him and using a branch as a makeshift carpet beater to swat them out of the air. Finally, they got away.

"Here: let's stop here," Fubbyloofah gasped. He shot Scott a grateful look as he plucked the last few out of his fur for him. The boys looked down at their forearms covered in red swollen lumps. They were by Swelterwater and the water was cool and welcome but the bites were just too angry and fresh to respond. They slumped to the ground exhausted and before long were all in a deep sleep.

They woke to the sound of heavy pulsing beats in the air. For a moment, Jack lay perfectly still before something inside made him jump to his feet.

"What is it?" Featherfae looked up sleepily. Jack shrugged, he couldn't see anything out of the ordinary. Over in the forest Fubbyloofah was busy foraging for something or other and Scott was still sleeping. He slowly made his way towards the lakeside where the sound was loudest. Suddenly, a voice rang out just as the throbbing beats intensified.

"I've been waiting to meet you again."

"Who? What? Where are you?" Jack swung his head round wildly but could see nothing. He darted to get back to the others but in his haste slipped and thumped to the ground. He was on his back and staring up at the sky when it appeared.

"Look what you have done to me!"

It was hovering over the pool and its wings worked hard to keep its large body airborne. It gestured to its sinewy body with huge leathery wings.

"Who? Me?" Jack scrambled to his feet.

"Don't take me for a fool. I know the Elven Prince when I see him."

Jack's skin crawled and he felt a pool of queasiness settle on his stomach. He jumped as he felt a nudge from behind. It was Featherfae and she was glaring at the creature.

"Then you know his power. Stay back and you won't be harmed."

The creature laughed malevolently and rose in the air as he smote the air more powerfully.

"He has not the wit to realise the power he has."

The moonlight shone brightly down on him. His skin was wrinkled green parchment pulled tight over a wizened skull. His eyes were waspish slits with a slash of deepest black in place of a pupil. He laughed again.

"Do you really think it in your power to deny me anything?"

Thick green slime dripped into the pool as he fluttered over it, excreting. It sizzled on contact with the water.

"Whatever it is you want, you're not going to get it." Jack's hands balled into fists.

"Fool! You don't even know what it is you carry! Give it up now and go back to your world whilst you still can."

He swooped forwards just as a cry rang out from behind them. Their heads whirled to see Scott dashing forward and swinging punches. There was a flurry of tiny wings as Featherfae launched herself airborne followed by a sharp cry as the creature's wings smote the air and caught her in the blast. There was a sickening crunch as she was flung against the rocks and crumpled to the ground fighting for breath.

"Featherfae!" Jack turned in horror before a leathery claw scrabbled for his collar. "NO! NO! NO!" he cried; his head spinning. "Arrgh!" The nails dug in and pierced his flesh. He was swaying on his feet. Any minute now, any minute and he would black out. He could feel it coming on. But then a voice broke through.

"Don't give in! Fight it, Jack!"

With gritted teeth he looked up. It was Scott and he was steaming forwards again. But he was too late. With powerful lazy beats, the moth-man scooped him up and carried him high over the lake.

"LET HIM GO!" yelled Scott. The waters bubbled with his rage as he charged into the lake oblivious to the corrosive slime that dribbled over him as the moth-man hovered in the air foraging for something that Jack had. It burnt and stung, yet a deeper fire was burning in him now. Through the flames of his rage, he could see the moth-man flapping furiously as he finally found what he wanted.

"NO!" bellowed Scott. He glimpsed the time-key in the creature's talons just as Jack's body dropped amongst a cloud of green spores into the lake. He choked in fury as a haze of white hot heat erupted from the furnace in his chest. Pure anger and rage consumed him now. Within seconds he was looking down on the heads of his companions as the djinn within him surged upwards and outwards. The moth-man veered away sharply.

"Give it back....NOW!" he shouted as his volcanic rage fused with the time-key and an acrid burning hit his nostrils. The moth-man shrieked as his skin smouldered and the molten time-key dropped from his grasp. Then with a squeal of pain he was gone leaving nothing but his shadow behind. Scott watched, as a shadow-sylph darted off into the inky blackness of the surrounding woods. Then the furnace inside him subsided as quickly as it had arisen.

"Jack? Jack? How's Jack?" He felt his eyes droop as he staggered back exhausted. He dimly caught sight of Featherfae pulling Jack from the lake, then collapsed.

The smoggilars mewed weakly. Their bodies were caked in bites and welts the size of walnuts. Featherfae cleansed their wounds as best she could and turned to Fubbyloofah.

"They're so tiny, they'll be lucky to survive."

Fubbyloofah nodded sadly feeling so helpless. He watched the light bounce off the lake and bathe their wounds in a golden mantle, then closed his eyes. The boys were safe and they had retrieved the time-key, but the forces aligned against them were growing stronger. He was suddenly brought back into the present by a tickling sensation at the back of his neck.

"What in La-Kelisland -?" He flicked a paw out and a bottle brush of bright orange hair flashed through the air to land on the grass in front of him. It wriggled furiously.

"Caterpillars! Look, Featherfae: big, fat, hairy caterpillars!"

"Excuse me! Kipwriggles is the name and I'm not fat, I'll have you know, just well insulated. There's not much sunlight to keep us warm these days. Thanks for nothing by the way." A large orange caterpillar glared up at him and rubbed at a fresh bruise.

"Oh, sorry, no offence intended Kipwriggles. You've just caught us at a very bad time, I'm afraid." He nodded towards Featherfae weeping gently over Tumbleweed.

"Stuff and nonsense! We're here to help you if you could just let us get on with it." He rubbed his recent bruise again and indicated towards his friends. Fubbyloofah turned. An army of caterpillars was streaming towards them: luminescent green ones encircled with concentric black stripes, big hairy orange ones with black legs like Kipwriggles, yellow ones polka-dotted for show and even a green and pink striped beauty who held back for fear of getting her foot pads wet. Within seconds they were everywhere.

"Bless my berriblods! They're neutralising the poison in the bites." Fubbyloofah laughed as he helped one down from the welt on top of his head then chortled at the sight of Jack with a big orange hairy moustache. The others looked equally ridiculous. Scott looked like a tribesmen, but with caterpillars rather than feathers in his hair, whilst Featherfae had sprouted a hairy wig that wriggled like an affable Medusa. Eventually, the angry redness subsided and Fumblepaw perked up enough to start sniffing and scratching at the earth again.

"He's eager to plant more pips," smiled Featherfae.

"Ooh, what a treat! That would be much appreciated," said Kipwriggles sucking in his stomach in order to look needfully undernourished. Featherfae laughed, left Fumblepaw to it, and turned towards Scott.

"I see the djinn has awoken," she said with a coy smile. Scott blushed as he shook the sleep from his eyes.

"Is Jack OK?" he asked. She nodded over to where he lay.

"Fubbyloofah will carry him the rest of the way. A shadow-sylph has touched him again. We can't wake him. How about you? You OK?"

"Yeah, I dunno what came over me. I just got so mad I -"

"It was the djinn inside you. Remember what I said at Waftenway? You have a smokeless and scorching fire inside you."

He sat motionless as he remembered. "I can't control it you know. It just happens." He felt Featherfae's hand rest gently on his shoulder in response.

They were soon on their way again and before long were catching the comforting whiff of woodsmoke from the outskirts of the town.

"Not long now," said Fubbyloofah, cheered by the thought of a frothy pint of rootbeer from one the Crambleside hostelries. Featherfae wasn't so sure.

"Do you think they'll let us in?" She looked over each member of the party. What a sad wretched rag-bag army they were. Fubbyloofah looked little different to a tramp. His fur was all smeared with mud from the pond. Scott and Jack were similarly dishevelled but with the added misfortune of having no fur to conceal the insect bites and as for herself: Featherfae was well aware that those large winged clasps buried deep within her flowing locks were nothing more than the wings of flying ants that had dive-bombed to a premature death.

"Ahh, there are far worse looking travellers than us," said Fubbyloofah with a dismissive sniff, "and anyway, after a pint or two of rootbeer who will care?"

Scott nodded vigorously in agreement. He would have agreed to dine on flying ants as long as it involved sitting down at a table for a while.

"Look out Fubbyloofah!" cried Scott a moment later as Fubbyloofah tripped, wobbled precariously and then crashed to the ground.

"What on earth are the groundluggs playing at?" said Featherfae as he scrabbled to his paws and kicked at the rubbish that littered the streets and lay strewn across their path. The houses themselves were even worse: doors were hanging off frames and window frames were slowly rotting. Everything spoke of long neglect.

"Remember what Flapbaggles said," muttered Fubbyloofah. "We'll need to be on our guard for sakratts. From the look of everything, they virtually run the place now."

They trudged forwards with a deepening sense of apprehension before finally spying a hostelry at the junction of two roads. It was a very public place and reassuringly busy with several tables outside, most of which were occupied by extremely large groundluggs who were literally spilling out of their seats.

"Coat your throat and treat your feet," grinned Scott, as Fubbyloofah returned with the drinks to find him with his feet up. Fubbyloofah raised his glass to all before a screech overhead made him slop the beer.

"Darn it! What now?"

"It's the magpies! You know; the ones that Flapbaggles sent over here." Featherfae watched as they screeched again before veering out of sight behind a stack of chimney pots. She frowned. What had startled them?

"Look: crows!" Scott pointed to the black smudges weaving in and out of the tendrils of woodsmoke.

"And the magpies are sounding the alarm! These must be the same crows that grabbed Lava," said Fubbyloofah springing to his paws and slopping more root-beer over Scott. He was just about to complain when he spotted a large white bird heading straight for the fracas in the sky. There was a small figure sitting astride its back.

"Chloe!" cried Scott with a grin as Silvertip dived towards the skirmish.

The black and white flashes of feather played well against the shimmering surface of Lake Wintersmere as Chloe pulled Silvertip out of a steep dive and climbed steadily in order to look down on the flurry of activity below.

Was there a flash of ginger amongst those birds, she wondered, as Silvertip circled closer? There it was again: no doubt about it this time. But she had left Lava with the others at Roughrigg Tarn. Her mind raced; perhaps the crows had picked up sun-threads from a bramble bush. But then, why would the magpies be making such a fuss? Her thoughts became blacker. What if Lava was injured; or worse? There was nothing for it. She pulled hard on Silvertip's reins and plunged straight into the turmoil of jabbing beaks and talons.

The first crow nearly took her eye out. The sharp beak jabbed fowards and glanced off her cheek. She pulled at the reins for Silvertip to re-engage. The magpies were re-grouping whilst the crows were more dispersed. Woodsmoke drifted across to obscure her vision. Was it Lava or just tufts of his iridescent fur? She still couldn't be sure. She took Silvertip back for another swooping dive. With wings folded back, she shot into the crows like a javelin. They barely had time to scatter. A swift downward beat of wing caught one. Stunned and out of control it fell to the earth spinning. Three others whirled and darted back, talons and beaks flashing. "Silvertip! Behind you!" As the swan swerved to avoid the attack, she saw instantly that there was a fourth crow clutching a large ginger bundle: Lava!

She threw her weight forwards and gritted her teeth. The swellings on her back were killing her but she had to steer through. Silvertip went into a brief free-fall drop before swinging past the three crows and towards the fourth. But it was almost across the lake and the other three were attacking again. She forced a full collision and knocked a second crow out, but time was running out. She flung a glance at the fourth crow but it was now almost across the far side of the Lake. Suddenly a deep primeval cry mingled with untapped passions came from within. Words spoken long ago rang in her ears: a voice strong and clear was banging, banging away, clamouring for her response:

"WAKE THE FIREFLAKES!"

Without knowing what or why, she pulled out the sunfruit. Unbidden and with no understanding, she yelled out to the wind, "AGNARO IGNITO!" On the ground below the fireflakes shimmered with a crimson sparkle whilst in the air the frostflakes glistened white in sympathy. The sunfruit throbbed and pulsed in her hand. The two remaining crows shrieked and flapped away like things possessed. Holding the sunfruit aloft, she turned towards Lava. As her emotion intensified, so did the pulse of the sunfruit, and before she was even half-way across the lake, a powerful golden beam shot out like a solar flare. The crows flew like demons, zig-zagging erratically to avoid it. They had almost made it across the lake and once amongst the trees Silvertip would be too big to follow. Chloe leant forwards, stretched out her arm and squeezed the sunfruit with all her strength. The golden beam diffused and seconds later a whole arc of sky lit up in burning orange. The crows had no chance! Caught in the blinding glare they fell tumbling out of the sky…and their ginger bundle fell with them!

13. The Chamber of the Grand Assembly

"If I get any trouble from that fool Barbletwist, I'll plug his ears with rancid mouse droppings." Jassaspy left the Tower of the Moon and drifted along the corridor towards the Tower of the Vedic Bells fully prepared to do verbal battle with its keeper. This journey was never easy. Granglethorn was full of surreal encounters: each corridor being named after whatever spectral phenomena people found there: and this was the Corridor of Fears.

"Get back! Begone with you!" He stumbled as a giant claw appeared out of nowhere and took a swipe at him. It faded as quickly as it had appeared. "Damn! This is going to take forever!" he muttered in irritation. He thought for a second about the alternative route down the Green Corridor then out along the Corridor of the Astral Plane. It was longer but much less arduous, especially as he could influence the spectral phenomena of the Green Corridor.

"The corridor linking the Tower of the Moon to the Tower of the Vedic Bells will be completed on the night of the winter solstice," proclaimed the Grand Assembly all those years ago. All had applauded at the time but Jassaspy knew what this would mean.

"Not on that night, please. It will be riddled with fearful spectres. I urge the Assembly to defer completion."

"Were you not the High-Lord pushing for completion, Jassaspy? Did you not argue that the northern half of Granglethorn be enclosed in ramparts rather like the head of an arrow, with your own tower in the north linking directly to the Tower of Reflection in the East, the Vedic Bells in the West and the Grand Assembly at the centre?"

"...and to isolate those of us in the south with only the Corridor of Dreams connecting us to the Assembly and thereby the rest of the castle," the High-Lord Hebradaigen of the Tower of the Sun added, his brow darkening at the recollection.

"Yes: but the spectres..." muttered Jassaspy dejectedly.

"...all our corridors are subject to spectral phenomena. None more so than your own: the Green Corridor. Many are the

Hebradaigese that have come to harm when attempting to pass directly from the Grand Assembly to your own tower."

"Yes: we have never heard you complain about that have we, Jassaspy?" said the High-Lord Hebradaigen of the Tower of the Sun grimly.

"No! You persuaded us to abandon the cross-formation by arguing that your own tower in the north needed direct links to both the eastern and western towers. This process is now almost complete and we shall not defer completion." The Steward slammed the gavel down and that was the end of the matter.

"Fuddled brained wind bags! Just wait! The gatekeeper's chair can't stay empty for ever. Sooner or later we shall have to elect another," seethed Jassaspy silently.

He wallowed briefly in his memories before a moment later the light in the corridor went out. With a deafening roar, the corridor split asunder. He whirled in panic, afraid his own tower might be crumbling. He sighed with relief as he realised it was safe and bit down hard on a cockroach to helped alleviate the tension. "Go on, wriggle! It won't do you any good," he muttered as the stress of the moment drained away. In front of him the chasm dropped hundreds of feet to the floor of Dragmines Valley. He inched forwards one step at a time until his feet were at the edge. He peered down and saw the river flowing through the valley bottom. But something was wrong.

"Why can't I feel any wind, and why is the front of my robe still brushing the ground?" For a split second he hesitated before chuckling quietly and stepping calmly forward into mid-air and continuing along the Corridor of Fears as the mirage faded. "If I can just get to the Tower of the Vedic Bells before -" he thought to himself as the tower door creaked open slowly. He caught his breath sharply.

"Are you looking for this?" said a defiant voice. It was Jack and he was holding a Hebradaigen time-key.

"- or this, perhaps?" Scott held the Mirror of Aggraides and a smokeless fire seemed to burn within him.

"No, I think he needs a blast of this." A girl was holding forth a burning globe of gold: the sunfruit from the old legends!

Jassaspy flinched. His head swung round wildly. Was there a way back? His breath quickened as they strode purposely towards him.

"Not all three of you. Not yet! I'm not ready for you yet!" Not with what they carried. But there was no time to flee. He couldn't out-run the blast from the sunfruit. He steeled himself as they approached. Three hands reached towards him, grasping and snatching at his robes and yet... not. He watched as their hands passed *through* him..... just like the wind. It took a second for what had happened to sink in, before he smirked to himself. Then he entered the tower.

His bald pate shone and his thin wispy moustache trailed on the floor having long ago given up its fight against gravity. He sat with his back to the door and snorted and snuffled as Jassaspy rapped loudly to announce his presence. There was a moment of silence. He rapped again.

"Barbletwist!" he said before entering. Jassaspy stood on the threshold and looked around his room. The lack of furnishings simply highlighted the exquisite quality of what he did have. "Ahh, the Shibayama cabinet," Jassaspy sighed enviously, eyeing the cabinet upon which was displayed the tusk of an ancient megathon. Somewhere in that furniture were secret drawers ideal for storing poisons and potions away from prying eyes. If only he could... He tore himself away.

"Barbletwist!" He said again, beginning now to get irritated. His lip curled as he caught sight of the roll-top desk with its painted panel of a valley bathed in golden sunshine. On top of the desk was a vase of flowers.

"Pah! Still obsessed with restorative treatments, eh?" He fingered the stamen from flowers long lost to La-Kelisland which were said to aid fertility. "You really have lost your way haven't you? You had so much promise when you were an apprentice in the Tower of the Moon."

Barbletwist had acquired a whole host of things since Jassaspy's last visit: powder dusted from the wings of butterflies which reflected and refracted light and could cure blindness and the scent glands of the blaggawob, an amphibious reptile whose glands produced a fluid so addictive that opium was used to wean addicts off it!

"Ugh! I can't bear it." Jassaspy turned away from the painted desk disdainfully, immersed in his own much darker world of excretions as he was. His eyes closed for a brief moment as he sought refuge in thoughts of potions scraped from creatures that had never seen the light of day and distillations from disembodied essences that hung like a fetid fume waiting to condense upon something living, something into which it could soak. He snapped back suddenly aware of the silence.

"BARBLETWIST! Don't keep a High-Lord Hebradaigen waiting. I'm no sewer rat from the kitchens." He strode forward angrily then froze. "Of course! The fool's deaf! No wonder..." He smiled as his rage subsided. It was what made Barbletwist so suitable as Custodian of the Vedic Bells. Who else could reside at the top of the tower in a room directly under four massive bells each weighing a tonne? He quickly scrawled his request on the parchment pad kept by the door for these situations, then prodded him in the back. Barbletwist turned and his eyes darkened. He grunted and snatched the parchment out of Jassaspy's hand keen to minimise all physical contact. He muttered to himself as he read it before responding.

"Not possible. Need three Hebradaigese to request Grand Assembly to re-convene."

He crumpled the parchment into an excessively tight ball then, with a flourish, dropped it into the bin. Jassaspy seethed quietly and a green vaporous plume seeped out from his cowl into the room. Barbletwist jumped up to quickly open the windows then very pointedly opened up a drawer in his Shibayama cabinet. Jassaspy visibly stiffened.

"So it's true then!" In front of him was the mummified eyeball of Anubis, the Egyptian God of the Dead. Just one eyelash plucked from this, was enough to kill someone through asphyxiation. "So you dabble in the dark side too, eh?"

Barbletwist shot him an inscrutable look and Jassaspy reached for the parchment pad once more but this time with a bit more respect.

"Meeting of the Grand Assembly requested under Land Policy, criteria 5.1 sub-section 3b 'information apertaining to a breach in the security of La-Kelisland'."

He pushed the note towards the custodian. Barbletwist cursed at being wrong-footed and shuffled slowly over towards the bells.

It took a good couple of hours for the Hebradaigese to fill the Chamber of the Grand Assembly: the 300 foot high hammer-beamed hall at the centre of Granglethorn castle. As the bells continued to ring out, they filed in to the terraced pews that lined the diamond-shaped chamber, the back row being a dizzying 50 feet above the chamber floor. In the centre of the chamber was a raised dais on which a circle of ornately carved wooden seats were arranged around a circular table. This was where the inner council sat and most seats were now filled, with the usual exception of a single high-backed chair. This was the chair of the gatekeeper which had been vacant ever since his disappearance at the time that the fire-cat had failed to return from World's End.

"Honourable colleagues! Honourable colleagues!" Jassaspy stepped forward, brushing down his robe from the dust of his moths and waving his application to address the Assembly. Scores of scrittlers, small winged mice, scuttled up the walls. You could hear their claws rattling against the stone hundreds of feet above ground level and their squeaks reverberated around the chamber.

"Honourable colleagues," he gasped, "I bring information of Hebradaigen Hagratty and a security breach." His voice echoed around the vast chamber and there was a sharp intake of breath from the Ro-Rillian, the reflective monks from the Tower of Reflection. Their heads dropped as they sank into deep thought about the implications of this.
Good! That was one group less to worry about! Jassaspy grinned behind his mask of concern.

"At this very moment, my sakratts are dealing with two intruders that have entered La-Kelisland through a time splinter. It is clear that they have no knowledge of how they entered, except that it was with the active assistance of Hebradaigen Hagratty and that dim witted Snarklepike."

"Suspend her!" shouted someone from the back benches. Further murmurs of shock rippled round the chamber.

"The security of the land has been compromised, and as such, I invoke the right to subject Hebradaigen Hagratty to an immediate suspension in absentia and to declare a State of Emergency as proscribed by the constitution of the Council of the Grand Assembly of Grangleth-"

"Yes, thank you Jassaspy: and I suppose your sakratts are to assume the role of policing this State of Emergency, eh?" said a voice from the Tower of the Sun. Jassaspy squinted painfully at the hostile ranks. They brandished their accursed sun-shafts: solid beams of light that had calcified and been fashioned into staffs. The golden light they emitted made Jassaspy wince. It would be the first thing he would outlaw, were he ever to become gatekeeper.

"A time splinter cannot be ignored so I would, of course, offer to deploy my sakratts should the Grand Assembly deem their services to be of use to preserve life in La-Kelisland as we know it."

"'As we *know* it' rather than as we *knew* it. Your choice of tense is noted Jassaspy. We all know how little you care for the plight of our sun."

Angry sparks shot from his sun-shaft. "You shall never get our vote so pray do not offend by asking."

"As partisan as ever, I see," spat Jassaspy.

The Tower of the Sun were never likely to support anything he proposed. He turned towards the other two towers. "Colleagues, what say you? Would you sit and bemoan the old days whilst a time splinter threatens what future we have left, or will you join me and declare the emergency to safeguard La-Kelisland from further harm?"

The High-Lord Hebradaigen of the Vedic Bells raised his hand to quell protestations.

"Honourable colleages, we request a recess before putting this to the vote. The implications are significant and cannot be taken in haste."

The massed ranks across at the Tower of Reflection clamoured their assent whilst the Hebradaigese of the Sun, having already voted, moved to leave the chamber. Many looked worried and more than a few cast anxious glances towards the Hebradaigese of the Vedic Bells.

"Very well; let us reconvene when the moonlight first slivers across the spires of Granglethorn: until then, adieu."

Jassaspy turned slowly, conscious of the need to make a dignified and graceful exit and retreated slowly down the Green Corridor to the Tower of the Moon.

"Everything depends on the Hebradaigese of the Vedic Bells, as the Ro-Rillian from the Tower of Reflection will almost certainly abstain," he muttered as he melded with the shadows in his chamber of moths. "I must get to the fire-cat before its presence here becomes common knowledge." Up to now, everything had been moving inexorably towards life *without* a sun. How many countless Grand Assembly meetings had been wasted where the Hebradaigese of the Sun had proposed fruitless policies to revive the sun, only for them all to fizzle in sympathy with each dying ray? Now, finally, he had begun to win the Grand Assembly round to approve his policy of underground excavation with a view to resettlement. The last thing he needed right now was the upsurge of hope that the fire-cat would bring. This would set him back months!

"I have to get the State of Emergency declared and then..." His thoughts skipped and jumped. He would deploy his sakratts everywhere with the number one priority of finding the fire-cat. He smiled as he remembered the Creatures of the Night Shade. He had a head start already. He reached out absent-mindedly for a handful of moths. He crunched down and felt their legs wriggle against his tongue. He took another bite, felt the juice squirt into his mouth and then something happened to make him forget all about his winged hors d'oeuvre.

"HACKWEEZLE, SPITTLEWHIP! He squealed in a voice an octave higher than normal. A flash of blinding white light tore across his chamber and struck him. He hit the floor hard and quivered.

"Sire?" Two heads appeared round the door just as the light flash struck him again. But It was a light that none but Jassaspy could see. He writhed and wriggled. At the door the sakratts shuffled uneasily. Slime that Jassaspy could no longer control oozed all around him. He stuffed his hands into his cowl rubbing his eyes desperately.

"HACKWEEZLE, SPITTLEWHIP!" His cowl turned towards them, "Go to the - sweat-pools. Bring them back!" Then he flopped as still as a rag and gasped in relief. The light had gone out as suddenly as it had struck him.

Over in Crambleside, Chloe doused the flame from the sunfruit. Lava had fallen into a place that Silvertip could not follow. With heavy heart, she turned back towards Crambleside to re-join the others.

Hackweezle backed heavily into Spittlewhip. A horny foot crushed his toe, he yelped and they both bumped heads in their haste to get out.

"Must change my robe," muttered Jassaspy, panting heavily. The spires of Granglethorn would be streaked with moonlight any moment now. He had to return for the vote.

The buzz of excitable debate was tangible as he approached down the Green Corridor. Waves of junior Hebradaigese parted for him as he took his place of prominence as the High-Lord Hebradaigen of his Tower, but before he could speak, a voice rang out from the Tower of the Sun opposite.

"Honourable Colleagues of the Vedic Bells, we would urge you to consider the possibility that a time splinter may not necessarily be a danger to La-Kelisland." There was a stunned silence. "For years we have seen our sun wither before our very eyes and yet during all this time, there has been no incidence of a time splinter occurring whatsoever. Perhaps in these desperate times, desperate remedies are required. Who knows whether the forces that could enter La-Kelisland through a time splinter are not forces for good?" Jassaspy tensed. "We from the Tower of the Sun, believe that all things are possible and everything should be tried first before we abandon hope and retreat underground. That way lies failure and the complete abdication of our primary function as Hebradaigese, that is, to safeguard the land and the life that lives and grows upon it."

"Hear! Hear!" cried voices from all sides of the chamber.

Jassaspy looked anxiously across at the High-Lord Hebradaigen of the Vedic Bells who had stood to address the chamber.

"Erstwhile colleague of the Tower of the Sun, we applaud your sentiment and desire for life as it was, but we cannot but feel that you are equally partial. You would risk anything to preserve the sun, however dangerous that risk were. The Tower of the Moon is not so readily blinded by your optimism and has worked hard to secure a future for all Hebradaigese and groundluggs should the land succumb to the sickness of the dying sun. Yes, we know that their solution is not ideal. None of us wants to resettle underground, but life is life and we need this option, if only as a back-up plan. It is for this reason that we vote with Jassaspy and for the State of

Emergency. We cannot afford to take any more risks, and we have no idea what the implication of a time splinter could be for our already tenuous hold upon the land."

Jassaspy very gently exhaled in relief, careful not to bleach the surrounding air with his breath. He turned towards the Ro-Rillian trying hard not to show his relief. The monks rose en-masse from the front bench and the Abbot cleared his throat before speaking.

"Grand Assembly, we are as always, honoured to be consulted and for our voices to be heard and our decision to be a vital part of the democratic process of decision making at Granglethorn. Long has this been the case and long may it continue to be so. For our part, life has taught us that a rash decision is one that the decision maker comes to regret. Contrary to taking a bad decision and living with the consequences, there are no feelings of guilt if one cannot decide a weighty matter due to a lack of certainty about the outcome. Indeed, it is most ego-centric to assume that one has all the requisite knowledge to make a decision either way, and, as you know, we of the Tower of Reflection are anything but ego-centric." He looked around him at the blank blinking faces that absorbed his words. "Reflection and contemplation are the inevitable recourse and for this reason, we abstain from this vote." His face was expressionless and retained its immunity to disturbance as he re-took his seat.

Jassaspy could barely contain his glee and keeping his cowl tilted down, and with it his grinning skull, he rose to proclaim his motion carried by a vote of 2 to 1. The Assembly disbanded to the streaks of moonlight that cut through the windows like heralding trumpets of the night. Jassaspy stood motionless, savouring the moment. The Ro-Rillian walked solemnly back towards their tower like pieces of driftwood carried on the passionate tides of others. The Hebradaigese of the Sun were still busy arguing the case: some with those from the Vedic Bells, others with his own junior Hebradaigese. Either way it mattered little. The vote had been taken. He looked up at the ceiling of the Chamber of the Grand Assembly for one last time. His head was giddy with triumph and sought the thrill of its dizzying height. As if in recognition of the outcome, the scrittlers scuttled quietly up to the high dome in a respectful silence and the dome was suddenly bathed with silvery moon beams that draped the auditorium like the gossamer threads of some large ethereal spider. A moment later and he was fully grounded again. His main concern now was back in his chamber with the two time-wards who held the key to his recent ordeal by blinding light. With quick and purposeful steps he returned.

"How much do you have left?" Flan heaved himself out of the pool of gloop that he had been lying face down in. A thick slimy globule hung heavily from his hair and stung his eyes. He could feel Sticklestabber's legs working furiously as it made itself a more comfortable nest in his hair. A wave of fresh sweat wafted over from Dog Bottom's direction. "God! You stink! What're doing in there?"

"Arrgh! It's back!"

A frantic splashing and sloshing came from Dog Bottom's pit.

"What's back? What's happening bro?" Flan strained to his feet.

"Get it away from me!" Dog Bottom sounded frantic.

Flan strained his neck then he saw it poised on top of the pit above them: the huge fat maggotty creature that had trailed them through the tunnels. Its needle-like teeth flashed in its open mouth.

"Jeez. Stay away from it bro!" yelled Flan.

"Uh, yeah! I think I've already worked that out, you numpty! Haven't you any better ideas?"

It hovered above them and twitched. Suddenly a voice rang out.

"Get ready, you dogs. Jassaspy wants you back in his chambers, NOW!" Hackweezle's voice echoed from down the tunnel. The tendrils on the slygorm's puckered mouth frisked the air in alarm before it reared up on its clammy belly. In a second it had humpfed off.

"Hackweezle! Boy, am I glad to see you," gasped Dog Bottom in relief when he walked up a moment later.

"Shut it! He wants you back. Don't expect it to be pleasant though!"

He dropped a ladder down into the pit for the Puddies and thirty minutes later they were face-to-cowl with Jassaspy and grateful that the only creatures to worry about were moths to which they had the distinct advantage of a vastly superior bulk.

Jassaspy poured out three glasses of the same smoky yellow liquid as before, pulled a worm out from the sleeve of his robe, bit off its head and squeezed out its innards. He dribbled it into all three glasses.

"Not for me. Thanks for the offer though, Jassi," said Flan.

Jassaspy pushed the glasses towards them and waited patiently for them to toast their renewed acquaintance.

"Guess he didn't hear you, bro." Dog Bottom glanced at his brother before holding his nose and bolting his drink down in one. He felt a globule of slime cling to his throat before it succumbed to gravity and flobbed down. They looked up from their empty glasses and steeled their stomachs against the involuntary heave that would follow. Eventually Jassaspy spoke and the inevitable blast of putrid breath wafted over them.

"Now that you have seen what awaits you should you sully my patience, are you ready to co-operate?" The Puddies nodded weakly. "Good. Then let me explain." He pushed a plateful of fried scorpions towards them. "Recently, in this very chamber, I was struck down by a foul, corrosive light: a light strong enough to warm graves that must stay mouldy and cold. Only one thing can produce such a light and it is something I thought died out decades ago. The vile creative sin I am talking of, is a sunfruit. It is not *of* this world and it cannot be handled by anyone *from* this world…." He looked fixedly at the Puddies. "….and that's where you come in." The Puddies exchanged glances before blurting out their own concerns:

"OK. So we can handle it but you can't? We get that. But you gotta tell us what's going on with that huge maggot and what's all this talk of sunfruit and graves. What's that all about?"

Jassaspy waved a silencing hand to quell the interjection. "You shall be billeted here in the Tower of the Moon and these sakratts," he indicated Hackweezle and Spittlewhip, "shall be your servants". It took a moment for this to sink in then Flan shot an evil glance towards Dog Bottom. This could be fun!

"Seek out and retrieve this sunfruit for me and then, and only then, let us talk of graves and worms and what moulders in your shrivelled hearts."

Dog Bottom smirked and thought of the centipede ball that he had thrown at Chloe and Lava at Caesar's Well. It was time to test its tracking abilities. Flan's thoughts were more immediate. Thinking of nothing but revenge he landed a heavy kick up Spittlewhip's arse. He grinned maliciously as the sakratt cowered and cringed in recognition of the change in their status. The air was filled with so much unearthly promise that nobody noticed the nightingale that fluttered off from the window ledge and back into the night sky to report her findings.

14. Of Groundluggs and Sakratts

Chloe bounced from Silvertip's back before she'd even landed. She was exhausted from the aerial battle and the lumps on her back were becoming more painful by the hour.

"Lava fell into the trees. We couldn't follow. It was too dense. The crows haven't got him though. I blasted them out of the sky with the sunfruit." She babbled breathlessly.

"Slow down, slow down!" Fubbyloofah thrust a root-beer into her hand. She gulped it gratefully. Behind them, Scott pulled out some grapes. Things were not looking good. The sky looked as if an artist had given it a wash with Fubbyloofah's insipid broccoli soup and now Lava had more than likely died in the fall from the skies. Suddenly a strange voice rang out.

"Don't tell me you're gonna eat those!"

They froze at the interruption and turned. A crop of groundluggs were behind them, noses already wrinkling at the sight of the grapes. They seemed jovial enough but to say that they were hulking great creatures was an understatement.

"Why ever not?" asked Scott. The groundlugg took in their shabby flea-bitten demeanour before replying.

"I can see you're all down on your luck, but nobody's eaten anything from the earth for decades. It's simply not clean. Come now," he smiled generously, "share some of our food."

He reached over to his knapsack but slumped back puffing from the effort. He tried again and this time heaved himself up so that his stomach was able to flop to either side of him.

"Now then friends, try some *real* food."

The sugar rush from the open pot of carbalix hit them in the face like an aromatic steam train. At the same time, a field mouse popped its head out of his top pocket and with a single leap bounded onto the table, twitched its nose and sprung head first into the gloop.

"Flamin' 'eck, Sniffy. Get outta there. That's for our guests." The groundlugg went red with embarrassment and then jerked spasmodically in his seat much to everyone's alarm.

"What's the matter? Are you Ok?" asked Featherfae, worried that he might be having a heart attack.

"Yip, ai-eee!" he cried as he wriggled and started to giggle uncontrollably. Seconds later he gave a huge hoot of laughter, kicked out a leg and a mole wriggled out from the top of his boot.

"By 'eck Blinker, it didn't take you long to smell the carbalix, did it? What you doing in there anyway?" He shook out his boot in case any other small creature had set up home there. Just at that moment, Fubbyloofah returned with the root-beers.

"Crush my berriblods! Don't eat *that* stuff!" he said as he eyed the carbalix with disgust.

"Now Sir, what wi the earth being so polluted an' all, we would have starved had it not been for the carbalix that those sakratts provide," protested the groundlugg.

"but it's not healthy!" blurted out Scott.

"Woa! Whadda you mean? I got all my faculties, hasn't I?"

"Yeah, but can you use 'em?" muttered Chloe under her breath. Featherfae shot her a disapproving look and Fubbyloofah sighed before continuing.

"My point, is that since you have taken to eating more and more of this -"

He never finished. There was a flash of black and white and a sudden screech. Sniffy yelped and sprung into the air whilst Blinker bolted straight up the groundlugg's sleeve.

"Stop it this instance!" Featherfae lunged forwards and sent two glasses of root-beer tumbling. At the same time, Fumblepaw bounced into the air, flashed his claws at Sniffy and landed splat in the carbalix.

"Strewth!" Scott was on his feet now as the root-beer swilled towards him yet again. He turned just in time to see Tumbleweed dart for the groundlugg's open sleeve and get stuck half way up.

"Serves you right, Tumbleweed," laughed Chloe as his bottom wriggled comically.

"Come back out of there at once!" Featherfae blushed with embarrassment as she got a firm grip on his haunches. Meanwhile, Blinker popped up from out of the groundlugg's collar, palpitating from the near fatal encounter.

"Don't forget about Fumblepaw" said Scott, pointing at the carbalix.

132

"Quick! Wash him down before he eats too much of the stuff." Fubbyloofah had him by the scruff but he was already grooming himself and quivering from the sugar rush.

"Now steady on sir! Who said anything about us losing relatives," said the groundlugg, as he proceeded to administer eye drops to little Blinker a moment later.

"He's right, Job," cut in one of his fellows. "We've all had family members taken to serve that slygorm, whatever it is. Only the other day, 'ole Pugg says he saw his missus being carted off but he could na keep up wi her abducters 'cos o' his weight and being out o' condition an all."

Fubbyloofah smiled sympathetically and pulled out a handful of grapes.

"Try the food of your fore-fathers. It won't harm you, I promise." Something in his voice and demeanour spelt out the word 'trust' and Job started to waver.

"Well I don't know about eating things that grow in this earth, I really don't."

"Oh, you silly chump," said Featherfae. "They won't harm you: look." She squeezed a grape into her mouth and a beam of light burst from her face. It was enough to make them all jump.

"By 'eck, that's mighty powerful stuff," said Job open-mouthed.

Soon the hostelry patio was a temporary light and sound show as one by one the groundluggs queued up to try one for themselves. But it was too good to last and eventually the black of the night screamed out a challenge.

"What's that flashing light?" croaked a guttural voice from the shadows. Fubbyloofah motioned for quiet.

"Light? There's been no light 'ere except what you see glintin' from the windows and the open door. Just messin' around wi' are. You knows how it is," answered Job. His fellow groundluggs shuffled into position so that their vast bulk obscured any sight of Fubbyloofah and his party. A warty sakratt loomed up out of the surrounding gloom.

"Well cut yer messin' or there'll be no carbalix for a week." He spat threateningly as he hobbled back into the night. They all stayed stock still for a good couple of minutes to be sure that he had shuffled off. When they finally dared to move again,

Fubbyloofah decided that they would be safer if they found lodgings for the night.

"OK well, best o' luck to you folks. Can't say I envy you trudging up the Striver though," said Job, who seemed to be perspiring just at the thought. Chloe gave Silvertip a big hug and was clicking away about heaven knows what, whilst Scott glanced over at Jack who was slowly coming round.

"Take care Job and don't forget to plant the pips wisely," said Featherfae handing him some grapes whilst giving him a hug that made him blush and his friends chuckle.

"Aw, don't you go worryin' 'bout that missie," said Job. "We'z gonna start up our gardenin' again, though I don't know how those sakratts'll take to it."

"Best not to mention anything, eh? Just remember to look out for sun-threads and you'll soon have a healthy crop growing!" said Fubbyloofah with an encouraging nod. Job and his fellow groundluggs grinned sheepishly from ear to ear before bidding the party good night.

"Now, follow me, everyone. There's a wonderful little place right at the foot of the Striver where we can get clean simple lodgings and a good hearty breakfast to boot," said Fubbyloofah, as he set off into the benighted side streets of Crambleside. Jack had shakily regained his feet now but was wheezing terribly. He exchanged glances with Scott that signalled delight at the mention of a comfortable bed but apprehension as to what exactly Fubbyloofah meant by a good hearty breakfast.

After what seemed an eternity of twisting through narrow darkened back-streets, they came upon a cobbled alleyway that snaked sharply upwards. They were all now coughing and choking in the thick green vapour that swirled around the foot of the Striver, so it was with a sense of desperate relief when Fubbyloofah finally announced that they'd arrived.

"Who said that? No use hiding! I heard you. Show yourself wherever you are," said a voice out of nowhere. Fubbyloofah motioned for silence but was too late! "A-ha! Got you! Over here boys!" said the voice gleefully.

There was a sudden scrabbling of boot on cobbled stone and a flicker of grey against a black background. A mouth of yellow teeth accompanied by an asphyxiating stench loomed up out of the darkness. A reptilian creature, the size of a horse and covered in scabrous sores and oozing pustules, charged forwards ridden by a sakratt. It was a raptaggadon and its tongue flickered rapidly; but it was its breath that was to be feared most. Strong and sulphurous, it choked and suffocated everything in its path. It steamed over Jack who suddenly fell to the cobbles with a thump. He just had time to see the time-key clatter away across the cobbles and a gnarled, scabby foot walk by before everything went black. The sakratt stopped in his tracks and simply stared at the key whilst another sakratt ran straight into the back of him. Fubbyloofah quickly took advantage of the confusion.

"Grab the smoggilars whilst I deal with this!" he said as he bounded forwards and knocked the sakratt off balance: he stumbled and narrowly missed stepping on Jack's head. The raptaggadon reared as its rider tried to turn and a plume of acrid sulphur belched in the air.

"This one's mine," shouted Scott as he kicked out and caught the back of another sakratt's knee. He crumpled like a pack of cards. Meanwhile, Featherfae scooped up the smoggilars and turned to see Chloe face-to-face with a sakratt who was waving a curved dagger dripping with thick viscous blood. She ducked and the knife whistled above her head but he had her backed into a corner. Then, just when things didn't look as if they could get any worse, a door in the alleyway opened and an enormous figure charged forwards like an express train. The hulk bellowed with a ferocity to chill the blood before it stopped, turned and thrust out a hand. A sakratt ran straight into it. Its head snapped back and there was a sharp crack of bone that made everyone wince. As it fell to the floor in a heap of stinking rags, the hulk spoke.

"Quick in 'ere all o'ye - and heads DOWN!"

Scott grabbed the key as the raptaggadon turned. His mind flashed back to the moth-man and how the djinn drove it away. Could he invoke it again? He screwed his eyes shut and clenched his teeth but nothing happened. Then he yowled in pain. His eyes owled in horror as the raptaggadon's teeth sank into his leg. Yellow pus oozed horribly from its jaws.

"No time to lose," urged the hulk as he twirled on the spot like a shot-putter and heaved an open bag of sand into the air. Chloe just had time to see Fubbyloofah grab Jack by the ankle before she felt a sharp push between her shoulders and tumbled through the doorway. Behind them they heard a howl of pain as the sand did its job. The door slammed shut behind them and a large groundlugg stood panting and perspiring heavily.

"I thought you needed a bit o' help out there. Things seemed to be getting' a bit hairy." A cheery grin creased his face.

"Why yes...thanks. *Very* well timed," said Fubbyloofah, "but aren't they just gonna wait for us?"

"Awh, if them sakratts wanna linger all night in an alleyway, let 'em. Personally, if I know them, they'll be all too eager to go for their grog, and besides - they'll need it to nurse their heads!" His grin widened before a flash of embarrassment crossed his face. "Awh, I'm so sorry. Forgettin' mi manners I am. My name's Blunt and I be very 'appy if ye'll all be mi guests for the night. See no point in ye wanderin' about what wi those sakratts lurkin' about."

"That would be fabulous," said Fubbyloofah, acutely aware of the grateful eyes all around him.

"Great. Then let me get you all a nice hot cup of carbalix to help you sleep."

"Whoa...steady on, steady on," said Fubbyloofah. "They're not from these parts. Dilute it to at least five times the usual strength."

Blunt looked horrified. "By 'eck, it'll taste like drain water," he muttered as he lumbered off towards his kitchen. He returned shortly with a tray full of steaming cups that smelt and looked like liquid sugar stars. Chloe's nose twitched with excitement.

"At last something to combat that stench!" she muttered whilst glancing towards Jack who was still out cold. The breath of the raptaggadon had crystallised all over him and it was as much as the party could bear to be in the same room as him.

"Well, I'm glad you like it. To me that's a sorry excuse for a carbalix drink. If a spoon can't stand up in it, then it ain't worth botherin' with," he muttered, as he looked at their watery brew whilst shaking his head sorrowfully. "Look: this is what you're missin' out on." He waited for their attention, then twirled a spoon around the thick viscous contents of his own drink and held it over his open mouth. A horrified fascination filled the room as the carbalix globulated as if gathering reinforcements for a fight against gravity before finally giving up. It flobbed onto his tongue in abdication. "'Up yer bottom!' as they say." He raised his glass to their stifled laughter and after exchanging a few more pleasantries the conversation turned to the incident with the time-key.

"That sakratt was over-awed by it. He couldn't bring himself to touch it, didn't you see?" said Fubbyloofah excitedly. Featherfae nodded but then was distracted by Jack who coughed and wheezed as he suddenly came round.

"Someone's gonna have to look after this time-key before it ends up in the wrong hands," he spluttered. "So much for my being the Elven Prince." He coughed and wheezed again.

"Yeah, 'Elven Stink', more like. Have you smelt yourself?" said Scott.

"Huh?" He sniffed the air and looked around. Scott had backed into the far corner of the room and Chloe was scowling at him. Both were holding their noses. "Oh, great! Great! Just what I need."

"It's the breath of the raptaggadon," explained Fubbyloofah. "Unfortunately it won't go away for some time."

Jack just stared at the ground dejectedly before breaking out into a flurry of wheezing coughs. This time a cloud of green spores shot into the air. Featherfae flashed a look of alarm before retreating with Fubbyloofah into a concerned huddle at the far side of the room.

"It's the spores of the moth-man. They're on his lungs!" she whispered frantically.

The next morning, after a night where Jack had moved into the Mouse-house and then taken to the air in a Feather-bed Flurry, he awoke to something very, very sickly. Fubbyloofah was in an armchair reading 'The Groundlugg Times'.

"Ugghh, what's that smell?" he asked whilst rubbing the sleep from his eyes.

"You!" said Chloe from across the room. "You absolutely honk!"

"Pay no attention, Jack," said Fubbyloofah, putting down his paper. "That, my friend, is your breakfast. Blunt is cooking carbalix-battered meal worms."

"I has only put in a tiny bit of carbalix. Most of it is big fat healthy worms," said a voice wafting through from the kitchen.

"NOOO. I think I'm gonna -" Jack ran from the room and violent retching sounds were heard from the bathroom. He emerged a few minutes later and muttered that he would be skipping breakfast today and that he might have an allergy to carbalix after all. Fubbyloofah nodded in sympathy and winked at Featherfae who calmly took out the bottle of grape juice and made him a cleansing detox.

Thanks and goodbyes were soon exchanged and they promised to call in the next time they were in Crambleside. It was early and the streets were deserted so they were soon on the open fell climbing steadily towards Treadmail Tower. Fubbyloofah was quick to point to the shimmering fireflakes that Chloe had awakened the day before by using the sunfruit.

"Look over there!" he said, pointing to the patches of crimson glitter. "How I miss the days when they would rise into the air and dance in courtship with the frostflakes."

The trudge up the Striver lived up to its name: relentless, uphill and not made any easier by Jack wheezing from the moth-man's spores and Scott limping badly from the bite of the raptaggadon. There was also a real fear that they would run into sakratts or slime trails. As they left the tree line behind them, the scenery became bleaker and harsher and the feeling of exposure increased, especially as alongside their route lay the remains of an old slate mine that was still worked by sakratts from time to time. Jack soon got spooked by it all.

"I feel we are being watched," he wheezed.

"- smelt more like," muttered Chloe.

"Oh do shut up, Chloe," said Jack, tired of the constant digs.

Fubbyloofah's eyes flickered around the fell-side. It was a distinct possibility. He picked out a criss-cross of slime trails on both sides of the road but nothing that appeared to be recent.

"I can't see anything, but let's push on to Treadmail Tower. We don't want to linger any longer than necessary."

But the mood was now set, and minutes later he piped up in alarm again.

"What's that over there? It looks like eyes: watching us."

"Shhh. Keep your voice down," said Fubbyloofah, picking out the carpet of orange and black eyes just as Scott started to groan.

"Oh no! It's happening again. Everything is fading to grey. I can't see!" Suddenly he was lurching forwards, groping like a blind man. "Featherfae? Fubbyloofah?"

"We'll all be spotted if he carries on like that," hissed Jack in alarm.

"Leave him to me," said Chloe with a determined set to her jaw. She darted forward and with a harder tackle than was strictly necessary brought her brother crashing to the floor. "Not nice when someone knocks you for six is it?" she whispered pointedly. "Now, keep still! We're being watched." She clasped a firm hand over his mouth. Scott struggled briefly before going limp. She winced as he stared up at her with lifeless black eyes. Behind her, Featherfae scanned the landscape apprehensively. Eyes were peering out from the rocks watching their every move.

"Crouch behind that rocky bluff whilst I take a closer look," said Featherfae as she and the smoggilars crept forward gingerly. Suddenly she stood up and beckoned everyone forwards. She pointed to the ground and her body shook with emotion. "They're butterflies, hundreds of butterflies, and all of them with broken wings," she said as she sobbed impulsively. Fubbyloofah reached across and placed a comforting paw on her shoulder until eventually she looked up again. "Help me gather them up. We must show Tanglestep," she said softly.

When they eventually got back to the track, Jack and Chloe took it in turns to lead Scott by the hand.

"God! When is this gonna stop?" said Scott, groping forwards. He ducked and dived erratically as dark shadows flitted in front of him.

"Tell me about it! I can't seem to stay awake whenever danger threatens," Jack replied wistfully.

They trudged on in silence, each buried deep in their own thoughts so that when the grey walls of Treadmail Tower finally loomed up it took them by surprise. Featherfae was the first to break the gloom that the broken butterflies had cast over them.

"I can't wait to introduce you to Tanglestep: dear, dear Tanglestep."

She rushed up to the huge creaking gates and rang the bell. They heard it peal and seconds later a second bell sounded deeper within the tower which was quickly followed by a single deep gong that resonated through the stone walls around them before finally subsiding into silence.

"Oh *please* tell me that someone's at home," said Jack, finding it hard to conceal the weariness that he felt was visibly oozing from his pores.

"It would be very odd were the tower to be left unmanned, Jack. Just be patient," said Fubbyloofah.

Moments later a face appeared over the ramparts. The face jumped and twitched as if its owner couldn't make his mind up whether to smile or not. Then the great door swung open and the party came face-to-face with a stooping, writhing, figure of a man whose body language screamed discomfort as he squirmed and wriggled at every word spoken.

"Hello there," he said with an uncertain smile and an eye that flickered from one to the other unable to settle on anyone or anything for more than a split second. His nose wrinkled as he caught a whiff of the raptaggadon but he did not acknowledge the smell much to Jack's relief.

"What brings you all the way up to Treadmail? We don't often get visitors up here." His fingers nervously fidgeted around his chin and his eyes flickered suspiciously from one to the other.

"We're here to see Tanglestep on urgent business," said Fubbyloofah, clearing his throat in an authoritative manner. The man's smile danced with uncertainty in response.

"Please tell him that Featherfae is here. He's a dear old friend of mine," she burst in. The man's lip tripped and twitched as she spoke and his grimace of a smile flickered for a few moments more before he waved his arm grandly in welcome.

"You'd better all come in then," he said as he put the weight of his puny shoulder against the door and grunted until the door slammed shut behind them. The echo of the closing door subsided and they found themselves in a cobbled courtyard facing a run-down tower. It was about 5 stories high with thin gothic windows running the length of the central tower. Strutting around the grounds were three or four peacocks which Jack recognized from the Conference of the Wing. The gangly man squirmed another smile before beckoning them into a rather dank outbuilding.

"Let me prepare some tea whilst I see whether Tanglestep can spare some time. He's extremely busy these days; never away from his papers: directives from Granglethorn, you know."

He cast them a lopsided grin before returning to the tea. Jack looked at Featherfae whose brow furrowed with concern.

"Who exactly are you?" she asked warily. The man visibly stiffened before turning round. This time he managed to rein in his facial muscles and his grin was glued to his face.

"They call me, Stunkensloop," he said with a low bow of mock formality. "And very pleased to meet you all … I'm sure", he added rather oddly. The troupe smiled a welcome back but inside Featherfae was frowning.

15. The Guardians of Life & Death

Creak....whine...slam. Without looking up from his mound of papers the man jumped from his seat and secured the window whose hinges were competing with a badly played violin. He wore the typical Hebradaigen hooded robe adorned with insignia of all four towers: the sun, the moon, the bells of Vedia and the clouds of reflection. On his robes the sun was the dominant symbol, it being the tower to which he belonged.

"A-ha," he exclaimed in satisfaction. "If they argue that the Hebradaigese shouldn't intervene because of the prospect of disturbing the peace, then we should point to clause 6.2, sub-section 3 which indicates a 'duty of care' to the landscape. This is an over-arching obligation...yes....must make a note."

He was a young slender man with an intense look and long wispy hair that frequently got in his eyes. He twirled his forelock at this thought, as he was wont to do when in deep concentration and scribbled frantically in the margin before adding a note to cross-reference with Appendix 13 of the document issued by the sub-committee for Standards in Community Service.

"Now, I must be ready to counter Jassaspy's proposal that the underground resettlement project be given priority funding ... mmm." A sudden knock at the door broke through his thoughts. "Come in," he shouted without turning from his papers. Stunkensloop stuck his head round the door, his face jumping through all sorts of emotional hoops.

"Sorry to disturb, sir, but I thought I ought to tell you that we have visitors down in the gatehouse."

"Visitors? Mmm, anyone I ought to meet?" said Tanglestep, still absorbed in his papers. "A- ha!" He spotted a mis-placed comma which he hastily corrected.

"No sir. A rag-bag bunch of misfits, if ever I've seen one. I'm making them some tea and then I'll send them on their way, if that's OK. Don't worry, I'll give them the usual excuse: Granglethorn business being so demanding and all."

"Well, you won't be wrong there. It seems that the faster I respond to the Grand Assembly, the more I am asked to do. Yes, ok, but, please don't forget to wish them well and a safe journey from me. Now, where was I? Ahh, yes - disappearing groundluggs." He thumbed through a large folio of papers. Stunkensloop paused in the doorway for a second and then backed out of the chamber smirking.

Back at the gatehouse, he paused to compose himself and adopt a look of feigned disappointment to fit the bad news that he would announce. He delivered about two sentences before the place erupted.

"Now listen here, Stunkensloop," said Fubbyloofah angrily. "We need to see Tanglestep and if you think we've travelled all this way just to be fobbed off with an excuse and a cup of tea, you're mistaken."

"I just don't believe it!" said Featherfae, twirling one of the sticks that protruded from her hair. "Tanglestep would never turn his old friends away like this."

"Times aren't what they were," stuttered Stunkensloop "He is just *so* busy responding to decrees from the Grand Assembly that I -"

"Codswallop!" expounded Fubbyloofah. Behind him Chloe snorted with laughter. "I want to hear it from him in person," he said as he pushed past him towards the main keep of the Tower.

"Oh no you don't!" screeched Stunkensloop wriggling past to bar entry. "Now I've been civil up to this point but not any longer. I want the lot of you out of Treadmail Tower: NOW!" he said, twitching with rage.

"We'll soon see about that." A paw shot out and grasped him by collar.

"How dare you!" squealed Stunkensloop as like an eel he squirmed free. He was nothing if not a contortionist.

"What's going on?" asked Scott groping about blindly. He thumped into the pair of them. Jack quickly spotted what would happen next.

"Look out!" he cried, as Scott over-balanced and fell against the table. He yelped in blind confusion as icy cold milk soaked his skin.

"Oh, my God! Do you see that?" Chloe's hand pointed to a mass of small worms wriggling out of the broken milk jug.

"We've just drunk from that! Is nothing safe to eat or drink here?" said Jack feeling wretched. Suddenly a bellowing shriek filled the gatehouse as a large loose bellied woman lumbered out of the shadows.

"Watch out, Fubbyloofah!" cried Jack.

With ankles long since buried in fat, she grimaced in tune with the gladiator sandals that criss-crossed the flesh they constrained. As if to show it meant business, a vein throbbed in her calves as she stepped forwards. But it was her face that mortified them most.

"What's that 'orrible smell?" She sniffed the air in front of Jack who cringed at the reminder of the raptaggadon breath that had crystallised all over him.

"STUNKENSLOOP! Get this rabble out of my Gatehouse: NOW!" Puckered lips crumpled with each vowel, whilst deep furrows of wrinkles assaulted the air around her forehead. She took a fresh lungful of air and fouled it again.

"OUT, RAT-FACE, OUT!" She glared into Fubbyloofah's face whilst Stunkensloop darted behind her.

"Throw them out, Flabblehogg! Throw them out!" He was springing about excitedly, safe in the knowledge that her loose belly fat provided a cushion against further attack.

"Listen: we just need to speak to Tanglestep. We've travelled far and have important -"

"GET OUT BEFORE I THROW YOU OUT IN A SACK OF MEAL WORMS!" she raged before advancing on the troupe, a large bag of flour at the ready. The sinews in her neck strained like over-tight strings and deep in her throat her periglottis flapped alarmingly. Behind her, Stunkensloop's face jumped and twitched with mixed emotions, of which glee was the most evident. Fubbyloofah steeled himself just as the door opened behind her.

"OUT: NOW! BEFORE I THROW YOU IN KITCHEN WASTE GARNISHED WITH THE PICKINGS FROM BETWEEN MY TOES."

She curled her toes provocatively hoping the small tufts of hair that adorned each toe-knuckle would cow him with revulsion.

"AND AS FOR YOU, MULCH HEAD - TAKE THAT!" With a grunt befitting her manner, she heaved the bag of flour into the air. Featherfae was about to launch into the air with her tiny wings but then something by the door caught her eye and distracted her.

"Featherfae - is that - really - you?" said a familiar voice as a shaft of calcified sunlight suddenly flared into life.The flour crashed over her head and through the cascade of white powder and the golden rays of his sun shaft, their eyes locked.

"Tanglestep: my dear Tanglestep. How long has it been?" Her hands darted to calm the leafy twigs in her hair as best she could before she launched herself through the dust cloud. A puff of flour went up on their floury embrace and the robin shot out, finally deserting the nest in her hair for quieter pastures.

"Featherfae: how are you my lovely wood nymph?" He returned her strong warm embrace. God; how he had missed her! He grinned ecstatically into her face then became conscious of the professional distance his role as a Hebradaigen demanded. She turned her face into the billowing flour, glad to powder over the blushes she knew were there, whilst she drew her garment around herself more tightly. There were curves where there shouldn't be!

Everyone dusted themselves down for a few seconds whilst Flabblehogg, to hide her embarrassment, busied herself by picking up the broken pieces of jug from the floor. She ignored the wriggling worms which Chloe jumped towards.

"One-nil to me." She grinned at Jack.

Tanglestep turned to his colleagues. "Stunkensloop, Flabblehogg, these are my dearest friends. Please make up accommodation for them in the main keep."

"Yes, of course, sir. I had no idea -" stammered Stunkensloop.

Tanglestep waved a silencing hand over the rest of his excuse.

"Two-one to me now," said Jack to Chloe, his eyes scouring the floor intently.

"No need, Stunkensloop. I know you were simply trying to protect my privacy." He turned back to Featherfae who shuffled uncomfortably, her hand once again nervously checking the leafy twigs in her hair: they could be so unruly.

"That's the lot of them. I win, three-two," said Chloe as all the worms from the milk jug had now been squished underfoot.

Stunkensloop slipped off into the shadows to prepare rooms, quickly followed by Flabblehogg, who cast a harried glance behind her. Tanglestep and Featherfae gazed at each other. There was just so much to say, but where to begin?

"Erm, do you remember Fubbyloofah?" She said through a fixed smile, her insides screaming for something more meaningful.

"Yes, the beluga-bear. It was some time ago. How are you?" Tanglestep shot Featherfae a final intimate glance before shaking him warmly by the paw and moving on to the three time-wards.

"So you are the one that the peacocks are talking about." He fixed his piercing eyes on Scott.

"What do you mean?" Scott asked uneasily, grateful that at last the shadow-sylph's touch was fading.

"The one who will find burnt gold and save our sun."

Scott's jaw dropped. Fortunately he was saved by Chloe who held forth a couple of the dead butterflies that she'd retrieved earlier.

"Look what we found on the way here. Do you know why all these butterflies have broken wings?" she asked to his sharp intake of breath. He looked crestfallen.

"I have only seen this once before. Kaleidoscopes of butterflies suddenly falling from the sky as their wings break in mid-flight. It's heart-rending. I believe it is caused by the polluted liquids and nectar that they have to feed on these days. Their wings are simply not strong enough to support their tiny bodies."

"Is there anything we can do to help?" asked Featherfae in concern.

He sighed wistfully before casting her a warm look.

"Keep on leaving flowers in your footsteps. You know the good that you do, Featherfae." He held her gaze just long enough for her to blush then tore himself away. "Now you must all freshen yourselves up and please excuse Flabblehogg and Stunkensloop. They are wont to be a little over zealous in guarding my privacy. I rarely get anyone up here at Treadmail bar rogues, misfits and sakratts. From your road-weary condition, they must have assumed you were beggars or robbers: not that there's much to steal except my papers for the Grand Assembly," he chuckled as he led them out of the gatehouse. "Now, I'm going to billet you all in the main keep close by my office. I am dying to hear what has been happening over at Dragmines Valley. Since I was posted out here over six months ago I have made very few visits. How are those streams and lakes? I do miss them all terribly." Fubbyloofah cleared his throat to speak but Tanglestep cut him short. "No, I'm sorry. I'm forgetting my manners. There's plenty of time for all this later. Get yourselves freshened up and we'll have a long chat over dinner."

He led the way to three small rooms high up in the central tower. As they got to the first one, Flabblehogg emerged with a grimace which they charitably interpreted as a half-smile.

"Put *him* in the bed by the open window." She nodded towards Jack and wrinkled her nose at his smell as she brushed past.

"Are you still in the shadow world, bro?" asked Jack, grateful that neither Scott nor Chloe had responded to Flabblehogg's jibe.

"Yeah, but it's fading fast. There's more colour and definition to things now. I wish this raptaggadon bite would heal though." He took a swipe at Chloe who was pulling a face at him.

"Yeah, if he could see that, he's coming back alright. More's the pity!" she humpfed, before grabbing the bed closest to the door. On the floor above was a room for Fubbyloofah, from which Stunkensloop slunk out as they entered, whilst the room at the top of the tower was for Featherfae and the smoggilars. Flabblehogg was still making up the beds when they entered.

"These two baskets down here are for the -" she nodded towards the smoggilars not knowing what to call them.

"Smoggilars," added Featherfae helpfully. "They'll like that I'm sure." The smoggilars cautiously sniffed and nosied at the baskets laid out for them. Flabblehogg was aware that everyone was watching her after her recent outburst and with feigned affection bent down to pet them.

"Yeeeoww!" She withdrew her hand sharply as the smoggilars bristled up. "*She's* quick with her claws!" she spat.

"Are you OK, Flabblehogg?" asked a concerned Tanglestep from the doorway.

"What do *you* think?" she snapped as she exited the room glowering and rubbing her hand.

"Don't worry about Flabblehogg," said Tanglestep on seeing the alarm on Featherfae's face. "She just needs a little time on her own. I'll check in on her later. I'm sure she'll be fine. Now, let me leave you to settle in and we'll - meet again - for dinner that is," he stammered. He tore his eyes away from hers lest he drown in them and quickly left the room. Featherfae's heart pounded. If only he would... She dashed to the mirror.

"Oh, these infernal twigs!" she said as they stuck out from her hair in an unruly fashion. She quickly rearranged the braids of love-lies-bleeding as best she could. "That will have to do!" She tried to bring her mind back to practical matters. Now that they were here Tanglestep would surely know what to do. He was so wise and... but there was so much to tell.... about Lava, the search for burnt gold, the talismans... oh, where to begin?

Dinner when it came was a somewhat surreal affair. Tanglestep was keen to use the old baronial dining hall which was splendid except that it was used to seating parties of 20-30 and appeared a little under-utilised with such a small party. To make matters worse, Tanglestep insisted on protocol and had the party seated so that Fubbyloofah was given place of honour at the opposite end of the table to himself which meant that there were about 12 empty seats between them. Featherfae was the first to speak up.

"Tanglestep this is absurd. You are practically having to shout over to Fubbyloofah in order to be heard, and I am beginning to wish my chair had wheels on it so that I scoot from one end of the table to the other to talk to you both. Can we *please* all cluster together and talk intimately?"

"He's arranged it this way because I stink of raptaggadon breath. I took a shower but it makes no difference," Jack said dolefully.

"I don't blame him," muttered Chloe as Scott sniggered beside her.

"Not at all, Jack. I just wanted a sense of grandeur," said Tanglestep. A quick glance around the table revealed that he was in a minority of one so they were all soon clustered round the fire together. It didn't take long before the subject of the talismans was raised.

"Ahh, an old Hebradaigen time-key from Granglethorn Castle," said Tanglestep as he balanced the large key in his hand. "You can see the representation of the berriblods here." He drew attention to the metal scrolling within the open lattice head of the key. "This is an integral part of the decorative stone and metal work of the older parts of the castle dating back at least 700 years."

"Take it. It's yours. You are far better equipped to use than I'll ever be." Memories of failing his father were never far from the surface with Jack, but Tanglestep just shook his head slowly.

"No. It's been given to you for a reason."

Jack's shoulders slumped but he wasn't that surprised. Nobody in their right mind would shoulder this burden willingly. He toed the floor coverings whilst his brother spoke.

"- and what about this mirror?" said Scott handing it over.

"Ahh, the lost Mirror of Aggraides." Tanglestep took hold of it reverentially and carefully tilted the mirror backwards and forwards to catch the light. Eventually he closed his eyes and his fingers probed into the gaps within the open wood carving of the frame and a strange wistful smile appeared on his face. Fubbyloofah motioned for silence. They watched keenly as his smile faded and a frown creased his brow. From his rapid breathing, it was clear that his mind was racing wildly, though to what end no one knew. Finally, his frown softened and his eyes flickered rapidly behind closed lids before he suddenly shouted out "SEEK NOBODY!"

Everyone froze. A second later, Featherfae put a concerned hand on his brow and his erratic breathing subsided. It took a while before he spoke again.

"Pass me my sun-shaft," he said shakily as he reached for a pitcher of water.

"What is it, Tanglestep? What did you mean by 'SEEK NOBODY'? Are you saying nobody can help us?"

"I mm, I don't - Did I say that? I don't remember saying anything." His hands shook as he poured himself a glass to steady his nerves. They waited for him to regain his composure. "Friends, what I do know is that within this mirror are powerful shadows: shadows of two females, one young, one old; one for life, one for death."

"Willow!" shouted Scott in excitement.

"- and the woman in black," blanched Jack. "That's the last time I'm looking into that thing if she represents death."

"These shadowy figures are the guardians of the time splinters and this mirror is the window to the keyhole. Much of it is still unclear, but I do know that its intrinsic powers will remain dormant until it is returned to the exact place in Granglethorn Castle from whence it came."

"Do you know the exact spot that it comes from?" probed Fubbyloofah.

"Yeah, we need to use the key to free Willow. She's the woman trapped in a time splinter," said Scott. "Can you take us there?"

"Unfortunately, I don't know where it belongs. It has been missing for years and section 3, sub-section b4 of The Security Charter of the Grand Assembly prohibits access to many parts of the castle for all except the Hebradaigese."

A creaking hinge behind them caused everyone to whirl round.

"Pardon the intrusion sir," said Stunkensloop slightly too quickly, as if the excuse for his presence had already been prepared, "but I was wondering whether you were ready for the next course." His smile jumped around his face obsequiously. Tanglestep indicated, with a brief flicker of annoyance, that they had barely started their first so he quickly bowed his way out of the room leaving everyone feeling that they had already said too much on the subject. Featherfae turned to the topic of Tanglestep's current work and why he seemed to be perpetually based at Treadmail Tower.

"It's such a remote posting. You can't possibly have enough to do up here. You are a Hebradaigen of the Grand Assembly and will be needed for the debates and votes that the Assembly takes. Can't this work here be delegated to your juniors?" she asked whilst reaching for a glass of snowdrop juice distilled from the dew of the dawn. It glistened and gave off thin wispy tendrils of mist. Scott nudged Jack and pointed at Chloe who was gaping open-mouthed in wonder.

"Apparently not," said Tanglestep wistfully. "The Assembly say they need Hebradaigese posted at all outposts so that they can't be accused of neglecting the provinces."

"But there's nobody here to object!" said Jack. The fire spluttered in sympathy and Jack half expected to see a couple of crocklepips sticking their heads out from under the chimney breast but none appeared.

"True, but it is a staging post of historic importance and besides the Grand Assembly can always summon me if they need me and I can always request to leave my posting and attend Granglethorn should the situation warrant it."

"Then that is what you must do," said Fubbyloofah firmly.

"Must do what?" asked Tanglestep.

"Request to leave Treadmail Tower and return to Granglethorn. We need you! Willow, the lady in the mirror, says that a Hebradaigen must be present when the keyhole to the time splinters is found."

"But I still have so much to do. It would be -"

"Willow said we would *fail* without the help of a Hebradaigen," said Fubbyloofah pointedly.

"Yes, OK, but there is a way of doing things. One cannot just storm off and abandon one's posting," said Tanglestep concerned.

He rose from his seat to distribute candied cuckoo eggs drizzled with thick honeyed hoar-frost. Everyone's eyes lit up.

"First I shall have to make a formal submission which will be considered by a representative of each of the four towers at their weekly meeting. You can rest assured that the Tower of the Moon will not support my application. I shall also need to convince the representatives of the Vedic Bells and the Tower of Reflection. It will all take time and careful thought."

Scott cracked the cuckoo egg between his teeth and found the warm soothing liqueur that flowed from the candied coating strangely intoxicating when tasted alongside the richness of the egg.

"For special guests only," said Tanglestep with a wink as he noticed Scott's eyes rolling in pleasure.

"But time is the one thing we don't have," said Fubbyloofah anxiously. Tanglestep did not reply and Featherfae, anxious that Fubbyloofah was becoming too pressing, brought everyone's attention to the fact that the next course was due. With the serving of the dinner came Stunkensloop and Flabblehogg and the lightness in the air quickly evaporated. A sullen silence lurked in their wake.

"Won't you join us after dinner for some coffee?" Tanglestep asked them kindly.

"Humpf. Far too much to do to waste time with idle chat, haven't we?" said Flabblehogg to Stunkensloop.

"What a shame," said Fubbyloofah through gritted teeth. She threw him a baleful glare before scuttling off to the kitchen. The sound of curses mingled with frantic whispering would occasionally waft through to remind them that they were not alone.

16. Flabblehogg Gets Burnt

The next morning the troupe came down to breakfast and were surprised to find no sign of Tanglestep whatsoever.

"He's received another urgent missive from Granglethorn," simpered Stunkensloop whilst squirming on the spot.

" - which means HE CANNOT BE DISTURBED!" said Flabblehogg, with a ferocious look upon her face that crumpled in sympathy with the large fleshy forearms which she had folded across her bosom like bull-bars. Fubbyloofah and Featherfae exchanged glances with each other before enquiring about breakfast.

"HUMMPF!" erupted Flabblehogg. "Expect us to skivvy for you, do you? Well you can think again."

She picked at her teeth and flicked the particles of food in their general direction. Fubbyloofah held her gaze whilst motioning for the others to stay silent. The last thing he wanted was another scene with this over-sized trollop.

"Of course not, dear. But if you could just point us to where things are kept we'll happily prepare it ourselves."

"Well, not that there'll be much left at this late hour, but try those cupboards over there. You might find a hunk of dry bread left over from a few days ago. I was going to give it to the pigs but hey - "

"We don't want dry bread!" Chloe piped up angrily. "Just tell us where we can find a proper breakfast: some fruit for example!"

"Fruit? Fruit? Where do you think you are?" asked Flabblehogg. A smirk appeared within her creased visage.

"There's been no fruit here for years, you little twerp!" added Stunkensloop his face wincing sharply. "I can't remember what it even looks like."

"It looks like this!" said Chloe, suddenly flourishing the sunfruit for all to see.

In an instant Flabblehogg's jaw dropped sharply revealing the periglottis that had flapped so angrily on their first encounter. "Yeoww!" It flapped again but this time in terror.

"Put it away!" yelped Stunkensloop who pirouetted on the spot such was the intensity of his twitch.

"What? Where - where did you get that?" squeaked Flabblehogg like a stuck-pig. Panicked eyes shot towards Stunkensloop who was in spasms. "Here, lemme see?" she said and before anyone could object she lunged forwards and snatched it out of Chloe's hand. For a moment time stood still.

"Stop! Give it back!" Fubbyloofah jumped to his paws all a-bristle.

"Oww, my toes!" winced Featherfae as she pulled back from under his heel, but he hadn't heard her.

"It's beginning to pulse!" cried Fubbyloofah. He sprang forwards but it was as if he was wading through treacle.

"Arrgh! What *is* this thing?" Flabblehogg staggered backwards, eyes wide in terror, as the sunfruit throbbed with a powerful light. Stunkensloop scrabbled to get out of the way. A deep groan came from his chest and his eyes popped out on stalks as he jerked and twitched as if at the end of the hangman's noose. Then suddenly, the time-warp was punctured.

"YEEEOOOWW!" Flabblehogg bellowed. Cracks raced across the window panes and deep thumping sounds came from the stairwell. Seconds later, Tanglestep burst in.

"What on earth - ?"

"She attacked me!" yelled Flabblehogg pointing at Chloe. The smell of burning flesh was in the air and Flabblehogg was clutching a hand so badly burnt it was if she had been holding red-hot coals. Tanglestep winced in sympathy before spotting something rolling across the floor that he had never expected to see outside the pages of a book.

"Bless my sun-shaft. Is that a - sunfruit?" he muttered as the orb pulsed and throbbed with re-awakened power. He swayed on his feet, whilst behind them the door slammed shut as Flabblehogg bolted from the room. "Don't touch it!" shouted Tanglestep to Fubbyloofah, who moved to retrieve it from the floor. "You saw what it did to Flabblehogg. Best leave it to the time-wards."

Chloe scrabbled over to retrieve her talisman and moments later, the party were shown to a full larder and left to breakfast.

"Now, I'd better leave you and see to Flabblehogg," said Tanglestep apprehensively.

"Just look what that brat has done. Just look at it!" She thrust her hand into his face. "I want her out! In fact, no: I want her taken before the Grand Assembly on a 'dangerous commodity' charge."

She was staring incredulously at her burnt and swollen hand and itching for vengeance. Tanglestep stared back at her and was about to explain how important a find the sunfruit was when she cocked her face to one side and with a look of great suspicion in her eyes said very pointedly, "You will support me on this, won't you?"

When Tanglestep returned to the breakfasting party, he seemed like he'd done a day's work already. He looked totally drained and strangely worried. The party could only speculate on what had happened with Flabblehogg. Featherfae spotted that he was clearly in need of sustenance and jumped up eager to be the one to supply it. His spirits soon lifted once he was handed a cup of smoked-tea and some snaptoast that crackled, popped and fizzed all the way from plate to mouth. He watched in fascination as Chloe played with the sunfruit. It pulsed and throbbed with a deep powerful energy and they filled him in on what had happened over Lake Wintersmere. When he heard how it had made the whole sky light up he jolted from his seat. The similarity that this image evoked with Stunkensloop's twitching made them all burst out laughing but Tanglestep was in no mood for levity.

"Does anyone from the Tower of the Sun know of the fire-cat's return?" he asked urgently.

"Not that we know of," said Fubbyloofah. "Once we'd made contact with Featherfae, she suggested we come straight to you."

"Well, we must contact them urgently. Crows are Creatures of the Night Shade. By launching this attack without first informing the Grand Assembly, Jassaspy must be trying to capture the fire-cat before its presence here becomes common knowledge."

" - and once we've informed the Tower of the Sun, will we have Granglethorn's support for a re-planting programme?" asked Fubbyloofah eagerly, as the last piece of snaptoast popped and did a double somersault in the air to land back on the plate. "Featherfae and the smoggilars have had some success already, planting pips and utilising sun-threads to aid germination. We've even managed to convince some of the groundluggs of Crambleside to help out."

Tanglestep shook his head sadly. "It's not that simple, I'm afraid. We are just one tower out of four and unfortunately, the gatekeeper has disappeared. He had a role independent of the four towers and could wield a casting vote to break deadlock. Since his disappearance at the time of the fire-cat's last visit, we seem doomed to forever wrangle amongst ourselves: tower against tower," he said as he stooped to light the pine kernels for a fresh pot of smoked tea. The smell was intoxicating and Jack jumped up to rummage around for some accompanying snacks whilst Tanglestep continued.

"Unfortunately, Jassaspy has already gained approval for his underground resettlement programme. We would need to present compelling evidence of successful attempts to nurture La-Kelisland back to health in order to gain support for a re-planting programme now."

Jack returned with some very strange looking objects that were giving off smoke.

"Bumblebulbs," said Tanglestep on seeing everyone's puzzled expression." They smoke just before they split in two. Cut a piece off just after the smoking stops. It's deliciously peaty and will complement the smoked tea perfectly. Good choice, Jack."

Jack grinned as he sat down to wait for the bumblebulbs to calm down. Fubbyloofah was looking concerned.

"What's our best course of action now then? Jassaspy must know that Lava will try to find burnt gold and get to World's End."

"We must go to Grangethorn," said Tanglestep simply. "But I shall have to draft an application first," he said as he rose from the table. "I shall retire to my chambers in order to prepare the preliminary draft." He made for the door before a thought occurred to him that the party might welcome some diversion to while away the time in the interim. "Would you like me to arrange for Stunkensloop to show you the tower and the environs, it can be -"

"NO!" shouted all three of them with enough force to make Fubbyloofah wince.

"I think they mean that they would rather explore alone," he added a little more diplomatically but with a hint of amusement curling his lips.

"No matter," said Tanglestep, too preoccupied with the task in hand to note the strength of feeling. "I've just had another thought: you might want to dust off the powder from the broken wings of those butterflies. I remember the Custodian of the Vedic Bells once saying how it reflects and refracts light. They are such beautiful creatures. Let us preserve what bit of their beauty we can."

Featherfae beamed in sympathy with the sentiment and he left them to it.

It was dusk before Tanglestep reappeared and Fubbyloofah was getting tetchy at the delay.

"May the sun bless you with an abundance of berriblods. I have packed all our things and we can be on the road within 30 minutes," he said in anticipation of a swift departure. Tanglestep looking shocked.

"Dear Fubbyloofah, what in La-Kelisland are you talking about? We can't possibly depart so soon. I have only prepared a preliminary draft. Once the draft has been finalised it needs to be sent to the Grand Assembly whereupon it will likely be passed to Committee to be discussed at the weekly meeting of the representatives of the four towers. Should they agree to my return, their decision will need to be ratified by the Grand Assembly itself who will then formally recall me should they agree with the Committee's proposal. It will take quite some time I can assure you, and that's providing the Tower of Reflection makes no special request for recess in order to ponder fully the consequences of an early recall."

"For the love of berriblods, pass me a piece of smoking bumblebulb," sighed Fubbyloofah, whose black fur positively blanched to the white of a polar bear's. He felt a sudden need of strong sustenance. "We can't possibly wait for this process to run its course. Can't you see how the sun is getting weaker by the day: not to mention Lava and the danger he could be in? For fireflakes' sake, can't you short-circuit this nonsense?"

"Friend, friend, listen to me." Tanglestep held up a hand to quell the agitation. "I am a Hebradaigen and bound by the conventions of the Grand Assembly. The best way you can help the process is by listening to my initial draft and advising me on any necessary revisions. Will you do that for me?" He gazed kindly into Fubbyloofah's face.

"Yes, yes, if you insist," sighed Fubbyloofah wearily. How could he resist such well-meaning kindness? The party settled down to hear what Tanglestep had been spending the last few hours drafting whilst Featherfae prepared a fresh pot of smoked tea and snaptoast. Tanglestep cleared his throat and looked up briefly to ensure he had everyone's undivided attention.

"Erstwile colleagues of the Grand Assembly." As if on cue a piece of snaptoast did a stylish back-flip. "I, Tanglestep, of the Tower of the Sun, at present residing at Treadmail Tower, do request leave to return to Granglethorn to address the Grand Assembly on a matter related to our policy of 'Duty of Care to the Landscape' and in particular, section B1 'Welfare of living things', sub-section 3.2, 'Preservation and Protection for Future Generations'. In respect of these policies, I am in possession of information that, if legends are to be believed, give fair prospect to the discovery of burnt gold and all the attendant ramifications that flow from that. I await the outcome of your considered deliberations and remain your most obedient servant, Horatio Tanglestep."

There was a brief and hastily stifled snort of laughter from Scott at the mention of Tanglestep's first name before Fubbyloofah spoke up.

"Personally, I would make a much more impassioned plea but I suppose it must be dressed up in legalese. Please can you get it dispatched p.d.q. as I fear that my fur will turn completely white with age or frustration if I have to wait around here for much longer." He reached for a mug of tea in the desperate hope that the smoke would permeate his fur and return some colour to him.

"Thank you Fubbyloofah. However, I was wondering if I ought to mull it over for a while," said Tanglestep with an affected twirl of his forelock. "Quite often I am able to get a more concise turn of phrase or strike a more convincing tone when I take a little more time over my drafts. As it stands it seems to me to be rather blunt and coarse and I fear that my colleagues will view me as having 'gone native' and lost the refinements of Granglethorn with my protracted stay here at Treadmail Tower. This is an impression I am anxious to avoid giving at all costs." He looked around at the gathering. Chloe was standing on tip toes trying to reach into a small pot of quail's eggs with a silver spoon and the smoggilars were getting increasingly skittish every time the snaptoast fizzed or flipped in the air. "So what say you all? Should I take the time to polish it or not?" he asked.

"How long would you consider necessary?" asked Featherfae with a reassuring smile.

"Oh, not long. A week or two would normally -"

"A WEEK OR TWO!" spluttered Fubbyloofah. "Crush my berriblods and use them for a foot balm! We haven't got a week or two!" He stood up bristling like a chimney sweep's brush. "You can talk and pontificate as much as you like but each minute that passes is another minute of fading sunlight that we won't see again. I, for one, will ready myself for immediate departure," and with that he stormed out of the room. Jack flashed a weak smile before darting after him anxious to avoid the party splitting up.

"Golly! I normally mull these matters over for much longer. A request sent in haste will more than likely be refused," said Tanglestep looking totally bemused and more than a little comic with his hair still ruffled from the thought processes that had gone into his draft.

"You silly noodle! Haven't you been listening to what we've told you about the smog and the slime trails?" Featherfae smiled tenderly as Tanglestep's face raced through confusion and offence before settling on a smile.

"In all my years as a Hebradaigen, I've never been called a noodle before," he said in earnest.

"Well there's a first time for everything isn't there?" she said, holding his gaze now. She reached up to stroke his cheek but Fubbyloofah's return distracted them both.

"Fubbyloofah, I've been thinking and I suppose I could risk sending this preliminary draft in the interests of group harmony." Tanglestep raised his eyebrows questioningly. Fubbyloofah nodded imperceptibly. "Yes...that is what I shall do. But the problem we have now is that the mail is not due for collection for another 3 days."

"Not to worry! I have a solution to that one," said Fubbyloofah with an enthusiastic look in his eye. "Flapbaggles sent a muster of peacocks up here who are in regular contact with a flight of swallows. Let's send the letter via the swallows. It'll get there faster than any other way that you can think of."

"By all that's good in the world, yes! Quick, one of you, please summon Stunkensloop whilst I just add a postscript. I shall request a receipt by swallow-mail too. That will raise a few eyebrows, I'm sure," he added with a chuckle. Chloe volunteered and found Stunkensloop lurking in the back kitchens boiling up some sticky black syrup and muttering what seemed like curses under his breath. As she approached his eyes narrowed.

"Whaddaya want?" he spat before instinctively recoiling as memories of their earlier encounter returned.

"Tanglestep is asking for you. He needs you now, please." She held out her hand as if to lead him back but he backed off sharply. The strong smell of the sunfruit was still on her hands.

"Keep away and don't touch me!" he said moving cautiously around her in order to get to the door. "I know my way around this place, thank you very much: so I'll make my own way, if you don't mind; and I'd be grateful if you didn't touch anything in here either, please. In fact, can you just leave!"

"Ok. Keep your hair on!" Chloe moved back towards the door. For once he controlled his twitching and stood rigidly still until she had left, then, with a badly shaking hand, he locked the door behind him.

"Can you pass this to the peacocks in the courtyard," said Tanglestep as he handed Stunkensloop a parchment roll addressed to the Grand Assembly. Stunkensloop raised an eyebrow and stared hard at it as if puzzling over the bizarre request. Whatever conclusions he reached, however, were not voiced as he simply clicked his heels smartly and with a quick "Toute Suite," bowed low and darted out of the room.

It would take 2 days to receive a reply from Granglethorn so there was nothing for it but to sit it out and entertain themselves as best they could. Mercifully, Stunkensloop and Flabblehogg had gone to ground, after last being spotted slinking into the courtyard looking for the peacocks. Featherfae decided to use the intervening time creatively.

"Wait here!" she said to Tanglestep, "and don't come into the courtyard for the next couple of days." Her eyes shone with excitement

"Why on earth not? What are you planning?" She didn't respond, but her tooth peeped over her lower lip cheekily. "Don't worry," he laughed, "I have to respond to Jassaspy's latest paper on underground re-settlement. There are policies to check and cross-reference." He turned back to his papers but not without giving Featherfae a winsome smile.

When the day of the expected reply came, Featherfae led Tanglestep down into the courtyard in a state of great excitement.

"You must allow me to blindfold you first," she said hopping about excitedly at the prospect of the surprise. He laughingly agreed and was soon blindly groping his way round the courtyard.

"What homespun wonder have we here?" he said as a honeyed smell filled his head.

"Try and guess," laughed Featherfae; but he was completely stumped. "OK," she said. "Let's try another tack. Do you notice anything different underfoot?"

He took one or two independent steps but squeals of laughter erupted as he stumbled and stretched out a hand for support. "Whatever it is, it's a trip hazard. Under Health and Safety poli -"

"Oh, do be quiet about your blessed policies," laughed Featherfae.

"I really, really have no idea," he said as he groped forwards.

"Put him out of his misery," chuckled Fubbyloofah.

"OK. OK. Voila!" The blindfold came off and Tanglestep found himself standing in a sea of purple. He drew the sweet fragrance up into his lungs and feasted his eyes on the splash of colour. Every corner of every stone was covered in lush purple heather.

"It's divine Featherfae I... I just don't know what to say."

There was a pregnant pause whilst Featherfae beamed up at him before he quickly drew her towards him, hugged her tightly and kissed her. The kiss radiated down through her footsteps and a moment later they both staggered as a sprig of heather sprung up so vigorously that it knocked them both off-balance.

"Wow! Some kiss!" cheered Scott as laughter rippled round the group.

"This calls for tea in the garden!" grinned Fubbyloofah, thumping his huge paws together in exuberance before making for the kitchen.

After the intervening period of tea, laughter and harmony was over, Tanglestep went to summon Stunkensloop to help with preparations for their departure. He returned almost immediately looking concerned.

"What is it?" asked Fubbyloofah, who was beginning to feel worried.

"It's Stunkensloop. I can't find him. Nor can I find Flabblehogg. I don't know where they can be," he said.

"Chloe said she found him skulking in the back-kitchens," said Scott. "I'll go and check in case he's hiding away for some reason."

He took off whilst the others racked their brains wondering when they had last seen them.

"It seems that they were last spotted in the courtyard with the peacocks," mused Fubbyloofah after much discussion.

"Presumably handing over the parchment for delivery."

"Well that's easy to check: I'll ask them. I can speak to the peacocks," said Chloe. She dashed off but returned with Scott within a few minutes. Both looked glum and down-cast.

"What now?" asked Fubbyloofah, suddenly very concerned.

"The peacocks say they both left the Tower over two days ago and haven't returned," said Chloe. "They were each carrying a small haversack so -"

She wasn't allowed to finish, as at that moment Scott threw a soggy bundle to the ground in front of them. They all stared hard as the fat from the kitchen bin slowly seeped away to reveal the remains of Tanglestep's un-posted parchment.

17. Fire-Cat Magic

Plummeting and toppling through the air, Lava fell in a blur of gold. Light was everywhere: golden light, white hot light, light of bright white titanium purity. Around him, weak smudges of black faded away in all directions. Then he hit the top branches of the pine trees. Through branch after branch, he crashed and tumbled until with a dull thud he hit the forest floor. He lay motionless and deathly still. Then, with the briefest flicker, he suddenly started to glow.

Over in the Chamber of Moths, Hackweezle was crouched on the floor acting as a foot stool for Dog Bottom who wiped his foot in his hair whilst looking into his centipede ball. It had reformed with those centipedes that had failed to latch onto Lava at Caesar's Well. He was revelling in the power he had suddenly acquired and even Jassaspy was hanging on his every word, eager to hear what was happening to Lava.

"Hold on! Wait!" cried Dog Bottom with his hand raised imperiously, much to Jassaspy's irritation. "There is something from the centipedes -"

"Well. WHAT - IS - IT?" hissed Jassaspy through gritted teeth.

"The fire-cat has fallen into Grizebale forest - the crows have lost him," said Dog Bottom, repeating exactly what the centipede ball was telling him.

"Ouch!" yelled Hackweezle, as Jassaspy kicked out in frustration.

"Wait! That's not all -" said Dog Bottom. "He is shining with a golden glow!"

"FOOLS! I should never have relied upon those crows," cursed Jassaspy. "An open display of fire-cat magic! He is getting bolder by the day. Whatever next? He must be taken before his presence is detected." He whirled round towards Spittlewhip. "Get Ripsnarl and his pack into that forest immediately."

The forest was dark and unwelcoming and there was little chance of picking out the black feathers of three filthy carrion crows.

After a few abortive attempts, the magpies whirled back to report to Flapbaggles.

"First the nightingales, now the magpies: quick! The time for action is now. Lava needs aerial cover!"

Ye Olde Dungeon Creek was soon buzzing with over-excited twitters as a cast of falcons and hawks gathered for the flight to Grizebale forest.

"Now I must attend to my sartorial needs. A general needs to cut a dash when leading his troops into battle," said Flapbaggles as he patted his rotund frame expectantly.

"Right you are," said Tappletock, the woodpecker, stifling a snigger.

Always one for travelling in style, Flapbaggles had decided it was time to give an airing to his old leather flying jacket, luxuriously adorned with a sheepskin collar to keep out even the sharpest north-easterlies. He made his way up to the attic and towards an old leather trunk covered in souvenir stickers from former trips: 'I've climbed Treadmail Tower' and 'Next Stop: World's End!' He smiled fondly at the memories before pausing gingerly. There was real danger of an ambush from Stinking Bishop and his mischief of mice. These were a band of rough field mice that had chased him out of his own loft one day through sheer weight of numbers. He shuddered at the memory. They'd come at him from all directions; nipping at his talons and dropping down from rafters to scrabble over his head like lice: no wonder he'd panicked. The worst part had been the end though, when Stinking Bishop himself swaggered up. Wearing a patch over one eye and a pirate's skull cap on his head, he had snarled rather than spoken. Flapbaggles could still recall every word.

"So, feather-bag: finally, the tables have turned. The day of the beak is over and the day of the whisker has begun!"

Flapbaggles shuddered as he remembered standing there frozen to the spot, blinking in fear as the mischief closed in on him from all angles. A second later, they surged towards him and in a panic he fell down into a pile of their droppings. He could still hear their delirious squeaks as he shot down the loft ladder in shame.

He peered cautiously about him. Thankfully, this time they were not at large. He could relax and savour some of the memories of his youth without fear. "A-ha!" He lovingly stroked the Jacket with his wing feathers, "and the goggles to boot! I'd completely forgotten about these. All I need now is the old leather flying cap and then I'm all set to go." Half an hour later he descended from the attic to quite a reception.

"Oh Lordy!" said Raffles, who forever seemed to be propping up the bar these days. "It's not the panto season already, is it?" A couple of young parrots squawked in laughter before a stare from their elders silenced them.

"Now, now, Raffles! You ought to think about what contribution you can make instead of poking fun at everyone else. You'll be the first to moan if your supply of G&T runs out or gets polluted by slime, heaven forbid!"

Raffles stiffened slightly before stating in a declaratory tone: "I shall man the bar in your absence, sire. After all, you'll need someone to keep the place going, not to mention to co-ordinate the messages that these busy-body swallows keep bringing."

"Mmm, just as long as you realise that I know exactly how much stock is behind the bar... and what it is worth," said Flapbaggles archly.

"Mortally wounded; mortally wounded, sire!" retorted Raffles. "That such a heinous thought could even flicker across your enobled brow strikes me to the core," he paused whilst affecting a dizzy spell. "I am sorry to say that after that verbal excrescence, nought but a G&T will steady my wing for the task ahead."

"Just the one then, Raffles," laughed Flapbaggles who couldn't help chuckling at his friend's impudent wit before strapping his flying goggles on over his monocle and going out to join the waiting cast.

It wasn't long before they were all airborne and heading for the forest. But, they were not the only party seeking the fire-cat.

When Chloe blasted the crows from the sky, they fell like tatty black rags dumped from the bin of a tanning factory.

"Jeez! What in the name of carrion was that?" asked Rag-wing as he thumped and thudded through the branches before hitting the earth. He looked around him, his head spinning, before realising that he had spoken to himself. "Worm-beak, are you there?" he called out to the darkness, before the sound of breaking and splintering branches filled the air above him. Seconds later, his friend crashed down besides him and squawked loudly with pain.

"Arrgh...I've...I think, I've broken a wing," he shrieked. He jumped to his feet and slowly and painfully stretched out his raggy wings, wincing as he did so. He cut a motley sight.

"Who's a pretty boy then?" said Rag-wing with a sarcastic snort.

Both crows looked round the forest floor and then up into the branches from where they had fallen. They quickly sobered up when they spotted one of their companions neatly skewered on a sharp branch about 40 feet above them. As for the remaining crow, there was no sight. They bounced around to get the blood flowing again whilst pondering what to do next.

"One of us ought to flit off to Granglethorn and tell 'ole moth-bag what's happened," said Worm-beak.

"Well don't look at me, he'll tear out my feathers and use them for a pillow."

"He'll find out sooner or later and then it'll only be worse for us and besides -" Worm-beak flapped his broken wing pathetically.

"I hope you get beak rot!" Rag-wing snorted angrily as he resigned himself and gathered his strength for the journey ahead.

Once alone, Worm-beak hopped around the undergrowth flexing his wings to test their strength. When he felt they would bear his weight, he launched himself into the air. Despite the pain, he was able to get up amongst the branches for a better vantage point.

The light was fading in the forest and the night creatures were beginning to stir. A couple of large earwigs crawled by making for a deliciously rotten piece of bark. They looked so plump and succulent.

"No, no! Gotta resist the temptation to gorge myself silly. There's too much at stake," he told himself. Then he suddenly had a brilliant idea. "Here, lemme help you 'wigs", he said as he hopped along the branch and started pecking away at the rotten wood. The wood soon crumbled under the impact of his beak, giving the earwigs easy access.

"Cor, thanks mate! We thought our time was up when we saw you perched there," said the 'wigs flexing their segmented bodies and waving their tendrils in graceful thanks. "I was just advising Wiggy here, to vomit if you came too close. I've managed to escape before by vomiting. There must be something in it that repels you birds."

Worm-beak had to bite back his irritation. Ear-wig vomit! Of all the things that could ruin a good snack!

"No problem. We night creatures need to stick together now that the fire-cat has returned," he said, putting his plan into motion. He fixed his beady eye on them to gauge their response. The mere mention of his name was enough to spook the 'wigs whose memories clearly ran deep.

"Fire-cat! That *is* bad news. If he revives the sun we'll have to retreat under stones forever," grumbled Wiggy suddenly realising what a treat it was to scurry about freely feasting on rotten bark.

"You're darned right you will, so you'd better help me find him quick. He's around here somewhere," said Worm-beak eagerly. The wigs needed no further urging and it wasn't long before they had introduced him to the local moths whose plump little bodies so tantalized Worm-beak that he had to use every ounce of strength not to skewer them and enjoy a long overdue supper. Feigning a complete disinterest in all things culinary, he got them to agree to spread the word and keep their antennae twitched for anything out of the ordinary. With a network of thousands of woodland moths now working for him, he soon had a bearing on both Lava and a pack of black wolves suffering with belly ache after a recent meal of grub-worms.

"That's got to be Ripsnarl's pack. What a comedown having to eat grub-worms," chuckled Worm-beak. He readied himself for the brief flight over when it suddenly occurred to him that he had all the information he needed from these moths. With a sharp rally of stabs, his beak shot out and skewered the three plumpest ones nearest to him.

"Ahh, well…. serves you right for being so trusting." He cackled to himself as others buzzed around him in clouds of panic; then he took off, hopping and fluttering as best he could with his broken wing.

He arrived to find the wolves hunched together at the roots of a very large fir tree. One of them looked like he was suffering quite badly as he was squirming around and whimpering quietly. Ripsnarl, himself, was resting with his eyes closed after the exhausting journey to get here.

"This'll be fun," muttered Worm-beak. He landed softly, bounced up to Ripsnarl's ear and let out a raucous scream. The wolf jolted awake, his bleary eye caught sight of Worm-beak and his snout creased with anger.

"What the blazes do you think you're playing at?" he snarled.

"Oh calm down, you dumb brute and listen," cackled Worm-beak. "This is no time for snoozing. The fire-cat is close by but I can't get far with this broken wing. It's time to join forces. With my aerial skills, we can track him together and share the honours that go with his capture," he said waiting for this information to sink in.

"Since when has anyone been able to trust you bird-brains?" growled Ripsnarl shiftily.

"You don't have any other option. Look at yourselves bellyaching on the forest floor. You'll not find him on your own. The forest is too dense and besides, do you really want me to report to the moth-bag that you refused to help?" said Worm-beak, thrusting his beaky face into his snout.

Ripsnarl growled again in disgust but knew that Worm-beak was right. He roused his pack and after a few minutes of bad-tempered snapping and snarling they departed with Worm-beak perched magisterially on Ripsnarl's back. It wasn't long before he was squawking in delight.

"What is it now, Wormy?" growled Ripsnarl, who was beginning to seethe with resentment at having to ferry the ragged creature about like royalty. Worm-beak fluttered down to retrieve something from the ground in front of them.

"It's a centipede scale and it's still warm. It must have fallen from from the fire-cat!" he squawked gleefully.

Up ahead, Lava's journey was getting increasingly difficult as the remaining daylight faded into night. Strange and hostile roots were snatching at his paws and small biting insects were emerging from their dank hidey holes to nip at his warm body. He began to pulse and glow to keep them at bay. Little did he know that when Dog Bottom had thrown the centipede ball at them back at Caesar's Well, one had attached itself to him. It was this that had led the crows to him at Ye Olde Dungeon Creek, and it was this that was leading the wolves to him now.

"Ha! Now we've got him," gloated Ripsnarl as he peered down at a small tuft of gingery fur that had snagged on a bush and was still warm with body heat. "Are you ready to finish it, boys?"

His pack gathered round and buried their snouts in the fur to lock onto the scent. A dribble of spittle drooled over it dousing what remaining body heat there was before the wolves howled to the moon in eager anticipation.

"Home in on that howling," spluttered an exhausted Flapbaggles, who was beginning to regret having embarked on this mission. His monocle kept steaming up under his flying goggles and what's more, within the first 5 minutes of flying with the falcons and hawks it was obvious that he was terribly unfit. He bobbed along in their wake barely able to keep his own body weight in the air. They had to fly in aerial loops to ensure that they didn't leave him behind. A couple of hawks immediately shot over towards the howling, whilst the falcons waited for Flapbaggles to bring up the rear like some giant lumbering booby. After about 10 minutes, there was an excited call. Sure enough, deep below on the floor of the forest they could just make out flash of ginger glowing brightly against the blackness of the night: but it wasn't moving! Flapbaggles looked around in concern. What had happened? Was Lava OK? Why wasn't he on the move as the magpies said he was? Suddenly the sound of howling broke through the tree canopy again and it sounded dangerously close. Peering down from the treetops, he could see Lava in the same position as before. Then, to his horror, he saw three grey shadows converging on him from different directions. If Lava didn't move fast…! There was no time for delay but how could they help from up in the skies? His feathers fluttered in panic for a moment, but then he had an idea…

"Get 'im boys!" snarled Ripsnarl, clearing a fallen branch that separated him from the sleeping Lava. He landed comfortably and bared his teeth for what he thought would be the final act. But it didn't end as he thought it would. With a terrific thud the whole forest floor was suddenly pummelled from above. Out of the corner of his eye he saw something hurtle towards him. He swung his head around and caught the full force of a falling pine cone on the nose. He yelped in pain, and then yelped again as the pine cone grew legs which wrapped tightly round his nose. The bug sank its claws into his tender snout and he squealed horribly. He glanced around and saw the rest of his pack was suffering the same bombardment. That irritating Worm-beak was flapping around and squawking which only added to the confusion and to cap it all, Lava was slipping away. He whined in frustration as he saw a gingery tail disappear into the undergrowth before another pine cone bug hit him smack on the top of his head and hooked its legs painfully into his ears.

Flapbaggles chuckled. It had worked a treat! By dislodging the pine cones, they had managed to wake the pine cone bugs and give Lava time to make his escape. "Next Stop Granglethorn!" he hooted as he noted the direction that Lava had set off in, his spirits now lifted by the welcome rest that he'd enjoyed whilst directing the operation from the tree tops.

Back in Granglethorn Castle a reception committee was being hastily convened. Dog Bottom was now strutting and swaggering around, having found favour with Jassaspy thanks to the centipede ball that had successfully tracked Lava since Caesar's Well and now Rag-wing had arrived with his up-date from the forest.

"Quick; sakratts, follow me!" Jassaspy shot Rag-wing a black look and jumped to his feet, barely able to prevent the green fumes from seeping out from his open cowl. "Fan out and sweep the valley floor. Find the fire-cat and bring him back to me unharmed."

He watched as his preparations got underway. There was just one more thing for him to do. He made his way over to the copse of trees where the rock-troll lived. A short while later the rock-troll appeared, his bloated figure coloured by the sudden exertion that was demanded of it. He glanced down the valley as if expecting to see Lava at any moment and then lumbered over to his store and started rummaging around. He soon had what he was looking for and thrutched off towards the portcullis at the entrance to the Castle, only to return a few minutes later to retrieve a huge box of iron nails and a large claw-hammer.

In the forest the wolves were re-grouping. "Come on, he can't have gone far. We nearly had him, and just think what our reward will be when we drop him at the feet of the cowled one." The wolves grinned, each imagining his own private heaven. "He's in my blood is this one," said Ripsnarl as they picked up Lava's trail again by the edge of the forest.

In the skies above, Flapbaggles and his cast were charting Lava's progress. The band of green smog that was previously at roof-top height was even thicker now and in many places was down at ground level. Flapbaggles was in despair.

"He would have had a clear run for Granglethorn if it wasn't for those noxious green fumes. How can any of us see, let alone breathe, with that everywhere?" Moments later, Lava emerged from the fringes of the forest. He looked up at the hanging green vapour waiting to choke his breath and sting his eyes and started to pulse and glow. A deep volcanic core of heat welled up inside him. Molten red with spots of deep black crimson speckled the air around his body. Then with a sudden flash, a tongue of fire seared into the hanging smog and an enormous sonic boom shook through the land and reverberated.

"Look out!" cried Flapbaggles, as the smell of burning stung his nostrils. The cast of hawks and falcons swooped and swirled acrobatically as huge holes began to appear in the noxious cloud which crackled and sizzled as the green vapour started to burn away. Down below, Lava set off on a direct trajectory for Granglethorn Castle, pausing only to scratch at his ear with his hind leg. The centipede that had tracked him since Caesar's Well dropped helplessly to the ground behind him.

Jassaspy screamed in pain at the sudden burst of fire-cat magic and collapsed in a pool of his own slime on the floor. No one dared help him up so it was some time before he had recovered enough to speak.

"This has set me back months!" he hissed. Dog Bottom flew into a panic of his own. With the loss of the centipede, he had lost contact with what was happening with Lava. Would Jassaspy be able to tell? He started sweating in fear at the prospect of discovery.

"Don't worry, he's approaching the castle sire," he said, his nose deliberately pressed to the centipede ball. "Not long now." The sweat was beginning to bead up on his brow. How much longer could he keep this up?

"Is he coming along the valley or the ridge?" asked Jassaspy, anxious to instruct the patrolling sakratts and retrieve something from the situation.

"He's ermm... approaching directly... sire," spluttered Dog Bottom weakly. He sensed Jassaspy tense next to him and heard Hackweezle start to snigger.

The wolves were closing in, and Flapbaggles could see that with their longer gait they would catch Lava in no time on this open ground.

"Time for the flying squad to spring into action!" he announced as he started to dive down through the crackling holes in the smog. Beaks and talons flashed from all directions. Ripsnarl jumped, twisted and snapped his jaws furiously. He caught a feathery wing before talons razed across the top of his head.

"Yeeow!" A sharp cut to a soft tender snout, caused his loyal lieutenant to veer off with a whimper.

"Back to the forest," yelled Ripsnarl, as hot sticky blood glazed his eyes and matted his fur. They ran for cover frantically and watched helplessly, as Lava scampered unheeded towards Granglethorn Castle, their reward of juicy ox-bones receding with each passing step.

"It's not over yet!" cried Flapbaggles. "We need to provide aerial cover until he gets into Granglethorn safely."

Flapbaggles and the cast fanned out, keeping Lava in sight at all times. The spires of the castle loomed up from the valley floor and punctured the poisonous green smog. Lava was heading for the portcullis but something was wrong. It all seemed too easy, as if Granglethorn was expecting him. Was Lava walking into a trap? Calling to the hawks and falcons to give him cover, Flapbaggles went into a sharp dive that took him down towards the portcullis entrance. As he swept closer to the valley bottom, he noticed sakratts emerging to seal off the retreat back down the valley should Lava try to escape by the way he had come. Flapbaggles put a brake on his speed. He had to time this perfectly. Lava was below him now and only a few hundred yards from the portcullis door where the rock-troll was hiding. Now it was only 100! Flapbaggles was careful to keep pace with Lava. Everything depended on the timing: 50 yards - 20 yards -10 - zero! The rock-troll sprang the trap and with a sudden spurt Flapbaggles flew straight up into a net that dropped like a cloak from the top of the portcullis. He bought just enough time for his gingery friend to slip unnoticed through the gates.

The weight of the net threw him to the ground with a bruising thump that he felt far too old to receive. The next thing he knew he was dragged through a cobbled courtyard, dumped in a darkened room and left there entangled to ponder his fate. He didn't have long to wait. The door opened and a chink of light flooded in along with the sound of footsteps. He tried to turn and see who it was, but couldn't move. Then an acrid, burning smell filled his head. What was it? Was something on fire? With a struggle he fit his monocle into his eye but still could see nothing. Then, to his horror, he noticed his wing feathers were curling up with heat. The singeing smell was coming from his own feathers. What were they doing? Were they burning him alive? Somehow he managed to summon the strength to spring to his feet. He looked around sharply and caught his breath. There, inches away from his face, was the open cowl of Jassaspy!

18. Jassaspy's Welcome

"No time, Tanglestep!" Fubbyloofah said firmly. "Bring the kitchen soiled parchment as evidence of your intent and of Stunkensloop's neglect of duty and let us depart at once."

"Fubbyloofah, I appreciate that further delay could prove critical. But to take such a unilateral course of action without the sanction and approval of the Grand Assembly, or even one of the sub-committees is unorthodox and could lead to recriminations. If only there were some sub-clause that I could justify -"

He never got to finish as between Fubbyloofah and Featherfae he was bundled out of the courtyard to get ready for departure. The rest of the afternoon was spent liaising with the peacocks and swallows for transportation to Granglethorn.

When the time for departure finally came, the courtyard struck a fantastic sight. Silvertip had returned with a lamentation of swans and several large wicker baskets like those used for ballooning. The idea was that they'd travel in the baskets carried by 4 swans, each gripping one end of a supporting bamboo frame like the aerial equivalent of a sedan chair. Scott and Jack were delighted.

"We'll show Chloe how it's done eh, Jack?" said Scott grinning from ear to ear. "First one to Granglethorn's the winner."

"You'll do no such thing young man," said Fubbyloofah, who had overheard the conversation. "These swans are doing us a huge favour by transporting us over to Granglethorn and we don't want to demean their gift by playing silly games."

When the swans finally took off, Chloe was more than a little sad.

"I'm sorry Silvertip. I'd love to fly with you again, but I've got such painful lumps on my back I can hardly move."

Silvertip dipped her head and clicked affectionately into her ear. Chloe stroked her long neck before climbing into her basket.

They were soon soaring high into the sky and it was so rejuvenating to get above the hanging green vapour.

"Look at Crambleside," said Jack. "It's virtually covered in green fumes."

"Look who's talking!" Chloe wrinkled her nose. Jack still stank terribly of the raptaggadon's sulphurous breath. Before he could respond she pointed to a convoy of carts driving out of Crambleside. "Hey, what's going on down there?" she asked.

"Let me check," said Tanglestep as he swooped low on the swan that he was riding solo. They heard a fizz and a crackle as a shaft of burning light from his sun-shaft sizzled through the claggy smog. He was soon back, looking very sober. "They're carting off groundluggs!" he said.

"Who? Where?" Questions came at him from all sides.

"Sakratts! Looks like they're taking them to Granglethorn."

"It's just as Job told us," said the Fubbylooffah. "Remember what he said about groundluggs being taken off to serve the slygorm once they put on enough weight."

Tanglestep broke eye-contact and gazed into the far distance deep in thought. When he next spoke it was with an air of renewed vigour.

"The sooner we arrive and awaken the powers in these talismans, the better," he said, as with a shake of the reins he took his swan out of earshot with a graceful swoop.

Far below they could just make out Lake Wintersmere as it shimmered in the early evening light. They couldn't help but notice how solemn Chloe was as she stared across the lake to where Lava had fallen after she had lit the sunfruit. The swans flew fast and steady with a rhythm that eliminated any turbulence, and soon they were over Swelterwater where they had met the moth-man. Jack hooked his wrists around the strands of wicker in case fear made him black out, but it didn't, and after a short while the outline of Ye Olde Dungeon Creek came into view.

"Can we stop for a piece of Feather-Bed Flurry?" Scott grinned across to Fubbyloofah. The answer was short and sweet.

"NO!"

It wasn't long before they were above Roughrigg Tarn where they had first met Silvertip. She couldn't resist plunging into a spectacular dive to skim the water with her proud white chest. Next they passed over the village of Onyx-Stone before beginning the inexorable climb up into Dragmines Valley. The spires of the Granglethorn castle shot up from the valley bottom to pierce through the claggy green smog like gigantic spikes. The swans circled the entire castle, gliding with extraordinary grace and beauty before Tanglestep motioned for them to land gracefully in the inner courtyard bounded by the Towers of the Moon and the Vedic Bells. They landed and disembarked and then a voice from the assembled party of Hebradaigese rang out to greet them.

"Hebradaigen Tanglestep. What a pleasant surprise!"

Tanglestep smiled a welcome back and scanned the assembled throng. The front line parted slightly to make way for the speaker who stepped through to continue effusively.

"- and what a stylish entrance."

He turned to survey the swans who were readying themselves for departure. "It has been so long since we've had the pleasure of your company here at Granglethorn. You simply must tell us all about what you've been up to, dear colleague."

Fubbyloofah and Scott were stunned into open-mouthed silence. There in front of them and gushing with a welcome befitting a long-lost cousin was none other than Jassaspy.

"Greetings, Jassaspy," said Tanglestep, "and thank you for your kind words of welcome. I realise that this visit is impromptu and more than a little unorthodox, but I come with urgent news for the Grand Assembly and request a preliminary hearing at tonight's sitting if that could be arranged," he said, before noticing the interest in his friends. "These here are my travelling companions," he explained with a wave of the hand.

"Ahh, may the sliver of the moon forever kiss the nights that you reside here at Granglethorn." Jassaspy surveyed the group. "I hope you find your stay here will *mirror* your ambitions and provide the *key* to unlock your deepest desires." He looked pointedly at Scott and Jack as he stressed these words. Jack had the sense to mask his feelings with a smile and an appreciative nod whilst inside the moth-man's spores rattled on his chest furiously. Jassaspy clearly knew what talismans they carried and the fact that he had signalled this knowledge left no illusions as to his intent.

"Now, as to your request to address the Assembly tonight, let me see what we can do. After all, it isn't every day that we get a Hebradaigen arriving with a lamentation of swans, and with such - *interesting* guests."

He turned to his colleagues to signal the end of formalities and a warm chuckle rippled around them as they surged forwards curious to know everything they could. The questions came quick and fast:

"Are you a type of under-nourished groundlugg?"

"What do you live on, if not carbalix?"

"How did you come to this land?"

"Why are you here?"

"What do you think of La-Kelisland?"

"Do you like Granglethorn?"

They all did their best to field the questions with harmless platitudes and eventually the hubbub subsided and the Hebradaigese invited the party to enter the castle. They walked across the courtyard towards the central tower. At the base of this was a door and a rather elderly Hebradaigen who looked like he was from the Tower of the Vedic Bells. As they approached he opened the door for them and spoke up.

"Please forgive us for forgetting our manners. We get so few visitors these days and we can get a little carried away. My name is Foggles and on behalf of my fellow Hebradaigese, I'm sorry if we came across as too inquisitorial." He smiled warmly before he continued. "I have just given instructions to prepare quarters for you all. I hope you will not mind if you are billeted in different parts of the castle but we have so few spare rooms these days." He smiled genuinely to reassure everyone before ushering them inside. Once inside they found themselves in the service tunnels that ran underneath the castle. They were labyrinthine and filled with a damp mouldery smell. "Quickly, quickly: we don't want to linger down here," said Foggles much to Jack's relief. The conditions were ideal for the moth-man's spores to multiply and he was struggling to breathe as it was. Foggles seemed very anxious to keep the party moving and kept looking furtively down each tunnel as if expecting something to emerge from them. They all followed close behind and Jack swayed as his fears ran riot.

"For God's sake, Jack, don't black out on us now!" hissed Chloe, nudging him from behind. Tanglestep sparked up his sun-shaft and shone the light down one of the tunnels.

"Uggh. Look!" said Scott. A sticky, tar-coated mass of droppings littered the tunnel floor. He staggered back and a high-pitched shrieking sound erupted around them. Jassaspy's robe was alive with a mass of small convulsions and a rabble of moths suddenly streamed out from his cowl and sleeves squealing in high pitched alarm.

"Fool! Show some consideration for the Creatures of the Night Shade," he hissed pointedly whilst waving irritably at the sun-shaft.

"My apologies, Jassaspy," said Tanglestep as he extinguished his sun-shaft. The moths squeaked before settling and showering them all with the dust from their wings.

"Come my children, come!" said Jassaspy, as one by one, the moths wriggled up the open sleeves of his robe and into the dark cavernous mouth of his cowl.

As they stepped into the anti-chamber of the Grand Assembly, Foggles shuddered and gave a sigh of relief.

"Well, thank heavens we're out of there safely," he muttered half to himself, but not before meaningful glances were exchanged. They quickly turned towards the Chamber of the Grand Assembly when Scott caught a glimpse of something ginger out of the corner of his eye. He nudged Jack furtively.

"Lava! I think I've just seen him: a flash of ginger. Over there," he whispered, taking care not to be overheard by the Hebradaigese. Jack glanced in the direction indicated and humpfed.

"There's nothing there, Scott. Just concentrate on how to use these talismans. Tanglestep said we were to seek nobody, so it's up to me and you to work it out."

Scott nodded. He knew this made sense, but he flung another glance back over his shoulder just to be sure.

Word of their arrival had obviously got round as the Chamber of the Grand Assembly was full of Hebradaigese all eager to meet the visitors. The place buzzed with their chatter and with the background squeak of the scrittlers, small winged mice, who were running up the Assembly walls and occasionally flying across the hammer-beams that supported the roof above. As the Central Committee called the meeting to order they saw that the large chair at the centre of the dais was vacant.

"Why is that chair empty?" whispered Scott as he nudged Tanglestep surreptitiously.

"It's the gatekeeper's chair," replied Tanglestep under his breath. "He hasn't been seen for years."

Scott was about to follow up with further questions when a pealing of bells rang out. There was a huge shuffle of feet as the Hebradaigese rose en-masse and the four High-Lord Hebradaigese, one from each of the four towers, took their places besides the gatekeeper's empty chair.

"Honourable members, and creatures from afar -"

Jack shot a look at Fubbyloofah, who looked faintly amused to be referred to in this way. Featherfae was more preoccupied with taming the leafy twigs in her hair, conscious as she was of everyone's attention.

"Tonight we shall hold a special sitting in response to the request from Hebradaigen Tanglestep who arrived here a short while ago on urgent business and in the company of the erstwhile guests that you see seated besides him."

Hundreds of heads turned towards them and Jack had to fight hard to control the desire to smooth down his own hair, windswept as it still was. The High-Lord Hebradaigen of the Tower of the Sun then rose to draw down the agenda for the meeting of which item number 9 was the accommodation of the travellers. At this point Jassaspy asked leave to interrupt.

"Whilst I am sure that the business of this chamber is of interest and concern to the Hebradaigese, it can be of little amusement to this party of weary travellers. Our debates are involved and detailed and will -" A sprinkle of droppings fell upon him from somewhere high up amongst the hammer-beamed ceiling. "Uggh, those darned scrittlers," he muttered to himself as he brushed himself down before continuing. "Our debates are protracted and will strain their comfort and shame our hospitality. I beg to move to recess until this has been taken care of."

"A most noble sentiment, Jassaspy, and wholly endorsed by us," said the High-Lord of the Vedic Bells, stifling his amusement at the interruption caused by the scrittlers. The other towers quickly concurred and the matter of accommodation was brought swiftly to the top of the agenda. The High-Lord Hebradaigen of the Tower of Reflection rose to introduce Auditicus, the junior warden that had been tasked with the job of finding suitable accommodation. He rose from his bench and approached the inner circle.

"Honourable members, visitors and creatures from afar, I have here the latest Room Utilisation Audit which reveals that the only free rooms in any of the four towers are the boiler rooms." A ripple of dismay ran around the chamber which he allowed to subside before continuing. "We are presuming that Tanglestep will wish to reside in his own tower," he nodded in the direction of the Tower of the Sun. "As for the forest dwellers, they can choose to reside in whichever of the other towers that they wish." Fubbyloofah and Featherfae quickly exchanged glances before electing to stay in the Tower of Reflection and the Tower of the Vedic Bells: both anxious as they were to avoid the Tower of the Moon. "However, as the others are strangers here," Auditicus continued, "the High-Lords of each of the towers have given special dispensation to make available one of their corridor rooms. These are superior rooms that we feel will meet with your expectations. I apologise on behalf of Granglethorn that you will be scattered around the castle but at such short notice we are limited in what we can do." His report delivered, he left the dais to await the visitors and handed the floor once again to Jassaspy.

"Before our guests retire to their comfort I would like to remind the Council of our policies regarding the recovery of ancient artefacts." A ripple of assent ran round the chamber and both Tanglestep and Fubbyloofah tensed uneasily. "It has come to my attention that a Hebradaigen time-key and the Mirror of Aggraides may be back within these castle walls. I am sure that the Council will join me in urging those who have knowledge of their whereabouts to come forward and declare it." He paused to allow the effect of his words to sink in. Jack froze, Fubbyloofah stiffened slightly and Scott, not knowing whether to acknowledge his words or not, simply looked straight ahead. Jassaspy's cowl swung round the chamber and seemed to linger on the boys as he continued to speak. "I need not remind this chamber of the penalties that are due if this does not happen. I would like to add that if the artefacts are delivered *voluntarily* to me, there will be no further questions asked." He bowed graciously and returned to his seat. The party got to their feet more than a little shaken and made to leave the chamber. Scott was about to whisper something to Jack, but was cautioned to silence by a prod in the back from Fubbyloofah's paw.

"We have rooms in the Corridor of the Astral Plane, the Corridor of Dreams, the Corridor of Shadows and the Green Corridor, although I'm sure you'll want to avoid the Green Corridor," said Auditicus as he moved to lead the way.

"Why?" asked Jack boldly.

"Oh, you'll see soon enough," he said cryptically.

The Corridor of the Astral Plane was their first stop and was strangely calm and infused with a gentle incense. It was also festooned with something that everyone immediately recognised.

"Gorse! Oh Jack, Scott, I've gotta stay in this corridor," shouted Chloe eagerly. "Who knows, maybe I'll find dad here somewhere. You know we got gorse signs when he disappeared and -"

"- quiet Chloe," snapped Jack, suddenly aware that Auditicus was looking at her strangely.

"Mmm yes, well at the end of this corridor is the Tower of the Vedic Bells."

"I'll take the room there," said Featherfae keenly. "It seems a safe place for the smoggilars to stay and it will be nice to be virtual room-mates again, eh Chloe?" she beamed.

"Yeah, but without any jumping or stabbing shoes for company this time," she said grinning as Featherfae blushed.

With Featherfae and Chloe settling into their rooms the rest of the party moved on to the Corridor of Dreams. This linked the Chamber of the Grand Assembly with the Tower of the Sun where Tanglestep would reside. Scott made sure he bagged it for himself.

"So we have two rooms left for you to choose from, and both link back to the Tower of the Moon," said Auditicus soberly. Jack's heart sank. It would be his luck. Still, he was the eldest and someone had to stay there. He guessed it made sense for it to be him. Glumly he followed on behind the junior Hebradaigen.

"Let's look first at the room in the Green Corridor. It will satisfy your earlier curiosity and may well suit you considering your penchant for malodorous eggs." He wrinkled his nose and sniffed delicately in Jack's direction. Jack winced and shot Fubbyloofah a look of utter misery. When would he be free of the stench of the raptaggadon?

Immediately they stepped into the Green Corridor, Jack's chest wracked as the moth-man spores flared up and the light faded to a sickly green hue. They walked on for what seemed like hours but in reality was barely a couple of minutes.

"Is it me, Fubbyloofah, or is there sticky green slime all over the floor?" His breathing rasped as he looked down at his feet but he could see nothing there.

"Relax, Jack, and keep your mind clear. This is why they call it the Green Corridor. Don't let the sickness in," said Fubbyloofah. Jack carried on but all the while the sensation of walking through slime remained with him. Eventually, they arrived at the room which was large and spacious with adequate furnishing. There was a window looking over to the Tower of the Vedic Bells and the Corridor of Fears and to an enclosed courtyard below that seemed eerily devoid of both light and life. Jack flicked the light switch and a green glow pulsed and throbbed as it began to fill the room with the same sickly light from the corridor outside. He felt his skin crawl with each wave of light that hit him.

"Can I see the other room please," he said quickly as he switched off the light.

"I said you wouldn't like it," said Auditicus knowingly. Jack, flashed a strained smile and, with an anxious look at Fubbyloofah, swiftly vacated. Every step back towards the Grand Assembly was a step into cleaner, purer air. He gasped, desperate for the rattle of the moth-man spores to subside within his chest. By the time they got back he was panting so loudly that debate in the chamber temporarily ceased.

"Is he alright?" asked the Chair of the Assembly looking across at them both in genuine concern.

"I'm fine," said Jack between gasps. "I just need to catch my breath. I've just been footing it all over this castle and I'm a little exhausted."

"Quite, quite," said the speaker. "Once again, we're sorry that your rooms could not be closer together."

"That's alright. Sorry to disturb your meeting." Jack moved around the perimeter of the chamber in order to proceed towards the Tower of Reflection and from thence to the Corridor of Shadows. The debate re-started but not before Jack felt his skin prickle horribly. He rubbed his arms for relief and at the same time became aware of someone watching him. Who was it? The Hebradaigese were debating again and had forgotten him, but yet? He turned to look back at the inner circle on the dais. The High-Lord Hebradaigen of the Tower of the Sun was gesticulating over some procedural point with his counterpart from the Tower of the Vedic Bells. Even those from the Tower of Reflection were signalling frantically for an opportunity to speak: but not Jassaspy. He sat motionless, looking straight at Jack: tracing his every step;

absorbing his very presence as he walked as fast as he could away from the Green Corridor.

"Even if there's nothing there but a bed of nails, I'll take it," muttered Jack quietly to himself. His thoughts soon translated into equally grateful words on seeing the room.

"That's quite alright. Just glad that we could sort something out at the last minute," said Auditicus. "I shall leave you now. Just to remind you that you can take breakfast in any of the towers. Just roll up in one of the banqueting halls between 7 and 9 unless you want the Tower of the Moon where you shall need to be there at 5am sharp for the 'moon salutations' that always precede it."

"I think we'll give the Tower of the Moon a miss," said Jack as Auditicus stepped back out into the corridor. He flopped down on the bed exhausted. "I am just so relieved to be staying here. Wasn't that Green Corridor creepy?"

"Enough to shrivel your berriblods. But let's not dwell on that now. It's been a long, hard day and I need to get back to my room in the Tower of Reflection for a good night's sleep. Let's breakfast with Tanglestep in the Tower of the Sun, 8 to 8.30am," said Fubbyloofah walking towards the door. Jack murmured agreement and seconds later was fast asleep.

19. The Daughter of Nobody

The sleep that overtook Jack as he lay in his bed in the Corridor of Shadows enveloped him like a wall of heat. With each stretch of his tired limbs he felt it press down on every muscle: soothing, relaxing, nurturing. Within minutes his mind was being swept away to sunny pastures and pleasant scenes from childhood. He drifted so deeply that when he was woken by a sharp clicking sound in the small hours of the night, he snapped awake feeling totally refreshed. It took a couple of seconds for his brain to register where he was and a few seconds more to realise that a strange sound had woken him. What was it? He lay still in the bed, straining to catch the sound again. Nothing! He turned over to go back to sleep. It was 4am. The castle was completely silent. Then he saw it.... a shadow....a woman...in the chair at the foot of his bed. He stared hard, trying not to move in case he attracted attention. The shadow started to move; rocking backwards and forwards in the chair. Then he heard the sound again: clicketty clack, clicketty clack. He stared as hard as he could without moving but could make nothing else out. Then, as quickly as it had appeared, the shadow faded away.

"It's hopeless. I can't sleep," muttered Scott in the Corridor of Dreams as he lay in bed staring at the ceiling. He was far too overexcited about being in Granglethorn and was still convinced that he'd spotted Lava. Perhaps if he explored the corridors whilst the castle was asleep he might see him again. Convinced by this thought, he threw on some clothes and quietly slipped out of the door. The Corridor of Dreams glistened from the starlight that sparkled through the gothic-arched windows that traced its length. He stood for a moment, transfixed by the play of moonlight, before looking across to the Corridor of the Astral Plane. His brow furrowed as he stared at something high above the valley floor. What on earth was it? At first it was too far away to make out any details, but then it drifted closer.

"A man?" he gasped in astonishment. The man was drifting on the wind, his arms flailing helplessly in the air. Did he need help?

Should he wake the castle? The man drifted closer. Something was wrapped around his head and obscuring his face. What was it? He strained to see. A bead of sweat trickled into his eye. Damn it! He caught his breath as he wiped it away. It smeared across his cheek and he blinked to clear his vision. The man was still there and he was coming closer. He could see what it was now: a long red silk scarf was wound tightly round his head. "Totally weird," he mumbled in awe as the wind carried the man over the top of the Corridor of Dreams and towards the Tower of Reflection. Slowly, he receded into the distance, his arms flailing helplessly in the air.

Chloe entered her room in the Corridor of the Astral Plane and immediately knew she was not alone. Featherfae was cooing and billing about the view down to the inner courtyard but Chloe wasn't really listening. She was more preoccupied with something that she could sense swirling around her. What exactly was it? Suddenly she knew. The room contained a patchwork quilt of emotional residue. Up around the ceiling were wispy bands of curiosity and satisfaction. At the back of the room, by the floor, was a small cloud of confusion and hanging in the centre of the room was a large swathe of calm. She walked into it, pausing to let it wash over her. It lapped around her body caressing her back with light feathery touches before going up and over her head like a cool balm. She immediately felt the painful lumps on her back tingle. Featherfae walked over to give her a hug, and walked straight into it, but appeared not to notice - why not? - She said something about breakfast before planting a kiss on her cheek and leaving. Chloe walked to the window where she saw a heavy claggy wisp of despair hanging about 3 feet off the ground. She observed it from a safe distance then raised both hands and with her mind reached into it and drew it to one side. When she looked again, it had moved to where she had mentally put it. She then opened the window and released it into the night sky. She stood by the window and watched it drift off over towards the mountain. She looked again at the emotions swirling around the room and repositioned the band of calm so that it hung over the bed like a floating mantle, then she climbed in. The painful lumps on her back were feeling so much better. Within seconds, she drifted off to sleep.

Breakfast the next morning at the Tower of the Sun was frenetic. Even at this early hour the Hebradaigen were engaged in their 'gaming-debates'. Gathered around the breakfast tables in small groups, they would jump to their feet and wave their debating booklets about frantically whilst outlining their argument. Meanwhile, on-lookers would toss coins on to the table according to how convincing they found them. When the speaker reached a crescendo he would slam his debating booklet down as loudly as possible. There was no aggression in what they did, it was simply an accepted custom and it was generally acknowledged that the louder and more emphatic the slam, the more convincing the argument was felt to be. The banqueting halls were therefore 'lively' places to say the least.

They all met up on the threshold of the hall and were about to go in for breakfast when a voice rang out behind them. It was one of the Ro-Rillian wearing their customary robe adorned with the cloud insignia of the Tower of Reflection. He signalled frantically to them over the heads of the breakfast crowd.

"Good morning guests; Pootlefopp's the name and I'm sorry to disturb you all at this early hour," said a comic, bald headed man with googly eyes and a moustache curled into two large spirals on either cheek. "I'm just checking whether you've got your R.E.S certificates," he asked with a sense of urgency.

"Our what?" asked Jack with a puzzled frown.

"Your R.E.S. You know: 'Room-Entry Safety' certificates. You can't be wandering round Granglethorn without having been certified for R.E.S. It's contrary to 'Health & Safety'."

Chloe looked confused and wrapped herself tightly in a cloak she had found in her chambers whilst Scott looked towards Jack who simply shrugged.

"We'll I suppose we -"

"Come! Come! It won't take a minute," Pootlefopp interrupted whilst ushering them towards a side door. "Now, just stand here whilst I demonstrate."

"Here?" asked Jack.

"Yes. Now, watch. First, grasp the door handle firmly." He checked to see that they were all watching. "Second, turn it to the right. Third, pull the door towards you, taking care not to pull too hard in case you hit yourself on the nose." Scott started to snigger but Pootlefopp was too engrossed in what he was demonstrating to pay him any attention. "Fourth: step through the opening and mind you don't trip! Finally, pull the door closed behind you. Easy, really! Here, have a go." He stepped back and twirled his moustache expectantly.

"But - it's a - certificate for opening a door! What possible use is that?" Chloe glared furiously. Pootlefopp jolted, made a few spluttering noises then recovered his composure.

"We've got educational targets to hit, young lady! Every student certified will earn the accrediting tower, 3 grangle-guilders. Come, come, it will only take a minute. Besides it's not difficult to pass and you can try as many times as you need until you do pass." He grinned foolishly as he opened the door and passed back and forth repeatedly in demonstration. Scott smirked, shrugged his shoulders and followed suit.

"Oh well done, well done!" effused Pootlefopp. "Good firm handling of the door handle. Now, next one please," he said invitingly. Seconds later he was bidding them all farewell. "Now, don't forget the 'Celebration of Achievement' ceremony will be held in The Tower of Reflection next month. See you there for your certificates. Oh, by the way, I recommend the mushrooms for breakfast, they're simply divine!" and with a flourish of a wave, he was gone.

"Absolutely bonkers!" said Scott as their laughter subsided and they went to join Fubbyloofah and Featherfae for breakfast. They followed Pootlefopp's advice and ordered the mushrooms as they were all looking forward to food that didn't wriggle, crawl or fly for a change. Scott grabbed the seat next to Chloe.

"What's with the new cloak?" He said, nudging her playfully in the back. Chloe whirled on him.

"Don't touch me there or have you conveniently forgotten that's where I got kicked?"

"Ok, sorry! Keep your hair on! It was just a friendly pat."

"Do I look like a dog?" she snapped.

"We'll no need to *bark* like one then," muttered Scott pulling a face.

"Oh shut up, Scott, before you disappear into that scarlet cloud of shame you carry round with you," said Chloe bitingly.

"What?" he blanched suddenly. "I'm not ashamed. What have I got to be ashamed of?" he said assertively, desperate to avoid any embarrassing reminders about what happened in the playground with the Puddies.

"Yes: I can see you all for what you are." She looked from one to the other before going through them one by one. "Jack: you live under such a brown cloud of muddy confusion and guilt, it's a wonder you can decide what pair of socks to wear each morning."

"Now wait a minute sis. Who gave you -"

"Stop, Jack! Let her finish. There's more to this than teasing. I think Granglethorn has awakened something in her," said Fubbyloofah quelling all further objections with a paw. He wanted to hear more

"Your aura is emerald green, Fubbyloofah. It has the strength of nature in it. And Featherfae: yours is golden, full of radiant joy!"

"What's she on about?" said Jack, irked but curious.

He never got an answer as they were all distracted by the arrival of Tanglestep who looked harried and worn out as he weaved his way through the tables of fellow Hebradaigese towards them. He jumped as a colleague to his left slammed his debating booklet down so hard that the book spine cracked. There was an instant cheer of "Bravo!" and his proposal that only slippers containing live silk-worms be worn in the Corridor of Whispers was passed for debate at the next meeting of the Grand Assembly. He sat down at their table but it was clear that his mind was still racing over the detail of last night's debate.

"Tanglestep?" said Featherfae. She gazed softly at him letting her eyes do all the talking. He acknowledged her concern with a smile.

"I can't stay long, I'm afraid. Further hearings are being arranged. I must get back to the policies and procedures," he said with a wan smile. "I have a horrible feeling that I may have overlooked something significant."

Fubbyloofah looked over at Featherfae and was sad to note that a little of her joyful spark had gone. Her face was lined with worry as she spoke the words that everyone felt.

"Dear Tanglestep, whatever it is, it can wait. You were on the road for a whole day yesterday and you were in council virtually all night. Just give yourself a break. Take an hour off. Have a leisurely breakfast and let's go round Granglethorn together before you dive back into those committees."

Tanglestep looked around at the sea of expectant faces and wavered.

"Please Tanglestep," urged Jack. "Weird things happened last night that we don't understand. We need you to explain."

Tanglestep hesitated for a moment before breaking out into a huge smile. "Ok, so be it. The breakfast sitting won't finish for another hour so I guess this time is yours."

Scott whooped with delight and relief flooded across Featherfae's face as she reached out to stroke the back of his hand tenderly.

"So what's for breakfast this morning then?" he asked sniffing the air. Jack described the various options and how they had each chosen the fried mushrooms. Tanglestep winced at the mention of this.

"I'm surprised you can bring yourselves to eat those; can't you hear them?" he asked, pursing his lips in recollection of something distasteful. Alarmed looks immediately shot round the table.

"What do you mean *hear* them?" asked Jack.

"Exactly what I said. Come and look for yourselves, if you want. It's an open kitchen." Seconds later they were watching the chefs at work.

"They're just mushrooms sizzling away, Tanglestep. I don't know what all the fuss is about."

"Are they? Listen."

At first they could hear nothing but the sizzle of the frying pan but then…. It was almost imperceptible but... Scott and Jack looked at each other in complete shock. It was not sizzling that they could hear.

"They're squealing! I can't believe it. They're actually hopping about the pan getting roasted alive!" Jack reeled backwards.

"Oh, my God - gotta change my order!"

"Me too," said Scott as the colour drained from both their faces. They signalled frantically to the chef whilst Fubbyloofah shook his head and muttered something about the sad state of culinary affairs these days. When breakfast finally arrived, the porridge that they had opted for had the texture and taste of sawdust. Needless to say, they were keen to distract themselves by recounting their experiences of their first night in the castle.

"I'm afraid I can't explain these happenings," said Tanglestep soberly after they'd finished. "Have you tried looking into the Mirror of Aggraides for answers, Scott?"

"Darn it! Of course, let's ask Willow!" After the events of last night who knew what she would reveal. Scott pulled out the mirror and she drifted into view.

"Scott, the time is almost ripe," Willow seemed anxious, "but you must wait for the keyholder. Only he will be able to find the keyhole. Be ready for the next time that the moon wanes: that is the time that the time splinters can be unlocked for ever."

He drew breath sharply then held the mirror out to his brother.

"Here, Jack," he said in a sober voice.

"No way, bro! There's no way I'm looking into that mirror again. All I see is the old woman of death. I can do without that, thank you very much."

"But Jack, you're the keyholder. You gotta be ready to use the mirror to find the keyhole." There was a heavily pregnant pause before Jack jumped to his feet.

"Come on, it's time we explored this castle," he said, keen to put some distance between himself, the mirror and his brother's suggestion. He strode towards the door purposefully.

"Hold on, Jack!" laughed everyone as they ran to catch up with him.

Once through the Chamber of the Grand Assembly, they were soon at the entrance to the Corridor of Whispers and Tanglestep motioned for quiet. A rush of wind immediately enveloped them all.

"What – afterwards – light – you," said Jack, his words whipped away by the wind.

"..tiful – always – their – red," said Scott to a sea of blank faces. Tanglestep signalled for silence and gestured for them to follow. They walked on for a couple more minutes.

"Will you dare refuse to give Jassaspy what he wants?" a voice whispered as clear as day. Scott jolted and swung round. There was nobody there.

"It's time to look in the mirror again. I am waiting for you there," said another voice that only Jack could hear.

"..step – out – voices," mouthed Jack and Scott helplessly as they tugged at Tanglestep's sleeve. He looked sharply from one to the other and signalled for them to cover their ears.

They were 50 yards from the Tower of Reflection when a flash of light through the corridor window distracted them. Chloe immediately ran to the window to investigate. The others quickly followed. At first all they could see were the imposing battlements of the Tower of the Moon opposite. But then their eyes drifted downwards. Far below, they could just make out the edge of a garden at the bottom of the light-well that encircled the basement rooms of the Tower of Reflection. Most of it was concealed from view by the angle from which they were viewing, but in the garden were three figures. One was a woman with long black hair and a cloak of exquisite colour and with her was something that was indistinguishable, apart from its colour, which was brilliant white. But it was the third creature which interested them most. Standing in the garden next to them was a small creature that pulsed with golden light.

"LAVA!" shouted Chloe. Tanglestep frantically signalled for quiet as the whispers started up again in earnest.

"Give up the sunfruit," they urged.

"Never!" shouted Chloe. She could see Tanglestep's blue swirl of honesty up ahead as he beckoned them into the Tower of Reflection.

"Not even to find your father?" promised the whispers.

"What? Is dad here somewhere?" Her fingers closed around sunfruit and it was half out of her pocket when she felt a hand on her back. Suddenly the breath was knocked out of her and the tower door closed behind her. There was a rush of wind as the voices stopped instantly.

"You were about to jump from the window!" said Featherfae shakily whilst at the same time casting Tanglestep a concerned look. His brow furrowed.

"Whatever it was that those voices were saying to you, you must ignore them," he said firmly. Chloe caught her breath. Her mind was a fog of confusion as were the others too. Gaping mouths fired questions like arrows but Tanglestep brushed them all away except the ones about the garden below. "That lady has barely moved from that garden in the last decade," he said soberly.

"Why? Who is she?" asked Chloe who suddenly felt an urgent need to meet her.

"She's the Daughter of Nobody. She has -"

"- NOBODY?" interrupted Scott, excitedly. "'SEEK NOBODY'." Everyone turned to look at him as if he'd gone mad. "That's what you said in Treadmail Tower when you were in the trance holding my talisman."

"Bless my berriblods! That's right. You did!" chimed Fubbyloofah. Tanglestep smiled with a dawning realisation on his face.

"Broken sun-shafts! Why didn't I think of it before? Seek out the Daughter of Nobody! Quick, let's get down there. I don't have much time before the committees start up again."

At the bottom of the tower Tanglestep used his master key on the old oak door. Moments later they stepped into the garden and a piercing shriek rent the air. Scott jumped back in fright and immediately felt the shadows closing in.

"Oh no; not again!" he wailed as inky blackness seeped over his eyes and everything faded to shades of grey. The woman was sitting on the grass enwrapped in a cloak of autumnal leaves and stroking a large white bird. She rustled her cloak and something in the ripple of colour broke through the shadow-sylph's icy grip. Scott jolted back with a coughing fit. His grateful eyes met hers and she smiled. Just then, the shriek reverberated around the light-well once more. It was coming from the bird, which just then got to its feet and fanned out its stunning white tail feathers. Time stood still for a moment as everyone gasped at its beauty.

"Now droops the milk-white peacock," said the Daughter of Nobody with a wistful smile, as the bird re-settled itself by her side. As it did so, a gentle shower of snow flakes started to fall down on the garden.

"Where have *they* come from?" said Jack out loud in wonder. Chloe and Scott were too enthralled to comment.

Her glance travelled from one to other and she shimmered with a brilliant white light as she breathed deeply. Her gaze lingered longest on Featherfae.

"A wood nymph. I see that you too live in the garden of your inner thoughts and desires." The Daughter of Nobody smiled as the twigs and the love-lies-bleeding in Featherfae's hair quivered at her words.

"Life is a cycle of hope and desires that are nurtured by memories of what is, what has been and what could have been," said Featherfae, as she stepped forwards and, with surprising familiarity, placed a comforting hand on the lady's arm. The Daughter of Nobody's eyes shone with empathy. She gestured for everyone to take a seat on the grass amongst the falling snowflakes before explaining that the fire-cat had already gone.

"I knew someone would come for him. I'm glad it is you," she said whilst stroking little Tumbleweed under his chin.

"Has he left for World's End?" asked Fubbyloofah anxiously

"Not yet. He still seeks burnt gold and then there is the matter of the time splinter. He is worried for you both." She nodded towards Scott and Jack.

"I'm worried about us too," said Jack. "We have both been touched by a shadow-sylph and I'm supposed to be the Elven Prince yet I haven't a clue about -"

"Ok, OK," Featherfae gestured for calm as Tanglestep was anxious to describe their night-time visions. The Daughter of Nobody grew wistful as she listened and the snowfall morphed into a shower of autumnal leaves: wonderful wine coloured leaves and flakes of a deep orange and brilliantine yellow.

"Wow! How does she do that?" mumbled Scott to himself as he revelled in the visual spectacle. Chloe just sat transfixed as she sensed the workings of something spectral.

"Ahh Granglethorn: so full of spirits and strange phenomena," said the Daughter of Nobody under her breath once Tanglestep had finished. They all looked at her quizzically. "It is all a question of spiritual alignment," she said. "Granglethorn has woken to your presence and speaks to all of you in different ways."

"But what does it mean? The man floating in the air with a scarf wrapped around his head and face?" asked Scott in frustration.

"- and that creepy woman at the foot of my bed?" said Jack.

"I can't say. It would be wrong for me to suggest a meaning. The visitations are for you alone to interpret. They may be manifestations of what is past or what might yet come to pass. Trust in your instincts and be true to them and to each other. That way you will weave your way unhindered through this spectral labyrinth."

She sighed deeply as if remembering something painful and then looked around at her garden and plants. Featherfae followed her look and reached out a comforting hand intuitively.

"So many bare patches these days," said the Daughter of Nobody shaking her head at the intermittent patches of bare earth where once flowers and shrubs grew.

"Please don't despair, dear lady," said Featherfae gently. "Let me help you. Flowers spring from my footsteps. It's one of the things I can do. Let me share my gift with you," she beamed warmly. The Daughter of Nobody smiled gently but remained lost in sadness.

"You don't understand," she explained. "Many, many years ago I lost all memories of my family and my past. I retreated here to piece the past together. Where I have been successful my garden has flourished but as memories slip through the hour-glass of my mind, my plants wilt," she explained sadly. "It is too painful to see the gaps where memories once were. Look over there by the Lily of the Valley. The earth around is bare. All I remember of that is a hot summer and laughter; lots of laughter. We were by the river that flows through Dragmines valley. But I can't even remember who I was with. I think it was my family but I'm not sure anymore." She stopped and squeezed Featherfae's hand.

"Let us help you," said Fubbyloofah. "I can dig up the soil in no time with these claws." He flexed them vigorously before moving towards a bare patch of earth.

"No, don't you see? It's the memories that matter. There is nothing anybody can do if the memories are gone. If you want to help then help yourselves and hold on to your thoughts, dreams and memories, however painful they may be."

"I know how you could be free of this pain," said Tanglestep softly. "Live in the 'now'. Forget the past and the pain it brings you."

"No, that way lies a life empty of meaning," she said, shaking her head. "The future exists only in the framework of the past. Life without it becomes a groundless void: an inevitable wait for death."

There was a pregnant pause before Featherfae's boundless enthusiasm spilled forth.

"Come with *us*. Help us! Help the fire-cat, and through doing this, journey in ways that you journeyed in the past. Through such journeys you will experience feelings that you had long ago before you shut yourself away. Through these feelings memories will seep back to nourish the present and water your garden."

At these words, the Daughter of Nobody exhaled deeply and as she did the autumnal leaves were replaced by a strong shaft of warming sunshine. Smiles broke out around the party as the scent of blossom suddenly filled the air. Then, as quickly as it had come, it subsided and a tear slowly gathered in her eye.

"I just wish I could remember something about my family but may the sun bless you, Featherfae, for your kind words." She rose from the grass and walked back towards the Tower of Reflection. "Come, you may be right. It is time for me to leave. Let's see if my old room at the top of this tower is still vacant."

20. Secrets of the Time Splinter

The door to her old room creaked open, and she gasped as recollections flooded back. A thick layer of dust covered everything and cobwebs trailed backwards and forwards like a giant cats-cradle.

"My, my, how long have I languished down there?" she said as she trailed a finger through the dust. Tanglestep gestured to the boys to take out their talismans.

"May I?" asked the Daughter of Nobody as both boys fiddled with them impatiently.

"Me, first!" said Scott pushing Jack out of the way and handing his over.

"Ahh, the Mirror of Aggraides. This is the window to the keyhole of the time splinter, but you'll also need -" she broke into a smile when she saw what Jack was twirling through his fingers, "- the key to unlock it."

"But what's so important about a time splinter?" asked Jack and Scott simultaneously, aware that everyone was listening intently. She sighed and drew her cloak of autumnal leaves tightly around her before replying.

"A time splinter is a link in time. When it occurs, time in your world and ours is the same for a very brief moment. It is a moment fraught with great danger yet also infinite promise"

"In what way?" asked Fubbyloofah, suddenly piqued with curiosity. She turned towards Tanglestep.

"Do you remember the Lost Runes of Rapgallion? The sacred texts that went missing at the same time as the gatekeeper disappeared?" she asked. Tanglestep shook his head solemnly. "Do none of the Hebradaigese understand what they are dealing with?" she added ruefully. "The texts explain how a time splinter allows our sun to draw power from another. If time splinters were never to happen, then our sun would simply die. It cannot survive long without a time splinter," she said soberly.

"So that's why Jassaspy is so interested in our talismans. He wants to kill off the sun?" said Jack angrily. Now more than ever he needed to offload the key. "Please, take the key and stop him. I know I'll fail if I keep it. I couldn't even use it to save my.." He tailed off despondently. It was just too shameful to put into words.

"But what about burnt gold and World's End? Isn't this the way to save the sun? asked Featherfae.

"You talk of the old fire-cat magic. If it is true, then this would indeed blast open the constraints on time and save the sun. The problem is that nobody knows in what form burnt gold can be found, or even if it still exists," she answered softly.

"So why don't we do it now?" asked Scott waving his mirror in the air eagerly. "I'll use the mirror to find the keyhole and Jack can use the key".

The Daughter of Nobody burst into spontaneous laughter and temporarily disappeared in a blaze of brilliant white light. "It's not that easy Scott. The window won't reveal the location of the keyhole until it is returned to the exact place from where it was taken."

"And where's that?" They clamoured in unison. A heavily pregnant pause followed before a familiar voice chirped up beside them.

"I know where it is!"

"WHAT? How would *you* know?" They whirled round open-mouthed to stare at their sister.

"It's obvious really?"

"Huh?"

"Of, course. If you could only step out from under those clouds of negative emotion, you'd realise it too." She swept the air above their heads as if trying to clear it away then gave up with a shrug. "It's the Corridor of the Astral Plane, of course!"

All eyes turned to the Daughter of Nobody but it was Chloe who explained.

"Yes. Didn't you notice it was full of gorse? It *has* to be the place!" The Daughter of Nobody smiled cryptically before continuing.

"Both talismans must be used together: at the right time and only by the right individual. Anything else would be -" she shrugged despondently rather than finish the sentence.

"Willow said that the time to release a time splinter is at the next waning of the moon," said Scott ominously.

"That's in a couple of days' time," said the Daughter of Nobody. Scott swallowed hard and shot Jack a glance, but Jack's mind was on something else that the Daughter of Nobody had said.

"But, how do we know which one of us is the 'right person'?" he asked tentatively. She looked them both in the eye and took hold of their hands solemnly.

"You won't. You'll have to trust to instinct," she said simply.

Suddenly, Tanglestep bolted upright: "The committee!" he shouted in alarm. "I'll be late for the committee." In a panic he apologised for having to leave so abruptly and promised to return tomorrow morning for breakfast.

"Before I go take some grangle-guilders," he said as he distributed some coins to the party. "They're very useful. Whatever the price of the goods you are buying they will always appear to the vendor as full payment." They were all fascinated but Tanglestep had no time to explain further and bolted down the staircase.

Overwhelmed by the significance of their talismans, Scott and Jack were both now anxious to secrete them away somewhere safe on their person.

"Why won't it close?" Scott muttered as his fingers fumbled frantically with the button on his pocket whilst Jack, meanwhile, was trying to hide the key as close to his skin as he could without swallowing it. The Daughter of Nobody laughed gently.

"Relax both of you! Nobody can steal them from you. If taken by force the talismans are rendered inanimate. Only if freely given can they be wielded successfully."

The boys stopped in their tracks.

"So that's why Jassaspy asked for them to be given up voluntarily at that first meeting in the chamber," said Scott.

"- and that's also why his sakratt didn't take the key when I dropped it during the ambush in Crambleside," said Jack. "I never could understand that."

Both boys felt a lot more reassured now and it was with a confident swagger that they trudged down to the banqueting hall of the Tower of Reflection for dinner later that evening. As they approached they saw an excitable cluster of Hebradaigese surrounding the newspaper vendors. The vendors were clanging their bells and shouting out the headlines desperate to be heard over the slamming of the debating books around them.

"Granglethorn Gazette….Granglethorn Gazette….. Cuss-Cuss Tatty claims new victim…..Read all about it!"

The buzz of activity that this ignited was too much to bear. Fubbyloofah grabbed a copy and passed the vendor a grangle-guilder.

"The exact amount, sir. Thank you."

"...*and* this copy of the Granglethorn Gossip too please," said Scott on spotting a more salacious rag.

"...*and* these candied fish eyes," said Chloe, shrugging cheekily. "Well, if you can't beat 'em, join 'em," she muttered in response to the look of reproach on Jack's face.

"That'll be an extra 40, squire."

"Oh, I think you'll find that coin covers everything."

"Nice try. Nice try," said the vendor whose grin faded as he looked again at the grangle-guilder in his hand. "Well, I'll be blown. So it does. I must be going blind."

They grinned in delight, and Scott reached for a packet of smoked bumblebulbs, eager to exploit the grangle-guilder's limitless potential. It took a glare from Fubbyloofah to rein him in. They were soon pouring over the articles in silence.

"THE GRANGLETHORN GAZETTE"

Cuss-Cuss Tatty claims new victim

For the second time this week the service tunnels under the Chamber of the Grand Assembly have played host to the horror that has come to be known as the Cuss-Cuss Tatty. At approximately 05.30 hours this morning, just as the moon was retiring from the skies, Hebradaigese from the Tower of the Vedic Bells discovered the mutilated remains of a sakratt. This is the second sakratt death in the tunnels in the last few days and bears all the hallmarks of the Cuss-Cuss Tatty. Both victims were found covered in thousands of insect stings and scoured with deep flesh-wounds. The surrounding area, in both cases, showed signs of a struggle with smears of tar marking the body and the scene of the attack. A strong mouldering smell surrounded the scene of death. The Central Committee of the Chamber of the Grand Assembly have issued a decree that none other than service personnel be allowed into the service tunnels and that they are required to consult their respective Tower Risk Assessments before doing so. Informed sources report that no decisive strategy is yet in place on how to deal with the mounting emergency."

"Well, well. What's all this about?" Fubbyloofah looked at the Daughter of Nobody but she was just as much in the dark as he was. Current events rarely percolated down to her garden.

"Let's see what this one says before jumping to conclusions," said Featherfae. They read on.

"THE GRANGLETHORN GOSSIP"

"Jassaspy fingers Tower of Sun over Cuss-Cuss Tatty"

In what can only be described as the clearest sign yet of deep divisions amongst the Central Committee of the Chamber of the Grand Assembly, High-Lord Hebradaigen Jassaspy flung moths in the face of his counterpart from the Tower of the Sun after hearing that another of his sakratts was found dead last night in the service tunnels. Furious that the tar-coated creature referred to as the Cuss-Cuss Tatty has now claimed a second of his sakratts in the last few days, Jassaspy accused the other High-Lords of "gross complacency" and threatened to pursue a policy of bureaucratic obstruction against all future Grand Assembly business if the other towers did not act decisively to rid Granglethorn of the Cuss-Cuss Tatty once and for all. Inside sources say this is Jassaspy's first move towards claiming the vacant seat of the gatekeeper. Intrigue! We at the Granglethorn Gossip applaud his no-nonsense approach and say, "Go, Jassi, Go!"

"This explains why everyone was so twitchy when we arrived in Granglethorn," said Jack. "They couldn't wait to ferry us up through those tunnels. Don't you remember?"

"Yes. It makes you wonder just how safe it is to go wandering round this castle," said Fubbyloofah.

"Don't worry, we're all certified," grinned Scott, thinking of his Room-Entry Safety certificate; but it was lost on Fubbyloofah who was more concerned about other matters.

"If they don't sort this out quickly, pretty soon there'll be open conflict above ground too. The Towers of the Sun and the Moon are squaring up for a fight by the looks of things."

They trudged into the dining hall to find that dinner consisted simply of different types of 'parchment pie': a classic Hebradaigen dish of filo sheaves of parchment pastry, encasing inky cubes of something indiscriminate but chewy.

"We'll need lashings of beetle juice to wash it down," said Fubbyloofah eyeing up the adjoining table where the Hebradaigese were already spluttering flakes of parchment everywhere. One of them looked up as they spoke.

"Don't worry," he said. "We like it extra dry! We specially requested a pie with pastry made from the minutes of the Sub-Committee on Administrative Affairs. It's partic…" he exploded into a coughing fit, his voiced clagged by the flakes of parchment.

"It's OK, we get the message," said Fubbyloofah, who nodded understandingly as the Hebradaigen reached for yet more beetle juice.

"As long as it doesn't squeal I'll be happy with it," said Jack.

"Beetle wings don't squeal and you complained about that bro," said Scott, grinning at the memory. Jack scowled back as Fubbyloofah passed the menu.

"Don't choose anything as dry as what those chaps are having." He lent over to point at certain dishes. "So I would urge you all to avoid this 5 year cyclical report on *'Room Utilisation Audits'.*" Featherfae wrinkled her nose in distaste over his shoulder.

"Uggh, we certainly don't want that one", said Scott, pointing to a pie made from a parchment entitled *'Hebradaigen Health Care vol. 6: In-growing toe-nails and the benefits of a silk-worm slipper.'*

"No, the subject matter doesn't exactly do much for one's appetite does it?" hummed Fubbyloofah.

"This sounds the best," said Jack indicating another entitled: *'The Corridors of Granglethorn: unravelling the spectral labyrinth.'*

"Oh yeah, for me too! Wonder if it'll explain about the floating man," said Scott.

"…or the bands of emotion I can see everywhere," said Chloe under her breath as she chose the same.

"I'll have this one," said Fubbyloofah pointing to *'Scrittlers: a scourge on the democratic process: a list of debates foreshortened due to droppings from on high'.* "Let's hope it doesn't taste of its subject matter." He looked around expecting a reaction but they were all far too excited by their own choice to notice that he had ordered a pie made from a paper on mouse droppings. Meanwhile,

Featherfae quietly opted for '*The Whys and Wherefores of a Granglethorn Gavotte: a study in Hebradaigen courtship rituals and 17th century dance*'. Fubbyloofah chuckled. "Three guesses as to what you hope to find in there," he winked.

21. The Trial of Tanglestep

Jack returned to his chamber in the Corridor of Shadows with a sense of trepidation. As he climbed into bed, he placed his talisman on the bedside table beside him and was asleep within half an hour. He slept solidly and undisturbed for the next 5 hours until he was woken by the same clicking sound as before. This time he was determined to face it down. Without bothering to feign sleep he sat bolt upright and looked straight at the figure seated at the bottom of the bed. It was the same shadow and she was making the same clicking noises as before but this time he could see what she was doing. She was knitting. It was the sound of knitting needles, clicking and clacking as she sat rocking in the chair at the bottom of his bed.

"Who are you?" he said in as deep a voice as he could muster. There was no reply. "I said, 'who are you?' Why are you here? What do you want with me?" The knitting stopped and Jack felt a moment of absolute panic at the void of possibilities that suddenly opened up. Then the shadow raised her head and looked him straight in the face. He choked back a cry as he recognised her face. It was her, the one in the mirror: the old woman of death!

Over in the Corridor of Dreams, Scott was buzzing with excitement. "I know I'll find the exact spot for this mirror. It's only a matter of time." He savoured the images of himself as the hero who saved the sun. The waning of the moon, a time splinter: nothing would be beyond him then. "The sooner morning comes, the better," he murmured as he tossed and turned in his bed in frustration. But sleep would not come. Finally, in a state of frenzied agitation, he got up and went out into the corridor. Would that floating man be outside again? He rushed to the window but there was nothing out there.

"Damn! What now?" he said to himself. Now that he was up should he explore the corridor or maybe go deeper into the castle? No sooner had the thought entered his head than he was there or at least he was somewhere else; but where? He was no longer outside his bedroom door that much was sure. He looked along the corridor but struggled to see more than a few feet in front of him. Then, a thick green mist swirled all around. He turned to run in the opposite direction but it was like wading through treacle. He looked down in horror to see them mired in slime.

"Not the Green Corridor?" he wailed in fright. But how had he got here? In a panic he pulled out his talisman. "Willow! Willow!" He shook his talisman desperately. Where was she? He felt a rush of air accompanied by a deep groaning sigh. Now the green mist was encircling him, clinging, burning his legs. He cried out in pain, and then...

"Scott. I'm here. You don't need to worry anymore. I know who the keyholder is," she said with a sympathetic smile. He gasped in both pain and relief before doubt washed over him.

"What do you mean? It's Jack, Jack's the key holder... *isn't he?*" When she next spoke it was in a soft, gentle voice.

"It is time to unkiss the oath twixt you and me."

"WHAT? What do you mean? I don't understand."

He bolted upright, breathing heavily. He was in his bed in the Corridor of Dreams. He looked around anxiously. The room was exactly as it had been when he went to sleep, except that he felt different. Something was wrong. His mind raced before he threw the bedclothes off and to his horror saw the burns on his legs. He sat and stared for a few seconds before he reached over to his jacket. His hands patted the pockets in a panic. The Mirror of Aggraides had gone!

Chloe now felt absolutely convinced that she was close to finding her father. The gorse festooned throughout the Corridor of the Astral Plane was a sign: a sign that she still had to interpret, but a sign nonetheless. She stood in the centre of her chamber watching the bands of emotion swirling around in a knot of confusion. Then slowly, ever so slowly, they started to unravel. She darted a look over her shoulder to check she was alone before she cast off her cloak. A huge pair of gossamer fairy wings unfolded from the lumps on her back. She twitched them lightly before launching herself airborne. She hovered and floated within the emotional sea all around her: sensing, probing, judging and slowly, ever so slowly understanding. Gradually she returned to sit down by the window. She folded her wings back up and thoughts of the day flitted across her mind: a time splinter, the talismans, and Lava. She made sure that warm bands of security were positioned over her bed before climbing in. Then she felt it; a hard object tucked under her pillow. She reached underneath and pulled out a silk-wrapped parcel, the size and shape of a small book. Where had this materialized from? Something told her not to unwrap it so she placed it on her bedside table before reaching under her bed to draw out a pale yellow band of compassion. She draped it over where her head would rest then closed her eyes and fell asleep. As she did so, her essence ascended into the air above her body and slowly floated out into the Corridor of the Astral Plane.

I've gotta find Scott and check whether that old woman's still in the mirror. Dawn had broken and Jack could wait no longer. He grabbed the time-key and dashed into the Corridor of Shadows. A split second later he was choking on dry dust and tiny scuttling legs were everywhere, scrabbling over his body. Insects! He brushed them off frantically. Deep inside his chest the moth-man spores rattled. *Can't breathe! So dark! So musty!*

"You need to look where you're going," rasped a voice in front of him. "I won't wish you a 'good morning', as no morning is ever good. But, I trust you were nourished by the night. Your brother certainly was."

Jack gaped at a loss for words. It was Jassaspy and in his haste to find Scott he'd run straight into him. This was too much to take in: Jassaspy right outside his room. His skin crawled at the close encounter: those horrible insects! He shivered as his eyes flickered over his arms and legs again.

"What ... what do you mean?" he stammered, still distracted by the moths which were still on him. He was aware of the dust from their wings peppering his clothes.

"Only that your brother visited the Green Corridor last night." Jassaspy smiled from deep within his cowl. "Now I wait only for your sister," he said. "Once all three of you have tasted the air of the 'Green' then you will be ready to surrender to me that which I am waiting for." His cowl tilted in the direction of the gothic key in Jack's hand.

"Never!" Jack choked on the words and felt himself beginning to sway. In a panic, his eyes darted along the corridor: it was deserted. Could there be a worse time to black out?

"You're being pulled into the world of the shadow-sylph, Jack. Spare yourself this constant torture. Give up the key and I swear I'll cleanse you of her touch."

There was a brief pause. Jack ached with the desire to be free from this nightmare and fidgeted with the key indecisively.

Why shouldn't I? Why not? I couldn't resist even if I wanted to. I won't be able to use it anyway; I'll just black out. And as for this Elven Prince that I'm supposed to be... He sighed heavily feeling nothing but a fraud. Jassaspy quivered in anticipation.

"Just drop it in my hand. That's all you need to do."

How tempting it was: the delicious consciousness of failure and submission: to be free of these expectations. His heart raced at the prospect. Then images started to drop into his mind: one by one. First it was daisies in the footsteps of Featherfae, then crocklepips grinning cheerfully from the chimney. Soon the images were coming thick and fast: puffleflies, poppletons, the smoggilars, Flapbaggles and the Conference of the Wing, not to mention his friends Fubbyloofah and Featherfae. All creatures that depended on him doing the right thing.

"No!" He croaked through the descending sleep fog. He looked up at the frayed moth-eaten cowl that hovered in front of him. A worm crawled back inside and a wave of revulsion swept over him.

"I SAID 'NO'!" He swayed briefly and then collapsed at Jassaspy's feet.

Breakfast in the Tower of Reflection was a sober affair this morning. Scott was sullen and withdrawn.

"The Mirror of Aggraides has gone!" he muttered guiltily whilst rubbing at his legs. He was in the process of explaining what had happened when a rabble of moths suddenly appeared out of nowhere. "I hate the ways these things leave you covered in dust," he said as, along with the others, he swatted them away. They were all so busy that no one noticed Chloe jolt to her feet in utter fascination.

A deep purple haze with an inky black centre was swirling towards them like a whirlpool. *What emotional turmoil was this?* Like a parched bedouin on the brink of an oasis, Chloe gaped in astonishment, eager to probe, feel, absorb. A deep primal force was pulling at her. Slowly the purple haze dissolved and she gasped to find Jassaspy standing in front of them. He was with two of the Ro-

Rillian from the Tower of Reflection. But then voices rang out around her as everyone saw what he held in his arms.

"JACK! What have you done to him?" cried Featherfae as she and Scott jumped to their feet. There was a sharp crack as Scott caught his knee on the table and groaned in pain.

"Put him down: now!" Fubbyloofah bristled in alarm. The dark cowl swung round to centre on him and a thin plume of green vapour oozed out. It hung in wispy tendrils around his head like a be-fouled halo. Jack lay limp and lifeless in his arms. A slug had settled on his lip and woodlice scurried freely over him.

If you're still inside me, then now is the time to show yourself again. Scott silently tried to invoke the djinn inside him from its slumber, but it was to no avail. Jassaspy stepped forward and gently laid him down in a chair beside them.

"The touch of the shadow-sylph is upon him. He will recover shortly." Jassaspy laid his hand on him. There was a brief flurry of activity as the flock of woodlice scrabbled back to the sanctity of his robes. With exquisite tenderness he prised the slug from Jack's lip and held it up to the light to admire its sticky secretions. Then he turned to observe everyone as he popped it into his cowl. They caught the flicker of a yellowed tongue then heard a faint slurp from within.

"What about the time-key?" Scott blurted out before he felt the jab of an elbow in his ribs. A glare from Fubbyloofah was enough to shut him up and he cursed himself silently for being so stupid. Suddenly Jack came to and felt his stomach heave.

"Oh my God! Where am I?" He whirled around towards Chloe who just stood as if in a trance. Jassaspy sniggered gently before clearing his throat.

"I am not about to take something unless it is freely given." He indicated Jack's pocket where the head of the key was clearly visible. "I am here on official business, so if I may be allowed to continue." He paused for a moment to allow the tension to ebb away.

"Hebradaigen Tanglestep of the Tower of the Sun and currently under posting to Treadmail Tower…" There was something unsettling about the stiff formality of address. "It is my sad duty to inform you that under Granglethorn Personnel Procedures I am suspending you with immediate effect following your neglect of duties that fall within the core remit of the Hebradaigese. The relevant policies for your information are: Duty of Care section 4.3 sub-section B3 and B8, and from the Duty Specifics, item 2.5 and 7.4"

Featherfae gave a heartfelt wail before a stunned silence fell like a cloak over the breakfast table. Tanglestep's face was lined with tiredness from the endless committee meetings he'd been attending. He looked at the accompanying Ro-Rillian before returning to Jassaspy.

"What exactly are you alleging I've done?"

"All will be revealed in due course," said Jassaspy. "Meanwhile, I must ask you to surrender your sun-shaft and accompany us to the Chamber of the Grand Assembly where special quarters will be assigned for you to prepare your defence. I need not remind you that in the interim you are to have no contact with other Hebradaigese nor with anyone seated at this table."

"Now wait a minute!" said Fubbyloofah, rising from his seat and sending a cloud of moths fluttering into the air

"Please don't," said Tanglestep softly but with a grateful smile. "It will only make things worse." He turned to Jassaspy before continuing. "If you would kindly permit me to finish my breakfast, I would be grateful." Jassaspy nodded slowly and with his two colleagues retreated to wait discretely by the door.

"What can we do to help? There must be something. He can't get away with this," said Featherfae anxiously.

"Try and find Lava. We know he's in the castle somewhere. My best line of defence is to prove that Jassaspy has acted with extreme prejudice towards him and sought to conceal his presence from the Grand Assembly." They nodded urgently but deep down were anxious. How could they hope to find Lava in this spectral labyrinth?

Half an hour later it was time. Tanglestep caught Featherfae's eyes and blew a sad silent kiss her way as they escorted him from the hall. She stood breathless and shaking, staring after him helplessly.

"We *can't* leave him in the hands of Jassaspy. There must be *something* else we can do." Her voice was cracking with emotion.

"Yeah," said Scott. "Remember what Willow said: '*a Hebradaigen must be present at the finding of the keyhole*'. Although, what can we do with the key now that I've lost the Mirror of Aggraides?"

It didn't look good and everyone fell silent for a moment. It took Fubbyloofah to rally their spirits again.

"We all heard what he said. The best thing we can do is to find Lava as soon as possible. We'll be quicker if we split into pairs and search different parts of the castle. Scott, Chloe can you take the Corri -"

"No way! Don't put me with him. Not after the last time when he stood by and let the Puddies attack me!" Her jaw was set with determination.

"Don't want to go with you anyway," Scott said sulkily. He felt wretched. When would she let it drop: as if he didn't feel bad enough about things as it was?

"Stop your bickering, the both of you! We've no time for this. Chloe, go with Jack instead."

"Humpf! He's not much better. He spends his life in a cloud of indecision. Fat lot of good he'll be in a crisis," she muttered under her breath.

Jack didn't respond being still shaken after his earlier encounter with Jassaspy so it was quickly settled. Featherfae and the Daughter of Nobody would search The Tower of Reflection and both corridors leading from it, Jack and Chloe would take the Tower of the Vedic Bells and its attendant two corridors whilst Scott and Fubbyloofah would search the Tower of the Sun, the Corridor of Dreams and the Green Corridor. There was not a moment to lose so with a businesslike nod they quickly set off.

"That's where I hid as a child, playing 'Hide and Seek' with my father," said the Daughter of Nobody. She was leading Featherfae through the library in the Tower of Reflection. "I just wish I could recall more about my family," she added mournfully.

"Oh, don't go worrying about that," piped up one of the bookworms perched atop the spine of an old leather-bound tome. He wore a long curly white wig, like those used by judges. "Family are like fish: lovely at first, but after a few days begin to stink."

"Very droll, bookworm, very droll: we're looking for the fire-cat. Have you seen him," asked Featherfae hopefully.

"Papelleticus is my name, thank you very much," he said with a mild air of affront. "A 'fire-cat' you say. I should hope not. That would be most irregular. The whole place could go up in smoke…and then what would become of us?" He blinked at them as if expecting an answer. "Cremation is not popular with us bookworms, you know. A good burial between the sheets of a nice dusty tome is what most of us want."

"But wouldn't that be a terrible shock to a young bookworm? I mean, if they stumbled across a dead elderly relative whilst reading," said Featherfae drawn instantly into his world.

"Humpf! Chance would be a fine thing. You won't catch young-uns today between the sheets of an old leather-bound. Oh no, it has to be 'bite-sized' and 'dumbed-down' to attract *them*."

"Yes, I suppose you're right" said Featherfae, laughing.

"I tell you, the only visitors to the old classics these days are senior citizens like yours truly. Now… where was I?" he said, as he peered down his nose to locate his place. They left him to it and moved on.

Tanglestep moved through The Corridor of Whispers with Jassaspy and his companions in a cloud of mixed emotions. He knew that his best defence lay in the others finding Lava but he also knew that this was a long shot. It would also be difficult to prove his innocence. The charges were deliberately vague and the policies and procedures were open to such wide interpretation that it would be quite possible to argue convincingly that black was white. They soon arrived at the Chamber of the Grand Assembly and Jassaspy led him towards a small windowless ante-chamber piled high with dusty tomes.

"You can work on your defence in here," said Jassaspy as the two Ro-Rillian departed. In the corner of the room was a pitcher of water and some dry bread.

"I see no expense has been spared on the refreshments then." Tanglestep gave a wry smile: even prisoners got better food than this.

"Now that we are alone for a while, we can drop the pretence," said Jassaspy. "The presence of your friends is a blight on Granglethorn that I endure because they have something that I need which they are not yet ready to surrender. That time is fast approaching. But you….you have nothing that I need. Your time is already overdue and this is my parting gift. Here…. take it!" Tanglestep looked up just as Jassaspy flung the contents of an old leather pouch into his face. He choked and blinked furiously as the dusty particles hit him full in the face. Jassaspy sniggered.

"Dried blackheads, squeezed from the pores of the night! Henceforth, your eyes will scream at the sight of daylight!"

Tanglestep felt his eyes immediately start to burn. He rubbed them frantically. Behind him the door slammed shut as Jassaspy left.

Water! water! He groped blindly desperate to rinse his eyes. He blinked rapidly in the dim light of the ante-chamber as water streamed down his face. His vision seemed OK, but the light in here was low; how would they be in daylight? He felt a wave of panic before he put it out of his mind. Time was pressing.

He worked feverishly, scratching away at his draft for several hours. *Have I included all the necessary clauses? Are all the subsections noted and annotated?* He checked and double-checked. Finally, when he felt that he could do no more, he summoned the Ro-Rillian.

They climbed the spiral staircase that snaked around the walls of the chamber before entering the ante-chamber at the top of the dome. It was a room with large sliding patio doors looking onto a terrace that hovered like a ledge well above the luminous green cloud that now thickened over most of Granglethorn Castle. Facing the patio doors behind a long desk were three chairs for the panel members. Half-way towards the patio doors was a solitary desk and chair, behind which Jassaspy sat scribbling last minute notes. He did not look up. Tanglestep was shown to a solitary chair out on the veranda facing the panel.

"YEOWWW!" The pain! Shafts of daylight splintered into his eyeballs as the blackheads from the pores of the night needled him relentlessly.

"Silence please, Hebradaigen Tanglestep. This is no time for histrionics," said the Chair of the Panel as he took his seat. Jassaspy smirked from deep within his cowl. Tanglestep screwed his eyes shut and sat down unsteadily. The wind at this great height was ferocious. It whipped around him whistling constantly. He heard the word "allegation" but strained to hear the details against the relentless buffeting. He caught the phrase "absent without leave" and "accept the charge". From the body language of the panel he guessed the latter was a question. The glimpse that he'd risked to ascertain this was excruciating. His fingers scrabbled for something, anything, to wrap around his head and protect his eyes. He found a red silk scarf. The panel glared at him with open hostility.

"I do NOT accept the charges," he shouted back.

"Speak up! We can't hear you." One of the panel members looked at the others in irritation but the chair waved proceedings on. Occasional words and phrases wafted out to the veranda where he sat blindfolded as Jassaspy presented the case whilst engaging in witty repartee with the panel. He heard himself accused of raising false hopes with tales of the fire-cat's return and phrases such as "deserted his post" came to his ears repeatedly. Finally Jassaspy sat down and the chair gestured for him to rise. In as loud a voice as he could muster he began.

"....indoors? .....that you........... words"

"Hey? What's he saying? For the sake of the sun, speak up!" asked the Chair as the wind whipped away his words.

"I think he wants to come inside," said another.

"Most irregular. Request denied." The Chair banged his gavel

Tanglestep battled on but it was useless. Then he had an idea. Squinting painfully through the blindfold he wrote out key words and policy reference numbers and held them up for the panel to see. "If they can't hear my words then at least they'll see my key points," he muttered to himself. Suddenly, it was looking good.

"Excellent point! He has something there," one of the panel said as Tanglestep held up his scribbled note. He wrote out another.

"Yes, point taken." The Chair nodded in agreement.

This was working well. Perhaps there was a chance after all, he thought, as he reached eagerly for another piece of parchment. But then, disaster struck. A sudden squall of wind caught all his papers and, like dandelion seeds on the wind carried them off to where the chance of them germinating into anything fruitful was remote. His head sank against his chest and there was silence for several seconds. He raised his head slowly and tried to summon the last remaining points from memory. But even this was denied him now.

"I think we've heard enough," said the Chair. "Call the first witness." The wind dropped for a moment and he heard the door open.

"Who is it? I can't see," he said as he squinted through the folds of the red silk scarf, but it was bound too tightly and he could make out nothing but a vague shadowy form. It was large and lumbering but he didn't have to wait long to find out who it was.

"In your own words, Flabblehogg, can you tell us what happened at Treadmail Tower," Jassaspy asked. She flung a sly glance in Tanglestep's direction then turned back to face the panel and affected an air of wounded frailty. Mercifully the whistling wind spared Tanglestep her more wretched self-indulgences.

At least the blackheads in my eyes have spared me from looking at that creased and bitter prune, he said to himself. His mind wandered to Featherfae whose smile radiated love and joy and it was enough to jolt him back and give him the strength to see this through.

"I suffered a burn thereof," Flabblehogg whined in cringeworthy legalese as she wound up her evidence with a twisted reference to how she had burnt her hand whilst trying to steal the sunfruit. With her evidence finished she heaved her vast bulk up and waddled off the stand. Tanglestep cleared his throat in readiness to respond but was cut short by the Chair who suddenly issued an admonishment.

"Could I remind you that it is not you who is subject to proceedings. There is no need to squirm with discomfort so."

Tanglestep stiffened in confusion. Who was he addressing? Then he heard another voice, one he'd heard before, and it was laced with venom and snide suspicion.

"Sorry mi 'lud: force of habit." It was Stunkensloop and he was equally quick to babble forth. "..attacked by his guests....humiliated....no support....just trying to do my job."

With a prayer for the gods to give spurs to his speech, Tanglestep raised the issue of the parchment he'd written to request permission to leave Treadmail.

"No such document was ever passed to me," said Stunkensloop with a declarative twitch.

"This will prove the false passage of your throat!" said Tanglestep as he pulled out the parchment coated in kitchen fat. Stunkensloop jolted and jerked like an intestinal knot but the panel failed to read his body language. Tanglestep heard the phrase, "One word against another," before a recess was announced.

Tanglestep turned to squint through his blindfold over the balcony high above Granglethorn. His paperwork still fluttered about in the same winds that had stolen his words during the hearing. He felt it strangely symbolic of the whole process.

"Lava, where are you?" he called into the wind. From his high vantage point he painfully scanned the castle and courtyards for any sign of him. It was a vain and hopeless effort, but just as he resigned himself he saw something. Down below from the windows in the Corridor of the Astral Plane was a faint flicker of gingery gold. *Lava! Lava!* It had to be him! But would his friends find him before the panel delivered their verdict?

"How will we know it's not a dream?" asked Scott despondently as they searched the Corridor of Dreams for Lava.

"We won't," said Fubbyloofah rather unhelpfully as they peered into the first room that they came to. Finding nothing, they moved swiftly on. Twenty minutes later they bumped into a very excited Hebradaigen.

"Come quickly, come quickly. Burnt gold has been found!" He raced ahead at an astonishing pace and they soon crossed the Grand Assembly and into the Green Corridor. "Come, come!" he urged, as he sensed their reluctance to follow any further. Scott took a tentative step forwards. The green mist swirled around him once more: clinging, burning, tearing into his skin. The next thing he knew, Fubbyloofah was shaking him.

"Scott! Scott! You drifted off. Wake up!" Scott looked round. There *was* no Hebradaigen. They were still in the Corridor of Dreams. It was empty and as silent as the grave. It was just a dream, but such a convincing one! He took a deep breath to steady himself. Then he saw it. It was the briefest flash then it was gone. He stared hard. Would it return?

"Fubbyloofah, look! There it is again." Scott pointed excitedly at a brief flash of gold that glinted through the windows of the Corridor of the Astral Plane. "It's Lava!" He felt his excitement surge them ebb as Fubbyloofah looked at him sceptically. He stared back in confused silence. Was it just another dream?

"Careful, Jack!" shouted Chloe in alarm. He was about to flop onto her bed in the Corridor of the Astral Plane.

"Huh? Why, what's up?"

Chloe grabbed his arm and pointed. A swirl of colour drifted past to reveal Lava curled up at the foot of the bed and bathing in the dying sunlight that was seeping through the window.

"Wow, we've found him." He grinned at Chloe but she was busy waving her arms gently around in the air above him. Lava looked up and purred strongly.

"I've discovered that burnt gold is in animal form not mineral as it was before," he said. "I just a little more time to identify which creature." He looked tired but oozed a quiet confidence.

"That's fabulous, Lava. It really is," said Chloe, pained that she couldn't rejoice more at his news. "But at the moment, Tanglestep's in real trouble. We need you to help save him. Can you come with us please? We don't have much time!" she pleaded. Lava glanced hesitantly towards the corridor and Chloe saw him recoil from the emotional currents that swirled towards him. "Don't worry about those. I can weave through them. I'll carry you. Come on: time's running out," she urged.

He shot her a final penetrating look before nodding briefly. She quickly grabbed the mysterious parcel that had appeared under her pillow the night before and then paused.

"Let me carry that for you," offered Jack, spotting her dilemma. "Where did you get it from anyway?" he asked. Chloe didn't answer and just clutched the parcel more tightly. "OK, no sweat: just thought I'd offer. Aren't you gonna tell me what it is, then?"

"I don't know what it is, Jack," she replied as she stooped to wrap Lava in her cloak with her one free hand. "But I do know that it's important and that when the time comes, I'll know what to do with it."

She opened the door and Jack followed her into the corridor with a puzzled frown which disappeared the moment he felt a warm glow seep up through his feet. Moments later he was laughing hysterically.

"Shh! Do you want everyone to know we're here?" Chloe flashed him a look of alarm. He didn't respond and just staggered into several bands of conflicting emotion before slumping to the floor. "What do you think you're doing?" she hissed. He looked up and straight through her before going limp. Then to her amazement his shoulders shook. He was sobbing. Chloe caught her breath.

"He's fallen into an emotional well," she muttered in exasperation. With great effort she managed to shield Lava whilst manoeuvring the swathe of despair that had settled around Jack's head. She had to wait for it to disperse into thin tendrils of minor effect before he recovered.

"What happened?" he said, shaking his head and breathing heavily.

"Never mind: just follow me. I can guide you."

It took Chloe a considerable time to negotiate the emotional currents of the Corridor of the Astral Plane, hampered as she was with Lava and the silk-wrapped parcel under one arm and the other used for guiding Jack. Eventually they arrived back at the Chamber of the Grand Assembly where Jack spotted his brother up ahead.

"Scott! We've found him! We've found Lava!" he shouted, unable to contain his enthusiasm anymore. He dashed forwards but fell to the ground dazed and confused as something darted out of the shadows and caught him off balance. Behind him, Chloe stumbled too as something grabbed onto her and swung her round.

"DOG BOTTOM!" she cried as his leery grin loomed up. He thumped her hard on her back: on her wings! She doubled up in excruciating pain and Lava fell amidst a flurry of stomping, kicking feet. Scott was over in seconds.

"I'm here Chloe; don't worry!" He screwed his eyes shut desperate to wake the djinn within him. But it wasn't happening. He glanced up, winced as Chloe shot him a look of reproach and felt sick to the stomach.

"Look, I'M SORRY, alright? I was trying to wake the djinn." Her gaze hardened and his voice tailed off. Then a hand pulled him off balance.

"FLAN!" he staggered, aware of a sticky black gunge dribbling over him. It was the worm-sponge that Hagratty had given him at the school gates. A mass of a wriggling nematoads now splattered over his foot. He flung out a hand and grabbed Flan by the hair. His fingers clenched around something warm and soft. Seconds later, he shrieked in terror as Sticklestabber emerged and sank its fangs into him. He fell to the floor with a sickening thump and shook his hand free. The spider scattered across the floor but was back on its feet in seconds. It reared up and scuttled towards Lava waving its front legs menacingly.

"Go, Sticklestabber; go!" urged Flan with a delirious leer as it herded Lava down the only route open to him; the Green Corridor!

22. Jassaspy's Triumph

Jack climbed into bed and felt completely numb. Now that Lava had been driven into what was perhaps the most dangerous part of the Castle there was little hope for Tanglestep. The only shred of comfort had come from watching Fubbyloofah kick the sorry asses of the Puddies out of the Chamber of the Grand Assembly.

Let the shadow visit me again in the night! What harm can it do now? Jack thought back to Willow's message and quietly despaired. She had said that a Hebradaigen had to be present at the finding of the keyhole, but with Tanglestep under house arrest and the Mirror of Aggraides lost, what was the point anymore? Also the time for a time splinter was at the waning of the moon which was now imminent. It looked as if everything now depended on fire-cat magic but with Lava stuck in the sickly heart of the Green Corridor things simply couldn't get any worse. He drifted off to sleep in quiet despair.

He awoke, as before, to the sound of the knitting. He lay awake staring at the ceiling. Should he ignore it? Suddenly, the knitting stopped. This was something different. He sat up and looked towards the foot of his bed. She was still there in the chair gently rocking to and fro. Then she spoke.

"I have something for you."

"For me?" Jack's mind raced.

"You are the key-holder, aren't you?" He noticed her eyes dart to the black gothic key on his bedside table and he nodded mutely. "Then this is for you." She held out the item she'd been knitting.

"What... what is it... and who *are* you?" Jack felt his skin crawl. The shadow looked down at her lap, her shoulders started to shake and she began to snigger. "I said 'what is it and who are you'?" repeated Jack, his voice mounting with alarm. The shadow looked up and stared at him with cold lifeless eyes.

"I am the Deathly Shadow and this is the key-holder's *shroud!*" she said, waving her knitting in the air.

"NO! Out! Get out! Leave me alone!" Jack fought for breath and felt his head spin as her sniggers flared into a deafening cackle.

Got to think positive thoughts! Yeah, that's it: think of my friends. Scott willed himself back to his first meeting with Featherfae and the flowers that had sprung up from her footprints. He saw Dragmines Valley like he had never seen it before, a vast ocean of wild flowers swaying in the wind. He saw streams cascading down from the hillside to fertilise the plain and nourish the flowers. He saw the streams swell into rivers. There was Fubbyloofah, Tanglestep and the Daughter of Nobody. They were signalling to him. What did they want? He approached but the signalling got more frantic. They seemed to... No! They were waving him away. Why? What had he done now?

"Fubbyloofah!" He rushed towards them anxiously; scared.

"Scott, no!" someone cried.

The djinn surged out from his chest, uprooting plants and trees before streaming towards the river. A deafening roar echoed all around as the river angrily burst its banks and flooded the plain. He saw seed heads, pollen and nectar wash around, trees break in half through the force of the water. The waters rose and rose. The tears of the mountain flowed and flowed. He saw the land drowning in sorrow... and all because of him! With a sudden jolt, he was back in his bed in the Corridor of Dreams, panting and perspiring heavily.

Through a haze of pain Chloe glimpsed Lava darting off down theGreen Corridor. A knot of mustard yellow fear swirled by her side.She knew that Scott was in the middle of it somewhere but the magnetic pull of the Green Corridor was too strong for her to care. There was so much spectral energy there: she had to test its depth. She probed into the emotional currents: so deep, so utterly deep. She felt the mysterious silk-wrapped parcel hum in her hands and her veins burned with a deep cold frost fire before screaming with a harsh narcotic rush. She withdrew in a panic, turned and ran back to her chambers panting heavily. She stood in her chambers and watched as the emotions swirled around her.

Of course! Why hadn't she seen it before? With a grunt of determination, she worked furiously; melding and merging different emotional swathes before climbing into bed. Within half an hour she was asleep and her essence was floating, shrouded in an emotional cloak of her own making. It snaked forwards down the Green Corridor.... exploring... seeking answers.

Up in the Chamber of Moths, Jassaspy crunched into a feathered snack in complete absorption. He smiled as he traced the essence of his visitor back along a gossamer thread to the body of Chloe sleeping under a mantle of forgiveness.

"Finally, the third time-ward has come. The time is ripe at last!"

"Here! Can you believe it? Read this!"

It was morning and Fubbyloofah shoved a copy of the "Granglethorn Gossip" under their noses. At the risk of bringing up their breakfasts, they read:

"THE GRANGLETHORN GOSSIP"

"The Tanglestep Tiff – Guilty as charged!"

Delighted with the verdict and in full 'battle dress', with her meaty calves straining the straps of her Roman sandals, Flabblehogg describes why she struck back at Hebradaigen Tanglestep.

"He left me nursing a severe burn after a ragged bunch of travellers ran riot at Treadmail Tower," she said to this paper, whilst wiping a tear from her eye. "I wouldn't care, but all I wanted was a little time for silent prayer and reflection, but every minute of every day I was on call to tend to the needs of his rag-tag army."

Her colleague, Stunkensloop, whose face still jumps in delight at the verdict, concurred:

"I felt put-upon and treated like a skivvy," he said. "It's high time he got his comeuppance."

Thankful for the chance to go on the record, the couple left our offices arm-in-arm, leaving all of us here at "The Gossip" wondering whether we will soon be hearing the slippy slither of tiny Stunkenhoggs"

"They're too dim to realise the fun that is being poked at them," said Scott in delight. His laughter choked off as he caught Chloe glaring at him. The events of the day before flooded back. "I was gonna help, honestly! I was just trying to invoke the djinn!"

She looked away in disgust just as Fubbyloofah cut in.

"They won't have acted on the verdict yet. Let's get over to Tanglestep's chambers FAST!"

He was sitting in a chair when they arrived with a red silk scarf bound tightly round his eyes. Scott jolted. Was Tanglestep the floating man from his dream? If so, what did it mean? Featherfae wailed and dashed forwards. The others rushed to join her but Fubbyloofah thrust out his paw.

"Stay back for a moment. Let them have a little privacy," he said softly.

"Tanglestep!" said Featherfae, her feelings bursting through with that one simple utterance. "Please let me help. There must be something we can do."

"Not for me, I'm afraid." He smiled weakly and shook his head. Featherfae rummaged amongst her bag and pulled out a small pot of powder.

"The verdict has been passed. I am to be cast into the corrosive pool of Fire-Fir Copse." He went silent for a moment as she unwound the scarf from his eyes.

"How I have *longed* to kiss every lock of your hair," he said tenderly as he fingered the love-lies-bleeding that hung from her head.

"My love -" Her voice choked off and she grasped his hand firmly.

"How I have *longed* to caress you and… too late, too late." He stammered as the emotional wave broke over him.

"Shh, shh, my darling. I live only for you." She kissed his eyelids and a tear trickled down her cheek.

"I have… I have… lost myself." He slumped forwards and shook with sobs.

"Darling! Darling! Somehow, we'll save you. You have to believe me." She stroked his hair lovingly and when he finally raised his head he was strangely becalmed.

"I have been granted a final dinner with my friends." He smiled, hoping to ease the sea of pain in the faces clustered round him. "I was wondering if you could do the honours so we can eat here in my chambers. I just can't face the noisy banqueting hall."

Featherfae caressed his face with a tender smile before turning away to hide her tears.

"Leave it to me. It will be a feast to remember," she said, almost choking on the words. "But first let me tend to your eyes. Do you remember the butterflies with the broken wings?" Tanglestep nodded gently. "Well here is the powder that we dusted off them. It reflects and refracts light and will help restore your sight."

The rest of the morning saw Featherfae as 'Master of Ceremonies' directing the troupe into preparing a feast of such exquisite refinement that none could remember one to rival it. Finally all was ready except the dessert: a flan full of irrebies sparkling like fireflakes with a dusting of white canker-blossom that glistened like frostflakes. Featherfae wanted this flan to be a personal act of love so they all left the room to leave her to it.

"You can all come back in now," she said, when she was finally finished. She opened the door to the corridor then caught her breath sharply.

"JASSASPY! What are you doing here?" she cried. Beside him Fubbyloofah looked tense and ready to pounce whilst the Daughter of Nobody stood apart and appeared lost in thought.

"What foul powder is that shining on your eyes?" hissed Jassaspy before shrugging irritably as Tanglestep stepped forward. "No matter: your appeal states that these fools are innocents and that you take full responsibility for all transgressions. Ha! High sparks of honour indeed! Well, it matters not. I have no interest in them beyond what they carry, and before the day is out, they will willingly give me that which I seek."

"Leave and take your poison with you!" said Featherfae through gritted teeth as she moved to shield Tanglestep. Jassaspy tensed momentarily before he looked round at the group one last time.

"It has been a pleasure, truly a pleasure." There was a flash of yellow, blackened teeth before he moved off down the corridor. "Enjoy your last supper," he called over his shoulder.

It took a moment for the shock of the encounter to dissipate before Featherfae reminded them that they had a feast to enjoy. They returned to the room where Tanglestep was determined not to allow his fate to spoil the occasion. He laughed and joked as they tucked into the most impressive banquet he could remember in years.

"This flan is laden with health-giving irrebies," said Featherfae. "Everyone must have a piece as it will help protect us from the dangers that lie ahead."

"Quite right," said Fubbyloofah. "That poison from the pores of the night is only part of the dark arsenal which Jassaspy can call upon."

Featherfae cut the flan into portions, saving the central piece with the impressive crown of chopped fruit and irrebies for Tanglestep.

"This portion contains extra berriblods," she said to Tanglestep quietly. "If the legends are true, they will help purify your blood."

It was truly heavenly. Every mouthful sparked memories, feelings and desires from a world of phantasmagoria: spices ground in thick mystery from far-away lands, fruits brimming with silky passion, and condiments from the kitchen of kings. Tanglestep ate with his eyes closed, savouring every mouthful of life. By the time he had finished, he opened his eyes to a sea of love and kindness radiating out from his friends.

"Thank you," he said quietly. "There is no wealth in this world but life, and you have helped me taste it afresh once more. Thank you for that."

After their farewell feast they set off back down the Corridor of Dreams in a confused state and wondering what to do next when something zipped past and landed with a splat on the wall beside them. Suddenly, the whole corridor erupted as things flew through the air from all angles and the silence collapsed into a frenetic squeaking.

"Scrittlers!" shouted Scott. All around were hordes of them: little winged mice that were usually found scuttling up the walls of the Grand Assembly.

"He's in trouble. You gotta do something!" said Flint-O, their self-appointed leader; a plucky little mite with a ruffled tuft of hair that bristled in tandem with his beating wings. He also had a ring in his nose which, glistened in the light and he was currently hovering in the air directly in front of Scott.

"Who? Waddaya talking about?" asked Scott.

"The fire-cat! They've got him trapped in a casket up in the Tower of the Moon."

Everyone's jaw dropped but there was no time to react as pandemonium suddenly broke out.

"Traitors! Sell-outs!" a cry rang out but from where and from whom? "Get 'em boys!" the voice urged.

Suddenly, wodges of soft blue cheese were lobbed from all directions. One caught Flint-O in the face, splattering his hair with oily pungence: it flobbed to the ground with a dull plop. He shook the globules from his eyes just in time to glimpse a pirate skull cap.

"It's Stinking Bishop! Scrittlers: to the wing!" he cried as he whirled away just as a mischief of mice swarmed down the walls and from behind the pipes. The party could only stand and watch as they ran up their legs and launched themselves at the hovering scrittlers. Most missed their target and fell to the floor with a painful squeal, others managed to grab onto a scrittler in mid-air. That's when it got ugly.

"Whaddaya doing trying to save a *cat*?" yelled Stinking Bishop as he grappled Flint-O to the ground and gave him a swipe round the head that mushed the smelly cheese even further into his hair. "I always said that those wings of yours were a disgrace to the whiskered community."

"Philistine!" Flint-O kicked out with his claws and severed the waistband of Stinking Bishop's trousers. "The cat will save the sun, which will mean fresh harvests again. Don't your retro-mob like eating grains?" he spat, as Stinking Bishop struggled to save his modesty. Fubbyloofah groaned in exasperation and beckoned to the others.

"We haven't got time to get involved in whiskery squabbles. If Lava's in trouble we'll have to take the Green Corridor. It's the most direct route to the Tower of the Moon!"

Everyone's face fell at the prospect but they all knew he was right. However, to their complete surprise when they arrived at the Green Corridor it was devoid of any signs of green mist or slime.

"Wait for me!" cried Scott. As if the raptaggadon bite wasn't enough, he now had the worm-sponge eating into his foot and it felt as if the poisons were getting stronger with each step he took towards the Tower of the Moon. He shuddered and quickly put the thought out of his head as he limped up to the others and they made their way along the corridor in trepidation. They were half way along when Jack mentioned something that was on everyone's mind.

"Something's not right about this. It's all too easy: as if we're walking into a trap."

"I know, but we've no alternatives. Just keep your eyes peeled." Fubbyloofah tensed as the Tower of the Moon loomed up in front of them silent and grey like a huge tombstone, a painful testament to their frail mortality. They gathered in a huddle summoning the courage to enter; then they heard it. It was faint at first but then quite discernible: a repeated mewing.

"Lava!" All three of them surged forwards. This time... this time...they would not fail. Jack got to the tower first. The door was locked. He turned just as Scott limped up and together with Fubbyloofah, shouldered the door. With her little wings working furiously, Featherfae managed a dozen steps at a time as the others darted up after her. Which floor? Which room was it? They froze straining their ears.

"Next floor up!" said Chloe in an urgent hush. With an air of anxious expectancy they crept up the final flight of stairs. Then the mewing stopped. Had they been detected? There was no time to lose! With a concerted cry they launched themselves at the door. It swung open to reveal a locked casket in the middle of an empty room. They stood and stared for a split second and then darted towards it. Suddenly the door slammed shut behind them.

"YOU!" cried Jack. They whirled round to see the Puddies barring the door and grinning oafishly.

"We've got something that you want," said Dog-Bottom indicating the casket on the floor.

"Lava!" Chloe dropped to her knees and peered through the keyhole. A faint mewing sound was heard from within.

"Yeah, and we have the key to set him free." Flan dangled the key provocatively in front of them.

"What is it you want?" asked Scott through gritted teeth. The desire to wipe that smug grin off his flabby face was almost irresistible.

"Oh come on, you muppets!" said Dog Bottom. "You must know." He turned to Jack who stared back filled with loathing. "A key, for a key, Jack. We want your key! Give it up and you can set the moggy free...but don't take too long thinking about it as there won't be much air left in there."

They all looked down at the casket which had become worryingly silent.

"Jack; no! You can't exchange keys; you'll condemn Willow. We need that key to free her," said Scott.

" - and what about Lava?" Chloe snapped back. "We've got to put Lava before some woman in a mirror that no one else can see and is probably just a figment of your imagination."

Scott winced but had no time to react as Fubbyloofah quickly spoke up.

"Lava's the fire-cat. We have to believe, he can look after himself," he said with a quaver to his voice that no one had heard before, "and we do need the key for the time splinters," he added with an uncomfortable squirm.

"I can't do this! I never wanted this darned key." Jack whirled round to look at his companions. His eyes were wide with fear and confusion. "What a decision... and all of it on my shoulders! Here, Fubbyloofah, you decide... you take it." He held out the key, his eyes pleading for him to step forwards and take it.

"Oh, dear, dear, you do appear to be in a pickle don't you?" chuckled Dog Bottom. "Tell you what Jack, why don't you just let us decide for you. Then you won't need to blame yourself when everything goes wrong." His lip curled into a sneer.

"Yeah, just like when you failed your own father," added Flan cuttingly. Jack wailed and from deep within his soul the pain flooded back.

"Open the door, Jack. Just open the door," - his father's last words as he scrabbled at the lock just before he disappeared out of their lives - his own frozen inertia as he stood rooted to the spot.

Was he to blame? If not, who was? .... and now? This was another decision that he was bound to get wrong. His shoulders slumped at the magnitude of it all. But then came a moment of clarity. No: it might be too late for his father, but it was not too late for Lava. And if it was the wrong decision, then so be it! All he could do was to be true to his instincts and his instincts were clear: rescue Lava and if that meant jeopardising the time splinters, then so be it.

"No Jack; NO!"

He heard their voices cry out behind him as he strode towards the Puddies, but he didn't care. He knew what he had to do. An uncertain smile flickered across the lips of Flan and the exchange was done! The tension snapped as Jack rushed towards the casket.

"Lava! Lava! Are you alright?" he fumbled with the key and then Lava sprung free.

"We've still got time. We'll find burnt gold. We'll get to World's End." Chloe babbled excitedly. Across the room the Puddies whooped with delight. Then the shadows parted and Jack caught his breath and started shaking.

"Oh no...what have I done?" he said as he gnawed at his knuckles in desperation. Chloe gasped at the deep purple and the inky black swirl that faced them. Why did it hold such a hypnotic pull on her? Jassaspy shook off his shadowy mantle and calmly held out his hand. With a sickening feeling they watched as the Puddies handed the key over...WILLINGLY!

"It's useless without the mirror!" shouted Scott. Jassaspy's cowl swung towards him and his voice died in his throat.

"It is time to surrender unto me what is mine," he hissed.

"I haven't got it anymore," said Scott defiantly. "It disappeared! Not that I'd give it to you anyway."

The hooded cowl tilted and a moth fluttered out of his robes. His next words were spoken with a soft, creepy gentleness.

"Now is the time. Come to me, my child!"

There was swish of fabric as Chloe discarded her robe.

"What the...?" Scott and Jack could only gape as her lace and gossamer fairy wings unfolded gracefully. With a brief flutter she was airborne.

"FATHER!" she gasped as she fluttered towards the inky blackness at Jassaspy's heart. Time froze solid for a second. A heart rending "NO!" filled the room, and Jack and Scott crumpled to the ground in horror. The echo died away to a malevolent chuckle as Jassaspy held out his hand and Chloe passed him the silk-wrapped parcel that she'd found under her pillow. In complete and utter defeat, Fubbyloofah and party watched helplessly as Jassaspy shook free the silk wrapping to reveal... the Mirror of Aggraides!

23. Burnt Gold....and a Kiss!

"Prepare now to see the sun extinguished forever." Jassaspy waved both the key and the mirror in the air. "Our sun has been drawing power from your world through time splinters for too long. Now watch, as once and for all, I break the link in time that keeps our wretched sun alive."

"You won't win. We've got Lava back now. He'll find burnt gold and get to World's End. You'll see." Scott babbled desperately.

"Do you really think old wives' tales of fire-cat magic can stop me now? Take a good look at me and feel the power I now wield."

With a flourish, he flung back his cowl and cast his robe aside. A plume of sulphurous gas leeched out to reveal a green shrivelled skull of throbbing veins. A moth crawled out from one of his nostrils and his mouth opened to reveal yellow blackened teeth and the twitching remains of other moths that wriggled in pustules of their own bodily fluids. But what made them reel most were the huge moth wings that sprouted from his back.

"It's the moth-man!" Jack's world swirled as he felt the pull of the shadow-sylph.

"Jack!" cried Scott as he limped forwards and thrust out a hand. But Jack crumpled, his arm cramped in her icy grip. Behind him Fubbyloofah crouched in tension. The dry leathery parchment creaked as the wings unfolded and flapped in the moonlight showering Lava and the party with a coating of moth dust. In the midst of the coughing and spluttering a voice rang out.

"Father! I knew we'd find you again." It was Chloe, hovering in the air around him.

"Fool! Do you think having wings means I'm your father?" He smote the air powerfully. There was a sharp crack as the blast threw her against the wall and her wings snapped. She shrieked in pain, crumpled to the floor and the sunfruit in her pocket exploded into an arc of light.

"YEEEOOOWWWW." Jassaspy was flung across the room.
As he hit the opposite wall he exhaled sharply and a dark spiky shadow darted out through the door whilst a slurry of slime spilled towards Lava. He squealed and the smell of burning fur hung in the

air whilst a rabble of moths swarmed towards them. Everyone spat and coughed as the moth-dust settled over them.

"Grab the talismans!" screamed Scott. They had scattered across the floor and were lying within easy reach. He lunged to retrieve them.

"NO!" shouted the Daughter of Nobody.

Was she mad? Scott pushed past her to grab the key then felt himself somersault through the air. He landed with a hard thump and groaned in pain.

"What was freely given cannot be taken back," said the Daughter of Nobody standing over him and breathing heavily. "Our only hope now is to get to World's End before Jassaspy finds the keyhole."

Lava bristled up his fur, sent the moths scattering, and together they limped and staggered down the stairs as Jassaspy screamed for his sakratts. They reached the bottom of the tower just as a horde of sakratts poured out from the Green Corridor to cut off their escape.

"Jack is still in the grip of the shadow-sylph, I'll have to leave him with you, Fubbyloofah. Hold them off as long as you can," said Lava, valiantly ignoring the burns he'd got from the slime.

"But what about burnt gold?" asked Fubbyloofah. "You can't go to World's End without that."

"I have found it already," he said with a knowing look before darting down the Corridor of Shadows. The others wished Fubbyloofah good luck and with an anxious look behind them quickly followed.

"Don't allow yourself to be distracted. Everything you see in this corridor will be a shadow of reality," said the Daughter of Nobody grimly. No sooner had she spoken when the door to one of the chambers opened. Standing there was her sister who smiled and beckoned towards her. The Daughter of Nobody swallowed hard then turned away. It was a pleasant memory but nothing more and too emotional to deal with right now. Just then, a ball rolled out into the corridor and stopped by Scott's feet.

"Scott!" Familiar voices called out to him. He couldn't believe it. His friends from back home were in the chamber to his left. How had they managed to get caught up in a time splinter? They grinned a welcome. "Come on. What are you waiting for? Join us."

"No!" Featherfae jostled him forwards from behind. "...and don't keep looking behind you. They're only shadows."

He tore his eyes away from them and trudged on.

Soon, the Daughter of Nobody indicated a small flight of stairs leading down towards the valley.

"That's the way out of the castle. I'll have to leave you now. I must try and stop Jassaspy from finding the keyhole. Good luck to you all," she said. Featherfae smiled her thanks before her eyes widened in horror.

"No; Chloe; come back!" They turned to see her disappearing into a nearby chamber.

"I won't be a minute. They're calling me; I can't ignore them," shouted Chloe from over her shoulder. She knew that such a strong emotional pull was no shadow, but it was pointless trying to explain. Nobody else could see or sense emotions. Ignoring their protests she walked quickly towards the back of the chamber. The room was dark with a pungent smell all around. Her heart pounded at what she might find. Suddenly there it was: a huge cage full of birds, mainly nightingales and thrushes and all of them in a dreadful state. She dived forwards clawing at the grill. In seconds it came off its hinges. There was a hive of activity as those birds that could, fluttered out. Most hopped out, smeared in oil.

"Shoo, shoo all of you, before someone sees you."

The birds chirped in gratitude. She waded into the cage fixated on one at the back. It was lying in a pool of oil and was the source of the emotional pull. What was it about this one? It raised its head weakly before tapping its beak feebly against the stone flags.

"Tappletock! What on earth..? You look dreadful! What are *you* doing here?"

"Thank daybreak, you're here. I got caught in a net by sakratts. They were after the magpies really – revenge for what happened over Lake Wintersmere." He tried to preen his feathers but it was no use: they were thick with oil.

"Gosh....you mean when I used the sunfruit?"

"I guess so. The magpies said you'd blasted those crows good and proper."

"Did the magpies get away then?"

Before he could answer there was a shout from the doorway.

"For heaven's sake, Chloe, COME ON!" It was Scott and the others and they were hopping around by the door in frustration. She shot them an irritated glance.

"I'm afraid not: roasted on spits for a sakratt supper," he said, as Chloe scooped him up and cleaned off his feathers. "They did give me this before they were taken away though. They said it was something important and to give it to one of you three time-wards." He reached deep within his oil smeared plumage and she saw a glint of something familiar in the half-light. It took a second to see exactly what it was. Then she staggered back as her head exploded into stars and an emotional spike fired her veins.

At about this time Fubbyloofah was in the midst of a maelstrom of flailing limbs, bruised bones and cries of pain. He fought like a demon to gain Lava the time he needed to get out of Granglethorn. He had taken out at least a dozen sakratts with his superior strength and weight, but he had to mind Jack who was out cold beside him and he was simply outnumbered. It wasn't long before a rain of blows descended on his head and he blacked out. When he came to he found himself bound tightly and being dragged by the scruff of the neck into the lower reaches of the Tower of the Moon.

"Fubbyloofah? Is that you?" Jack winced in pain as he found himself being bumped down the stairs like a sack of potatoes.

"Hey, Spittlewhip, this one's awake," chuckled Hackweezle.

"All the better to appreciate what we have in store for him then," cackled Spittlewhip. "I wish mine would wake up. He weighs a ton does this one."

Eventually they arrived at the bottom level. "Save your strength. You're gonna need it!" said Spittlewhip as Fubbyloofah came to his senses and started flailing and thrashing about.

"What's happened? Where are we?" he mumbled before wincing as the lumps on his skull reminded him of recent events.

"You'll see soon enough," said Spittlewhip as he opened a large cast-iron manhole in the floor. A damp mouldering smell wafted up from the stale interior and Spittlewhip screwed his nose up in distaste. "Phoarrr it stinks down there!" He dragged Fubbyloofah towards the opening and thrust his head down into the open cavity. "Time to get acquainted with yer new home!"

Fubbyloofah wailed and a rush of ammonia choked off his breath as he tumbled through the hatch. Seconds later, Jack followed and landed on top of him. He rolled off into something unpleasant and sticky that didn't bear closer examination. He looked up through the open hatch which Spittlewhip and Hackweezle were about to close.

"Wait!" cried Jack. "Where are we? What are you doing?"

Hackweezle exchanged a glance with Spittlewhip.

"You're in the service tunnels; that's where!"

"Service tunnels?"

Hackweezle guffawed at his confusion.

"Oh don't you realise? It's supper time ...but not for you....No: supper time for the Cuss-Cuss Tatty!" he cackled and with that the hatch slammed shut on their fetid mouldery world.

Back in the Tower of the Moon, the Puddies were tasting Jassaspy's wrath once again.

"Louse brains! I've got a good mind to mulch your brains for moth-food. They would never have escaped without that sunfruit. Your job was to retrieve it and you have failed me like the sun fails the centipede!" He kicked out at the empty casket and paced up and down the room. Down below he could hear the battle with Fubbyloofah but knew that his sakratts did not have the skill to capture the fire-cat. He turned to face them.

"Follow them to World's End. If the myths are true and burnt gold exists, then they must be stopped before I get a chance to use the key to the time splinters. First, I have business with the slygorm." He threw on his robes again and a rabble of moths flew out from his cowl in alarm.

The moon was already out when Tanglestep was taken from his chambers in the Tower of the Sun to begin the long walk to his final resting place at Fire-Fir Copse. A small party of Hebradaigese had gathered to accompany him: friends, colleagues and the morbidly curious. Tagging along at the back of the group, like criminals revisiting the scene of the crime, were Flabblehogg and Stunkensloop. The procession left the gates of Granglethorn to begin the slow ascent to the copse. Some kind and tender soul had taken the care to line the pathway with fairy lights and Tanglestep looked back at the accompanying throng with a grateful smile to whoever it was. He walked on steadily, filling his lungs with the crisp night air and marvelling at the beauty of the night sky. The moon was strangely alluring this night, twinkling and peppering the land as if shedding silvery tears at what was due to pass.

"How sad that there are those who can't rejoice in the beauty of *both* the sun and moon," he muttered to himself.

Fire-Fir Copse was an ominous resting place: a small marshy hollow with a wooden jetty leading out into the centre of a dank and corrosive slime pool that glowed with an iridescent blue-green hue. He stepped onto the platform with his official escorts and walked calmly towards the end of the pier. At the end, he turned.

"I'd like a moment to myself, if that's alright."

"Please," the escorting guard was holding something out to him. He looked pained yet strangely hopeful. Tanglestep glanced down at what he held and smiled.

"Thank you, you have no idea how this lifts my spirit." He exhaled with joy as the guard handed it over before withdrawing. He took a moment to survey the landscape. He saw a painfully wounded land: ridges scoured by slime trails, the earth cracked by lack of rain, weak and anaemic plant life. But he smiled. He looked over to the high hills. Somewhere...somewhere over there was World's End. Somewhere out there was the burnt gold needed to heal all this sickness and Lava would find it. He looked down at his hand still clutching a tuft of ginger fur. "Yes; Lava will find it, I'm sure." The moon soaked up his words as he turned, walked to the end of the jetty, stretched out his arms and with a heavy sigh fell forwards into the bosom of the pool.

His skin screamed: nerve endings danced feverishly, exploding with fire. It consumed him: burning coals, sharp blades, stabbing thorns. The acidic waters burrowed into him like needles. Then: it was over.

The guards and the assembled throng filed away and as their footsteps receded, the moon reclaimed her lonely vigil. Fire-fir copse was quiet and still and Tanglestep's body floated on the surface of the pool: a silhouette against the night sky.

"He's still there!" hissed Stunkensloop.

"We'll soon see about that. Come on!" Flabblehogg lumbered her way towards the end of the pier and peered down at the body.

"Why's he floating?" asked Stunkensloop, his lips twitching nervously.

"How should I know? But let's put an end to it. Here, take hold of my arm."

With Stunkensloop as her anchor, she leant out over the pool, and stamped viciously down on Tanglestep's head. But each time it bobbed back up to the surface.

"Sink, you bully!" she bellowed, as she practically jumped on his head. This time it went deep under the surface but then jolted back with such force that she was caught off balance. "ARRGH! Pull me back, Stunkensloop!" She wobbled on the brink of the jetty. Stunkensloop strained desperately to counterbalance her weight but it was no use. His withered mass of intestinal knots weighed little more than one of her meaty calves. With an enormous cry she started to toppled but at the last minute she managed to twist and land in the shallows. Moments later she let out a huge bellow as Stunkensloop fell on top of her forcing her under. She gulped a bellyful of slime which quickly burnt its way down to her stomach lining. She lashed out and heard him yowl in pain.

"You wriggle-some git!" she cried, as she let out a sulphurous belch. She could hear the acidic slime gurgling inside her doing something nasty. In a panic she looked down at her belly. A once proud muffin-top was now sagging with multiple flaps of sweaty flesh. She heaved her way out of the pool and was aghast to see how she wobbled and slobbed with every step. She let out a low moan of despair then glanced about. Had anyone seen her? Her head swung nervously from side to side before she flabbed off into the surrounding wilderness.

Stunkensloop fared little better. In the kerfuffle with Flabblehogg, she had pushed him face down into the slime. The acidic rot had penetrated deep into the pores of his face and his innate wriggling only made it worse. He got to his feet gasping for breath and felt the skin on his face racing with fiery needles. He squirmed his way back down to Granglethorn frantically scratching his skin with the dawning realisation that his face was slowly dissolving.

"I can't breathe Fubbyloofah! I can't breathe! It's the spores, they're clogging my lungs!" Jack looked panic stricken.

"Not helped by these droppings from the Cuss-Cuss Tatty either, I'm sure." Fubbyloofah wrinkled his snout at the sulphurous residue smeared over the tunnel floor. "This must be a feeding spot. Come; we'd better get out of here before it returns."

Together they weaved their way through the labyrinth according to the vagaries of Fubbyloofah's twitching nose. Eventually he stopped dead in his tracks.

"Sshh! Jassaspy's down here somewhere."

"WHAT?" Jack slumped to the floor, barely able to breathe. Fubbyloofah's ears twitched frantically before he honed in on a spot where he could excavate a spy hole big enough for the two of them. They peered through to the same huge cavern full of sweat-pools which the Puddies had been in earlier. Some were occupied by groats whilst others....the colour quickly drained from their faces.

"Groundluggs! So this is where they end up," gasped Fubbyloofah in shock. "Look: that's Cob down there in that sweat-pool, and look how gross he's become!" His mind raced with what to do next when a sudden wail from Jack brought him back.

"They're being fattened up on groatmeal....and becoming groats!"

They stared in horror. Across the cavern, sweat-pool after sweat-pool contained bigger and fatter groundluggs until they came to the sweat-pools occupied by groundluggs so bloated that their limbs had withered through disuse. These were the groats!

Back In the centre of the cavern on a huge dais was the slygorm: the larvae-like queen maggot. It was busy secreting a gelatinous gloop that the sakratts were shovelling into giant vats. On the side of one vat was written the word 'Groatmeal' whilst the other read 'Carbalix.' Jack's stomach heaved.

"I think I'm gonna be sick." He closed his eyes and fought the revolt in his stomach. When he opened his eyes again he saw that the slygorm had finished and was shivering from the deep chills of the underground cavern. Jassaspy's voice rang out.

"Take her to the sweat-pools. She needs to stabilise her body temperature and don't forget the vapours." Sakratts scurried forth to do his bidding and soon the slygorm was wallowing in the sweat-pool of a morbidly obese groat. As the warmth from the sticky sweat coated her body, noxious green-tinged vapours exuded from the folds of her gelatinous flesh. Other sakratts scrabbled to open a vent and the green fumes quickly escaped to mingle with those hanging over Dragmines Valley. Jack and Fubbyloofah could only stare open-mouthed in horrified realisation as the source of the poisonous fumes was finally revealed. Jassaspy walked over to where the slygorm was soaking and reached out a hand to caress her.

"Ahh, my beauty: so pure in your aversion to sunlight: soon, soon you shall be able to emerge from your lair and feed....feed on the flesh of this land."

The slygorm reared its huge head and turned its puckered mouth towards him. A deep rasping hiss was heard as it exhaled a vapour so powerful that even Jassaspy spluttered for breath.

"Magnificent!" he gasped before stifling a cough deep within his cowl.

Suddenly, Jack felt Fubbyloofah stiffen with alarm besides him. Then he smelt something nasty: a warm rank mouldering smell.

"THE CUSS-CUSS TATTY!" he hissed, eyes wide with fright. They scrabbled back as fast ass they could but it was no use. Seconds later, a large feathery, straw-covered monster caked in tar and with a writhing black mass of a beard emerged from the shadows. As it rushed to make them its next victim, its beard exploded into a swarm of angry wasps.

"I'm not gonna make it. Best if you go on without me," said Chloe. Their route was a long one, snaking up the valley towards The Swirl of Vows, the peak at the end of the ridge. Chloe felt wretched. Her gossamer wings hung broken from her back and Lava had slumped to the ground, his own paws burnt horribly from Jassaspy's slime. "It's no use. Our hopes lie with Jack and the time splinters now."

"Well don't look at me. It's not *my* fault! My foot is rotting from that worm-sponge and the raptaggadon bite still hasn't healed," moaned Scott. Featherfae couldn't help either as she had taken a different route, hoping to act as a decoy and buy them time. She was already half way to gaining the mountain ridge and clearly exhausted as not a single daisy or buttercup had sprouted from her footprints.

"Forget it, Scott! We all drew the short straw relying on you." Chloe looked at him reproachfully. She struggled to her feet but overbalanced as she tripped over her broken wings. She began to crawl wearily over the boulders. To her side Lava squeaked with every painful step. Scott burned with shame. So what if he did have his injuries? *They* weren't feeling sorry for themselves, battling on in their own way. He looked behind at the castle. It was still so close. They could be recaptured at any time. If ever there was a time...

Chloe looked up and saw him limp over to her.

"Come on, wuss! Let me help you."

She saw him wince in pain as he reached down. The next thing she knew, she was in the air and over his shoulder. He stifled a deep groan as with his other hand he bent to scoop up Lava.

"I - you - I didn't..." Her voice cracked with emotion. Suddenly she sobbed with a long pent up release and a tender swathe of forgiveness diffused into the air around her and embraced his aura. The air turned a soft turquoise in colour and the scarlet swathe of shame that he'd carried since the playground ebbed away.

"If we gain the ridge early we can jump 'em at the top," said Flan. Sticklestabber emerged from the nest in his hair and waved a purplish leg in the air but quickly re-settled himself the mountain winds being simply too blustery. The Puddies doggedly puffed their way up to the mountain track until finally they reached the ridge. Ahead was The Swirl of Vows and beyond that was the Arctic Spears: a cluster of huge rusted spears that legends said had been thrust into the earth by the fallen Gods of Thunder.

"We've got the advantage. They don't know they're being followed," said Dog Bottom.

"Yeah, and the disadvantage of wondering what old moth-mouth will do to us if we fail," muttered Flan dejectedly.

Even with shouldering the burden of Lava and his sister it took Scott longer than he thought to climb to the top of The Swirl of Vows. Every step caused pressure pads on the rotting pulp of a foot left by the worm-sponge. Every step on the other foot spread the poison from the raptaggadon bite deeper into his leg muscle which throbbed and twitched in spasm. But this was his penance. Every step of pain was countered by something that revitalised and resuscitated. The turquoise aura of forgiveness settled around around him, nourishing, replenishing. The tension left his chest. He found himself able to take deep lungfuls of cool fresh air. His brow, for so long furrowed with tension and guilt, unfurled. A broad smile played across his face. Finally he was free of the burden he had carried for so long.

"Scott, what's happened?" Featherfae gaped as he staggered up to the Arctic Spears carrying both Chloe and Lava. They were all in such a sorry state. Lava had slime burns on his paws, Chloe had broken wings, Scott a rotten foot that stank to high heaven and all were still smeared in moth dust. But he was grinning: grinning with a lightness of spirit that Featherfae had not seen in him before. He slowly lowered Chloe and Lava to the floor.

"I must get over to the Grey Friars of Aggraides," said Lava indicating a solitary peak out on a promontory separate from the main ridge. "Stay here by the Arctic Spears and be ready to use the sunfruit."

"The sunfruit? So Chloe's talisman is key to everything after all?" said Scott.

"Of course, you idi- " She left the sentence unfinished and flashed him a warm smile instead.

"What's going to happen, Lava?" asked Featherfae apprehensively.

"I'm going to light up the sky. Put the sunfruit on top of the Arctic Spears and form a circle around it. Don't break the circle whatever you do. If nothing happens and I don't succeed, go back to Granglethorn and try and help Jack. Whatever you do, don't wait or come looking for me."

"But what about burnt gold? Where it is?" asked Featherfae. But her words found only the wind as Lava had already left. Chloe placed the sunfruit on top of the spears and Featherfae turned to them both and held out her hands. It was then that the Puddies broke cover and attacked.

"Keep the circle! Don't break hands for anything," shouted Featherfae as vicious kicks and thumps rained down upon them. Featherfae kicked back and heard a satisfying yelp before launching herself just high enough into the air to be out of their reach whilst still keeping the circle intact by holding hands with Scott and Chloe. But her wings were not large enough for sustained flight and she was tiring rapidly. Meanwhile Chloe was taking a pummelling and wouldn't be able to last much longer. It was then that Scott did something remarkable. Gritting his teeth and with a yell of defiance he leant across to shield her. Blow after blow he took on his back, shoulders and legs as the Puddies kicked and punched but they did not break the circle.

"Scott. I'm *so* sorry!" Chloe turned to him with streaming eyes. Rich, warm emotion streamed out from her. The orange swirl settled over him, offering him a protective cloak. He looked across to the Grey Friars of Aggraides but Lava was still some way from the top. Suddenly the Puddies caught the direction of his gaze and stopped. A second later, Dog Bottom leant in to whisper in his ear.

"WHAT?" Scott asked incredulously, as he turned to face him.

"I said that your useless brother failed. He is already dead!"

Scott's jaw dropped in horror. Seconds later, he reeled as a mass of wriggling meal-worms heaved out of Dog Bottom's mouth and hit him splat in the face. He felt Chloe's grip tighten and had to summon every ounce of inner resolve not to break the circle. When he finally shook the last remaining wriggler from his hair, it was to find the Puddies gone. They'd spotted Lava and were giving chase.

"There's nothing we can do now except pray and hold the circle," said Featherfae. The sun, weak and watery at the best of times, was now breathing its last.

"Oh, no, they're closing in on him!" said Chloe.They watched as the silhouette of Lava and the Puddies converged against the globe of washed-out yellow that was still discernible under the green hue of the sky.

"What about burnt gold? Do you think he'll find it in time?" Scott asked. Lava was almost at the summit cairn but the Puddies were almost there too. In horror they saw Sticklestabber spring down from his nest in Flan's hair. And then...the silhouettes merged! What was happening? Had he made it? Had he found burnt gold? The pain in their fingers reflected their tension as they crushed each other's hands in their own. Then slowly the silhouette became clear. A wail of despair circled skywards from the Arctic Spears as a boy holding a cat by the scruff of its neck was silhouetted against the dying embers of the day.

The moon was waning as Jassaspy strode quickly along the Corridor of Fears. He had decided to avoid the unwelcome publicity that would come from entering the Corridor of the Astral Plane via the Chamber of the Grand Assembly. For obvious reasons the Corridor of Fears was rarely used so there was a strong chance his journey would go unnoticed. He had both the key and the window to locate the keyhole. It was now only a matter of time before he could the seal off the time splinters and let the sun drain away. But what was this? A slightly stooped man wrapped in a golden robe adorned with the bells of Vedia was approaching. His head glinted in the moonlight that shone through the windows and a long thin wispy moustache trailed on the floor either side of his feet.

"Barbletwist, outside his tower and wandering down the Corridor of Fears of all places?" Jassaspy quickened his step just as Barbletwist looked up.

"Jassaspy; it's not too late for you. You can still be saved, you know." His eyes shone with a steely sadness as if he knew that his words were wasted.

"Get out of my way - oh, what am I saying? Barbletwist, out of his tower? Ha; what a ludicrous idea!" He laughed out loud. "Illusions, more illusions. When will I learn?" He swept forwards confidently. Within minutes he would pass through the Tower of the Vedic Bells to the Corridor of the Astral Plane where he would have to take extra care in order to negotiate the emotional currents.

"By the smoke of what's..."

"Ha! Thought I was an illusion did you?" Barbletwist grabbed his arm. His face leered up into his cowl with gritted teeth. "Look what I've got for you. Do you want to taste the eyelash?" Jassaspy's eyes caught sight of the mummified eyeball of Anubis. He recoiled but felt Barbletwist's nails dig sharply into his flesh. This was a dark power equal to anything he could muster.

"Raka si-raja, Raka si-ji!" Jassaspy whirled towards the moon as he dredged up the darkness against him.

"I see your lips move but you know I cannot hear. Your curses and invocations can't touch me, Jassaspy." Barbletwist's nails dug deeper.

Of course, the fool's deaf! Jassaspy scrabbled deep within his robes. "Let's see how you deal with these then. Blackheads squeezed from the pores of the night!" The pouch exploded into the air but Barbletwist was quicker. A flourish of red silk swirled in the air and the blackheads dispersed on the wind. The scarf drifted off with them just as Jassaspy broke free from his grip.

"You don't know what I keep under my nails," cried Barbletwist as Jassaspy steamed away towards the Tower of the Vedic Bells.

"You'll regret this," hissed Jassaspy. He glanced over his shoulder but the corridor showed no sign of Barbletwist ever having been present. "Was he here at all? Did this just happen?" He glanced down at his arm. Small bumps were already appearing under the skin and his arm itched like fury: or did it? He wasn't sure any more. He shook his head in confusion walked through the Tower of the Vedic Bells and into the Corridor of the Astral Plane. Soon, soon he would be at the source of the time splinters. But... what? A swirl of emotion blocked his way along the corridor.

"Who has roused these long-forgotten feelings?" he mused aloud. He closed his eyes and meandered along with arms outstretched, groping like a blind man and feeling the emotion rather than seeing it. He knew it was vital that he got this right. He smirked at how he had managed to weave just enough emotional intrigue around himself to fool Chloe. But, a mistake even at this stage could be fatal. He stopped outside one of the chambers and looked inside to see a bed under a band of envy and surrounded by competing bands of love and hate.

"No, that's not right: too much inner conflict." He moved on and entered the next room. "Laughter, joy, love and tenderness. Pah! It reflects nothing of life's bitter trials." He slammed the door shut just as his skin exploded into itches. "Damn! So it wasn't an illusion after all!" Without thinking, he scratched at the bumps on his arm. Tiny red spiders hatched out from under his skin and began to crawl along his veins. He brushed off what he could but saw others moving under the skin. "Curse that Barbletwist! He'll pay dearly for this!" But he had no time for this now. He had to find the keyhole to the time splinters. He moved on down the corridor and stopped suddenly in front of a room full of gorse in full bloom. His jaw dropped in shock.

"What? Who has? ... and ... WHY?" He stepped inside and a rabble of moths flurried out from his robes and flapped lazily around the chamber. The bed lay under a shroud of forgiveness. He noticed a distinct absence of despair and the careful positioning of curiosity and satisfaction. This was the place! Yes: definitely. He jumped as the door slammed behind him and whirled round to find the Daughter of Nobody. A flurry of moths settled onto her cloak of autumnal leaves. She drew a sharp and sudden breath, as if a long-lost memory had finally broken through the crusted mulch of time. It was several long seconds before either of them spoke.

"I remember now!" she said softly.

"You remember NOTHING!" He spat the words and turned away. "Now where is the keyhole?" His eyes roved the room frantically.

"I remember a father -" she said quietly.

"What?" He tensed suddenly.

"- a father who kept moths... but who turned away from me and.....I never knew why." She sighed deeply and drew her cloak of autumnal leaves tightly round herself.

"Pa!" Jassaspy stepped forwards and shoved her back against the door. Her cloak of leaves curled and crinkled from his touch. Suddenly he jolted.

"That's the place!" He whirled on his heel, stepped across the room and placed the Mirror of Aggraides on the wall over the bed. This was the spot. No doubt about it. For a brief second he saw the Daughter of Nobody reflected back at him. Then she was lost to him forever as the mirror became a window. He stared and stared deep into it all the while holding the key up in full view. For a second nothing happened and then slowly, ever so slowly, Willow materialised.

"Speak keyholder, and let me show you the way."

"I seek the keyhole to the time splinters," his voice quavered. The image was silent and simply stared back at him. "I said 'I seek the keyhole to the time splinters'. Will you show me where to find it or not?"

"I will do more than that. I will take you there, but first - we must - kiss."

"WHAT?" Jassaspy reeled.

"There is an old saying that only when gorse is out of bloom is kissing out of season. Look around you."

His eyes flickered up to the sprig of gorse in full bloom above the bed and then over the window and around the room. She looked at him softly.

"Only after a kiss can you decide whether to open up the time splinters and embrace life or lock them shut forever. A kiss will change you more than you can dream, Jassaspy, and change is the only evidence of life. Take this final challenge."

He quivered, hovering between a desire to take the kiss and the consequences and between falling back on the comfort and security of his role as the High-Lord Hebradaigen of the Tower of the Moon. Yet, how else would he get to the source of the time splinters? He had to shut them down, to kill off the sun, to see the slygorm emerge from its lair. There was no alternative! He lunged into the mirror and Willow's fair head dipped under his cowl. They kissed for what seemed like an eternity. Round and round they span together locked in a swirling embrace. He kissed her greedily, ignoring the moth wings stuck between his teeth as his tongue stabbed into her mouth. But something was wrong. Her mouth was flaccid, there was no firmness and why so many missing teeth? His eyes snapped open in concern. He swirled round and round in his passionate embrace. The frame around the Mirror of Aggraides was now a distant porthole through which he could glimpse Willow bathed in golden light. She was in Chloe's chamber standing next to the Daughter of Nobody. They were both staring in through the porthole watching him.

"What witchcraft is there in this kiss?" he shouted as he pulled back from the embrace. He found himself deep within the timeless void of a time splinter: but who was he kissing? The woman sniggered and suddenly lifted her face to his, a face of utter toothless decay: the face of the Deathly Shadow. He gasped in shock and her sniggers flared like fire in his face.

"Here, key-holder; take your shroud." She proffered him her knitting. Jassaspy looked around in alarm. He now found himself in a stone corridor with a door at the far end: the door to the time splinters? It had to be! He rushed towards it, frantic to unlock it with the key that Jack had willingly surrendered. The key slotted into the lock perfectly. "HA! Not long now!" He was exultant: only moments away from shutting them down once and for all. He heard the door unlock and stepped through into a second corridor. At the far end was a figure in black seated in front of another door. He bolted forwards eager to pass through to the other side. He skidded to a halt as he approached the door.

"No, it can't be!" The figure at the end of this second corridor was the same woman: the Deathly Shadow. In a panic he used the key again and passed through the door beside her to enter yet another corridor, but this time with three doors at the far end. One of these had to be the one for the time splinters. He darted off towards them.

"NO!" he slumped to the floor. There she was again. "It's not possible!" His heart sank as he approached the three doors. It was! The Deathly Shadow looked up and smiled, before slowly taking out her knitting. Clicketty clack, clicketty clack, went her needles, as Jassaspy tried first one door then the other: all three of them led into further stone corridors... and at the end of each of them was the Deathly Shadow!

Scott, Chloe and Featherfae watched tearfully as the sun started sinking below the horizon for the last time. It was in its death throes and Lava had failed.

"Of course!" said Featherfae. "The Grey Friars of Aggraides: the mountain at the end of a promontory beyond which is nothing but the vastness of sky and the faint pulse of a dying sun. *This is World's End.* With tears streaming down her cheeks she squeezed the hands of Scott and Chloe before looking back at Lava wriggling helplessly in the hands of Dog Bottom: unable to break free, unable to get to the burnt gold! But then... as the last few flickers of light spattered over the horizon, he started to pulsate with restrained power on the brink of something magical that just needed a trigger to release it. Suddenly, the golden moth dust that covered him, tingled and shimmered before sparking into life. He started to glow like he had done that first night when they had taken him home for the very first time. He fluffed out his fur and pulses of orange and gold started to mingle with his natural gingery colour to cocoon him in light. The Puddies dropped him in alarm and started running back towards the Arctic Spears but it was too late. Soon the waves of light were deepening and burnishing, as his fur released all the shafts of sunlight and heat that he had soaked up on his long journey to World's End: the heat from the crackling log fire in Rascal Howe, the sunlight that he had grabbed on the journey to Crambleside whilst Featherfae was planting pips, the warm nourishing rays by the bridge at Ye Olde Dungeon Creek and the tender gentle warmth of the evening sunshine that he had caught on Chloe's bed in the Corridor of the Astral Plane. All this warmth, heat and natural energy he had stored for this very moment. Nothing now stood between World's End and the dying embers of the sun as it soaked up the energy he radiated. From the corner of her eye, Featherfae saw the moth dust on Scott and Chloe spark into life.

"Burnt gold" she laughed. "It was the moth dust all along!" Scott and Chloe could only gasp in amazement.

"AGNARO IGNITO!" shouted Chloe instinctively. There was a split-second flash of diamond and crimson light, before the sunfruit went molten red like Lava. Then Scott staggered.

"Keep the circle!" urged Featherfae. But he was swaying badly.

"It's the shadow-sylph again," he cried. "Everything's going blurry round the edges and my arm's frozen solid!" But then from deep within, a surge of white hot heat emerged. It whirled upwards feeding off the swathes of emotion left from Chloe's embrace.

"What's happening to him?" cried Chloe as Scott jerked and jolted beside them. The next minute, his chest exploded with smokeless fire. "It's the djinn!" cried Featherfae excitedly.

The fiery being surged out, pulling with it a dark essence that leeched from the back of Scott's eyes. He bucked and strained from the force before slowly crumpling. This time it was Chloe that shouldered his weight. A deep orange band of her affection cushioned the turquoise of his emotional core.

"The shadows are fading, and my arm...At last I'm free of it!" Scott sobbed.

The djinn streamed upwards carrying the shadow-sylph into the air desperate to meld with the burnt gold. A second later, the sky exploded cataclysmically with a sonic boom and solar particles scattered across the sky streaking its cloudy cheeks with an eye-blinding flash. Instinctively they shut their eyes as they gripped each other's hands to maintain the circle. A wave of intense heat washed over them and then.... receded. As it did so the shadow-sylph vaporised and a black plume whirled frantically around the valley before streaming back to Granglethorn. It swirled through the castle corridors before finding an open ink-well where it dissolved into the black ink with a gentle sigh.

Slowly their breath returned and they opened their eyes. The Puddies were gone and in their place was a lingering sulphurous plume which gently broke up in the wind.

"The sky: just look at the sky!" Featherfae could barely contain her joy. The languid green hue was gone and in its place was a soft iridescent beauty; a golden protective glow that pulsed with a life long denied. They stood in silent awe as around them diamonds sparkled with dazzling crimson as the air shimmered once more to the dance of the frost and fireflakes.

Scott, Featherfae and Chloe returned to a hero's welcome at Granglethorn but not before a strange thing happened concerning Scott. He'd arrived back alongside a very irritated Featherfae and Chloe. Whenever either of them spoke or said a word, he would start sniggering privately to himself. It drove them mad! And when he started doing the same to everyone he met back at Granglethorn it was the last straw.

"He'll get banished from Granglethorn if he keeps offending everyone like this," muttered Featherfae to the Daughter of Nobody as they relaxed in her chambers prior to the meeting of the Grand Assembly. The Daughter of Nobody listened carefully to all that had happened at World's End but as soon as she heard about his fight with Dog Bottom she grabbed Scott by the arm and began thumping his back with all her strength. Featherfae was horrified.

"Stop, please stop!" she cried in distress. The Daughter of Nobody paid no attention, until, with a final choking splutter, Scott spat out a small worm. They all stared in horror as the Daughter of Nobody explained.

"It's a brain-tickler. He must have accidentally swallowed it when Dog Bottom's meal worms hit him in the face."

Scott looked at them all sheepishly but no one mentioned it again. He was back to his normal self and that was all that mattered.

Pennants were flying from all four towers and the Chamber of the Grand Assembly was draped in banners reserved for visiting dignitaries when they were ushered inside in hushed reverence. It was packed to the gunnels as even the Hebradaigese on annual leave had returned to be part of this historic event. They were about to take their seats when an odd looking man with a bald pate and a spiral moustache waved frantically for their attention.

"Well done, well done! I knew you had promise when I met you earlier. There was something about the way you opened that door to achieve your 'Room-Entry Safety' certificates: such panache, such confidence!"

"Pootlefopp!" They cried in unison, trying hard not to laugh.

"- and touched that you all remember me." He bowed gracefully before continuing. "Now, I just need a quick word about 'progression'. All students must show 'progression'. It's proof that education works, you know."

"This'll have to wait, they're about to start," said Chloe, glancing anxiously towards the gathering crowd. Pootlefopp paused, aware of the settling silence.

"Of course, of course, but if I can just quickly sign you up to take your 'Room-*Exit* Safety' certificates. You can't go entering rooms safely if you don't know how to exit them safely, can you?" he asked with a look of expectancy. Scott exploded with laughter which died in his throat when Fubbyloofah and several Hebradaigese suddenly shot him disapproving looks. Pootlefopp's eyes briefly mirrored his spiral moustache as a couple of ushers darted forwards, grabbed hold of him by each arm and forcibly bundled him away. "Progression, we do need to show progression," he cried as his voiced tailed away in the crowd.

Featherfae looked confidently around at the sea of faces as any wood nymph would once well groomed: she had finally managed to tame the twigs in her hair. She noticed a vacant seat on the benches of the Tower of the Sun and a hard lump came to her throat but she had no time to dwell on it. They were quickly ensconced in high seats of honour on the central dais before trumpets announced the arrival of the Central Committee. One by one the seats were filled until finally an old man entered wearing a long purple robe covered with symbols from all four towers: the sun, the moon, the clouds of reflection and the bells of Vedia. He sat down in the vacant chair of the gatekeeper followed by a young woman with long flowing blonde hair who stood behind him. There followed an unusual silence as all eyes turned towards Scott and Chloe. The old man in the gatekeeper's chair started chuckling to himself. Scott blushed with embarrassment and then couldn't stop staring. There was something familiar about this man; something very familiar. His sister got there quicker.

"Peek!" she cried as she rushed forward to embrace him. Cries of joy and laughter echoed around the chamber as, against all protocol, Scott hurdled over the table to hug and greet their old friend.

"Bless you all and thanks for the harvest!" squeaked a familiar voice from on high. The advance warning was all they needed to dodge the 'confetti' from above.

"At least they're wholewheat now!" Peek laughed as Flint-O and his scrittlers waved down to them from on high, their droppings landing harmlessly close by.

"It was my daughter who showed me the way back," said Peek to their enquiring eyes.

"Yes, but I needed to be released from the timeless void of a time splinter first," said the woman with the long blonde hair. She smiled before reaching out to gently tug Scott's shirt. "Hello, Scott. Remember me?"

"Willow? Is it really you? How? ...what? ...when?"

"Later, later," laughed Peek as he turned to deal with the remaining formalities. One by one they worked through the agenda until, at an appropriate point, he could hand the chair over to his deputy and give them his undivided attention.

"Come, I want you to meet someone," he said as they followed him down the Corridor of the Astral Plane. They stopped outside Chloe's chamber where inside they saw a large shaggy beast on the bed. It took them a few seconds to register who it was.

"You old black and white fur-ball," shouted Scott in glee as he pushed open the door and rushed to embrace his old friend Fubbyloofah. But then he checked himself and looked round frantically as Dog Bottom's words came flooding back to him: *"Your useless brother failed. He is already dead."* The room was otherwise empty.

"Oh no!" he wailed as the loss of his brother suddenly hit him like a block of ice that no shadow-sylph could even hope to replicate. He felt a comforting hand rest lightly on his shoulder. His head sank and he turned to seek comfort.

"Peek! I don't believe it," he cried, head down, before starting as a hand pushed him away firmly.

"You're not gonna blub on me now, are you?" said an all too familiar voice.

"Eh?" yelled Scott, looking up sharply and blinking away the tears. "Jack! Where did - ? How - ? JACK!" He cried in delight as behind him he saw his brother grinning from ear to ear.

With everyone tumbled together in an informal sprawl on the bed, Jack told them all about their adventures in the tunnels, about Jassaspy and the slygorm and about the attack of the Cuss-Cuss Tatty and how at the last moment it had broken off its attack in mid-flight.

"It was then that I spotted it...amongst the straw, feathers and tar....dangling on a chain....a cracked monocle!... It was Flapbaggles!"

Scott's jaw dropped.

"Apparently, he'd got into that state by crawling through a sewer pipe after being left for dead by sakratts. He's terribly embarrassed by it all and refuses to be seen in public until all the tar is out of his feathers," grinned Jack. They couldn't help chuckling at the thought of the dapper Professor Flapbaggles being pariah-ed as the tar-coated Cuss-Cuss Tatty. "Luckily he has already managed to re-home the wasps that had taken up residence in the sticky tar he was caked in."

"And the shadow-sylph?" asked Scott apprehensively.

"Gone: streamed out of me when the sun was revived. Same with the moth-man spores too."

"Yeah, me too ....and look!" Scott pulled up his trouser leg. The raptaggadon bite had completely healed as had his foot from the effects of the worm-sponge. "So, what happened to Jassaspy and the time splinters?" he asked a moment later. Willow beckoned them over to reveal the Mirror of Aggraides tucked behind a picture above the bed.

"His one burning desire was to use that key," she said as they peered inside to see Jassaspy running along a corridor at the end of which sat the Deathly Shadow.

Jack shuddered at the memory of those night-time visitations and a chill trickled along his spine at the thought of how, if he hadn't given up the key, it might have been him in the void of a time splinter instead of Jassaspy.

"Yes, and now he shall spend eternity using it to open doors to corridors whose stony bosom shall never relinquish him," said Peek. The party watched as Jassaspy used the key to pass into another corridor identical to the one he had just left.

"So when you said a Hebradaigen needed to be present to open the time splinters, it was him all along?" said Scott to Willow.

"Yes, but you would never have really wanted to give him the mirror. You would only have done so out of duress, that's why I had to use Chloe and her desire to find her father. I'm sorry I had to play it that way." Willow reached out a comforting hand to Chloe who blushed with embarrassment.

"OK, so I made a mistake with Jassaspy, but I was right to look for father," she said with a sudden burst of remembrance. "Look what Tappletock gave me in the Corridor of Shadows. Don't you recognise it?" She waved a small gold trinket in the air. The boys leaned in for a closer look.

"I don't believe it; that's dad's signet ring! I recognise the swan motif," said Jack looking totally dumbstruck.

"So he *is* here!" muttered Scott in awe.

"Yeah, he must be, so stop going on about me and Jassaspy. Somehow the key and the mirror had to end up with him and you two would never have given them up willingly."

"*I* did, even though everyone was telling me not to," said Jack more to himself than to the others.

"Yes, Jack you did. You followed your convictions and thanks to you, Jassaspy is now trapped inside a time splinter." The Daughter of Nobody radiated a shimmering golden light as she spoke and Jack felt a wave of self-belief suddenly wash over him.

"That's part of your aura now," said Chloe smiling, as she helped settle a deep bronze emotional band around him.

"I hope so," he said quietly.

"..and Tanglestep?" asked Featherfae in a hushed voice. She knew from the sea of heads that suddenly drooped that the news was not good. But when she heard what had happened to him up at Fire-Fir Copse she couldn't control her sobs. "We can't leave him up there", she cried. "Let me cleanse his body and find him a suitable resting place." They all fell silent and Peek nodded and promised to arrange for the body's immediate retrieval.

The waters of Fire-Fir Copse shimmered with a sheen of purple hues when it finally surrendered up the body of Tanglestep. A burnt husk was all that remained. His hands, gnarled and twisted by fire, were not those that had gently brushed her cheek: his teeth, bereft of the lips that had once gently kissed her, were no more than lifeless bone bared in defiance at what had been done to him. Nothing remained of the warm flesh that had cushioned her head or the arms that had enfolded her when she had felt most at need. She swallowed hard and steeled herself for the task ahead.

"Now, I'll need agrappa; and lots of it," she said as she rummaged amongst her bags desperate to stay focused lest her grief overwhelm her. Fubbyloofah was deeply concerned.

"Can't we spare her this pain?" he whispered softly to Peek as he was preparing to release the body for cleansing.

"She would want nought but weeping eyes to dig his grave. Let's not dam her emotional well," said Peek gently.

She had chosen a burial spot for him in a quiet valley setting just below the pass at The Swirl of Vows and it was there under a mound of stones and boulders that he was finally laid to rest. She was inconsolable.

"I will cry him a river," she vowed once the final burial stone was laid. "And with rainy eyes, I shall remain to lie sorrow on the bosom of the earth."

For days afterwards, she could be seen weeping up at the pass overlooking the burial mound... and it broke everyone's heart.

Granglethorn was a hive of activity over the next few days as the national re-planting programme got under way. The Daughter of Nobody had offered to oversee this as her garden was now a positive jungle of health thanks to all the memories that had flooded back. Her first act was to get the gorse adopted as the national emblem of Granglethorn in recognition that its constant bloom was a life-affirming symbol. It was universally endorsed. Peek then sent news to Ye Olde Dungeon Creek authorising a pardon for Flapbaggles.

"Oh, you'll never get that old booby to show his face round here again. He's far too vain," said Raffles the Jay, to a sea of grinning faces, as he dusted down his velveteen Jacket and twirled his gold cane. He had flown up especially to deliver Flapbaggles' reply. He also brought some very alarming news for Fubbyloofah.

"You've got a flood in your kitchen, you have," he said nonchalantly whilst sipping a G&T in readiness for his return flight.

"A WHAT?" Fubbyloofah gaped.

"A flood, my good man. You know...water streaming out from under the door."

From the dropping of his jaw to his kitchen door took less than an hour. Raffles wasn't kidding either. The ground was swimming in water. A voice from the chimney reached him as he stood on the threshold.

"We're not coming out until it's dried out. It's a waste of our fire scents. You're making everything musty." It was Snuffmeakin the crocklepip, but who was he talking to? Fubbyloofah unlocked the door and the water gushed out.

"What the..? Podwhiffle! What on earth has happened here?"

"Oh thank heavens, you're back! I thought you'd deserted the place. I felt so unloved." The kitchen work-top was awash with his watery tears. "Just look at me. What kind of a broccoli am I? All that nice 'purple sproutin' gone to waste."

"Fubbyloofah! Not a moment too soon. For the sake of a sooty supper, stop his tears. Have you any idea what happens to a crocklepip if it gets wet feet?" cut in Snuffmeakin, from the chimney.

"OK, Snuffmeakin, I'm onto it. Ssh! Calm down, Podwhiffle. I haven't deserted the place," said Fubbyloofah, thinking fast. "In fact I've just returned especially for some of your lovely florets: so please stop your infernal sobbing won't you?"

Podwhiffle sniffled out a promise and Fubbyloofah trimmed off some of his rubbery, half-wilted stalks. "For the 'high table' of the Grand Assembly no less!" he grinned. Podwhiffle swelled with pride and a short while later all his sobs had subsided.

Household emergency over, Fubbyloofah returned to Granglethorn where he was pleasantly surprised to receive a very special invitation.

"We'll be havin' a fruits-o'-the-forest party to celebrate gettin' back 'ome and yer all invited!" said a cheerful looking groundlugg.

"Well, bless my berriblods! I'd be delighted to come. What say the rest of you?" he asked expectantly. His face quickly fell when he saw Jack's furrowed brow.

"I'm afraid we really should be getting home," he said, thinking of his mother and wondering who on earth this cheery groundlugg was. Scott quickly interrupted.

"Well, you won't stop me from coming! How are you Cob?" Scott grinned at his old friend. "And where have you been all this time? Hiding from smoggilars again?" Cob blushed at the memory from Yuletree Tarn before introducing his wife, Florabunda.

"I met up wi 'er again in them sweat-pools, 'fraid we both put on a kilo or ten what wi that groatmeal. We both still got a bit to lose hasn't we mi dear!" He squeezed her ample waist and she giggled coquettishly.

The groats were slowly reverting back to groundluggs as their new diet of fruit and vegetables took effect but it was not going to happen overnight.

Everyone was deeply moved by Granglethorn's new policy of reconciliation and it proceeded with remarkable pace. The slygorm was allowed to retreat deep underground where it could live out its life peacefully whilst the sweat-pools were busy being converted into living quarters for the sakratts as they found life under the newborn sun intolerable. But it was the service to commemorate Lava which moved everyone most. Tears of pride mingled with tears of loss as they sobbed and shook through a minute's silence for their gingery friend.

24. Epilogue

It was some time later when a stranger was seen picking his way slowly along a valley awash with wild flowers. His gait was unsteady as he stumbled towards the solitary figure that was the source of the valley stream.

"I'm here," he called out weakly before pain choked off his voice.
The figure looked up. Her grief overwhelmed her, but she simply couldn't ignore another's pain. She looked out at the world for the first time in a long time. The sky was blue and filled with sunlight. Life was all around and as her tears stopped the valley stream started to dry up. Through her grief her inner beauty had condensed all over her leaving her more beautiful than ever. The sun bathed the stranger with a golden aura as his silhouette approached. His gait and posture were strangely familiar. Slowly, he stepped out of the sun …and streamed straight into her heart.

"How can - ? Is it really you?" she gasped.

"Yes, my love!" He rushed forward and snuzzled her cheek with kisses. "In love, you dissolved yourself to dew and washed me fresh again." He dipped his fingers in the stream of tears that flowed over his burial mound and smiled. "Did you ever think that we could part? Hand from hand….and heart from heart?"

She sighed a rush of wind as her face opened with joy and a tear pooled in her eye.

Back at Granglethorn Peek was trying one last time.

"Can't I convince you all to stay? You will lose your wings if you leave Chloe. And Jack: it is true, you know. You are the Elven Prince. If you stay we can help you tap into memories that will awaken those powers."

"We do still need to find father," said Chloe, her jaw set with determination as she looked hard at the signet ring. She shook her long gossamer wings which were slowly healing; but Jack was already shaking his head.

"We've no idea where he could be or even if he's still here: another time, Chloe. We need to get back home now."

"Yeah, mum'll be going spare. Besides, the djinn is no longer in me. What magic would I have?" Scott asked despondently, unaware of the crimson fireflakes that now sparkled behind his eyes. Peek smiled knowingly but said nothing.

To manage La-Kelisland's replanting, Featherfae started a land management partnership: 'Noodle & Nymph', though the 'noodle' of the partnership was yet to regain his health before he could deal with all the associated paperwork.

"He should never have put his faith in those labyrinthine policies," she said before shaking her head and laughing. "He is *such* a noodle, but he is *my* noodle and he's a *lovely* noodle," she said with such feeling that flowers threatened to sprout through the stone flags under her feet.

With her round-the-clock care, Tanglestep was soon able to sit up in bed and they all gathered round to share a tender moment before going home. They promised to return, if only to surprise Fubbyloofah by crashing through the brass porthole in his bathroom. Tanglestep smiled fondly before catching sight of a file of policies and procedures. He frowned and reached for a pen.

"This could be useful in clearing my name - just for the records...."

"NOODLE!"

Suddenly fruit juice splattered over his dusty documents and he looked up in alarm. Featherfae was standing over him with an empty glass and a grim expression. She strode quickly to the window and flung open the curtains. Sunlight streamed in and there was a powerful flash as it reacted with the juice. Papers, pens and all things legal were coughed out of the room like a lungful of stale air. They all burst out laughing at her no-nonsense approach to nursing and hugged them both one last time before starting back down the Corridor of Dreams to begin their return journey home. They got as far as Scott's old chambers, before Chloe started.

"I can't leave without giving them this," she said as she fished out something that she'd been saving for the occasion. The boys smiled when they saw what it was and waited patiently while she dashed back. At the door she paused and knocked gently. She opened it to find Featherfae cradling Tanglestep's head and surrounded by the red hot aura of love. She walked in to give them her parting gift. It was another piece of fruit: a passion-fruit and Featherfae blushed deeply.

   Jack, Scott and Chloe are long gone now and the story of Lava and the burnt gold has been recorded in the Castle archives. The ink well is empty and the book is safely stored under lock and key: a strange hunch told Peek to make sure the ink stayed dry.
   Tanglestep's strength is returning now. He can get out of bed for long stretches and has taken to sitting by the open window. Everyday he looks down the valley as the light dances off the bright ginger coats of the smoggilars, recently rejuvenated by the sun. It streams down warming and nourishing everything it touches. A peal of laughter circles skywards and his heart leaps as he spots Featherfae. He watches lovingly as she skips and frolics, re-populating the land with wild flowers.

~ Glossary ~

Characters:
Auditicus: a junior Hebradaigen at Granglethorn
Mr Bagwapple: a bookworm
Barbletwist: a Hebradiagen (Keeper of the Vedic Bells)
Blinker: a mole
Blunt: a groundlugg
Cob: a groundlugg
Dog Bottom: a bully (one of the Puddies)
Featherfae: a wood nymph
Flabblehogg: Tanglestep's housekeeper
Flan: a bully (one of the Puddies)
Flapbaggles: a large tawny owl
Flint-O: a scrittler
Florabunda: a groundlugg (Cob's wife)
Foggles: an elderly Hebradaigen from the Tower of the Vedic Bells
Fubbyloofah: a beluga-bear
Fumblepaw: a smoggilar
Glob: a glow-worm
Grubgragga: a rat (Creature of the Night Shade)
Hackweezle: a sakratt
Hagratty: a Hebradaigen
Jassaspy: a Hebradaigen (High-Lord of the Tower of the Moon)
Job: A groundlugg
Kipwriggles: an orange caterpillar
Lava: a ginger cat (believed to be the fire-cat)
Papelleticus: a bookworm
Podwhiffle: a weeping broccoli
Pootlefopp: Hebradaigen Health & Safety Officer
Prod: a groundlugg (wax-pie maker)
Pugg: a groundlugg
Raffles: a jay
Rag-wing: a crow (Creature of the Night Shade)
Ripsnarl: a wolf (Creature of the Night Shade)
Silvertip: a swan
Sniffy: a field mouse
Snuffmeakin: a crocklepip
Snarklepike: a scout from the Tower of the Moon
Spittlewhip: a sakratt
Sticklestabber; a large purple-haired spider
Stinking Bishop: Leader of a mischief of rough field mice
Stunkensloop: Tanglestep's assistant at Treadmail Tower
Tanglestep: a Hebradaigen of the Tower of the Sun, posted to Treadmail Tower
Tappletock: a green woodpecker
Twitchetty-poos: a bespectacled white mouse
Tumbleweed: a smoggilar
Worm-beak: a crow (Creature of the Night Shade)
Wiggy: an earwig

Creatures:

Beluga-bear: a 7 foot tall black bear with a large white strip running from snout to tail
Blaggawob: an amphibious reptile whose glands produce an addictive fluid
Cork-bug: a bug that sits atop a bottle like a stopper.
Creatures of the Night Shade: creatures that serve the moon eg. centipedes, wolves, crows & rats
Crocklepips: small black spindly creatures that live in the chimney.
Fire-cat: the ginger cat of legend that saved the sun by travelling to World's End
Groats: obese creatures with withered limbs that live in sweat-pools.
Groundluggs: honest, simple folk with large ears and long arms.
Glow-worms: worms that supply underfloor heating.
Hebradaigese: Guardian-Priests of Granglethorn whose principal duty is to care for the land.
Pine cone bugs: Pine cones that morph magically into bugs.
Puffleflies: insects that reflect a different colour of the rainbow with each beat of their wings.
Raptaggadon: A large scabby reptile the size of a horse and with highly sulphurous breath.
Rock-troll: A troll living by the gates of Granglethorn castle.
Ro-Rillian: Hebradaiges of the Tower of Reflection.
Sakratts: thick-necked hulks with grey wrinkled skin and covered in tattoos and stubble.
Scrittlers: winged-mice
Shadow-sylph: a vile essence that afflicts its victims' sight or consciousness.
Slatherwelts: six legged blood-sucking insects.
Slygorm: A horrifying subterranean creature.
Smoggilars: small furry creatures with bristly coats
Spleeworm: An intestinal worm that lays a sulphourous egg inside its host
Time-wards: those able to travel back and forth in time
Waxenwaifs: small visceral fairies that appear at moments of great peril to save the natural world.

Misc:

Agrappa: rare grapes containing a healing juice
Berriblods: small health-inducing berries, long since disappeared.
Brain-tickler: a worm that induces stupidity
Bumblebulbs: delicious bulbs that emit a peaty smoke
Carbalix: a sugary unhealthy slop forming the major part of the groundlugg diet.
Centipede ball: A ball of tightly bound centipedes used for tracking others.
Dried blackheads from the pores of the night: a powder that blinds the eyes.
Fireflakes: particles of fire which lie dormant until woken by the sunfruit to help heat the land
Frostflakes: particles of frost which lie dormant until woken by the sunfruit to help cool the land
Grangle-guilders: the currency of Granglethorn which always appears to the vendor as full payment
Groatmeal: a viscous white sugary gloop eaten by groats
Irrebies: scarce forest berries
Mime-clock: a clock that chimes whatever words are spoken on the hour
Mummified eyeball of Anubis: a source of lethal asphyxiation
Poppletons: Plants that flower by shooting tiny coloured petals into the air.
Pulsecake: a soothing cake that pulses with calm.
Quaggles: nuts that jump out of their shell as if on springs
Snaptoast: toast that snaps, crackles and jumps in the air
Sunfruit: An orange fruit of legendary power
Sun-shafts: calcified shafts of sunlight carried by the Hebradaigese of the Tower of the Sun
Wipwaffle: an ivy plant whose tendrils wrap around the head to give a massage.
Worm-sponge: a sticky mass of insect larvae that rots whatever it is squeezed upon.